THE
LOST GIRL

THE
LOST GIRL

SANGU MANDANNA

BALZER + BRAY
An Imprint of HarperCollins*Publishers*

Balzer + Bray is an imprint of HarperCollins Publishers.

The Lost Girl
Copyright © 2012 by Sangu Mandanna

Library of Congress Cataloging-in-Publication Data
Mandanna, Sangu.
The lost girl / Sangu Mandanna. — 1st ed.
    p. cm.
Summary: "Sixteen-year-old Eva is the clone of a girl living far,
far away on another continent—and when this 'other' dies, Eva
must step in and take over her life."—Provided by publisher.
ISBN 978-0-06-208231-2
[1. Cloning—Fiction. 2. Science fiction.] I. Title.
PZ7.M31219Lo 2012   2012006548
[Fic]—dc23   CIP
                                                       AC

Typography by Torborg Davern
12 13 14 15 16   LP/RRDH   10 9 8 7 6 5 4 3 2 1

First Edition

For Lekha, for whom I'd have stitched
an echo if I'd had a Loom

Life and death appeared to me ideal bounds,
which I should first break through, and pour
a torrent of light into our dark world.

—Mary Shelley, FRANKENSTEIN

PART ONE

1

OTHER

I remember being in town with Mina Ma. I must have been about ten. She wanted to buy a lottery ticket, and I stood outside the corner store and looked in the window of the toy shop next door. There was a man in the shop, sitting on a stool with a knife and a large piece of wood in his hands. He worked at the wood with the knife, chipping and whittling away, shaping the wood into arms, little legs, a face. I watched him smooth the rough edges with sandpaper, then pick up a wig of soft, almost black hair and fasten it with glue to the doll's head. Finally he sewed a tiny white dress and buttoned it around the doll. The whole thing looked like dancing. His hands moved so delicately, so *lovingly*.

When I imagine how *I* was made, that's how I imagine it. I don't know the reality, of course; no one will ever fully explain it. Mina Ma once told me there was fire. Erik said they stitch us together. So I imagine my Weaver sitting at a great oak desk in a workshop. The sunlight glints off the wood. I imagine he's got a bit of my other's skin, a bit of her *self*, and he uses it to make me look just like her. To put a bit of her soul into me. As for the rest, he stitches me together from pieces of someone else, someone long dead, perhaps. He smokes out the old bones to clean them. He burns the old flesh to whittle it down. He uses fire to make me fit the mold he wants to cast. He stitches my infant self to life, weaving in little organs, a few fine baby hairs, a tiny white dress. He glues my edges together. It looks like dancing. But his hands—no matter how many times I imagine my creation, his hands never move like they love me. Because they don't.

I suppose it's one of those things I have always known. The Weavers create us, but they don't love us. They stitch us together. They make sure we grow up knowing, always, that we belong to them.

It's early. I can smell the wet grass outside, the sharp, clean morning air that turns warm and breezy over the lake later on. It's too early to be awake, but I get dressed and tiptoe out of my room, past Mina Ma's, to the French windows at the foot of the cottage. The windows gleam in the sunlight. Only a few weeks ago, they were dirty and splattered with eggs. The town kids thought it'd be funny. I remember looking at the pattern of egg yolks and having the strangest idea that it spelled MONSTER. That was what they called me, when they cornered me down by the lake a few days before the egg-splattering. I think they came because they wanted to know if the rumor about the girl in the cottage was true. It turned nasty fast, and I hit one of them in the face. He was twice my size. I got away with a black eye, a bloody lip, and a sense of savage satisfaction because I did what *I* wanted for once.

My other would have walked away. I don't think she fights against something if she doesn't like it; she has this soft, sensible way of accepting it. Erik and Mina Ma tell me that kind of grace is a more admirable quality than ferocity. They tell me that is how I should be. *Her.* Mina Ma thinks I like being contrary. "Sometimes," she says, "I think that if she were a rowdy, angry little thing, you'd be soft and quiet *just* to be difficult." But it's not true. It's simpler than that: I don't think I'm much like her. I threw her favorite food on the floor when I was five. While she sat on her father's knee and polished dusty artifacts, I secretly made sculptures of birds out of wet paper and candle wax. When I was seven, I begged Mina Ma to take me to a movie in town even though I knew my other hadn't seen it. These are small things. Risky, but not dangerous. I've learned the difference.

I touch the glass of the French windows. I was very lucky to escape that fight without lasting consequences. My guardians were appalled. Ophelia should have told the Weavers about it. Only she didn't.

Erik didn't say much, but the disappointed look on his face spoke volumes. "We can only lie for you so many times," he told me. "We can't protect you if you defy their laws."

Sorry tripped to my tongue, but seemed inadequate. It didn't matter. Erik hadn't finished. "It's not just the Weavers, either. What about those little brats? Don't you think they might tell their parents they've found an echo? People *talk*."

I knew what he was really afraid of: hunters. That they might find out about me. Only I guess the kids didn't talk, or Erik stopped word from getting out, because nothing has happened since. There has been no witch hunt, no flaming torches at our door. No quiet attacks in the dark.

I check the mail, littered under the slot in the front door. There are two bills for Mina Ma and a blank postcard for me. I know it's from Sean, the youngest of my guardians. No one else sends me anything in the mail. He knows that, and he lives less than an hour away from us, but he still sends me postcards once a month. I've got them tucked between *Oliver Twist* and *These Old Shades* on my bookshelf, tied together with ribbon.

At the time, Sean made it clear he didn't think fighting was a clever thing to do either. His tone annoyed me enough to say, quite unjustly, "Well, if it had been *you*, I bet they'd have battered you."

"I don't batter so easily, thanks very much," he replied. "And if you'll notice, *I'm* the one who can still eat without having to aim for an uninjured bit of my mouth."

It was difficult to argue with logic like that.

I watch telly until Mina Ma wakes up and bustles out of her room. We make breakfast. Eggs and bacon. I don't like eggs. It's the yolk. The way it squidges out makes me feel ill. I try not to touch it when we wash the plates afterward.

Mina Ma laughs. "Don't be so insufferably idiotic, child. It's not *infected*."

It's like her to laugh and scold me in the same breath. I love her more than anything in the whole world. She left India close to fifteen years ago, when the Weavers offered her a job as my caretaker. We live here together. She raised me. Ever since she took me from the Weavers' Loom as a baby, she has loved me. And ever since she chased a doctor out of the house with a rolling pin, after he referred to me as "it," I have loved her.

Once we've put away the breakfast dishes, it's time for my lessons. I put together a neat pile of textbooks and notes.

I have a routine that doesn't change much. I study a girl far away. She's the original to my copy. She haunts me. Everything I do depends on her. And on her parents, my familiars, the two people who asked the Weavers to make me.

I learn what she learns. I eat what she eats. I sleep. Mina Ma teaches me small things every day. How to make rice in a pressure cooker. How to pronounce Indian names and words properly. She tells me about Bangalore, where my other lives. I could find my way around that city blindfolded by now. On Tuesdays and Fridays, Ophelia comes to the house to check me over. She asks me questions, examines me, takes blood. No one would call her medically qualified. She struggles to do subtraction in her head, fumbles with her instruments and notes, and I often hear her saying rude things under her breath about "stupid big words." But she's learned enough about echoes to keep me healthy. All I care about, though, is that she's friendly and funny and I can trust her. I don't think I'd let a real doctor anywhere near me.

On Mondays, Wednesdays, and Thursdays, my lessons are with Erik. He homeschools me in things like English and math, from big textbooks and lesson plans that my familiars have gotten from her school. He gives me information about my other, helps me learn it. He also tells me about *my* world. About the centuries-old Loom in London and the Weavers who stitch echoes there.

And on alternate weekends, Sean turns up for a couple days. His job is to help me understand what life is like among regular people our age. I need to be prepared if I'm ever sent off to live her life.

"Do you have all your notes ready for Erik?" Mina Ma asks, coming out of the kitchen to find me.

I show her the pile I've put together. She glances at the clock. She wants to teach me how to sew a button onto a dress.

"Easy," I scoff.

She chuckles. "If you can keep your restless fingers still for ten minutes to do it, I'll eat my hat."

It would have been nice if she'd had to take that back, but she's right, as always. I have trouble even threading the needle.

When Erik arrives an hour later, I'm ready for his lessons.

In fact, I am perched on the sofa with a look of such sweetness on my face, he stops short in the doorway. Erik is in his late fifties. He's tall, with brown hair and eyes the color of a Mediterranean ocean. He can do anything. He's the only one of us the Weavers will listen to.

"You want something." His voice is resigned, but he gives me a twinkly-eyed smile. "And I'm sure I won't want to know what it is."

"A pony."

"A pony," he says, straight-faced. "I'll get right on that, shall I?"

I laugh but hesitate over bringing up the zoo question. My other went on a school trip to the zoo last month, while I had to make do with photographs and a description. I open my mouth to ask if I can go to one of the zoos within a hundred-mile radius of Windermere, "to get a better feel for what her experience was like, Erik" (a lie—I just want to go see exotic animals), but I bite back the words before they come out.

It's Erik's expression that stops me. His face does a funny thing. It's like watching a light turn off. The amusement in his face, his smile, it all drains away, sucked out with the flip of a switch.

I've seen it before, and it always means bad news. My face transforms in response, and I watch him anxiously as he sets a thick envelope down on the table.

Officially Erik is a go-between. He is the only one

of us who speaks to my familiars, through secure emails and disposable phones so that the Indian authorities won't know about it. We have to be cautious because echoes are against the law in India, and my familiars could be arrested for requesting my creation. They send Erik school reports, descriptions of events and birthdays, and photos, all the tiny details about my other's everyday life that I must know if I am to be as much *her* as she is.

And I learn these things. I learn to love or dislike people the way she does, or at least I try to, even on days when I want to hate them all.

I'd have given up years ago if Erik didn't make me sit still and do it. When I have questions, he tries to answer. He helps me understand the laws, the rules, truths about the Loom and my creation. Nine years ago he told me what I am. He told me about the Weavers in London. About how ordinary people, who can't bear the idea of losing somebody they love, can ask the Weavers to make an echo. He told me how they spend weeks, sometimes months, making each of us. When they're done, we live. We breathe. Echoes. And one day, if our others die and we are wanted, we replace them.

And until we replace them, we learn them.

I set my jaw. "What is it? What's wrong?"

Erik opens the envelope and lays things down on the table. First, the week's Lists: what to eat, what to drink, what to watch, what to read. Next, a CD. It has a recording of my other's voice on it. I'm supposed to learn how to speak like her, but I don't do a very good job of it. Her accent is slightly less neutral than mine, and she uses different words for some things than I do.

Among the sheaf on the table is a set of journal pages. That's where she writes about what she's done this past week, where she talks stiffly about herself, her friends, and her family. She has to do it, but it's obvious she hates it. She hates *me*.

Erik coughs. "I'm sure it will be mentioned in the journal."

"Can't you tell me first?" I ask, my fingers tightly knotted together.

He hesitates. Then: "She got a tattoo."

My stomach drops. "Where?"

"Her left wrist. On the inside, between the bottom of her palm and the place where you wear a watch. There's a photograph here somewhere."

"Erik," I say, and my voice breaks. "Erik, you *promised*. Do you remember when the stray dog bit her on the belly? I was afraid I'd have to let a dog bite me just to copy her, but you told me copying scars wasn't allowed."

"It was what I fought for twenty years ago," he says softly. "I fought to keep your bodies your own. I wanted the Weavers to stop making you mimic injuries and intimate experiences. It seemed too cruel. I eventually persuaded them to decide that having a description of those kinds of things should be enough."

"So *this* is—"

"It's a tattoo," he says. "It's allowed. This is a change she *chose* to make, and one that will do no harm to her or you."

I think of the needles I have seen on telly, that needle in my blood, spilling fine ink into my clean, untainted skin. It would be all right if I wanted the tattoo myself. But not like this.

I recoil. "I won't do it," I say.

"You must," says Erik, very quietly.

I seize the journal pages and flip through them, fast, frantic, until I find the words I'm looking for.

Got a tattoo today. It hurt a lot more than I thought it would.

My jaw aches with fury. I know it's probably not true, because it's not like her, but I imagine she's satisfied, knowing she may do what she pleases and I will have to bear it. She will always win.

I crush my fist around the pages and fling them violently across the room.

"That was childish," says Erik.

"I don't mind being childish," I say. "It must mean I'm a *little* bit human."

"It's a beautiful tattoo," says Erik. "Small, delicate, very like you. You might grow fond of it in time."

"I don't know what it means to her," I say, "but it will always remind me of what I am and what I can never be. I'll hate it," I add, passionately, "forever."

"I know you don't like hearing it," says Erik, "but this is

what your existence means. You *are* her. You must *be* her. Or all of this will fall to pieces." His face softens. "It won't help to fret. Put it out of your mind until it's time."

Later, after he leaves, I watch the sun fading away outside. The summer is almost over. I put my fingers to my wrist, touching the soft, translucent skin between the edge of my palm and where I wear my watch. The skin is cold, but in my head I imagine it's no longer clean, or mine, but is instead *hers*, and is on fire.

2

LAW

Mina Ma feels sorry for me. I know this because she comes into my room that night with a tray of freshly baked scones and clotted cream.

I'm trying to concentrate on *Romeo and Juliet*, which I'm supposed to be writing an essay about, but I can't. I can only think of the tattoo. A stupid thing to get upset about, really; people get tattoos all the time. But it's the point she's making. That's what I can't bear. I think I may hate her as much as she hates me.

I smooth my fingers over the clean skin on my wrist. I don't count. Only she does.

Behind the image of the tattoo, another one surfaces: a mark, black, curving around itself and up to meet a lightning bolt. I always think it looks like a lightning bolt and a small letter *e*. E for echo. I've had that mark branded in my skin since I was born. It's on the back of my neck, so I've never seen it. But I know what it looks like.

I don't know how to be a better echo. I don't know how to stop banging my fists against my cage and feeling bitterly resentful of everything my other does. I don't know a lot of things. I only know the cold mornings, the woods, the lake, and this tiny town called Windermere. In a city thousands of miles away, my familiars live with storms and heat and a sun that bakes the earth.

So Mina Ma tells me. I'll never know it for myself. Not as long as my other is alive, not as long as her star remains firmly fixed in the night sky.

When Mina Ma comes in with the tray, I sit up on my bed and turn away from the homework I've been ignoring for the last half hour. I feel slightly cheered. I know scones are delicious because I sneaked one off the tray on my eleventh birthday. My other has never had one.

"You're living on the edge, Mina Ma," I tease her. "Breaking the rules, what will the Weavers say?"

She snorts. "And which of us is going to tell them?"

"Good point." I keep my smile pasted on, but we both know Mina Ma doesn't break rules for the sake of breaking them. If she has brought me scones, it's because she feels guilty enough to take that risk. She feels like it's her fault she can't protect me from my other's whims. I widen my smile. "I'm okay. You don't have to try making me feel better."

She smoothes hair off my brow. "There are many things I don't *have* to do. But I am going to do them anyway."

She waits until a real smile tugs at the corners of my mouth before getting up to examine the window. She makes sure it's bolted fast, with only a slim panel at the top left open to let fresh air in. She measured the panel herself. She wanted to make sure no one could slip an arm through. I used to think she was worried about burglars, until the day I realized she was afraid of hunters.

There is a pistol hidden away in her bedside table. She once told me the Weavers gave it to her for my protection. I still find that hard to believe. The Weavers have always been something dark and wicked on the edges of my life. The idea that there could be something more frightening out there is ridiculous. The Weavers are the beginning and end of me. They made me. They can unmake me, too.

Mina Ma gives the window bolts a shake, testing them for weakness. When she's satisfied, she turns back. We eat a scone each, and I ask her a question.

"What would you have named me if I'd been yours?"

"This again!" She blows a breath, her cheeks puffed out. "What good are these what–if games to either of us?"

I don't answer. She scowls. "I don't know," she says, in a tone that suggests she's heartily sick of the subject.

My name is Amarra. Like my other. It means "immortal one." I have always wanted to choose a name of my own. I hate it when my guardians call me Amarra.

Just last year, I had to read the old Indian epic, the *Mahabharata*. Inspired by it, I wished I had been named Draupadi. After all, she, too, had been born *differently*, even abnormally. She had stepped out of fire, a gift from the old gods to her father the king. There had been no Hindu

16

gods involved in my birth, but the loose parallels gave me a delightful sense of grandeur.

Sean didn't bother to hide his dismay. I had known him only a few weeks then, but he had no qualms about telling me that he, Erik, and Ophelia would only end up pronouncing it "Drow-puddy," and there was nothing grand about *that*.

Fortunately for him, Mina Ma put her foot down. "Sad life, that one. Five husbands at the same time, ay Shiva, what a scandal! And have you forgotten all that bloodshed? No, thank you. No sense absorbing such a legacy."

"Maybe I want five husbands," I said, laughing.

"Maybe you won't have a choice in the matter," Mina Ma retorted.

I stopped laughing and scowled. It made Sean laugh. "Five husbands?" he said. "With a temper like yours, Drow-puddy, you'll be lucky to find one."

That was when I decided he and I were going to be friends.

After a second scone and a long monologue about the fact that nobody sells good mangoes in England, Mina Ma gets up. "It's late," she says. "Rest."

"I still have homework. And I don't think I could sleep yet anyway."

"Fine," she says. An unholy gleam of humor flashes over her face. "I might as well teach you something useful."

Ten minutes later, she's exasperated. "Stand *still*!" she cries. "I've never known a child as fidgety as you."

I do my best to comply as she wraps a long section of chiffon around my waist. I try to hide my complete lack of interest as she shows me how to form crisp, neat pleats out of the cloth. I'm not very good at obeying people. I try, but all kinds of inconvenient questions and objections pop into my head.

"Mina Ma," I say, "if you want to know what I think—"

"Which I do not," she says.

I bite my lip, but almost immediately burst out with, "If you *were* to ask me what I thought, I would say this was pointless. Why do I *need* to know how to put on a sari?"

She tugs hard on the blouse. I gasp as it tightens across my chest. I look at her reproachfully, but she only says, "You *are* going to need this knowledge. You will need to know how to wear a sari if you go to a wedding, say."

"I'm never going to go to a wedding," I tell her.

"You will, if you're *her*."

"But she's young and healthy. It's never going to happen."

"Young and healthy people have accidents, don't they? Trip down the stairs, fall off trees, get mauled by panthers."

"That's an awful thing to say."

Mina Ma pulls at the chiffon, draping it over my shoulder. "I want you to live until you are old and grumpy," she says. "I don't want you removed in ten or twenty years' time because your other wants to get rid of you, or because you have upset your familiars, or even just because no one thinks they'll need you anymore. There are so many ways to lose you. I won't have it. I won't have someone passing the Sleep Order on you."

Erik told me about the Sleep Order years ago. Officially it's called a Request for Removal, but most people call it the Sleep Order. Someone thought it sounded nicer. Whatever you call it, though, it boils down to the same thing. When a familiar passes the Sleep Order on an echo, they're signing away the echo's life. Returning the faulty toy to its creator. And when that happens, he or she comes back to the Weavers, who always have the last word. They *could* keep the echo, they could do whatever they want, but instead they always shrug and say it's a pity, and the echo dies.

"Crushed like a mosquito," says Mina Ma, as though I had put my thoughts into words. "You exist by the Weavers' grace. Only as long as you are what they expect of you. Do you not understand how *fragile* that is? But if you replace your other, you might be safe. You might make your familiars happy, and then they will always keep you. So if only for my sake, child, *hope* that happens."

"I won't wish for her to die!"

"Then I will wish it," she replies, ruthlessly, "because I don't know or love *her*."

We gaze fiercely at each other. She is unapologetically stout and sturdy. I am quite small and slight. Her skin is a rich brown, darker than mine. My face is delicate, while hers is round and impish. But in spite of these differences I think we could be related. We both have dark hair. Hers is cropped to below her ears, mine is longer to match my other's. We have dark brown eyes with soft eyelashes and neat dark eyebrows. And our eyes are ferocious. She can make a grown man cower with a single look. I learned to be fierce from her.

She looks away before I do, which is rare. She tweaks the last folds of the sari into place and takes a step away.

"It will do," she says.

I take off the sari, and she gathers it up into her arms. She turns to the door. I can't shake her outburst. She must worry constantly that at any moment I might be taken away from her. That my familiars might decide they no longer want me and I will be destroyed.

"Mina Ma?"

Her beady eyes focus on mine, resigned. She knows that tone. She knows it means I'm about to ask a question.

"Do you ever . . ." I hesitate. "Do you ever wish we could run away?"

Mina Ma stares at me for a long time. Then she sits down next to me, her face very tight. "It would kill you if we did." She brushes a lock of hair off my face. In her touch, there is a universe of words and thoughts and emotions that narrow to a fierce point, like light shining into the sky to find a single star. "Running away would mean giving up your right to live. The Weavers, they would feel they could no longer trust you. They wouldn't even have to consult your familiars. They would send their seekers after you, and they would destroy you." I hear her voice in my ear, almost desperate. *"Don't run."*

"I won't," I say. "It's just that with this tattoo, and everything, sometimes it feels like it's too much. I wondered if you ever felt like that too. But I don't mean to *go* anywhere. I know about that girl. The echo, years ago, the one who ran. I know the seekers found her and the Weavers unstitched her."

Mina Ma huffs. "I suppose you 'accidentally' overheard me talking to Erik about her."

I blush.

But she only nods. "Good," she says, her eyes so intent they could have pierced holes through me. "At least you know what it would cost you."

Before she leaves, I ask one more thing.

"Why did my familiars bother having me made? They could go to prison. For all they know, I could be nothing like her. So why risk that?"

Mina Ma smiles slightly. "You've asked me that a thousand times."

I wait.

"Because they cannot bear the thought of losing her."

But like all the other times I asked that question, that answer isn't enough. If Amarra died, what would her family get? Me. Not her. How is that worth the risk they've taken?

I know that's not how it's supposed to be. I'm imperfect. We all are, all the echoes who exist right now. We're a stepping-stone. What the Weavers *really* want is to be able to transfer the human soul from one body to another. One day there will be echoes who are vessels for the human soul. They will lie peacefully, like Sleeping Beauty or Snow White, for years, perhaps forever. Unless their others die while they are still wanted. And if those others do, their bodies will die, but their minds, their souls, will survive. They will awaken in the echo. Their spare body. But *we* are not like that. We have our own thoughts, feelings. It's a flaw. The Weavers haven't yet figured out how to make us perfect. But we have their faces, their voices, bits of their skin, threads of their mind. That has to be enough for now.

I watch the door close behind Mina Ma. I push thoughts of imperfection and tattoos and Sleep Orders away. I pick up another scone, lick the clotted cream at the edges, and go back to finishing my homework.

When I've made my notes for my *Romeo and Juliet* essay, I read over Amarra's journal pages. There are events that happened this past week that I have to memorize. One of her aunts fell down the stairs and broke an ankle, her physics test went badly, and her little sister, Sasha, had a fever.

I put the pages aside and study the new Lists. Some of the books are new; others we've both read before. Maybe this time she'll actually finish *Bridget Jones's Diary*. I could have killed her a few months ago, when she picked it off her mother's bookshelf, read half, got distracted, and never went back to it. Mina Ma had to physically wrestle the book out of my hands.

I notice *Sense and Sensibility* is on the list of movies. I sigh. This will be the third time I've had to watch *Sense and Sensibility*. My other has a passion for Jane Austen that I don't share. I can't help thinking that if they transplanted us into the story, she'd undoubtedly be Sense and I'd be Sensibility. And no matter how many times I watch it, Sense always wins.

I reread the journal to make sure I haven't missed anything, stopping right before the bit about the tattoo. When Erik or Ophelia asks me questions about the journal in our next lesson, I'll be able to give all the right answers.

"What did she eat at Coffee Day?" one of them will ask. If it's Ophelia, she'll probably add, "What's this Coffee Day place anyway, love? Is it nice?"

"She ate a brownie with vanilla ice cream. It's the place she often goes with her friends; she's talked about it before."

"Who spilled half a bottle of juice on her leg at school?"

"Sonya, by accident. They laughed so hard they got scolded by one of the teachers."

"Which teacher?"

And on it will go. It's about as exciting as brushing my teeth. I never forget, never give them a wrong answer. When we're finished with the questions, Ophelia will go make a cup of tea, or Erik and I will play cards, and we'll pretend for a while that it's a normal house and I'm a normal person.

I drop the pages onto the floor and turn off the light. I crawl beneath the covers of my bed. I try to sleep, but behind my eyelids I see the town kids bloodying my lip and a lady at the supermarket shuddering and backing away when Mina Ma accidentally let slip what I was. I see a murky mirror and a tattoo and a girl with eyes like bruises. Me? Or the echo who ran away all those years ago and died for it? I shiver in the dark.

It's so quiet I can hear Mina Ma's bed squeaking in the room above, the gurgling of water in the pipes, an owl, something creaking softly. I open my eyes again and glance at the window. Beyond is the back garden, and the creaking is the sound of the swing, *my* swing, swaying back and forth.

My guardians made me the swing as a gift on my seventh birthday. I woke in the morning and it was there, like magic. I've spent hours in it, kicking myself high into the air or simply lying back to stare into the sky.

In the dark I think about the fight. I think of Mina Ma telling me she wants a girl to die because she believes that will save me. I think about the swing. It was a kindness my guardians didn't have to show, a gesture of their affection in spite of what I am. It was a gift, rare and precious, and gifts don't come often to echoes in this world that despises us.

3

NAME

"There you are," says Sean.

I turn around and look at him, standing at the top of the path. The sun is a hard orange ball behind him, and he looks like he's only a shadow.

I've known him about a year. Before that his father, Jonathan, was my guardian instead. Then they found cancer in Jonathan's brain and he had to stop working. Somehow Erik and Jonathan got the Weavers to agree to take his fifteen-year-old schoolboy of a son on as his replacement. When Jonathan died nine months ago, I thought Sean wouldn't have to come anymore, and my grief doubled. I didn't want to lose them both. But he came. He turned up the weekend after his father's funeral, and I tiptoed around him, terrified of saying something wrong, until he snapped at me and told me not to treat him like he had smallpox. And on every other weekend since then, like clockwork, he's here.

It takes him a few seconds to come down the path to the bottom and meet me by the edge of the lake. I wasn't expecting him.

"I thought you weren't going to come this weekend," I say. "Isn't your girlfriend's birthday tomorrow?"

His girlfriend's name is Lucy and she's in his year at school. They're both sixteen, a year older than I am. After much badgering, he showed me a photograph last time he was here, and she *looks* older than I am. Gorgeous. Confident. Mature. They've been going out three weeks now. She likes dogs and volunteers at a local thrift store, and after once hearing her on the phone with Sean, I discovered she has a way of making every sentence turn up at the end like a question. I try and talk like that just to wind Sean up, but he never reacts.

"She's doing something with her friends," Sean says vaguely.

He has the perfect poker face. It drives me crazy because I can't mask a single thing *I* think or feel. But I've learned to read his eyes and the little ups and downs in his voice.

"Erik told you about the tattoo."

Sean nods.

I glance up at him. "Thank you. For coming."

One corner of his mouth crooks upward. "You're welcome."

We stand there for a minute, facing the water. Sean's hands are in the pockets of his jeans; his short, untidy dark hair flickers in the wind. He is tall and lean, with his shirt rolled up past his elbows and green eyes the exact color of the marbles I had to play with when I was little. I look down at the skin on his forearms, lightly tanned from PE and after-school soccer with his friends. He has a scar below his left elbow. I wonder how he got it. I wonder why he cares more about an echo and her tattoo than his human girlfriend's birthday.

"I hate those words sometimes," I mutter under my breath.

He doesn't ask me which words I mean. I think he knows. Sean always knows. He can see what move I'm planning to make in chess and counters before I can do it. He always knows who the killer is in a detective story. I think he could make a career out of detecting, but he wants to write plays for theater. Maybe he could be a Shakespeare instead of a Sherlock. He could be anything. Anything he wants to be.

"We'd better go back inside," I say, trying to shake off visions of Sean growing up and Lucy kissing him when he gets home, their kids running up to hug him—

He watches me turn away, eyes narrow. "What's the matter?"

"Nothing," I say with painstaking cheer.

He doesn't push it. He follows me back up to the cottage, and possibly to distract me, he kicks off one of our lessons: grilling me about social groups and stereotypes and etiquette. What is a goth? What is "emo" short for, and what kind of music would I classify as emo? I need to give him examples. What words might an average teenager's parents disapprove of hearing from their child? And would these parents frown upon similar words in Amarra's India *and* Sean's England alike, given that they both come from English-speaking families, go to English-speaking schools, and live in towns or cities that are largely if not entirely English-speaking and are subjected to similar TV shows, movies, news, sports, and music?

I get all the answers right.

"Well done, you!" he says, in an exaggeratedly hearty tone of voice. "You can have a cookie for being so good!"

I throw a dishcloth at him.

Sean goes to help Mina Ma with dinner. I'd help too, but I have to finish reading *Wuthering Heights* and email Erik an essay on whether Nelly Dean is a reliable narrator. I love *Wuthering Heights*, one of the few things I share with Amarra, so this assignment has been far more fun for both of us than the one on *Romeo and Juliet*. While Sean and Mina Ma mash potatoes and fry sausages, I sit at the kitchen table with the book and my notepad.

"Nelly"—I read my words out loud, scribbling my introduction—"obviously hates Cathy and Heathcliff, so her judgment is far from objective. Quite frankly, she's also a bitch."

Mina Ma and Sean burst out laughing. Mina Ma hastily stops herself and shouts at me for my language.

I'm halfway through the essay when Mina Ma goes out of the kitchen to take the washing off the line and Sean sits down at the table across from me.

"I have a question," I say.

"What a surprise," he says. "You, with a question? Unprecedented."

I grin. "Never mind. It was only about the book, anyway."

"Well, I have a question, too," he says. "I happen to have two tickets to the zoo for tomorrow. Want one?"

"What would I do with it?" I ask him. "You might as well give it to somebody who can use it, Sean." I clench my teeth. "Wouldn't Lucy like to go as a birthday present?"

Sean sighs. "I'm going to let that slide, because you've never been asked this type of question before. Obviously I haven't done a good enough job of teaching you how to recognize the situation. For future reference, it might help you to know that when a friend tells you they've got tickets and asks if you want one, they usually also mean that they would like you to *go* to the event in question."

I don't even notice the sarcasm. I look up at him, taken aback, the book and essay forgotten. "You mean, you're asking if I'd like to go to the zoo? Like, *actually* go?"

"Well done," he approves.

How could he have possibly known how much I have wanted to go to the zoo?

I fly out of the chair. "Sean, do you mean it?"

"Of course I mean it," he says, exasperated. "Why would I ask you if I didn't mean it, you daft harpy?"

I falter. "Is this about the tattoo again?" I can see my life unfolding in front of me, filled with pitying gestures like scones and zoos. I can't bear to imagine that I will always be someone Sean feels sorry for.

He pulls out a pair of tickets. "Here," he says. "These are the old tickets I got before I changed them. Look at the date on them."

"These are tickets for next month."

"And at the bottom, see, there's my receipt for the day I bought them."

"You bought them two weeks ago."

"Right," says Sean. "Meaning I bought them long before I knew about the tattoo. I've changed the date so we can go tomorrow instead, which I will admit *is* about that bloody tattoo. I thought you could use some cheering up. But I was always going to ask you."

"Why?" I ask, bewildered.

"Everyone should get to go to the zoo," he says. "So do you want to?"

"Yes," I burst out, my chest tightening with excitement, "thank you, yes, of course I want to go!"

"You're not allowed," Sean reminds me, "so it'll be tricky. It's more than an hour away on the train."

I tip my chin, refusing to let such a consideration destroy this moment, this flare of hope that I may never have again.

"No one needs to know," I say.

"Not the others," he concedes, "but Mina knows. I asked her when I first came in today. It took some persuading, but she's agreed. I think she wants you to get out for a bit. But only as long as I, and I quote, 'don't let you out of my sight for an instant.'"

"I don't need looking after," I say indignantly.

"You may be able to handle yourself in a scuffle, but you don't know the first thing about the country beyond this town. If you got lost, you'd probably wander straight into a hunter. Wouldn't *that* be the prettiest pickle?"

I point a dirty look his way, but I'm too euphoric and grateful to stay annoyed. A lock of hair falls over my forehead, feathery and wayward, and I blow it impatiently out of the way.

"Do we have to take the train through Lancaster to get to the zoo?" I ask eagerly.

"Yeah."

"So can we stop off and go to your house on our way back?"

Sean gives me a strange look. "You want to go to my *house*? Of all the places—"

"I'm curious."

He rolls his eyes. "Well, if that's what you want, why not?"

I am so excited for the rest of the evening that Mina Ma says she has half a mind not to send me if I can't act my age. When Sean says he could get a ticket for her too, she declines, announcing that she's quite happy not to go "racketing about the countryside." Yet this doesn't stop her from muttering about "unaccompanied girls, with *boys*" and "*zoos*, of all things" and "if *they* find out."

It's the last bit that worries me, a knot of fear battling the excitement. What if the Weavers *do* find out? For me to actually leave town, go somewhere even with a guardian, is punishable. I am not allowed to leave Windermere. I am not supposed to spend time in busy places. Someone might see the Mark on my neck and recognize me for what I am.

"What will they do if they catch us?"

"I don't know," says Sean.

His voice gives nothing away, but I am looking at his eyes, which are honest and very green, and they're troubled. I believe him. He doesn't know what they'll do to us. But he knows that because I belong to them, they have every right to dispose of me if I defy them.

Sean might not belong to anybody, but that doesn't mean he's in the clear. Guardians are not allowed to help us. To interfere with the laws. The Weavers can punish them, too.

"They won't find out," I say.

"Course they won't," says Sean. "So finish your broccoli, it's good for you."

I have trouble sleeping all night. Tonight my dreams are mine, which is not always the case. Sometimes I dream of things from Amarra's life, bits of memories and emotions that slip through the cracks from her consciousness to mine. Like the time the dog bit her. It preyed on her mind for weeks, the memory of that terror. Or the time she had an enormous crush on a pop star and I dreamed of his face for days. Erik says it's normal: when they made me, they had to put bits of her into me. This means that sometimes traces of memories and feelings cross over from her to me.

I dream of strange things—not of zoos, like I'd expected to, but of an abandoned carnival in a deserted dark city. Men and women in green, swinging back and forth on trapezes. Elephants rearing up on their hind legs. Brightly painted clowns. Each time I wake, my heart races with a mixture of fear and excitement. In my dreams, the clowns and the Weavers look eerily alike.

On the train the next day, I am too excited to sit still. I bob up and down in my seat, jostling Sean, who gives me a look that mingles amusement with exasperation. I can't contain myself. I haven't left Windermere since I arrived as a baby. As the familiar town disappears, the English countryside meanders in. It's like a snapshot lifted off a postcard, with endless fields and sheep-dotted hills.

"It's so beautiful," I say softly.

Sean points things out, like the low stone fences that he says are a northern thing, you don't see many of them in the south.

"Have you been to the south much?"

"Now and then," he says. "London, mostly. Cornwall, too. My parents used to take me there on holiday when I was younger. Except for one year when we went to Egypt. Echoes are illegal there, too, so Dad had to lie about his work whenever anyone asked. I met some kids in Cairo who weren't even sure echoes actually exist."

"So you and your mum don't go on holidays anymore?" I ask.

He shakes his head.

"Is she all right?" I ask tentatively.

He shrugs. "She misses him."

"You do too, don't you?"

"Yeah. Do you?"

"I try not to," I confess. "But I keep thinking about that rhyme Mina Ma used to sing for me. You know, about the five little ducks? And how they went out one day, over the hill and far away. And the mama duck quacked, but only four came back." I try to smile, but there's a lump in my throat. "It's silly, but I keep thinking Jonathan's the one that didn't come back. And in the song it goes on until none of them come back."

"You know how it ended, don't you?"

"I always made Mina Ma stop because it upset me so much."

"Silly," he says. "In the end, the mother duck followed them, over the hill and far away. And she quacked and quacked, and all five little ducks came back."

"Really?"

He laughs. "Yes, really."

I laugh too.

When we pass through Lancaster, I pay special attention

to it. I can't quite imagine how Sean lives his everyday life in this place, with its storybook castle and cobbled streets and old bridges. I've never known Sean in any setting except our cottage by the lake.

It's almost noon when we finally pull into Blackpool. Sean seems to know his way around, so I follow him out and down the street to the nearest bus stop. I can smell the seaside, all salt and fish and vinegar.

"What do you want to do with your life?" Sean asks me unexpectedly. We're on the bus. I can see the ocean as we rattle down the road. It's a bluish gray, sparkling in the pale sunlight.

I have the answer ready, slotted in place in my memory. "I'm going to study archaeology," I say. "My other's father, Neil, is a historian, and she really loves that kind of thing. We could be the next Indiana Jones."

"No," says Sean. "What do *you* want to do?"

"I'm not supposed to think about that," I say flatly.

"I'm asking."

"I don't really know," I admit, "but I like not knowing. I could go to university when I'm eighteen, maybe, study art. I think I'd like that."

It's a nice thing to dream of. I look out at the sea and the sky, and then I look the other way at the passing street. And though I try not to, I see the laughing teenagers, the mothers and children, the families outside the restaurants and the pubs, and I think of how different I am from every single one of them.

Sean carefully touches my hand. I try to smile, and it's easy to do with the sun in my eyes and the salty sea air blowing around us.

When we get there, the zoo is beautiful. Filled with brightly colored signs and little stalls and animals from the far-flung places of the world, it's everything I ever imagined it would be. Sean has been here before, but he lets me take the lead and drag him every which way as signs and animals catch my eye. Many of the cages and enclosures have big signs with names on them: a chimpanzee is called Molly; a python is called Eduardo; the hippos are Daisy, Ju-ju, and Tom. Sean and I laugh over some of the names. He can't believe anyone would name a hippo Tom.

"Clear lack of imagination, that," he complains.

I try to remember the last time I was this excited, but the memory eludes me. Memories never elude me. Maybe this is the most excited I've ever been.

But I'm careful. I keep my eyes open; I glance over my shoulder. Once, I catch Sean with a tiny frown between his eyebrows, searching the crowds as though worried someone might be watching us. I let myself enjoy every minute, but the Weavers stay in the back of my mind. I can't forget that I'm not like the happy, chattering crowds. I check my hair, making sure my Mark is covered.

"There," says Sean, as we stop in front of a large enclosure. "That's what I really wanted to show you."

The elephants.

"Mina told me Amarra went to the zoo for the first time when she was seven," he says, "and she wrote in the pages about seeing the elephants, but she didn't put a picture in. And you cried and said you wanted to see them too."

There's a lump in my throat. "I can't believe you know about that."

"I know a lot of things," he says. "You're their favorite thing to talk about. Mina and Erik, I mean. You're everything to them, you know."

I wipe my eyes and watch the elephants. There are three adults and a couple of smaller ones nuzzling up to their mothers. They look happy, like they're enjoying being out there in the sun with the grass to nibble on. One of the elephants uproots a tuft of grass with its trunk and dumps the grass and dirt on its back. They're so beautiful.

I glance to the right and see a sixth elephant. This one is very young, smaller than the others, and seems to be in a separate enclosure. The sign at the front says she's Eva.

"Why is she on her own?" I ask indignantly. "Won't she be lonely?"

"Does seem weird, doesn't it? There's someone in a uniform right there. I'll ask him."

I watch Eva the elephant. She has a restless energy. She stomps at the grass beneath her feet, kicking up small mounds of dirt and soil. Occasionally she glances at the other elephants, and I imagine her expression is wistful. Then she lets out a defiant trumpeting sound and turns her back on them. I want to stroke her trunk, the short, bristly hairs on her back.

Sean reappears. "Apparently, she's—"

"Difficult," I guess.

"Yeah. When they're all together, she is generally disruptive. So they put her on her own whenever she's particularly difficult."

"It won't make her behave," I say with certainty. "Look at her. She's stubborn. They'll just have to accept her for what she is."

There's a smile in Sean's voice. "You like her."

I nod absently.

After another half hour, I regretfully leave the elephants behind and follow Sean back in the direction of the reptiles. For a while there, with the smell of elephant and wet grass around us, I forgot about the Weavers. Now they're back. I push them into the furthest corner I can find, but their murky, half-remembered faces keep coming back like a persistent jack-in-the-box.

Sean and I buy a box of popcorn and a Coke to share and wander around while we finish them. I sip the Coke noisily through my straw.

"Which way?" Sean asks me when we reach a fork. "Reptiles or birds?"

"Is a turtle a reptile?"

"More reptile than bird, I reckon," says Sean, grinning,

"so we'd better go that way."

There's a girl on the path ahead of us. She has dark hair and eyes like me. She falls and starts to howl. Her father leans down and kisses her knee and wheedles a laugh out of her. And for no reason at all it makes me think of the Weaver who made me. Of how he will never pick me up when I fall.

I want to be human so badly it hurts.

"Look at me," says Sean, and the tone of his voice makes it clear he knows how I feel. "You're different. We've always known that. But it doesn't have to be a bad thing. Being different doesn't make you something *less* than the rest of us." I open my mouth, but he cuts me off. "And it does mean that you are *not* Amarra. You're someone else. And you're important. As a *girl*, not an echo. No matter what the Weavers take from you, you matter. To all of us."

I stare at him. "I've always wanted to be a girl. Only a girl. To not be 'the echo.'"

"You're not 'the echo' to me."

"But it doesn't make me any less of one."

"So?" he demands. "There's nothing wrong with being an echo. You step in when someone else dies. That's pretty glorious, don't you think? You're an angel among mortals. Echoes are asked to sacrifice everything to make another family, other people, happy. To give them hope. *You* are hope."

He gestures at the little girl and her father on the path ahead. "Think of how he would feel if something happened to his daughter. But if that girl has an echo somewhere, he might find her again. He might get her back."

I've never looked at it quite that way before.

"Dad used to say that if he could have an echo made for every person he loves, he'd do it." He looks me in the eye. "You shouldn't be ashamed of what you are. Or of not being like us. You should wear it like a badge of honor."

I stare at him for a long time, and he stares back, until I can no longer see anything beyond him but a blur, and he's the only clear thing in the world.

Then his phone vibrates and the spell is broken. He checks his text. "It's Lucy," he says.

Lucy. It takes a second to pierce my thoughts. For a moment there, I had completely forgotten he had a girlfriend.

But I still can't help smiling. Because no one has ever said those things to me before. I look at the father and his daughter, but not with envy or longing this time. I imagine the man losing the little girl, like one of the five little ducks vanishing over the hill, and I think of the echo who could be good and perfect and replace her. I am not perfect, but I could be the thing that gives somebody hope. The thing that makes the loss of each little duck a bit less painful.

It doesn't make everything okay, it doesn't fix much, but it does fix *something*. It does force me to look at things differently. For the first time I see my own face through someone else's eyes.

I'm not like these people around me, and I am not Amarra, but I can wear all my differences without shame.

Sean puts his phone away. "You look happier," he says, smiling crookedly at me. "I must be good for something."

"I've wanted a name, my own name, for so long," I say, "and I think you just gave me one."

"What is it?"

I smile. Here it is, at last, the one thing that belongs to me. "Eva."

4

STORY

We get off the train in Lancaster and walk to Sean's house. It takes us ten minutes, across a bridge, down two cobbled roads, and onto a street lined with old, pretty houses. Sean leads me to the third house from the top of the street, fishing a set of keys from his pocket. I stare at the house in interest, marveling at the fact that in all the years I'd known Jonathan, I'd never seen where he lived. Where Sean lives. Or Erik, or Ophelia. When they enter my world, they leave theirs behind.

I hope Sean's mother's not home. I always got the impression, from things Jonathan would let slip, that she doesn't like me.

I'm sure she adores Lucy.

Something funny happens to my throat when I step into the house and smell the faint scent of cigars. Even nine months after his death, it feels like Jonathan is still here.

It reminds me of those late evenings at the cottage, when he would sit on the steps with his cigar and Ophelia would sit next to him and fish for a cigarette in her bag and the smell of smoke would waft into the house and mingle with Mina Ma's hand cream and the tea brewing in the kitchen. And I'd hover in my pajamas outside the door, listening to them talk quietly about grown-up things. Now and then I would hear Erik laugh at something one of the others said. I always waited for that sound. If Erik was laughing, it meant nothing was wrong.

And one day, just like that, the cigars stopped wafting in through the door and it was only the three of them left. And the sound of their voices was different, no longer an old soothing lullaby but something new and, at first, strange.

It's been a long time since I've missed Jonathan this fiercely.

"I know," says Sean, like every thought is written clearly in my expression, "I can never walk in without it hitting me either. I think my mum lights his old cigars sometimes."

"It must be hard letting him go."

"I don't think anyone ever really lets go of the people they love," he says, putting his keys down in a big bowl by the door. "You're living proof of that, aren't you?"

"But is that the right thing to do?"

"I don't know. Maybe there's no right answer."

I think about that. "No, I guess not."

"Anyway," says Sean, gesturing vaguely at the room around us, "this is home. We—" He cuts himself off, watching my eyes drift across the bookshelf and settle on one volume in particular.

"Don't even think about it."

It's the novel *Frankenstein*, and it's utterly forbidden and it's so beautiful I want to snatch it off the shelf and read every last word.

"You can't expect me *not* to think about it when it's right there staring me in the face."

"I can hide it if you like," says Sean, unmoved by my piteous, pleading eyes. "You can't break that law. You are not allowed to read it. The Weavers would have my head if I let you. And God knows what they'd do to you." He crosses the room and plucks the book off the shelf. "So you're pronouncing it *E*-va, then? Not *A*-va?"

A terribly unsubtle attempt to change the subject, but I let it go. "She was more of an Eva than an *A*-va. And I am too, I think."

He cocks his head at me. "I think so too. I can't wait to see Mina's face when you tell her." He grins wickedly.

I stick my tongue out at him, but have to admit I'm slightly anxious about Mina Ma's reaction. Naming myself goes against everything that is expected of me. How will Mina Ma and Erik and Ophelia take to *that*?

"We have another half hour before the next train," says Sean. "Do you want something to drink?"

"Yes, please," I say, still eyeing *Frankenstein*.

"I'll put some tea on."

He leaves, taking the book with him. He knows I have few scruples when I'm curious.

While he's out of the room, I look around. At the magazines piled neatly on the coffee table and the books stacked in order on the shelves. The house is tidy, but not pristine; it looks lived in. On the mantelpiece above the fire, lined up, are framed photographs. A younger Jonathan and a woman with blond hair on their wedding day. Baby Sean. Jonathan and Sean by the seaside. Sean and a group of boys in soccer shirts. There's so much in Sean's life that he leaves behind to come to us. He has given up a great deal, all that time he could be a normal kid, all that time he could spend with Lucy or his friends.

I hear him come in behind me, the teacups clinking in his hands, but I don't turn around. "Why do you come?" I ask quietly.

I feel him approach, his voice by my ear. "Because he asked me to."

This is so surprising, I turn. I notice he hasn't got any tea for himself, just milk. Sean loves cold milk.

"Jonathan asked you to take his place?"

Sean nods. "When he got too sick to work, he asked me to go instead. He didn't know what kind of guardian another replacement might be. He worried you'd get someone who was unkind, who would tell the Weavers every time you did something wrong. Ophelia's supposed to, but we both know she doesn't, and Dad was afraid someone else might. He thought I was your best chance."

"That doesn't seem fair, to ask you that when he was so

ill and he knew you wouldn't refuse."

"I could have refused."

I smile. "But you didn't. You never would have."

"It's not as bad as it sounds, anyway," he adds. "He only asked me to come until he died. He said, 'When I'm gone, you can quit if you want. But you might find you don't want to leave her.'"

"But you never quit."

"No," he says, "I stayed."

I watch him with wide eyes.

"Why?"

"We should go," he says, looking past me at the clock, "or we'll miss the train. Drink your tea."

I want to push the question, but I don't. My nerves feel wobbly, and I drink the tea quickly to soothe them.

"Eva," says Sean.

The sound of my new name is thrilling, and I look up at him, my skin as hot as the tea.

"I don't agree with what they do to you," he says. He lifts my wrist and turns it over to reveal the small, delicate stretch of skin where my tattoo will go. "But I like you a lot more than I hate this." His fingers feel so light against my wrist, it might be my imagination. My pulse throbs faster under his thumb.

"Don't," I say unsteadily, pulling my wrist away.

He drops his hand. "I didn't mean . . ."

Of course he didn't. Why would he have meant anything by it?

"I know." I force an easy smile, but it comes out a bit twisted. "I felt one of those static-shock things, that's all."

He doesn't point out how lame that sounds. "Okay," he says simply, "ready to go?"

It's still light out when we get back to Windermere, the streaky pinkish-gold light that means the day is ending. The sky looks like it's melting.

I check my watch. It's almost seven. It's starting to get dark earlier. I shove my hands in the front pockets of my jeans to keep them warm. It's not as easy as it used to be in my old jeans: these are new, in the skinny style that Amarra recently discovered.

We turn the corner and are less than a hundred feet from the cottage when I feel Sean's hand clamp down on my elbow.

"Keep walking," he says in my ear.

"But—"

An exasperated breath hisses through his teeth. "Do it."

I look quickly at his face. It's completely calm. Wooden. Taking my cue, I try to hide my alarm. I keep walking, not slowing down or approaching the cottage. I look casually around and try to spot the thing that's set him so on edge.

There's a small park up ahead with a playground for children. I've been there a couple of times, always when it was empty because I wasn't supposed to play with other kids growing up. It's full of laughing children and parents and old couples strolling around. The road is mostly deserted, but there are a few people passing by and two teenagers standing outside a house, talking.

Then I see him. He seems ordinary, a regular guy in his thirties, but he's the only one who might have spooked Sean. Unlike the others, he's on his own and he's standing quite still, leaning against a lamppost and consulting a map like he's a tourist. This isn't an unusual sight, and I open my mouth to tell Sean so, but then the man's eyes flick upward and settle on the pair of us. I look away quickly to avoid eye contact, and my heart leaps into my mouth. There was something about the way he glanced at us. Something hopeful.

Sean turns abruptly and heads into the park. I follow him, glancing once at the man watching us. I could swear he looks disappointed.

"What's going on?" I ask Sean once we're by the edge of the playground, well out of the man's earshot.

Sean shrugs. "Being careful, that's all."

I give him a disbelieving look. "You think he's a hunter."

"I think he might be."

A hunter. The word rattles around my head like loose change. I found out about hunters years ago. No one told me. I suppose they didn't want to frighten me. Getting a secret out of Mina Ma is like trying to pry open a sealed pistachio, but she couldn't stop me from eavesdropping. I used to hear her talking to Erik about the people who hunted and killed echoes all over the world. On the news they call them vigilantes. An old secret society set on stopping the creation and survival of unnatural things like me.

They are the reason I mustn't tell people what I am. It's why I'm tucked away in our cottage and not allowed to hang around normal people. It's why Mina Ma has a pistol and double locks the doors and looks suspicious if strangers talk to us in town.

I've never been afraid of hunters. I think it's like standing in a field, caught between a blind tiger and a healthy one. You can't watch them both. So you ignore the blind one. It doesn't know where you are; it can only try to sniff you out in the dark. You watch the other tiger, because it doesn't have to find you. It can see you. It can catch you with a single leap.

I have always kept my eyes only on the Weavers. On their laws. Until now. Now, with Sean tense at my side and a stranger nearby, I feel a tiny prickle of unease.

"Sean, he's just a *guy*."

His teeth clench. "You think I'm being paranoid?"

"Yes, actually," I say, trying to cast off my unwelcome doubts. "How would a hunter have even found me?"

The look on his face tells me the answer. The fight. Of course. Erik tried to stop the kids and their friends and their parents from talking, but one word slipped to the wrong person would have been enough. Any one of them could have tipped a hunter off about the rumor. Anyone could have told him which house to watch.

"He looked awfully disappointed when we came in here,"

says Sean. "He was expecting us to go to the house. Or he hoped we would. If he *is* a hunter, he was probably waiting to find out what you look like. If he finds out, he can follow you, get you alone—"

"Stop," I say sharply. "This is ridiculous!"

"That's what they do."

"He's probably a tourist—"

"And if he isn't?"

I've never tried so hard not to be scared. I bite my lip. "If he isn't, then no harm done," I say, trying to sound uncaring. "We walked right past the cottage, so he has no reason to think I'm the one he wants." I put on my best brave face. "Sean, I know you're just trying to be careful, but I think you've got him all wrong."

"Either way," says Sean, glancing over his shoulder, "he keeps looking at us, and I'm not going back to the cottage until he's gone."

Sean turns around and walks a few steps, to a young father playing with his daughter on the slides. I stay where I am, trying to hold on to my conviction that hunters are not worth being afraid of, that there's no way even one of them could have found me.

When my palms feel less clammy, I approach Sean, in time to hear the father say, "Yeah, it *is* sort of weird. Think it would be overkill if I rang the police?"

"Might be," says Sean, shrugging. "Dunno."

The other guy rubs his jaw. "Ah well, it won't do any

harm. If he's just waiting for someone or whatever, they'll sort it. I'd rather look silly than risk the kids."

I open my mouth to protest, then shut it again. I give Sean a dirty look as soon as the father walks away. "You told him there was a weird guy staring at the children?" I demand.

He's unmoved. "Whatever it takes to make him leave."

"Not exactly playing fair, though, was it?"

"Hunters don't play fair."

"We don't know—"

"*I* know," says Sean. "Everything about him is wrong. He's pretending to be a tourist with a map, but you can see the date on the cover and that map is ten years out of date. He's also got padding around one of his ankles. See, his jeans don't quite sit right. What if that's where he's hiding a knife?"

I stare at him in silence, nauseated. How did he even notice such small things? How did I miss them?

For a minute he looks bitter. "You don't consider them a threat. But hunters have killed others like you, all over the world, and there's always a chance, however small, that they'll turn up on your doorstep. Like *he* has. Maybe I'm wrong. But maybe I'm not. I just like knowing what to look for."

I don't say anything for a long time. I want to ignore everything he's saying, but he makes sense. He always makes sense.

"Still think I'm paranoid?"

I shake my head. "Well, maybe a bit. But that wasn't what I was thinking. I was thinking that Jonathan should have given you a chance to be a regular boy. He shouldn't have ruined that for you."

"If he hadn't raised me the way he did," says Sean, "I wouldn't be here. Is that really the way you'd rather have it?"

I don't know how to answer that. I glance at the lamppost. The man is gone, and a police car is vanishing back down the street.

"Don't tell Mina Ma, Sean. You'll scare her."

"She'd rather know."

"Please."

"Fine. But I'm telling Erik. He'll want to kill the rumors for good. It's the only way to make sure they don't come back."

As we walk out of the park, I realize my hands are shaking. I knit my fingers together to keep them still.

"You might have just saved my life," I say, trying to make it sound like a joke.

Sean smiles for the first time since we left the train station. "Not if he was a tourist."

When we get back to the cottage, Mina Ma is in the living room, waiting for us. Sean looks at ease, and I do my best to seem the same.

She asks us about the zoo. I describe it for her. Then we offer to help her with dinner, but she shoos us away. So Sean kicks an old ball around the back garden and I shower and try to wash away a lingering sense of fear. Over dinner, I tell Mina Ma about my new name. She is silent for a few minutes. I prepare myself for the worst, but she only watches me and chews. Then she glances at Sean. I can't decipher the expression on either one's face. Mina Ma turns back to me.

"I see," she says at last. "Well, don't complain to *me* when you cause a stir."

I eye her fondly. "That's it?"

"Yes, child, that's *it*. If you want that name, then you can have it, with my blessing." She shakes her head. "Naming yourself after an *elephant*. Why am I even surprised?"

After we've finished eating, we settle down in the living room, Sean and I on either side of a chessboard and Mina Ma picking stitches out of an old blouse that no longer fits her. And she tells us a story.

"All this talk of elephants make me think of a fable I told you when you were very small," she says to me. "You might not remember it. It's the tale of the farmer and the mongoose."

"Why did talking about elephants make you think of that?"

Mina Ma does not look happy about being interrupted. "Because this was in a book of folk tales and the picture on the cover was of an elephant. Now if anyone mentions elephants again, I will jump in the nearest well. As for the story—"

"Wait," says Sean, "what's a mongoose?"

Mina Ma is taken aback. "Ah," she says, "they look a bit like foxes. But they are smaller. They are very fierce creatures, very bold." She raises her eyebrows at us. "Anything else?"

"No," we say together.

"Good. Then I will begin. Once there lived a young farmer and his wife. This farmer came home one day, when his wife was expecting their first child, with a wounded mongoose in his arms. It was only a little thing, with enormous black eyes and soft fur. They looked after it most tenderly, the farmer and his wife, but they worried that when their baby was born, the mongoose would be jealous and try to hurt the child.

"They needn't have feared," Mina Ma continues, "because from the moment their baby came into the world, the mongoose loved it and guarded it. He protected it so fiercely that its mother could leave the baby alone, even though their house was surrounded by treacherous woods and poisonous snakes."

I bite my fingernail. "Is a panther going to come get the baby?"

"Who is telling this story?" demands Mina Ma.

I subside into silence, adopting my most contrite expression.

"Thus did they live together, for a year. The mongoose grew big and strong. As did the baby. One afternoon the farmer and his wife went out to a festival, where they danced and ate mango pickle and fat chilies. When they returned home, all was unnaturally quiet. The farmer and his wife ran to the door, and what did they find on the threshold? It was the mongoose, watching them, with its big black eyes, and its face was stained with blood."

I gasp. Sean, opposite me, is watching Mina Ma intently.

"The farmer's wife screamed. The farmer picked up a stick and beat the mongoose until it was dead, aghast that any creature they had nourished could have turned against their baby.

"With the mongoose dead on the floor, they rushed to the baby's room. But there was their child, laughing and gurgling in her cot, with not a scratch on her. The farmer couldn't understand, but then, with a ghastly face and a trembling hand, his wife pointed to something lying on the floor, close to their child.

"It was a cobra, the most poisonous snake in the land, and it lay dead, with tooth marks in its body."

Stupidly, ridiculously, my eyes have filled with tears. My memories of this story have awakened in the back of my mind.

"There are many versions of this tale, of course," says Mina Ma, briskly threading a needle. "Hundreds."

"I remember now," I say, gazing at the French doors, where our reflections are deathly pale. "I remember that in every version I've read, the mongoose is killed."

5

MERCY

I wake at four in the morning, jerked out of an Amarra dream by something strange. I sit up in bed, listening, and realize it is the sound of the front door. It's not a normal sound this late.

"I'm sorry, Mina." I hear a muffled voice, out in the living room. Ophelia. "I know you weren't expecting me until the morning, but I couldn't sleep and I thought I'd save time and drive up early. . . ."

"Naturally," comes Mina Ma's voice, groggy with sleep. "Who would want to stay *there* any longer than necessary?"

She must mean the Loom. She never uses that tone for anything else.

"That's not what I meant," says Ophelia, sounding hurt. "I don't mind being there, I . . ." She trails off, obviously realizing it's useless. Ophelia has always defended the Loom. She has believed in it, in the Weavers, for as long as I can remember. I think she realizes she and Mina Ma will never see eye-to-eye on that subject.

After a pause, Mina Ma says, more gently, "Was it very difficult?"

There's no reply, so I assume Ophelia has nodded, because Mina Ma says, "So it went badly, then? No," she adds quickly, "you're upset. Let's go into the garden and talk."

"The kids asleep?"

"Yes."

There's a long pause. I open my door and peer out. I can see the corridor and the doorway to the next room, but no more than that. There don't seem to be any shadows moving against the wall of the living room, so they must have gone out.

A shape materializes at the foot of the stairs, inches from my bedroom door. I squeak and jerk back.

"Don't *do* that!" I hiss at Sean.

He's in the T-shirt and boxers he wears to bed, but he looks wide awake. I make myself stare at his face.

"What the hell's going on?"

"Ophelia's here," I whisper. I pull him quickly into my room and shut the door. "I guess she's been in London. But she left quite suddenly, and she seems really upset. Do you know if anything was happening at the Loom last night?"

"Weaving?" Sean asks drily.

I frown at him. "Anything else?"

"There may have been a trial," he says. "I saw something about it in the weekly update we're sent. An echo *and* her guardian. They must have broken a law."

"Well," I say, "my room faces the back garden, so we could find out."

His disapproval is obvious, but he doesn't stop me. I pad across to the window and open it a crack. I kneel down beside the sill. With a resigned look, Sean crouches across from me.

We can hear them talking. Ophelia's voice is quiet. Her hands must be shaking because I hear her lighter click several times before I smell the smoke of her cigarette.

"She must have been twenty-three, twenty-four," says Ophelia, between desperate drags, "and she was screaming. God, how she screamed. They weren't hurting her, but she was scared. I had to sit there with her." She pauses. "Her and two of the Guard. You know what they're like. They don't speak unless they have to. They just stand there, watching. Always *watching*."

Who are the Guard? I mouth the words at Sean. This is the first I've heard of them.

He hesitates, then says very softly, "They're echoes. If an echo goes wrong and can't be used as a replacement, the Weavers keep them. Raise them. They become the Guard. They protect the Loom and the Weavers. They're completely devoted."

I hadn't even known echoes could go wrong. I look down at my own fingers. I'm not broken.

"Do regular people know about them?"

"I think they've heard rumors."

That doesn't surprise me. So little of the Loom is *fact*, is understood. Until recently there were no facts at all. The Loom first started stitching life two hundred years ago, or something like it, anyway, and back then it was a secret, smoke and stories to frighten naughty children, a mysterious thing no one was ever quite sure about. And over time it's become more and more a part of the ordinary world. Now people know it exists. They know about us. And many of those people hate it. *Unnatural.* That's the word they use. I wonder how they'd feel knowing it's possible for an echo to go wrong.

"Are they treated badly?" I ask Sean. "The Guard?"

"No, they're treated kindly enough. But even if they weren't, they wouldn't betray the Loom. It's the only life they've known. They do anything, everything, the Weavers ask them to. A few of the Guard double as seekers, too."

There is a sudden sound outside. I stifle a gasp.

Sean stops speaking. I hold my breath, but no one comes to the window to confront us. I don't relax until I hear their voices again.

"And the girl?" That's Mina Ma.

"The moment they came to take her to her trial, she broke down. She wouldn't stop screaming, *begging* them to give her another chance—"

There's a silence out in the garden. I lean my head against the sill, a sour taste in my mouth, and watch Sean's face. Something solid to hold on to.

"How did they vote?"

"Oh," says Ophelia. I can tell she doesn't like the question. "Well, naturally they felt that they couldn't trust her, and I—I mean, of course they had a long think about it, but I . . .

well . . ." I hear the sound of her blowing smoke in a short, ragged burst. "Elsa wavered. She might have voted to save that poor girl. But Adrian and Matthew voted first, and they both voted to get rid of her, so Elsa gave in."

"What will happen to the guardian who broke the law with her? Prison?"

"I don't know," says Ophelia. "But he did break the law. . . ."

Mina Ma lets out a long, sad breath. "I keep hoping, with every trial, that it will change. That they will show mercy to *somebody*."

"It's not about mercy," says Ophelia. "They can't make threats and not follow through. They can't make laws and forgive if the laws are broken."

"That doesn't sound like you," says Mina Ma, rather coldly. "Is that what Adrian says?"

"That's not fair!" Ophelia protests. "They're doing what they believe is right. *Adrian* is doing what he believes is right."

There's a long, tense silence.

"Come"—Mina Ma's voice is softer now—"never mind that. You need rest, you haven't slept, and you've driven a long way. Go upstairs, use my room. I will stay with Eva for the rest of the night."

"Eva?" Ophelia demands in surprise.

"She's named herself. She says she's tired of feeling ashamed of not being like normal people. She wants something of her own."

"Good for her."

Mina Ma's voice is stern. "You'll forget to mention that to the Weavers, won't you?"

The first trace of a smile creeps into Ophelia's voice, and I feel a rush of love for her as she says, "Mention what?"

I reach to close the window. Cold creeps up my spine like icy fingertips. The Weavers never show mercy. I lean back against the wall, my leg pressed against Sean's for warmth, and neither of us moves or says a word for a long time.

6

TATTOO

There's a dream I have sometimes. It's always the same. I dream of a Weaver who made me because he loved me. I hear a dark, rough voice singing me lullabies in a room painted pale green. He talks to me. He holds me and throws me in the air and laughs. I can't make the dream go away, but I know it's false. Silly. I know not to fall into the trap of believing any kind of love ever existed.

The Weavers must never know about my name or the zoo. They must never know about how it felt when Sean touched my wrist. Or how we sat together in the dark and listened to Ophelia talk about broken laws and dying girls.

And while I keep my secrets, I must go on with Amarra's life, and Amarra's life now includes a tattoo.

The Weavers wanted to send one of their own people to do the job, but Erik suggested I go to a place in town instead.

"It's not much, a day out," he said to me over the phone. "But you'll enjoy it more than staying in the house. Mina will pretend to be your mother; they need to have a parent's permission if you're underage. Take the photo with you."

So on Monday morning, instead of lessons with Erik, I go to the tattoo artist's studio. Mina Ma and Ophelia come with me. The former is tight-lipped with disapproval, but the latter chatters to keep my spirits up. In spite of the fact that I have lived here all my life, Ophelia still feels compelled to point things out to me: the cemetery, a pub, the Beatrix Potter museum. She means well, so I pretend the pub is a novelty.

The artist's studio is down one of the alleys, and when we walk in, I am surprised it doesn't fit the seedy image I had built up in my head. It's a pleasant set of rooms with pictures of tattoos on the walls. There's an ominous sound coming from the next room, a drill whirring merrily away. I grimace, my stomach feeling heavier by the minute.

"You must be Amarra."

I turn at the sound of the light male voice. The artist is short and chubby, his pale face a study in self-alteration. I try to count his piercings, but there are too many in his eyebrows alone.

"Eva," I say before I can stop myself.

He glances questioningly at Mina Ma and Ophelia. "That's her name," says Mina Ma, in a tone no one would dare challenge.

"Okay," says the artist pleasantly. "I'm Tim. Your uncle called and made an appointment for you. Are you under the age of eighteen?" I nod. "Then you'll need one of your parents' permission."

"I'm her mother," says Mina Ma.

"Great! Then if you'll all come with me, we can get started." He leads us into a private room and shuts the door. "First time?"

"Second," I say.

It's not really a lie. I don't remember getting the Mark, which is odd because I remember just about everything, but I know it's there, burned forever into me, that lightning bolt with the curl like a small letter *e*. Mina Ma says the same mark is on the gates of the Loom, too. It's the Weavers' crest.

Tim sits me down on a stool and gets me to hold my wrist out to him. He swabs the skin with something that smells strong and medicinal, and then rubs Vaseline gently over the spot the needle will touch.

"You're nervous," he says, probably feeling my galloping pulse. "Don't worry. If it hurts too much, we'll stop right away."

We can't, not really, but he doesn't know that. He doesn't know I have to do this.

Tim turns on the needle and it starts to buzz. It's the sound that so unsettled me before. I see Mina Ma shudder, but her face stays calm. Ophelia utters a squeak, and Mina Ma elbows her. I eye the needle, gulping. It's enormous. It makes me think the slightest touch will tear straight into the fragile skin.

But I must be tougher than I thought. When he traces the ink into my skin, it's a shock because it hurts less than I expected it to. This is no worse than having somebody press hard into my skin with a pencil.

"Not so bad, is it?" says Tim, smiling.

The needle does draw blood, but Tim deftly swabs it away with a wet cotton ball. I watch him lose himself in copying the photograph of Amarra's tattoo. He's an artist and he works like one, brow fierce with concentration, hands perfectly steady.

I focus on my companions' faces, lingering on Mina Ma's eyes, the set of her lips and chin. It is strange how much stronger and safer I feel when I see *her* so strong, so firm.

In ten minutes, it's over. The tattoo is small, I hear, only about an inch long. I haven't looked at it. I flung the picture as far away from me as I could when reading the journal pages.

Tim wipes away the last of the blood and stray ink, and tells me how to help the tattoo heal faster. "Diaper cream will keep it from getting too sore or dry," he explains. "Make sure you reapply it regularly. Some people find their tattoos scab over and get itchy, but you can avoid that by keeping it moist."

I keep him talking, asking questions about looking after the tattoo, putting off having to see it. But eventually I have to look down.

I suck in a sharp breath. Erik was right. The tattoo is strangely beautiful. But it's also a tattoo of a *snake*.

The snake is delicate. Its head is turned up, looking at the sky in longing, as though it wants to fly. But all I can think of is a snake that came to bite a baby and a mongoose that slew it. A mongoose that died because of it. And now we, *I*, bear the snake.

After we've paid Tim, they take me to lunch at a nearby pub. I set my wrist carefully down on the table and try to eat a steak one-handed.

Ophelia drives home when we've finished lunch, and Mina Ma and I go back into the cottage. I wonder what I'm going to do with the rest of my day. Without the usual lessons, I have the afternoon free. After making sure Mina Ma is safely in the next room, I unearth the box beneath my bed. It's full of things I have collected over time: scrap paper, old newspapers, bits of cloth, unused candles, broken clocks, feathers, pebbles from the lake.

I melt one of the candles in a bowl and, while it's still warm and soft, start to mold shapes out of the wax. Mina Ma likes to joke about my restless hands, but this is one time my hands stay quite steady, focused. My mind goes quiet when I draw or make things. I'm not supposed to, of course. My other would rather spend her time learning about old things or out with her friends or helping Neil, her father, with his work. This is my one great secret, one I keep from everyone except Sean. It is another thing the Weavers could destroy me for. I don't think my guardians would tell them, but I don't want to force them to make that choice, either.

It's interesting that my other's mother, my familiar Alisha, is an artist. She paints and sculpts for a living. Maybe that passion skipped Amarra and I got it instead.

I am just finishing up my wax bird, a crane, when I hear the unmistakable sound of Mina Ma coming to check on me. I leap to my feet and meet her in the next room first.

"What have you been so busy with?" she asks.

"I . . . er . . . I was making something for Sean." Not strictly a lie. Sean sends me blank postcards, and I give him the bits and pieces I make. Birds and elephants and other things. "As a kind of thank-you for the zoo."

"That's nice," says Mina Ma. "Maybe it will cheer him up."

I give her a sharp look. "Why does he need cheering up?"

"Did he not tell you?" Mina Ma raises her eyebrows at me. "Well, I don't think it's a secret."

"What isn't?"

"That girl he's been—what do you call it—*going out* with," says Mina Ma. "They're not going out anymore."

I blink. "What? Why not?"

Mina Ma shrugs. "I don't pry, child. I only asked him how his girlfriend was, and he said they'd broken up. Something about her not liking that he missed her birthday."

"He told you this yesterday?"

"Not long before he left, yes."

"It's my fault!" I tell her, dismayed. "He's unhappy and it's because of me. If it wasn't for that stupid tattoo and me being so upset about it, he wouldn't have come this weekend."

Mina Ma rolls her eyes. "Don't be silly, he chose to come—"

"He wouldn't have if I hadn't made such a fuss," I say. I feel awful. "Can't we go see him? We could take him a pint of milk and the cra—the thing I made. It might cheer him up."

"Eva," says Mina Ma, sighing, "don't be ridiculous. We can't turn up out of the blue on the poor boy's doorstep. Just because I let you go to the zoo one time doesn't mean everything has changed. Why don't you call him or wait for the next time he's here?"

"That's not good enough! You can't give someone milk over the phone, and seeing as I've gone and ruined his life, I want to do *something* to fix it—"

"Ruined his life!" she says with a snort. "Ay Shiva, everything isn't life or death just because you're a teenager."

I scowl.

"There are only so many risks we can take," Mina Ma says firmly. "Is that understood?"

I hesitate before giving her my sulkiest look. "It's not fair," I tell her, in the most annoying whine I can muster.

She shakes her head. Then, satisfied that I've given in and am in a right sulk because of it, she stands and goes upstairs for her afternoon nap.

The moment I hear the telltale creak of her bed as she turns over in her sleep, I spring up and run to the fridge. I retrieve a pint of milk and shove it into my bag. I put the crane in as well and hurry into my room. I pull on my boots over my socks and leggings, swap my holey dress for one in slightly better condition, and search my desk drawer for the spare change and notes I've collected over the years. I have £21.45, which, having watched Sean buy our tickets on Saturday, I know is more than I will need for the train to Lancaster. I put the money in my bag and snatch up the phone Erik gave me for emergencies. I write a note to Mina Ma, apologizing (underlined several times) and promising her I'll send her a text as soon as I reach Sean's safely.

I have to do *something*. Lucy could have been the girl he wanted to spend the rest of his life with. I bite my lip. That thought chafes at me and I don't know why. But I do know it's not fair that he could have lost her because of me.

I hesitate at the door, thinking of the consequences if the Weavers ever find out. Of Mina Ma's anxiety when she wakes up to find me gone. Of going to Lancaster on my own, when I've never taken a step farther than the lakeshore alone before.

I close my eyes, then walk out.

The afternoon sunlight flashes across the water as I walk up the familiar road, leaving behind the cottage. The leaves on many of the trees have turned red and orange already, and tour boats bob on the main lake, flanked by sloping green hills. I pass the old church and the cemetery.

The road up to the train station feels very long. It winds gently around many bends and rows of tall, dark trees that whisper to one another in the fading sun. A bird swoops over my head, cawing, and it sounds like it's saying "Eva's gone, Eva's gone!"

I pass a lamppost and remember the man leaning against it with his old map. What if there's someone else out here watching me? What if he really *was* a hunter?

I get to the station and buy my ticket. As the lady behind the counter punches in my request, I touch the back of my neck, smoothing wayward wisps of my hair, making sure my Mark is well and truly hidden. The lady gives me my ticket with a smile and I smile back, enjoying the freedom of being a girl, no more or less. The train is waiting and I climb aboard. When we jolt ahead, I know it's too late to go back, and I sink deeper into my seat, my nerves rattling on edge.

It gets darker as the next hour wears on. Flashes of light from the motorway signal the cars moving along at blistering speeds. Fog rolls in across the hills. It slips over the road and the trees and I have to screw my forehead up to see properly through the window. I try not to think of how easy it would be to not go back at all. When an echo replaces their other, the Weavers plant a tracker in their body. But I haven't replaced Amarra, so I'm tracker-free. If I wanted to, I could flee. It would take them weeks to find me. If they found me at all.

The sun's completely gone by the time I arrive in Lancaster. I have no trouble finding my way out of the station and down the road. I never forget my way around places. I rarely forget anything.

At the top of Sean's street, my phone rings. A heavy sense of dread sinks into my stomach. I answer the call and silently accept Mina Ma's shouts, questions, and criticisms of my character. She's furious and anxious, but when I tell her I'm only yards away from Sean's house, the anxiety vanishes and leaves only the fury. After threatening to throttle me ("Who needs the Weavers? Wait till *I* get my hands on you!"), she asks how I plan to get home. I tell her I was going to take the train back. She says she'll be waiting, in a tone so ominous I shudder, and hangs up.

I put the phone away, enviously watching a pair of girls at the other end of the street. They're wearing pretty dresses and high heels and look like they're going somewhere nice for dinner or to a party.

By the time I get to Sean's house, I feel drained, drawn taut by the terror and thrill. I hesitate outside the house, catching my breath, wondering what to do if his mother opens the door.

But here I have an unexpected splash of luck. Before I can knock, the door opens, and there's Sean. He must have just gotten out of the shower because his hair is damp, like dark sparrows' feathers. His jaw is rough with stubble. He never shaves until he starts looking scruffy. His face is stony and his eyes are blazing.

"What the *fuck* are you doing here?" he demands, very quietly.

I sway slightly on the doorstep. I try to show him my bag, but my arm refuses to move. "I brought milk," I say.

7

CREATOR

Sean stares at me in disbelief. "Milk," he repeats. He covers his eyes. I wait, impatiently, on the doorstep. "Milk," he says again.

I show it to him, to clarify the matter.

"I thought it might cheer you up," I say. "I brought you a bird, too. See?"

A series of expressions crosses Sean's face. His eyes are very dark and narrow, which means he's angry. But his face softens slightly, which I think must mean he's a *little* happy to see me.

He steps aside to let me in. "Mum's fallen asleep in front of the telly—long day at work," he says. "We'll go upstairs."

I'm relieved. I've dodged another encounter with her.

I follow him up. There are three doors branching off from the landing, and two are closed, the third a bathroom. Sean leads me up one more flight of stairs. Beneath my light feet, the floor is carpet, the walls creamy and lined with small paintings and photographs. Sean's room is a converted attic. It has a sense of organized clutter about it, things piled or tucked away in various places.

Sean's shoulders are stiff. "I could kill you."

"I know." I make myself look at him, though my eyes are drawn to the floor. "I'm so sorry about Lucy. I didn't mean to—"

"What?" he barks. I jump. "You can't actually think *that's* why I'm ticked off! If you were a few inches closer, I'd shake you."

I take a prudent step backward. "Are you angry I came?"

"Of course I'm bloody angry you came," he says, "D'you know what they'll *do* if they find out? Jesus Christ, you're—"

"An absolute idiot?" I supply. "Hopelessly impractical?"

"It was a—"

"Reckless thing to do? I know."

"The Weavers—"

"Would have every reason to destroy me if they find out."

"Stop doing that," he growls.

"They won't find out," I tell him. "I wouldn't have come if I'd thought they might. You and I won't tell, and Mina Ma is the only other person who knows, and she won't breathe a word to them about it."

"You shouldn't have come anyway," he bites out. "Have you forgotten that you may have had a *hunter* watching your house only a short while ago? One day you'll do something else like this and you won't get away with it. One day you *won't* be able to escape facing the consequences. What will you do then?"

"I don't know," I say. "I won't know until I'm there and it's happened. Look, I didn't come here to fight. I was sorry about Lucy. I knew it was a risk, but I thought it'd be worth it if I could cheer you up. It's my fault you didn't get to spend the weekend with her."

He sighs. I hold out the wax bird. He hesitates but takes it. "It's not your fault," he says. "But thank you. For wanting to cheer me up."

"Was it really because you missed her birthday?"

"Yeah, she wasn't happy about that."

I open my mouth to say something, then close it again.

"You can say it," he says, a crooked smile wiping his angry look away. "You think that was a tad unreasonable."

I nod.

"Maybe." He shrugs. "But it wasn't exactly fair of me to say I'd do something with her on her birthday and then say I had to go away for the weekend instead."

"You don't seem very upset," I say, trying to keep the accusation out of my voice.

He grins. "Feel cheated, do you? You came all this way, risked everything, and I'm not even a sobbing wreck. Doesn't seem worth it?"

I laugh and bite my lip. "I thought you liked her."

"I did," he says.

I press the issue. It feels suddenly and unbearably important to me that I know. "*Past* tense?"

"I suppose," he says. "I don't know. We have a lot in

common. We both do theater at school. We both like watching soccer, we both like going to the pub around the corner. And she's very—" He rethinks whatever word he was about to use, something crude, no doubt. "Pretty. Maybe that's all it was. I did duck out of her birthday. I wouldn't have done that if I liked her as much as I used to think I did. And I don't think she'd have been so keen on splitting up if she liked me all that much either."

I don't say anything. Sean shakes his head like he's shaking off the subject, and he gestures at my hand. "Can I see?"

I show him the tattoo, just visible under a layer of cream.

"Mmm, dried blood," says Sean. "Very fetching."

I say a rude word.

"Swearing is so unbecoming, love."

I laugh in spite of myself. "I need to reapply the cream, actually. Do you happen to have any in the house?"

"I'll have a look. Does Mina know you're here?"

"I slipped out while she was having her afternoon rest, but she rang before I got to your door. She was *not* amused."

"You astonish me."

"She's going to cut my heart out and hang it to dry. Then, for good measure, she'll feed me mango pickle for the rest of the year."

"Woe is you." He walks to the door. "Put the telly on or something. I'll be back in a minute."

I flick the telly on, but look around the room instead. This is his territory. I want to explore it, like fingers tracing contours on someone's body.

Pieces of paper with notes and scribbles, a laptop with books stacked beside it, a school jacket hanging over the desk chair, books and DVDs on the shelves, crammed in because there are so many, an MP3 player, CDs, a grubby soccer ball in the corner of the room, scratched-out scenes from a script or a play he must be working on, phone numbers for a couple of theaters in London, notes from a director with a funny name, homework, a row of wax birds on top of his bookshelf—

"—that echoes have no souls is certain."

I jerk my head around. I must have flicked the telly onto the news. Someone is speaking over a news story of a hunter killing an echo in Bristol. It's not the first time I've seen a story like it, but it doesn't exactly happen every day, either. The clip cuts back to a live studio, where there seems to be a debate about echoes. A young, pretty host is interviewing a tall man wearing dark robes.

"Don't you think that's a little harsh, Father MacLean?" the presenter asks. "Can we be certain of anyone's soul, human or otherwise?"

"I have nothing but pity in my heart for these unfortunate creatures," the man says. His face is severe, solemn. "But they are abominations. God is our creator. No Weaver has the right to create life out of materials too horrifying to ponder. What good can come of grave-robbing and *buying* the dead from morgues? The Weavers are playing an ungodly game with these echoes."

"That's not—"

The priest interrupts her. His tone changes, like he's quoting from something. "'Frightful must it be,'" he says, "'for supremely frightful would be the effect of any human endeavor to mock the stupendous mechanism of the Creator of the world.'"

"*Frankenstein*, I believe," the presenter replies, rather drily. A chill goes through me. "An odd choice for a priest."

He dismisses that and says, "How do these creatures hope to find heaven? Without souls, God will not welcome them."

There's a movement at the corner of my eye. I turn my head to see Sean standing by the door. It's difficult to tell how long he's been there.

"Is that true, Sean?" I ask him. "Does God hate me?"

"Course not," he says roughly. "God doesn't hate anyone. Isn't that the point? Look, I don't even know if he exists, but it doesn't matter. Who cares about heaven? We're on Earth. And *I* know you have a soul, or whatever else it is that makes us human."

He gives me the cream and goes to turn off the news.

"Wait," I say.

The man in the robes is leaving the armchair, and there's a different man coming on. He's tall, and too thin, with a sharp, handsome face. He must be fifty-five or so. His hair is dark brown and short, growing back from his forehead like a lion's. He has a lion's gold eyes and lazy grace, too. He unsettles me deeply, like there are spiders crawling along my skin. What's worse is how familiar he seems. Like I've seen his face before.

"Is that—?" I whisper.

"Adrian Borden," says Sean, and there's a note in his voice that makes me think he might be aware of that spidery feeling too. He hesitates. "A Weaver."

"I know." I feel like ice has filled my lungs. I've always known their names. Adrian Borden, Matthew Mercer, Elsa Connelly. Sometimes I think I even know their faces. I used to ask Erik questions about them, but I stopped when I was eight or nine years old and it struck me that *not* knowing made it easier to pretend they couldn't hurt me. I must have seen all three of them, as a baby, when I was born and stitched in the Loom, but this is the first time I've looked into one of their faces since. All the years of terror, of fearing and resenting that dark thing on the fringes of my life, focus now on the face on the screen. It's a funny thing, to realize that somebody you are looking at may have made you with his own two hands. To know those hands could unstitch you again.

"Adrian Borden didn't make you," says Sean, as though he can see the conflict and fear in my face. "I asked Erik once. Matthew made you."

I suppose that makes it better, knowing it's not this man on the screen. But what if Matthew is worse?

"Erik knows them very well, doesn't he?" I say, remembering the way I would pester him for answers as a young child.

"He used to, anyway."

Sean sits down on the bed next to me. We watch the gold eyes and sharp marble face of the Weaver. "I met him once," Sean says. "I used to go down to London a lot with Dad when he was still your guardian. I was quite little the one time he took me to the Loom. It was such a strange place. It seemed to belong to a different time. It was so *old*. Dad met him while he was there. Adrian, I mean. I don't remember what they talked about, but I remember he scared me."

"I don't like his eyes," I say. "He looks like nothing would stop him if he wanted something."

Sean smiles wryly. "The Weavers have achieved the impossible, creating life," he says. "But Dad once said Adrian wanted more. Now that he knows how to create life, he wants to find a way to *prolong* it. He experiments. He doesn't stop. There have been rumors . . ." He hesitates. "About things he's been doing. Grave-robbing. Strange tests on echoes."

"How do you hear about these things?" I ask him.

"Dad and Erik, mostly. Also by skimming the Loom records. But a few stories have leaked into the news, like the grave-robbing. That was on the news last week, but no one's been able to prove it."

I point at the screen. "Why is he doing an interview?"

Sean shrugs. "To keep up appearances. It's not like it used to be, before we were born, when the Loom could get away with staying completely in the dark. The Weavers do interviews every year so that people will think they're normal. Respectable. Trustworthy."

I focus on the conversation happening on-screen. The presenter has grown agitated. I wonder if she, too, finds him unsettling.

"But you must realize," she's arguing, "the secrecy is a problem for them. Don't you think they might become less controversial if you talked to the world about how you create them? Echoes might have an easier time of it."

"I don't Weave for the world's peace of mind," says Adrian Borden. He has an unforgettable voice. Smooth and tightly leashed. "I do it for the awe of creating life from nothing."

"But—"

"Echoes aren't here to have an easy time of it. They are here to be somebody else. I am not concerned about their individual standing in the world. They are echoes of others. They are living proof that humankind might, ultimately, cheat death. I create *life*. That is the rarest of all gifts."

I can't believe my ears. "No wonder people think we're just mindless, soulless copies," I say bitterly. "You'd have thought he might feel *some* paternal concern for us."

"Why don't you ask Ophelia about his capacity for paternal feelings?"

"Why would she know?"

"Because he's her father," says Sean.

My eyes pop. "He can't be! She's *nice*. And she would have told me—"

"Why?" he asks. "She knows how you feel about them.

81

Why would she willingly admit to you that a man you fear and hate is her father?"

It's suddenly clear why Ophelia defends the Loom when the rest of us criticize it. Why she so passionately believes in it. When she first arrived, years ago, it didn't take me long to get Mina Ma to tell me why she was there: she would be the link between the Weavers and me, reporting my progress back to them. I hated her instantly, but she was so friendly, so eager to please, she eventually won me over. She has never told the Weavers about my defiance, about the things that could put me in danger. She has always stood by me.

"He's her father." It's such a strange thought. "She was talking about him, in the garden with Mina Ma. She cares about him."

Sean nods. "Adores him. They've had their problems in the past. He wasn't around much when she was little, and she's heard the rumors. But she doesn't believe the bad things are true."

I watch Adrian Borden's eyes glitter. "Do you think I'll ever go back to the Loom, see them again?"

"Hope you don't," says Sean. "When an echo goes back to the Loom, they're usually about to die."

We stare at each other in silence. Eventually I look away and start smoothing a fresh layer of the cream into my tattoo. Sean sits down at his desk, spinning the chair around to face me.

Onscreen, the presenter is struggling. I have to give her

credit for braving the quicksand of Adrian Borden. "Aren't you concerned the stigma will attach itself to *you*, as the Weavers of echoes?" she demands.

"Why would I fear that?" Borden asks. "Nobody blames the creator. It was the monster people feared, not Victor Frankenstein."

This time, I can't stop Sean. He turns off the news.

"So close," I complain.

"Yeah, nice try."

I finish treating the tattoo. I run my fingers over the snake, misty and distorted under the layers of cream.

"I wish I was human."

"You *are* human."

"Really human. A proper human with a proper soul and everything."

"Ever read about the Little Mermaid? She wanted to be human. She got what she wanted. Then she died."

First a mongoose, now a mermaid. Why don't these stories ever end happily?

"I should probably go soon," I say reluctantly. "I don't want to miss the last train back. Mina Ma will be waiting, ax at the ready, and a shovel to bury my body once she's done chopping my head off."

He chuckles, stands up again. "Will you be all right getting home on your own?"

I give him a nasty look. He raises his hands. "I'm only asking."

"I got here on my own, didn't I?"

"You did," he acknowledges, "but I can walk you to the train station."

I want to tell him he doesn't have to, but I stop. His eyes are greener than usual in the light from the lamp. I don't want to go. I'm a girl, but I'm also an echo, and I shouldn't *want* to stay. But I do. Have I always felt this way? I don't know. All I know is, I want to stay and that's wrong.

Sean swears under his breath. "Stop looking at me like that," he says.

"I wasn't looking!"

"Were."

"Wasn't."

"If I could—"

"If I wasn't—"

We both stop. Whatever we were going to say, we won't say it. I turn around and start for the door. Sean follows me. We cross through the house, without waking his mother, and walk out into the night. The air feels good, cold and sharp against my warm skin. I watch the cobbles on the street until Sean takes the plunge and starts talking about the *weather*, of all things, and I go along with it, leaping from there to discussing a song that's been overplayed on the radio recently.

"I had a dream last night," I tell him, when there's nothing left to say about the stupid song. "I was flying. I had wings."

"I used to have those dreams. When I was six, I used to

dress up like Peter Pan, and every time I lost an eyelash, I wished I could fly."

I give him an innocent look. "Wow. So *your* eyelashes made airplanes!"

He laughs.

We sit together on a bench at the train station. For one minute I allow myself to think of those movies, where the couple goes to the train station and they kiss good-bye, and it's sweet and sad and lovely all at once.

My train pulls in and we stand up and I almost do it. Almost lean up on my toes and kiss him, wrap my arms around his neck, feel his fingers on my skin. But I don't. I don't know how.

And I think of Ophelia, smoking her cigarette and talking about a dead girl. Of Erik telling Mina Ma, years ago, about an echo dying because she—or was it a he?—ran away. Broke the law.

That's enough to stop me, this time.

"What do you dream about?" Sean asks me. "When you're not dreaming about flying away? Is it always Amarra's life?"

"No, I only have the Amarra dreams now and then. Otherwise it's cities. I always dream of cities." I don't tell him about my dreams of the green nursery.

"What about people?"

"Sometimes. People in those cities."

I step onto the train and turn back to look at him. He's quiet, says nothing.

"What do you dream about, Sean?"

He's staring at me, but he takes a step back as a whistle blows. I raise my hand to wave as the compartment door starts to slide shut.

"You," he says, before the door closes all the way. "I often dream of you."

8

DESIRE

It's a good photograph. Beautiful. The sunlight falls perfectly against his face, reflecting sharp and clear off its angles. Brown eyes squint at the light. And that smile, so sweet, sincere, spontaneous, a happy moment captured on film.

Yes, it's a splendid piece of work, but it doesn't change that awful question. Can I love the boy smiling at me from this photograph?

No, not at me. Smiling at *her*.

"Oh."

I spin around at the unexpected voice. Sean is standing behind me, staring at the picture I've been examining. I want to hide the photograph from him, but I can't move my hands. I've never seen a deer caught in headlights, but I've heard it's like the poor thing's been frozen, pinned in place, and I feel a little like that now.

"So this is him?"

"Yes."

"Bit pasty, isn't he, for an Indian kid?"

"He's not *pasty*."

"He's fairer skinned than you. But you don't get much of a tan, seeing as you spend your life in this marvelous climate. What's his excuse?"

"He's half French."

"How unfortunate for him. Is he called Pierre?"

"No, as a matter of fact, he isn't called bloody Pierre. His name's Ray. I think his mother's French."

"I'm sure you'll make a lovely pair."

"He and *I* are never going to make a lovely anything," I snap, "because I'm never going to meet him. Odds are Amarra will outlive their sweet little love story. And me."

"Stop saying things like that. She won't outlive you."

"Then you don't say rude things because you don't like him."

"Don't *like* him? I don't even know him. But you"—he grimaces at me—"you're defending him already. I suppose you're well on your way to falling in love, then, like you're meant to."

I spring out of the chair and stomp away.

We've never acted so angry with each other before. It's been months, a whole autumn and winter and spring, since the night I snuck out to his house and that moment as the train doors closed. In all that time we've never got to arguing like this. I thought we would. We jumped like scalded cats every time we accidentally touched, we avoided each other's eye if the room was full—it was *weeks* after that evening before we went back to talking and acting like we used to. I had expected something to snap in that time. But it never did.

Yet now—

I storm out the back and throw myself into the swing. The sky is gray, overcast, and grim. Soon it'll start to rain (what a surprise, rain in England!) and I'll have to go back indoors.

The photograph has turned everything topsy-turvy. I should have seen it coming, but I didn't. It startled us all.

The first time I saw the face of the boy in the picture, it was the night before my birthday. At the end of April.

After I slipped away to see Sean, Mina Ma went angry lioness in the extreme and scarcely let me out of the house for months. She still doesn't trust me not to do something reckless again. I can't blame her. I haven't exactly given her reason to think of me as a steady, cautious type. So I spent most of my time at the cottage, as snow came and went over the lakes and I got a lopsided haircut for the New Year because Amarra, for reasons unbeknownst to me, let her best friend, Sonya, go at her hair with a pair of blunt scissors.

Really. I'd expected more sense from her.

And on the night before my sixteenth birthday, I dreamed about a boy with black hair and dark, flashing eyes. He looked familiar. Maybe I had dreamed about him before, but I have no memory of it. My chest tightened. I felt like I knew him, which was strange, and the way I felt looking at him was even stranger, until I woke up and realized that it must have been some snapshot of Amarra's life. Someone she knew from school or a friend of the family's.

Those feelings, the feelings I shared with her in the dream, should have tipped me off, but I didn't pay attention.

I woke up and I was sixteen.

The rest of my birthday went so normally, so perfectly, there was no reason to stop or to ask questions. Sean and Erik and Ophelia came, with presents, and Mina Ma made me a cake in the shape of a baby elephant. We cleaned the house and put up balloons for my party. I thought I was too old for balloons, but Mina Ma said she'd rather it was balloons than kisses with boys in a corner. Sean coughed and stared at the floor. I examined the tablecloth. Mina Ma coughed, too, only hers sounded suspiciously like a laugh.

I didn't give Amarra's boy another thought. Not for many weeks. Then the photograph turned up. With his face on it. Now it has a name, too. Ray. Now it's almost *all* I can think about.

The wind whips my cheeks. I close my eyes and open them again. I'm still in the swing and the weather hasn't changed and the world has still gone on turning. The photograph of Ray is on the damp grass below me. I don't remember dropping it.

What did Erik say to me?

"Learn him the way she knows him and try to love him the way you've learned to love her family."

But have I genuinely learned to love Neil and Alisha? I

know their faces. I know so much about them. Over time, I've even grown to feel attached to them, like something vital would be missing if they were suddenly gone. She loves her parents. I should too. And her brother, Nikhil, and little sister, Sasha. I keep the photos of Sasha getting older and bigger and I sometimes even smile fondly at them. I don't know if that means anything. I don't know if these are leftover feelings passed on from Amarra or the product of a lifetime of *acting* like I love them.

Now must I love this boy too, because she does?

Ray.

"They've been together over a year," Erik told me on Wednesday. "She kept it a secret as long as she could. I expect she would have kept it quiet even longer, but Sasha saw them together. She says she loves him. So you must too."

"Why?" I demanded. "What's the point? They'll probably break up in a few months, anyway; doesn't everyone our age fall in and out of love?" I sounded bitter, but I couldn't help it.

"Eva," said Erik, very gently, "please. I know this is hard, but it's the law."

I looked into his face, saw the lines in his forehead, the worried look in his eyes. And I said okay, I'd do it.

He had some notes about Ray, basic things that my familiars had told him. He also had the week's journal pages for me.

I opened them and suffered a shock—for the first time in

our lives, Amarra wrote *to* me. And even stranger, as I read her words, I didn't see them. I heard them. Soft but rigid with outrage. I knew her voice so well.

They want me to tell you all about him. They want me to tell you everything, everything we did, the places we've been, secrets we've told each other. All that stuff. But you're crazy if you think I will. You're a thief. You've stolen everything else. But you can't have this. You have no right to him.

She was right. I *am* the thief. I've taken everything that belongs to her. She's had to give it all up. What must that be like, to know that every single thing you wear, every last thing you know, is being copied, mimicked, duplicated halfway across the world?

I may not like her much, but she shouldn't have to tell me a thing. I feel nauseated at the very thought of being given a window into a love I have no right to.

A treacherous, dangerous idea crosses my mind. Wouldn't I feel the same, if it were Sean? Wouldn't I refuse, passionately, fiercely, to tell *my* echo anything about him? She would have no right to him, *I* have no right—

Yet it's the law. One day if I exist and she doesn't, I will have to go there and love him as best I can, the way she would have done. Her life is a relentless wave coming at me, crashing against the shore, again and again and again.

The rain starts up, water trickling slowly between my

fingers, along my nose, onto my lips. I taste it, then get up and walk back inside, closing the French windows to keep the heat in. Through the windows and the water running down the cold glass, I watch the wet swing sway. What will they do with the swing when I'm gone?

Sean's reflection appears in the windows behind me, flickering with color in the mixture of rain and daylight. He leans against the door frame beside me.

"I'm sorry," he says.

"Me too. Shouldn't have stormed away."

"Shouldn't have made you," he replies. He smiles faintly and lets out a breath, but it's not very steady. "He looks all right," he says. I glance around at him, puzzled by the struggle in his voice. "Nice enough."

"Ray?"

"Yeah. He's probably all right, I reckon."

I think of the boy in the photograph. There was a look in his face that made me envious, made me feel a powerful surge of longing. To be looked at like that, to be so obviously *loved* . . . it had been so *clear* how he felt about her, like looking directly into the sun.

I nod. "I could learn to like him, or pretend to, if I had to. Maybe it wouldn't always have to be pretend, either. Sometimes you can make yourself feel something for real if you will it hard enough."

"Can you?"

I shrug. "On the other hand," I say very quietly, "maybe

I don't want to. Maybe I don't want him and won't *ever* want him."

He's silent. Shadows of the rain trace a path across his face. I can see him struggling, his eyes flickering over the garden. Sweet, bitter heat shoots across my skin, right into my blood. I know his eyes so well. I can map the tiniest shift onto his thoughts.

"There's nobody else you're allowed, as long as she chooses this," he says eventually. "No one but him."

I strive for flippancy, because what else can I say? "Despite him being half French?"

"That *is* a serious flaw."

"Do you think they say the same about you?"

"The French? They love making fun of our cold English reserve."

I count raindrops on the glass.

"Why does he bother you so much?" I ask before I can stop myself.

Sean is very still. We're so close I can feel his breath on my hair. It feels electric; it turns my skin to goosebumps. I want to look away. I don't. I keep my face tilted up, my gaze fixed on his.

"Dunno," he says at last. Carefully.

I swallow, my throat tightening. I should just leave it here, but my unruly tongue, my reckless soul, will not be quelled.

I hear my next words before I can stop myself from uttering them.

"I think you do."

"Eva," he says, so quietly I can hardly hear it, "don't you know what they'll do to you? Echoes have died because they've loved the wrong person. That's how the Loom's justice works. It scares the hell out of me every day."

There's a thick, heavy taste on my tongue. Before I can think of a reply, the front door clatters open.

We separate like someone shot flames between us. Mina Ma bustles in, her arms full of bags. Sean goes to help. His muscles look tense and knotted up. I follow. My throat feels so tight I don't dare speak.

I envision a pair of hands reaching for me and touching my hair. I picture the hands pulling at a lock of my hair, pulling and pulling because it doesn't stop sliding out, it's a thread, unraveling my head and my lips and my body and my feet, until I am lost, gone, unpicked and unstitched, unwoven from the strands that made me. It's the cost of trampling on the Weavers' laws.

Over dinner, Sean's eyes are far away. I look at Mina Ma, my most faithful, the one who has loved and protected me longest. I reach across the table and touch her hand. A tiny smile crosses her face, and she pushes my hair back from my forehead. Things have been tense lately. I think we're all unraveling already. We don't need the Weavers to do it.

I sleep restlessly that night. I drift into cities, dreams. Churches and spires, temples and dust. Old gods, Shiva the destroyer, merry blue Krishna raising a hand as though he wants to warn me, stars transforming into angels. Cities, cities.

I follow a deserted cobbled road to a clock tower, dark and forbidding with the silver slant of a cold sun in the sky. The tower is the color of wine, a red-purple so dark it could be black, and I can see eagles crying out from the sky. A woman stands at the top of the steps, clad in gray silks that ripple in the wind. She's older than Erik. Her hair is still gold, but her eyes give away her age.

I stop a few steps beneath her, looking up at her, and she smiles very sadly. "What do you desire?" she says. "What does your heart want?"

I don't speak. I can't. Images flicker in my memory. A green nursery and a man laughing. He has a voice like thunder and lions. A broken vase with water spilling across the floor. Cutting my foot on the glass and crying because I made a mess. Erik telling me not to worry. He will clear it up. A cold-eyed doctor fleeing Mina Ma's rolling pin. A boy with damp hair.

I leave the clock tower behind and walk away. My bare feet contract against the cold. I walk faster, as though the clock's shadow is a curse, but the shadow lengthens as I run and I can't get away. I turn into a house and push the door open and run inside. It's warmer. In the light slanting through the window, I see Sean, standing by a fireplace with his back to me.

"It's cold outside," he says.

"Yes."

There's a pause, a silence that hangs in the air like droplets of the finest silver. Slowly Sean turns around.

"Eva," he says.

I go to him without hesitation and touch his lips, the taut line of his jaw. He does not move. I put my palm on his chest. Beneath it, I can feel his heart beating.

He takes my hand, easing out my elbow. He bends his head low and his lips touch the crook of my elbow, so faintly I gasp,

and open my eyes.

I blink. The dream is gone, vanished like smoke. I am awake. Alert.

In the silver of my moonlit room, I look at the inside of my arm, bent slightly at the elbow, held out at an angle. I touch the spot where the skin tingles. I breathe in and out, but it doesn't stop my heart thrumming too fast, frantically.

I look up and there's someone else in the room. Sean is by the wall, watching me.

"How long have you been there?"

"A few minutes," he says.

"Why?"

"I don't know," he admits uncertainly. "I came to talk to you, but then I didn't want to wake you."

We look at each other for long, silent moments, and I see something flash briefly into Sean's face and then disappear again. But there long enough that I recognize it. Despair.

"I don't want him," I say. "I want you."

"That's punishable."

"I don't care about the laws."

He laughs softly, but it's a funny sound. "It doesn't matter."

"Why not?"

"Because I do."

"Don't you care about me more than you do the laws?"

"No," he says quietly.

I stare at him silently, my throat tight and my eyes raw. "No," I repeat, wrapping my arms around my knees. "I see."

He crosses the room and comes to me, his feet brushing softly against the floor. I look up at him. He touches my face with his thumb. "I'd rather spend the rest of my life without ever seeing you again," he says, "than watch them destroy you because of me." His hand slips to the back of my neck, skimming over my Mark, and stops in my hair. He leans down and kisses my forehead. I long to reach up, close my fingers over his arm, keep him here. He pulls away but not by much. His mouth lingers on my forehead and then, as if with an effort, he straightens.

"Want *him*," he says, his face hidden in shadow, "not me. He'd love you more than I could."

Then he leaves me alone.

Sean doesn't believe in superstition. But when the world collapses in on itself, I remember him telling me he'd rather never see me again than watch the Weavers destroy me because of him. I can't help thinking that when he said it, he somehow turned those words into reality.

At the end of August, I have another dream and it's different from the others. I dream of a city, but it's a real city. It's Bangalore as it exists right now.

And it changes everything.

I recognize the city from Mina Ma's descriptions and stories, from the photographs, from the snapshots of Amarra's mind. There's the ice-cream shop down the road from her house, with the Baskin-Robbins logo dark and unlit above the windows. It stays with me, that image. It's the only clear spot as light flashes through everything else, setting my skull on fire.

Then fragments, pieces flying one after another: the bright lights, a speeding car, streetlights that I try to count as they spin by, Ray, Ray's face, laughing.

A motorcycle comes around a corner too fast; the car swerves to avoid it. The car skids off the road. I'm scared, so scared. We're scared. My body crashes through glass.

Screaming, I thrash to life, fighting my own sheets. It happened so fast, I couldn't stop it. We couldn't even move.

Mina Ma is there, holding me while I scream. I search my body, but there's no blood, no car, no shattered glass. I am safe, I am alive.

She pushes me gently back into bed and goes to fetch some water. Without her there to hold me in place, I flounder. Understanding seizes me, prompted by some unspeakable instinct. By a dark, empty thing in my chest. An absence. I curl up on the bed, shivering, and cover my face with my hands. "Amarra?" I whisper between my shaky fingers. As though she might answer. She doesn't. She'll never answer anyone again.

Erik comes to visit us in the afternoon. Mina Ma is surprised to see him because it's not one of his days, but I'm not. I know exactly why he's here. I watch him, blank and unsurprised, as he tells me what I already know: that my other is dead and I have to go.

PART TWO

GOOD-BYES

I don't want to go. I say it, over and over, but it doesn't make any difference. I have to. This is why I was born.

"You're all your familiars have left now," Erik reminds me. "They want nothing more than to have her back. They're grieving. They *need* you."

"But they know I'm not actually her!"

"Yes," says Erik, "but you have to understand that all they have is hope. They're hoping you *will* be perfect. It's a one-in-a-thousand chance that Amarra's soul could have survived her death, but that's all they can think of. That's what you must be for them." He gives me a long, sad look. "You've been Eva too long. It's time to be Amarra."

I'm going. I'm really going.

And I will never see my guardians again.

"Eva," he says more gravely, "there's something else we have to talk about. You know, of course, that echoes are illegal in India. And you understand that if the police discovered that your familiars have you, they would go to prison." I nod. "What you may not know is if the police *do* find out, they will also take you into custody. They could choose to destroy you themselves. More likely, the Weavers will be able to win you back, but even so, I fear they would destroy you anyway." Erik looks me in the eye. "Under normal circumstances, it is essential that an echo does not reveal what they are to anyone apart from their familiars. That's even more important in your case. You will soon be breaking a law simply by existing."

"I understand, Erik."

"I don't particularly want to see Neil or Alisha go to prison," he adds with one of his twinkly-eyed smiles, "but I'm more concerned about you. Be careful."

"I will, Erik," I promise.

"Good."

"Will you be taking me to Bangalore?"

He shakes his head. "No, unfortunately. Matthew has decided to take you instead. He's better acquainted with your other's family."

My family now. I don't know which thought is more sickening. The idea of becoming part of someone else's family and pretending they are mine? Or the idea of traveling across the world in the company of the Weaver who stitched me with his own hands? They've controlled me, kept me all my life. If I slip up, they're the ones who will unmake me. How do you face someone like that?

"What's he like, Erik?"

"That's a difficult question," says Erik. "Matthew is a

difficult, if not downright insufferable, human being."

This is hardly reassuring. "But you're friends."

"We met at university. He, Adrian, and I. Elsa taught history. Matthew and I have been friends since. Sometimes against my better judgment." A smile crosses his face. "When they became Weavers and took over the Loom, I became the first guardian. I thought I'd do better to protect you than create you."

I have a brief, chilling flash to what my life would have been like if Erik had chosen not to be involved.

"You've saved me more times than I can count," I say. I will have to leave him soon and might never have a chance to say this again. "You're the only human thing about the Loom."

He shakes his head. "That isn't true. The Weavers aren't your enemy, Eva. At least, they don't have to be."

"Only if I follow their laws."

He doesn't answer that, which is acknowledgment enough. He stares out at the lake and his sea-colored eyes grow astonished. "It's been thirty years. Sometimes it feels like it was yesterday. Matthew and Adrian were just boys then. So was I. Sometimes I look at them and still see those boys. Not the men they've become."

"What's wrong with the men they've become?"

Erik only sighs.

"Can I trust Matthew?"

That makes his mouth turn upward. "To get you to

Bangalore safely, certainly. With anything else? Let me put it this way. Would you drink cyanide for breakfast?"

I smile bleakly. "I'll take that as a no."

We go back inside. The Weavers have given me a week, in which time I am expected to tie up my life in England like a present with a ribbon and bow. A week for two parents, far away, to tidy away the last of their daughter and await a copy.

I pack my things over the next few days. A lady from the Weavers arrives. She puts me under anesthesia and places a tracker in my body, tiny and undetectable. I don't know where it is, and no one will tell me for fear I might try to take it out. I must not be allowed to slip free of the net.

After the tracker lady has left, I spend an hour running my fingers over my skin, hoping to feel some sort of bump or lump. Nothing. So I give up and go back to packing.

My guardians give me things to take with me. Last presents. Ophelia hands me a box full of makeup. "Something silly and fun," she says. "You don't have enough of it." Sean's gifts are a bracelet made of seashells and a book called *British Romanticism* that looks so boring I'm somewhat surprised he'd even considered giving it to me. Mina Ma gives me a beautiful black dress, knee length and elegant, and it's so unlike anything Amarra owns that a lump forms in my throat.

And Erik gives me a single envelope. "There's a key in there," he says. "Don't lose it." When I look blankly at him, he explains, "It opens a safe-deposit box we set up years ago for you. You'll have access to all of Amarra's possessions now, so you may never need it. But if you do, if you're ever desperate, it's there. And Eva," he adds, "I need hardly add that it would be best if the Weavers never found out about this."

I burst into tears.

Right now I would give anything to stay, but Mina Ma, incredibly, is *happy*. She can live with the thought of never seeing me again because she believes I will be safe now. Hunters won't find me while I'm playing the part of an ordinary girl. The Weavers won't hurt me unless I break their laws. My familiars want me. Mina Ma is determined that I will live a long time.

"You have learned her all your life," she says to me with fierce intensity. "Be what they need now. Give them an illusion. Make them believe she's still here. Give them that hope. If you do, if you make them see her when they look into your eyes, they will keep you. For *years*. And if you are good, when they are gone, no one will be able to take your life away from you." She touches my cheek. "It's the only consolation I have."

So I smooth the lines of worry and ferocity from her face. I promise her I'll do what she asks. I promise I will do my best to forget myself.

I sit on my bed the evening before I leave. I will never come here again. I am not supposed to see my guardians again. This existence is over. I am Amarra now.

My room looks bare, naked. It's silly to think so, because not much has changed, I've only had to pack my clothes and a few other things. But the room already looks unlived in. It looks like I left a long time ago. I lie back on the bed, fully clothed, and try to swallow something hard and knotty in my throat. My guardians will all be here tomorrow, to see me one last time. We'll say good-bye.

How will I *bear* it? How am I supposed to spend the rest of my life with half strangers, never seeing Mina Ma again? And Sean . . .

I close my eyes and try to sleep.

By three o' clock the next afternoon, Ophelia has arrived. Mina Ma is keeping herself busy, making everybody a drink and somewhat ferociously offering food. I sit quietly. I can't eat or drink anything. Sean isn't here yet. Erik will be bringing Matthew soon. I can hear the second hand on the clock on the wall, ticking so loudly it hurts my brain each time. Mina Ma keeps looking at me as though she wants to tell me something but doesn't know how. This worries me, but I can't focus on it. My attention flits from one thing to the next. Ophelia is sniffing into a tissue, wiping tears away. I want to comfort her and tell her I'll miss her, but I can't move. *Tick, tock, tick, tock*, the clock is relentless.

Where is Sean?

After I've looked hopefully at the front door for the hundredth time in about half an hour, Mina Ma seems unable to stand it any longer. "He's not coming," she says.

"The Weaver's not coming?" I ask, puzzled but pleased.

She's struggling, then says very quickly, "Sean. He's not coming."

I can't quite digest this. "Why not?"

"He's ill."

This is a lie. Ophelia can't even look at me. I have no idea what to do or say. So I turn back to the clock, squinting to keep it in focus because my eyes have begun to water. Unbidden, an image of Sean creeps into my head. I picture him under his slanting roof, at the window. I imagine him saying "Just go, Eva. I don't care."

Tick, tock, tick, tock, and then the sound of Erik's car pulling up outside the cottage. I stand. It's time.

Mina Ma goes to open the door. Erik comes in first. I look past him, into the eyes of the man who wove me.

He is about as tall as Erik, and probably as thin, and about the same age. He reminds me of a polished predator, immense brilliance hidden beneath an urbane smile and shrewd dark blue eyes. His beard stubble is short and rough, salt-and-pepper like his cropped hair. Dressed in shirt and trousers, he has the strangest vest on over his shirt. It looks like thin chain mail, glittering silver like that of a knight from a forgotten time.

I've seen him before. I've dreamed him before.

"I know you," I say.

"You have a good memory, even for an echo," he says,

teeth showing in a smooth, feral smile. "You must remember your early months."

If Sean's voice is layers of wood, and Mina Ma's is a copper pot, then Matthew Mercer's is the voice of a wild animal. I suddenly think of a movie Amarra and I loved when we were little, and I think of Scar, the lion who murdered his brother to become king. *That* kind of voice.

"How like your mother you look," he remarks.

I shrink back, but say defiantly, "Alisha is not my mother."

Mina Ma gasps. It's not a good start, but I can't help it. He sets my teeth on edge. He scares the living daylights out of me.

"Now, now," he says. "Claws are unattractive on kittens. You have a latent temper, I see. I suppose I'm to blame. I did make you."

Erik frowns. "Don't be flippant, Matthew. She's having a difficult time."

"Aren't we all?" the Weaver demands in indignation. "Are we or are we not recovering from a global recession? Difficult economic times, you know. We're all suffering."

I look at him in disbelief.

"Sir Matthew," he says, sweeping me an elaborate bow, "at your service. But I wouldn't take that literally if I were you. I'm notorious for only being of service if I feel like it, and I don't usually feel like it." He studies me a moment longer, and the strangest look crosses his face. His drawl fades. He becomes curt, an irritable stranger instead of the flippant one. "Shall we set off? We have a flight to catch in seven hours."

"I'll get my things," I mutter.

"Sullen, too," he says as I turn away. "I think we'll get along *marvelously*, don't you?"

We pack the car in record time. My legs begin to drag and I try to draw it out as long as I can. The good-byes become a blur, an exercise in trying not to cry. Ophelia sobs openly as she hugs me. Erik is driving us to the train station, so I go, finally, to Mina Ma, blinking away tears. She grips me very tightly and whispers in my ear, "Be good. Be happy."

She is the last thing I see before the car turns the corner. I catch Matthew's dark, amused eyes in the passenger mirror and I look away, hating him.

At the train station, letting go of Erik is unbearably difficult. He is the last one left. The only trace remaining of this world that I so railed and stormed against and loved in spite of it all. Matthew hums as he watches a seagull above us, but I watch Erik as he walks back to the car and gets in, lifting a hand to wave to me. I wave back like a small child. As he goes, I think of the way Jonathan used to spend hours in the garden with me, pushing me back and forth on that swing, how Ophelia kept my secrets for me, and Erik kept secrets *from* me because he would have stopped at nothing to shield me—and Mina Ma, who loved the baby the doctors loathed, who scolded and teased and protected and loved me, no matter what I did. I was so lucky to have them.

2

CREATION

Erik's car vanishes. I follow Matthew into the train station. My mind trudges away, back to the cottage by the lake, but I keep my eyes on him. Warily.

On the train, we don't speak for the first quarter of an hour, apart from Matthew telling me we're changing at Preston. I look out the window, watching the now-familiar English countryside pass us by. We're taking the usual train to London and one of the stops is Lancaster. I allow myself the indulgence of wallowing in self-pity for a minute and wonder if it's possible to feel more miserable than I do right now.

"Yes, it is," says *Sir* Matthew, yawning, "Try childbirth. I hear it's far more painful."

I jerk my head in his direction. There are any number of things I'd like to say to him, but I bite them down. "You can read minds, can you?"

"Just faces."

"In other words, a lucky guess."

"I am never lucky. I am always right. I," says Sir Matthew, "know everything."

Under any other circumstances, I might have laughed at him. But considering how horrible this day has been, and how unwise it seems to laugh at a Weaver, I settle for being skeptical.

"I doubt that."

"Well, that settles things, doesn't it? I see I shall need all my wits about me to counter your ruthless intellect."

I glare at him. Matthew's expression is a testament to complete boredom. But his eyes are watchful, watching me, relentlessly. I watch him back.

"You can't possibly know everything."

"I think you'll find I can."

"So you know, say, ancient Greek?"

"Indeed I do, especially as I am a renowned scholar of ancient languages."

"I don't believe you."

"Clearly you know best," he drawls, pulling a magazine out of the seat pocket in front of him. He yawns elaborately again. "Now I expect you will embark on a quest to prove me wrong by asking questions. Do. I'll play along. Being clever is, to me, like stealing sweets from an infant. I do it *very* well."

On principle, I want to refuse, to tell him I'm not interested and I'll be reading my book for the rest of our trip, thank you very much. Unfortunately, I can't do it.

"Do you know the capital of Turkey?"

"You'll have to do better than *that*," scoffs Matthew. "That would be Ankara."

"Which came first, the chicken or the egg?"

"The egg," he says with a yawn.

"You can't possibly know that, no one does."

"That is a transparent lie. Haven't I made it clear that I know it? Now don't be insufferably imbecilic. It's quite clear the egg came first, as anyone with the slightest grain of intelligence would know."

"What is four hundred and sixty-two multiplied by sixty-nine?"

"Thirty-one thousand, eight hundred and seventy-eight."

He gives me a feral smile. I don't know the answer myself. I grit my teeth. Several questions later, my Weaver has not gotten a single question wrong nor even appeared to have taxed himself at any stage.

"Tell me about *Frankenstein*," I say, goaded, "if you know so much."

He is disdainful. "Why on earth would I do that?"

"Because I want to know and you want to show off."

"It's against the law," he says deceptively softly. "Is that really what you want to do?"

I fall silent.

"Why don't you tell me about yourself?"

I stare at him in astonishment. "Like you care."

"But I do," says Matthew. "I am very interested to know what my creation has grown up to be. Did I go wrong? Did I create perfection? Of course I must know! Not that one would call you *grown up*, per se, but—"

"I'm not telling you anything."

"No matter," he says, smiling maliciously. "I know everything about you already."

An ice-cold finger trails up my spine, spreading fear through my skin. There's something about his voice that makes me believe him.

"If I had done something wrong," I say, "would you have destroyed me?"

"Naturally."

"That doesn't sound like somebody who cares."

"You can't be powerful without being ruthless," says Sir Matthew. "If we weren't powerful, we would crumple like a house of cards. The world is divided. We must remain powerful, and ruthless, and in favor with our supporters. Or our detractors would tear us down. So yes. If we have to destroy any of you, we will, without hesitation."

I stare at him for a long time. "Would it hurt?" I ask. "If you destroyed me?"

He considers me. "It wouldn't be . . . nice," he acknowledges with a kind of ghoulish humor. "You do realize you have to be unstitched, don't you? *Unmade.* It is akin to watching somebody come apart."

My stomach flops.

"You were lucky to avoid that fate, you know," he says, as though I should be on my knees thanking him for it. "I gather Amarra didn't care for you. You were lucky she had her accident before she could find a way to get rid of you."

"Others can't pass the Sleep Order. Only familiars and Weavers can have an echo destroyed."

He smiles slowly. "And who told you that?"

I turn away.

The train pulls into Lancaster. I glance out at the familiar station rolling in, then at the bracelet of seashells on my wrist. *Sean.*

There's a sharp tap on the other side of the thick window glass. I look up, startled. My eyes fly wide open. I blink, certain for an instant that he's an hallucination, that I conjured him up.

Sean steps back from the window, watching me. He looks out of breath, like he's run all the way here to catch us.

My heart stutters against my ribs. I leap to my feet and am about to run to the compartment door when a hand closes over my wrist. It's too tight, too strong.

"Do you *want* to die?" Matthew demands, his voice dark and disbelieving. I shudder at the sound of it. "Sit down." Gone is the drawl, the boredom. He is a Weaver. My Weaver. His eyes are blue and dangerous. His warning is clear. But I don't care.

I stare back at him. "Let me go."

He narrows his eyes. Abruptly the pressure on my wrist is gone. I don't stay to question it. I run for the door. I might only have seconds before the doors close and the train leaves. I race through the compartment, jump onto the platform, and run to Sean. He crushes me to him. I grip my arms tight around his neck. My eyes feel raw with tears.

"I'm sorry," he says in my ear, "I'm sorry, I thought it'd be easier if I didn't see you, but I *had* to—"

I look up at him. His green eyes. Like marbles. Vivid and brilliant. "I can't never see you again," I say to him desperately. "I *can't* do that, I won't. I'll find you. I'll come back and find you when I'm older—"

"You can't see me, Eva—"

There's a whistle, sharp and shrill. I have to go or break every promise I've ever made.

"Sean," I say.

"Go," he says quietly.

I let him go. I don't know how, but I do. His hand tightens against my back before he releases me and steps away.

"We'll pay for this one day, you know," he says. "We're standing here and there's a Weaver on the train. He won't forget." He swallows and takes another step back. "Get on the train, Eva, or they'll leave you behind." And then he turns around and starts walking. I turn, too, because I know he won't look back, he won't dare, and I shouldn't either. I hurry onto the train, just in time, and feel the jolt beneath my feet. And then he's gone.

How can I never see him again? How can they ask that of me?

I go back into the compartment and sit down across from the Weaver. I don't know what to expect from him, knowing he knows so much, knowing I defied him. But he doesn't say a word. He sits there and watches me. He doesn't speak for hours.

But he doesn't stop watching, either.

When we arrive in London, the station is a shock to my system. I never realized just how small and uncrowded Windermere is. I've never seen so many people in one place before. The bright lights, crowds, and flashing boards are overwhelming. I stand in the middle of the crowd, trying not to get jostled, as Matthew studies our surroundings. I notice he seems impatient, in a hurry, but I know we have plenty of time before our flight.

I look once again at his chain-mail vest. Is that why he's so impatient? He's afraid of being out in the open in case someone *gets* us?

I break our long silence.

"Why are you wearing armor?"

"*Armor*, is this?" he demands scornfully. "Have you ever seen a real knight? I assure you, they wear more than light chain mail. This is for protection."

"Protection?"

"Knives. Wicked thing, knife crime. Most upsetting."

"Why would you encounter a knife?"

"I know you're only an echo," says Sir Matthew irritably, "but I take exception to any echo *I* have woven behaving in such a dense fashion. Haven't you heard of hunters? They loathe us almost as much as they loathe you."

"Yes," I say, trying not to think of the maybe-hunter

leaning against the lamppost so long ago, "but I hardly think they'll stumble across us here."

Matthew gives me a long, flinty look. "You seem to underestimate the dangers in your little world. You defy me, you scoff at hunters. Is that simply a brave face you put on, or are you really that stupid?"

I flinch. His cutting contempt is humiliating. But I won't let him make me feel like an idiot. "You say that," I say, hoping my tone could freeze hell, "but if you'll notice, I'm still alive."

"And it's a wonder, I assure you," he replies.

I don't back down from his stare. "I don't see any hunters. We appear to be quite safe."

"Nevertheless," he says, patting his vest with satisfaction, "I don't take chances. As I have put myself in charge of getting you to Bangalore safely—and lord, I can't remember why I ever thought that would be a good idea, you are positively *irksome*—it is now a question of my pride to make sure you get there. Imagine if you were killed on my watch. Or worse, *I* was! If I allowed myself to be slain by hunters, Adrian would mock my memory for years!"

I don't want to think about the hunters. They won't find me. How could they?

"Is Adrian your friend?" Changing the subject seems like a good idea.

Matthew nods. "Oh, indeed. Oldest friend in the world."

This only makes me feel worse. I haven't forgotten Adrian's cruelty in the interview, his utter indifference to us and his obsession with his art. I haven't forgotten the things Sean said, about grave-robbing and experiments and other strange, dark rumors about Adrian Borden. It sounds to me that if the rumors are true, he and his oldest friend would probably be hand in hand in it all.

"Come along," says Matthew. "We mustn't dillydally any longer."

I make sure I've still got all my bags. He has already started walking. I follow, several steps behind, wondering what would happen if I turned around and walked away. Would he chase me? Would he call on the Loom's seekers, ask them to find my tracker and hunt me down?

"I understand you make birds," he says a few minutes later, quite abruptly, while we're on the Underground.

My throat feels knotty. "How do you know about that?"

"I know everything. Do keep up."

I consider denying it. Telling him I don't do anything so un-Amarra-like. But he won't believe me. And why should I act like I'm ashamed of something that is so essentially me?

"Yes. I make birds. And other things."

"And how would you feel if one of these birds, or other things, decided to leap off the table and shatter onto the floor?"

I wonder if he's a little bit mad. "Excuse me?"

"Would you be angry?" Matthew drawls. "*Irked*, perhaps? Would you be frustrated by the way this creation, one you have spent so much time and strength on, simply threw all your effort away and destroyed itself?"

"I suppose," I say.

"*That* is how I feel about you," he says, teeth flashing white. "It is how we feel about all the echoes who break the laws and force us to destroy them. It is a waste of the time and trouble we took to stitch them."

"We're not wax birds!"

He clicks his tongue in a sympathetic way and pats my cheek. His hand feels like steel. "You are to me."

The cold, sour taste of hate fills my mouth and I have to look away to keep my temper. I stay quiet for the rest of the trip underground and only speak when I have to at the airport. Matthew has a passport for me, and a false one for him, both bearing the same last name. Like I'm a genuine human being. Like we're father and daughter. I almost laugh at the bitter irony.

And then he does something strange. It's very cold in the airport. With hot, sunny India firmly in mind, I didn't bother to pack a coat or fleece in my carry-on luggage. I stand shivering by the queue for security.

"Here," says Matthew, handing me a jacket.

I don't want to take it, but I'm cold and I have a feeling being stubborn will only amuse him. I put it on, muttering a thank-you under my breath. He is delighted by my attitude and whistles a cheery tune as we join the queue for our security checks.

"How many of us are there?" I ask him. "How many *creations* do you have?"

"Hundreds," says Sir Matthew. "That is, between the three of us, we have created hundreds. I believe most still live. But then there are the hundreds and hundreds our predecessors made. Few of *them* are still alive."

Considering how many ordinary people exist, "hundreds" barely dents the surface. But it's still an awe-inspiring number. It's hard to imagine so many of us.

"Have there always been three Weavers at the Loom?"

Matthew looks at me like he's not sure he's enjoying all these questions. But he tells me, "No, we are the first generation of three. Before Adrian, there was only one Weaver at a time. It's been in Adrian's family for two hundred years. There has always been a Borden at the Loom."

"Why did Adrian break the tradition, then?"

"With three of us making echoes," drawls Matthew, "Adrian has time to spend on his other . . . ambitions. Creating life still thrills him, but it isn't enough for him."

"Is it enough for you and Elsa?"

"You ask too many questions," he says wearily. "Do stop. It's exhausting. I can't speak for Elsa, but I, at least, still take pride in the act of stitching a life. I'm beginning to regret stitching *yours*, but that's neither here nor there."

I ignore that. "Is that why you decided to take me to Bangalore yourself? So you could make sure no hunter destroyed your creation?"

"How quaint," says Matthew. "In spite of everything, you still attribute good intentions to me. You mustn't, you know. I am not kind. Handsome, certainly. And undoubtedly brilliant. But not kind. You will learn that yourself, in time." He yawns. "I think I shall have a little sleep on the plane. Do try not to be noisy."

He does sleep. Or at least he pretends to. Even with his eyes closed and his body relaxed in his seat, I still feel him watching me. I don't know why. He can't expect me to try to run away from him in midsky. And I stare ahead, hating him with all my heart and longing for *something*.

It becomes easy to ignore him as the flight wears on. With ten hours to sit in one place and do very little, it's impossible to forget everything I've left behind. I can't stop thinking about Sean and the way he looked as he walked away. Or Mina Ma, who I miss so much it feels like sand on my tongue. Or Erik or Ophelia. I can't fathom not seeing them again. I can't process the idea of an existence without any of them in it.

Sean.

And beside me, instead of a friend or a guardian, I have a Weaver. A man who could end my existence with a word.

It's an ugly thought.

I can't fail.

As the plane draws nearer to Bangalore, anxiety bubbles up in my stomach, tightening each of my muscles until they ache. I feel sick. Here is my chance to survive, to live a long and normal life. True, I have to be perfect, but it makes me feel better, knowing I can fight for myself, that it is in my power to live.

We land all too soon, and I totter a little unsteadily out of the plane. They've attached one of those great steel stairways to the door. As we cross a strip of the runway to the airport, the heat is astounding. Like a blanket, the humidity sinks over us, and I smell wet earth, and dust, and something strangely like the sea, though I know we're nowhere close. Maybe it's that raw, salty air.

Out in the sun, before we can step into the airport, Matthew's hand closes like a vise over my arm again.

"Understand this," he says, urbane, friendly, "it is not clever to test me. I *like* being tested. I like to win. I have watched you break a law in the last eighteen hours. You defied me and I let you, but you mustn't fall into the trap of thinking that means you got away with it. I know enough to destroy you this very minute. I don't need a further excuse. At any time, I can take away the rest of your life. Tread more carefully in this city, or you will fall. Have I made myself quite clear?"

And before I can reply, before I can shake off the steely hand that has blotted out the sunlight, he delivers his final blow.

"And while we're on the subject, Eva," says Sir Matthew conversationally, "what *is* Blackpool Zoo like these days?"

3

STRANGER

I have no appetite. I move my hand mechanically, taking the fork to the pasta and bringing it to my mouth. It's difficult to swallow. I am aware of every sound. The chink of cutlery, fork on plate. The steady breathing of the people on either side of me: Matthew and a young boy with a lean, pale face and soft, dreamy eyes exactly the same brown as mine. He doesn't say a word. Matthew's foot moves against the leg of the dining table, *tap, tap, tap,* and it's annoying. There's the occasional crunch when the youngest person at the table, a little girl of five, bites into her peppers. I keep glancing at her. I can't help it. I've watched her grow from a baby to a little girl from a distance, and it's surreal to see her in the flesh. She smiles at me without reserve. Her teeth are small and even, and her smile is sweet, her dark hair soft and unruly. People always said Sasha and Amarra looked very alike. Sasha swings her feet to and fro. They don't touch the floor, she's too small, and there's a rush of air every time they swing. *Swish, swish.*

There's no conversation at the moment. Even with my

head down, I sense their eyes flicking to me and then away again, all of them except eleven-year-old Nikhil, who has a peaceful, faraway look on his face, as though nothing in the real world can shatter him.

It was a long drive from the airport. The house is close to the city center, set on a quiet cul-de-sac flanked by trees. It offers some breathing space in this busy, brightly lit city. Through the window, I can smell the wet trees, and they smell clean and raw and untouched by the city scent, the dust and hooves of town-bred cows that stand in the middle of streets and refuse to budge.

We saw one of those cows on the way. It had planted itself in the middle of the road and stood there peacefully, swinging its tail back and forth. When cars slowed down and honked, the cow did little more than lift its head to note our plight. I leaned out of the window to gawk at it. I was so sure that Mina Ma had been lying the time she told me about this particular phenomenon.

Alisha, Amarra's mother, met us at the airport. It was a shock to see her brought to life. I had only ever known her in photographs and videos. But there she was.

She stood outside the sliding glass doors of the terminal. Behind her, I could see rain slowing to a halt, the red sign of the airport Coffee Day, the cars in a line waiting to pick somebody up or drop them off.

We saw her before she saw us. She was beautiful, still slender, and didn't look like she was in her forties. She had a soft, earthy look, with wide brown eyes in a heart-shaped face and thick dark hair. She wore jeans and a blouse open at the neck but made them look more glamorous than most cocktail dresses. As we got closer, I could see her fingers were stained with paint and pencil. It was the only thing that made me smile.

She spotted us as we got to the doors, the blood draining from her face. She was wringing her hands so hard they were nearly white. I couldn't help noting how familiar the gesture was. How many times had I caught myself knotting my fingers together, knitting and twisting my hands?

She reached for me, then stopped. Her eyes swept across my face, drinking in every detail. She stared into my eyes for the longest time, until I couldn't stand to see the agony, the grief, the wild, desperate hope.

I was about to look away when her face split into a smile so happy it hurt to look at it. She put her arms around me and held me tight, her entire body trembling.

"It *is* you," she breathed, and I looked up to see tears start down her face. "I wasn't sure—I didn't know if it would work—but your *eyes*. I'd know your eyes anywhere."

I didn't know how to feel. Part of me felt like the lowest form of flea for letting her believe this pretense. Another part of me was just so glad to see that awful grief fade off her face. I stood very still, too scared to hug her back.

"People are staring, Alisha," said Matthew, his lazy drawl firmly in place.

She stepped back and wiped her face. "It's an airport, Matthew," she said. "Everyone cries!" She smiled at him, a sweet, slightly tentative smile, as though she wasn't certain of his reaction to her. "Thank you."

He nodded and for once resisted the urge to be flippant. It intrigued me. They acted like they knew each other, better than I'd imagined a familiar and Weaver would.

"What's the matter?" Alisha asked me, concern widening her still-wet eyes. I didn't know if I looked sick, or scared, or uncomfortable. I certainly felt all three. She rubbed my arm.

"It's been a long journey," Matthew answered for me. "She's tired. I did warn you. She'll be disoriented and confused for some time. It's hard adjusting to the new life. So don't expect too much of her."

He might as well have said "new body" instead of "new life," because it was quite clear Alisha saw Amarra when she looked at me. I should have been happy. It meant my familiars will keep me, and to disillusion her would have been to give her back her pain. But I couldn't shake off the guilt.

"I didn't think," she said, stricken. "I'm sorry, darling, you must be badly shocked. The trauma of the accident— and the change—"

"Don't lose sleep over it," said Matthew, giving me a darkly amused look. "She'll recover."

Alisha frowned at him. "You sound more like Adrian these days. There's an easy cruelty in you that I don't remember."

"I daresay you're right," said Matthew.

"Was he kind to you on your way?" she asked me, and she suddenly reminded me of Mina Ma, angry and protective. "Did he behave?"

Matthew feigned high injury. "I always behave impeccably." He grinned at me. "Don't I?"

Alisha laughed. "I know better than that, Matthew." She gave me another concerned look but, to my relief, didn't push me to speak. "We'd better go find the car, baby. You look tired. Do you need a bed for the night, Matthew?"

"I expect Neil will have something to say about that," he said, "so no. I do have a hotel. But thank you for the offer."

"Well," she said, carefully avoiding his eye, "you can at least stay for dinner."

I couldn't understand them. Were they friends? Did they used to be friends but now no longer were? Alisha knew Adrian. Matthew seemed to think Neil didn't like him. This was no average familiar-Weaver relationship. She showed none of the suspicion or awe Erik had once said characterized most familiars. She seemed uncertain of him, but it wasn't because he was a Weaver.

They talked as we made our way to the car. I sat in the back, and Matthew folded himself into the passenger seat. His face held no expression. In spite of their too-casual conversation, I had the odd idea that he hated her.

I focused on the city.

Seeing the city was stranger than seeing Alisha. I had been

sent pictures all my life, of course, and Mina Ma had told me long stories about Bangalore. She had described streets, places, pieces of her life. As a child, I sat at her feet and drew pictures, inspired by her voice and by the flickers of memory passed on through Amarra's and my consciousness. So many of those pictures had been *true*. There were ashoka trees down the middle of a long road, just the way I'd imagined. Mina Ma would always joke about them. She used to say the mushroom-shaped foliage of the dark green trees was exactly like her hair. There were little stalls along the roads, open late, tea stalls with clinking steel cups and sweet shops with packets of crisps hanging from makeshift roofs. Or chips, as Mina Ma called them. Coke and Pepsi in glass bottles with steel bottle caps. Men crouched on the edge of the road, smoking tiny not-quite cigarettes. It was all so impossibly familiar.

Watching the city come alive made me feel an unbearable pang of homesickness and longing for Mina Ma. The cow was a welcome sight toward the end. Between them, the ashoka-trees-like-Mina-Ma's-hair and the cow kept my spirits from sinking too low.

Alisha's attempt to park her car in front of the house was a fiasco. Driving was not her strong suit, though on the roads she had seemed positively talented compared to some of the motorcycles whizzing by. She reversed badly, hit a coconut tree, swore, and shot forward again, bumping into the back of Neil's car. I held on to the back of Matthew's seat. It was an old car, obviously made in the days when backseat seatbelts were an unnecessary affliction.

When we stopped, I thought of the story Mina Ma once told us. Of the mongoose and farmer, and the snake I always think of when I look at the tattoo inked in my skin. I thought of how the farmer brought a stranger home to his family, and how they loved the mongoose but never really trusted it. And when disaster seemed to have struck, they turned first on the creature they had cared for.

I tried to put the story out of my mind. I followed Alisha and Matthew through a front door, which was unlocked, and into a hallway full of light.

"Neil? We're here!" Alisha sounded so excited it was heartbreaking.

A man emerged from the next room, holding a dishcloth in his hands. He was very thin and wore glasses. His hair and clothes were untidy but scrupulously clean. I recognized him too, down to the disarray.

"Hello, Matthew," he said in a pleasant tenor, and he held out a hand.

Matthew's eyes glittered. "Neil." I recognized the smooth, feral good humor I had come to loathe and mistrust. "You look well."

"Thank you, so do you." His eyes, a paler brown than mine and full of light that reflected off his glasses, shifted to me. I stood stiffly in the corner. Neil smiled carefully and drew closer. I saw that beneath the kind smile lurked a deep, terrible sadness.

"Hello," he said, deliberately avoiding the use of my name.

"Hi," I said. I should have added "Dad," but I couldn't make my tongue form the word. I had never used it in my life.

He scanned my face, much like Alisha had done, but I could see that there was no hope in his. He might have hoped once, but he must have known the moment he set eyes on me that it had been in vain. He was the logical one, Alisha the passionate one.

"Don't you see it, Neil?" Alisha asked. "Don't you see her?"

"I see her face, Al," he said, but gently.

While Neil asked Matthew something, Alisha glanced quickly at me, as though worried that I would be hurt by his reaction. It was the way Amarra would have felt, after all.

"Give him time," she said in my ear. "You know your father. It'll take him some getting used to, but he'll see you're there."

Or *she* would see that Amarra wasn't, I thought sadly.

Footsteps clattered on the stairs. A boy and a little girl appeared at the top. I felt a sharp tug on my chest, which surprised me. I had pretended to be fond of them since they were born, but I hadn't realized that somewhere along the way it had stopped being pretend.

The boy moved cautiously. His face reminded me of a saint's in a painting: sweet, unflappably calm, faraway. He looked at me curiously. The little girl bounded down and ran to her mother.

"There, Sasha, see? I told you I'd bring Amarra home with me."

"Hi," said Sasha shyly. "How was your holiday?"

I had to clear my throat, painfully. "It was nice. Have you been going to school?"

She grinned and hid her face behind her mother. Alisha laughed. "She's been home every day this last week. She's a little devil, aren't you, baby? Neil lets her get away with anything if she makes her sad face at him."

From behind Alisha's legs, Sasha lifted a shy hand to wave at me. It occurred to me then that Sasha had sensed, in spite of her mother's promises, that the girl in her home was not her sister at all.

Things began well at dinner. There was food to compliment. Sasha demanded extra peppers and made everybody laugh by spilling them, and Alisha kept up a lively stream of chatter. But even she couldn't do this indefinitely, not on her own. When Matthew went suspiciously silent, the talk died.

I glare sideways at him now, knowing his silence stems from a malicious desire to see what we do, to watch how we struggle to find level ground to stand on. But my glare has no effect on him. He smiles and continues to tap his foot, *tap, tap*, against the table leg. I wonder who he's punishing. Me? Them? Is he simply doing this out of interest, the way someone might put a rat and hawk together in a cage to see what happens?

My stomach is knotted tight. I wonder if I will ever be able to relax in this house.

Dinner has to end at some point and it does, after what felt to all of us like an entire historical era. I watch Matthew leave with mixed feelings. He was something from my old life, my own world. He made me. But he's also the man who knows enough about me to destroy me.

"Why don't I take your things upstairs?" Neil says.

Alisha frowns at my bags, as if noticing them for the first time. "Why did you need to bring so much? All your things are here."

"It's, erm—" I stammer. "It's just stuff."

"Oh." Alisha catches Neil's eye and lets it go. She touches my cheek. "Do you want me to come up and say good night in a bit?"

I shake my head. "I'm going to go straight to bed now."

Watched by eyes that are pretending not to, I walk up the stairs and to Amarra's room without error. Even if I struggle with pretending to *be* her, my memories of her life, whatever they told me, are crystal clear. I don't hesitate when I reach the landing that splits off two ways, and I find it very easy to choose the right bedroom door.

I hesitate on the threshold, in the dark doorway. My hand reaches automatically up to the light switch on the right. I remember that this is not my room. The switch here is on the *left*. No one ever told me that. I learned it from the photographs. Why would you tell somebody where switches are? It's not something anybody would think of. It is only by the grace of memory that I recall seeing them.

Neil follows me in and puts my bags down.

"Thank you."

"You're welcome." He hovers by the door for a moment. "If you need anything—"

"I'll ask. Thanks."

He turns for the door, then stops and looks back. "Who are you?"

"Amarra." He doesn't look satisfied. Hesitating, I add: "An echo of Amarra."

"Is she there?"

It's almost funny. Is she here? As though my body is a house and everyone is knocking. They want to know if she's home.

"I am," I answer, and let him make of that what he will.

He nods. "Good night."

The door shuts behind him. My shoulders drop. I realize how stiff, how tense they have been all evening. There's a stabbing ache between my shoulder blades. I relax now that I am alone. Now I can take off the mask. I close my eyes and take a deep breath before opening them again.

I face the room squarely, taking in every stark detail of the life a girl has lost. It's a funny sort of word to use at a time like this, *lost*. You lose your keys. Your phone. Your favorite shoes. And often you find those things again, days or weeks later, under the sofa or buried in the back of a closet. But it isn't quite the same for a lost life. A lost girl. Can you find *those* things again?

Everything—from the clothes strewn on the bed to the photographs on the desk to the books on the shelves—breathes of somebody else's world. Where has she gone? Her clothes are here, her ancient teddy bear, her computer. Nothing has been touched. The room smells of a girl, but it's not me. She wore something with a soft mango scent. If I listen, I can almost hear her voice. On the phone with Sonya or Jaya. Brushing Sasha's hair. Giggling with Ray on the bed, shushing him so her parents won't hear them. Where is she?

By the time I'm finished unpacking, there are two nearly identical sets of clothes in the room. I'll have to pack her things up and put them away in the back of the closet. I can see why they let me bring my own things. The thought of wearing her actual clothes is sickening. The thought of making this room my own, of using her money and sleeping by her teddy bear, is appalling. How do other echoes stand this?

But I don't have a choice. I promised to be Amarra for Mina Ma, and I will. I'll do my best. But I don't want Eva to disappear.

Over the next few days, the family and I circle one another, feeling our way in the dark. Only Alisha acts no different from how she would otherwise. She seems frenzied, joyous, filled with the kind of thrill you must only feel when you find something you were afraid you'd lost forever. I watch her when she isn't looking. Does she *really* believe she sees Amarra when she looks in my eyes?

Nikhil doesn't say much to me. He is not unfriendly, simply content to keep his distance. From what I have learned of him, I know he's wise for his age. He can see me exactly as I am. I will have to earn his trust.

Sasha is different. Her world is uncomplicated. Once her shyness wears off, she's the one who crawls onto my lap and asks me to braid her hair; she throws roasted peppers at me when her parents aren't looking; she sits beside me, inching closer and closer, while I watch telly. *No, TV.* I have to start saying that now. I think Sasha knows I am not her sister, but she accepts me as I am: I am just another person she now lives with. She is the only one with whom I can be Eva and not be caught doing so. She laughs at my vocabulary. She loves the word *mint*, which I teach her to use in the context of something wonderful, and she goes around telling people they look *minty*. She is the one thing that is not difficult in this new world.

When I have been in Bangalore a week, Neil has a question for me over dinner.

"How do you feel about going to school on Monday?"

I feel no pressure from him. He's encouraging me to go but is giving me the option to say no. Everybody else at the table, except Sasha, goes still.

"Neil, give her time to adjust," Alisha protests. "The accident was hugely traumatic! And she must still feel disoriented in the new body—"

"If she needs time, she only has to ask," he says reasonably, carefully avoiding confronting her about the "new body" part. "But you know Amarra's friends have been asking after her."

I look at him, horrified. My stomach tightens painfully. School. Her friends. I gulp. *Ray.*

The fear grates on me. I didn't come here to be a coward. I came here to be convincing. I made a promise to Mina Ma that I'd do my best. I have to do everything Amarra would have done, and she would have been dying to see her friends again. She would have longed to see Ray.

So I say just the opposite of what I really want to do. "I'm okay," I tell Alisha. "I want to see everyone. I'll go to school."

4

ILLUSION

We walk to the bus stop together, Nikhil, Sasha, and I. With each step, I feel a little sicker, my schoolbag heavier.

I've got a ham sandwich in my bag, a packet of crisps (*chips*, I have to remember to call them chips like they do here), a chocolate bar, a copy of Amarra's schedule, and the books that seemed to fit the lessons she has on Monday. I am prepared but not prepared. I don't know what to expect. What if they take one look at me and, like Neil, realize I'm a fake?

The only difference is that Neil knows Amarra's echo exists. Her friends don't. They'll have no reason to question who I am.

Unless I make a mistake.

"It's a private school," says Nikhil, quite out of the blue. His voice is mild. "International. It's quite small, about five hundred kids. So everyone knows who everyone else is, you know?"

Great. That's all I need. To *not* be anonymous. But I

appreciate the warning.

"You'll be in the high school bit. Your classroom door is supposed to be yellow, but I think it's more like the color of puke. The watercooler by the football field's always broken, so don't try using it 'cause Amarra always knew it was broken and used the one in the high school courtyard instead." He hesitates. "You probably know most things already. But I just thought there might be stuff you never learned."

"I never knew about the watercooler," I say softly. "Thank you."

He will never look at me and see Amarra. I understand that he's telling me so. Nikhil reminds me of Sean, not physically, but in that sense of a boy older than his years. The comparison is so painful I have to turn away.

When I've recovered, I smile at him. He either doesn't see it or pretends he hasn't. I mention the heat. I've never known heat like this.

"Nik," says Sasha, "will you play the swinging game with me?"

"Yeah, sure, Sash."

Nikhil holds out a hand, and Sasha grabs it. She reaches with her other hand for one of mine. She hangs off our arms, giggling and kicking her legs up. I laugh in spite of myself, and a furtive grin flickers across Nikhil's face, and this is how we arrive at the bus stop.

The trip on the bus is less stressful than I expected. It gives me more time to brace myself for our arrival at school.

I know one of Amarra's best friends, Jaya, is on the same bus, but she doesn't turn up. I'd recognize her if I saw her. Straight haired and friendly, the kindest of them. Then there's Sonya, who hates her nose, is loud, and has a temper. Responsible for that messy haircut. Then there are a few other names that often cropped up in her journal pages. And Ray, of course.

I close my eyes and let the humid air through the bus window hit my face. Air is not like this in England, so heavy and warm and salty. The city passes by in dust, concrete, and trees. I watch vendors hawking their wares by the roadside. Corn on the cob, green mangoes, coconuts, fat gooseberries wrapped in newspaper and spiced with lime and chili powder. As each thing passes me by, my tongue tingles, tasting the phantom flavors.

I've never been to school. I don't know how I am going to figure out the classroom politics or get used to the atmosphere. I wish I had a road map or how-to book.

Suddenly it's as if Sean is sitting right beside me, his jean-clad knees braced up against the seat in front of us, his eyes twinkling.

"Ask me nicely," he says, "and maybe I'll write a play about it. It would sell out in hours, don't you think? Gripping things, how-to guides."

I turn my head back to the window, tears prickling my eyes. I reach blindly for the bracelet clasped around my wrist. Shells woven together. Touching it makes me feel better.

When we get to school, I move as though I'm in a trance,

following pictures in my head. It's a simple enough campus to find your way around. It's pretty, with its courtyards and trees and an open green soccer field. The grass is overgrown, stamped down by all the feet that have run there. Over the field, sparrows arc through the air and disappear into the sky. I watch enviously. If you fly fast and far enough, is it possible to vanish forever?

I find my way to the high school, a courtyard of its own surrounded by classrooms, a stairway leading up to an open terrace. There's so much light and color.

There are people around my age everywhere, chattering, laughing, vanishing in and out of classrooms, frantically scribbling last night's homework. My hands are clammy, and sweat breaks out on the back of my neck. I glance at the faces around me, recognizing several from photographs.

"Amarra!"

I stop in my tracks and turn.

"You're back," says a boy standing a few feet behind me. "We thought it'd be a while longer before we saw you, the way your mother was going on about your injuries. You look okay, no scars or anything. Feel all right?"

I nod.

"Cool," he says. "Glad you're okay." He turns back to his friends, most of whom are glowering at him.

"Can't believe you mentioned injuries and scars," someone hisses. "Seriously?"

The first boy is bewildered. "What?"

A girl, rummaging through her schoolbag on the ground, glances up. She has thick, wavy hair and beady, birdlike brown eyes. She's pretty in a sturdy, snub-nosed way. "You are tactful as always, Sam," she says. Her voice is high and clear. "Tact *bleeds* out of you."

"Says you," one of the other boys scoffs good-naturedly. "You wouldn't know tact if it bit you."

"Was it *me* who accosted the poor girl first thing in the morning? *I've* got better manners than that, unlike *some* people—cough, Sam, cough. As if anyone would bombard somebody so early. I can't even process basic math before lunchtime."

I slip away. I flip through my memories to find their names. The boy is Sam. *Samir.* The girl? *Lekha.* I remember now. She sat in class photos with her chin in her hands. She has the brightest eyes, like there is always something to laugh about. Neither one featured much in Amarra's journal pages, but it's a small class and they all know one another.

Nikhil's tip about the yellowish door helps. I take a shaky breath and go in. Of the twenty-three people I know are in this class, most have settled down already. I brace myself for instant discovery.

Instead, a girl approaches me, pointy-faced and sharp-eyed. "Hey," she says. She's trying to be gentle, but her voice is loud. I wince, convinced it will draw everybody's attention. "You recognize me, don't you?"

What an odd question. My heart skips uneasily. Does she know?

"Sonya," I say.

"Yay!" she says happily, tucking her arm in mine. "I *knew* it'd be fine." I stare at her, brow tense, and she explains, "Oh, your mom told us. You know? About the head injury? She said you've been having trouble remembering stuff, so to be gentle with you. But I knew you couldn't have, like, forgotten *us*." She tightens her grip on my arm. Her lip trembles. "I cried so much when I heard. You're okay, right?"

Incredibly, Alisha has given me room for mistakes, diminished my chances of exposure. Amarra's acting different? Blame it on her head injury. Amarra can't remember something big? It's that memory problem.

I clear my throat, trying to find a suitably Amarra-like reply. All I can come up with is "Oh, sure. I'll be fine."

I'm doing a poor job. I struggle to pull myself together, to regain my wits and force myself to get used to lying.

"Come on," says Sonya. "You should sit down, rest. Your mom will kill me if you collapse or something."

We slip into their usual places at the back of the classroom. The seating's not assigned, but people pick their favorite spots and stay there most of the year. I spot pencil scribbles on Amarra's desk, notes between Sonya, Amarra, and Jaya— and there, scratched into the wood at the edge of the desk, the names AMARRA and RAY with a slightly demented-looking heart scratched in between.

I swallow. She was just a girl who did sweet, silly normal things like scratch her boyfriend's name into wood. Then she went away, and none of these people who loved her know that she never came back.

I'm lucky. I don't have to speak much. Sonya does most of it for me. She flings books onto her desk, chattering nonstop. "Have you seen Ray? He looks rotten. Serves him right—I mean, seriously, he could have killed you! You haven't talked to him, have you? Your mom told me she didn't want anyone disturbing you while you recovered, so I guess that includes Ray. She's not happy with him right now. He's a dumbass. Is your cell still broken? I'm sick of calling the house."

Cell? It throws me for a split-second before I remember. Cell phone. All my guardians called it the British *mobile.*

"I think I'm getting a new phone sometime this week."

"Good. Do you know how weird it is not being able to talk to you for hours every evening?"

I try to hide my alarm. "God, I know," I say. I rub my clammy palms on my knees. I could give myself away at any second. Head injuries don't make someone's skin almost a different color, for a start—a life in another climate does. Amarra's accent was never hugely different from mine, but her speech pattern was more like Sonya's. I'm not sure my tongue wants to work its way around the word *dumbass.*

Sonya is still chirping on. "Amarra, you and I need to have a serious talk about this almost-getting-yourself-killed hoopla. I don't want to get all mushy, but I really, really hate the world without you, so could you kindly refrain from doing it ever again?"

The words stick in my throat, but I make myself say them. "Okay," I say, forcing a twisted grin. "I promise."

Sonya makes me "pinkie promise." I comply, my jaw aching from biting back the urge to be sick all over her. I pull myself together. I *have* to do this.

"Ray's not sitting with us," Sonya pipes up, a little too loudly. "That was weird. He stood at the door staring at you, like he couldn't believe you were actually here. Then he made this funny face and went and sat in the middle." It takes all my willpower, but I don't look around for him. "Does he think you're pissed off about the accident? Or is he doing his angst thing and blaming himself? I won't be surprised if he makes like a tortured vampire and tells you he's too dangerous for you." Before I can reply, she straightens slightly. "Damn, she's here."

A teacher walks in. Mrs. Singh, all bones and elbows and sour faced. She's in charge of the eleventh grade, and she also teaches English Literature. Very few people like her. According to Amarra, she's too strict and she has a twisted sense of humor.

Everybody falls silent and settles into their places. Mrs. Singh opens her class register. As she runs through the names, she makes the odd dry remark, including casting serious doubt on Sonya's claim that Jaya is sick today. When she gets to Amarra's name, she sniffs and says, "Oh. I see you've recovered, Amarra. How nice to have you back," in a tone that doesn't sound like she takes pleasure in seeing any of us.

I suppose I should be grateful. If she knew what I was, she might have followed my name with "Well, children, I'm sure you've noticed Amarra's echo by now. Remember, we must try to treat her like we did dear, departed Amarra and not like the unnatural life-stealing stain upon our world that she is. Is that clear?"

At the sound of my name, a black-haired boy two rows ahead of us stiffens. He turns his head to look back at me, then turns quickly forward again as our eyes meet. I catch a glimpse of his profile—flawless like marble; gorgeous.

Ray.

Why did he go sit there? I wipe my damp palms on my skirt, wishing I could see into his head, work out what he's thinking. I can't imagine why he wouldn't come straight to Amarra, hug her, hold her. Unless he knows that I am not the girl he loved.

I swallow hard, trying to make my heart slow down. It isn't necessarily *that*. He could just be hunched up there blaming himself for the accident, like Sonya thinks he is, convincing himself Amarra's better off without him. Sonya seems to think Ray capable of such tortured angst.

"Enough dawdling," says Mrs. Singh, banging her register closed. "Anyone doing economics needs to be out of here in one minute. Mr. Fernandes isn't in school, so you'll have the class upstairs with a sub. Literature students, stay where you are—Karan, pull your trousers up this instant. I won't stand for this nonsense of wearing one's trousers below one's bottom."

"I have stupid economics," says Sonya to me. "Will you be okay?"

I nod. She collects her things and disappears with half the class. I study Amarra's schedule, memorizing it. She had three different lessons on Mondays. Double English Lit, then a break, followed by double geography, lunch, two free periods, and a single slot of English language. I know what she had been learning before she died. I learned it too.

I search Amarra's bag until I find *Macbeth* and *Wuthering Heights*, her notebook, and her locker keys, which will give me access to everything else. The rest of the class, the ones still here, go through a similar ritual. I take note of the way they tuck their hair behind their ears or slouch in their chairs. Their conversations drift around me.

"Did you manage to finish chapter six?"

"I couldn't be bothered. It's such a stupid book. I mean, it's not like anybody acts like this is real life—"

"It's meant to be *gothic*, you idiot, you know, like Keats—"

"Personally"—I recognize the owner of this voice. Lekha, bright-eyed and wise-voiced—"I think you're being absolute Palestines about this. Don't you have any sense of Victorian culture at all?"

"Did you just call me a country?"

"No, I called you a person with no sense of culture."

"No, you called me a Palestine. That's a country."

"Is it really?" says Lekha, sounding fascinated. "How odd. I always thought the country was called Philistine."

I smother a giggle in spite of myself. Then, from two rows ahead of me, I hear: "Why is she sitting by herself, do you think?"

"Ray won't look at her, it's weird."

"*Shhh*, she'll hear you."

I realize the last conversation is about me, and my face goes warm. I hastily look down at my copy of *Wuthering Heights*. I try to focus on it, shut out my awkwardness, my anxiety, but distracting myself from the classroom only makes me think of my guardians. Of Mina Ma. Of Sean. I swallow back my longing for my cottage by the shore of the lake. I can't bring myself to accept that that life is over. That I will never see them again. I *can't* accept that.

I know *Wuthering Heights* backward by now, so I don't find the lesson hard. I stay quiet and let Mrs. Singh pick on others for answers to her questions. It cheers me up a little, knowing that I know as much, if not more, than they do about the book.

I try to imagine what Sean would say to this, his good-humored mockery, his wry voice in my ear. But it's hard. I'm painfully aware that Sean is not really standing by my shoulder. I know the air rustling by my ear is not the sound of his breath. I imagine Mina Ma snapping her fingers in front of my nose, saying, "What use is this? Is it helping you? Get back to their world, child."

So I push them away. My chest aches for them, but I pretend it doesn't. Pretending has begun to get easier.

By the time the last bell rings, I am thoroughly drained by the day and the effort of being alert and tense all the time. I collect my things and follow Sonya to the buses. She gives me a hug and races off to catch her bus, at the front of the line outside the gates. Mine is fifth in line. I hover by the gates, waiting.

A familiar face joins me. "Hi," I say to Nikhil. "How was your day?"

"It was okay," he says. "How was yours?"

"It could have been a lot worse," I tell him truthfully.

"Must be hard to pretend."

I hesitate, then say, "I don't know if it's all right to talk to you about your sister, or if it's too hard—"

"It's all right," he says. His eyes are like an undisturbed pool of water. "I don't mind. But don't ask me if I miss her or if I'm sad. Those are dumb questions."

I acknowledge that. "I was only going to say that your mother's told people Amarra had a head injury and now has trouble remembering some things. It's made it a bit easier for me to get away with mistakes."

"Mom believes you're Amarra," says Nik, starting toward our bus, which has drawn up level with the gates. "She says she's not stupid; she knows you're different. But she says she really, truly sees Amarra when she looks at you. She says she's still here."

"Your father doesn't agree."

"No," says Nik, "but he won't tell her that she's wrong. He says that if we force her to believe something else, it'll just cause her a lot of pain."

"What do *you* think?"

He shrugs. "I don't know. I want her to be here, but I don't think she is. At least not the way Mom thinks she is. She's not *you*."

"Do you resent me because of that?"

"No, but Dad does. He doesn't like looking at you." He catches a glimpse of my expression, and a tiny frown skitters over his brow. "Sorry."

"It's okay."

"He doesn't *mean* it," Nikhil offers. "It's not his fault. You don't know my parents. You don't know how much they loved my sister."

"Don't I?" I ask him. "I know they loved her so much that I was made."

He smiles.

We're at the steps of the bus when I stop, like I've walked into a wall. Ray is a few feet to my right, and he's crouching down to talk to Sasha. My pulse jolts in panic, and I clutch the strap of my schoolbag very tightly. Sasha knows I'm not Amarra. She calls me by that name, but she knows. What if he asks her? What if she tells him about my "holiday" and my mysterious arrival with a strange man?

"Sash!" Nik calls, and I almost faint with relief. "Come on, we have to go!"

"Okay," she says brightly. "Bye, Ray!"

He watches them as they get on the bus, then turns his gaze on me again. I can't move. I don't know what to do. Every instinct wants to run, but I know that's not what she would have done.

Ray gives me a sad, confused look. It's familiar by now: that look of someone searching my eyes for something. I try to look relaxed, shy, happy. But it's so hard. He's searching for her in me and I'm terrified that if he looks long enough he'll realize she's not there.

I know what I'm supposed to do. I can't *kiss* him. But I could go to him, touch him. Only I don't know if I want to touch him or not. I don't know how to feel about him.

I compromise by standing still.

"You've been avoiding me," I say.

A conflicting mixture of emotions cross his face: relief, and delight, and confusion.

"I thought you might be angry," he says. "I could have gotten you killed."

I make myself smile. Her smile, practiced from photographs. "I don't do angry."

"Well, you *should*. I'm so sorry."

"It was an accident," I remind him. There's perfect truth to that, because I was there too. I was watching as she died.

He shuffles his feet. "Are you okay? I heard about your head—"

"It's made my memory fuzzy," I say, taking the only route I can. "I have blanks, bits I can't remember, especially the last year. I know you. I know that we . . . that you and I—well, you know. We were together. But there's so much that's foggy, and the doctors say it could be weeks before it starts coming back. I just . . . I can't remember *us* as well as I should."

My heart is pounding so fast I'm afraid I might faint. The words trip out, much too quickly, but he doesn't question me.

"Sorry," I add softly.

"It's okay," he says. He very carefully takes my hand. I swallow. "We could go out sometime this week, just to talk? You can ask me questions and I can tell you stuff you've forgotten. Amarra," he says, and his voice is so tender, so desperate to believe every word I'm telling him, that it's agony to listen to him. "I love you. I'll always love you. But right now we don't have to be what we were. We can start again if you want."

This is it. This is why I came here. This is what I was woven to be. She loved him and I must give that a chance.

There is only one answer I can give him.

"Yes," I say. "I'd like that."

His eyes light up. I feel so guilty I could break something.

"Saturday?" he asks.

I nod.

"Okay." He glances at the bus. "You better get on or they'll leave you behind." He kisses me on the cheek, so lightly his lips are a breath. I blush.

I reach for the handle by the bus step, but before I can leave him behind, he says, "Amarra?"

"Yeah?"

"It *is* you, right?"

My heart plummets.

Lie.

I have to.

Lie.

I force a smile. "See you tomorrow," I say. And I get on the bus.

5

GLASS

After dinner that night, I sit at Amarra's desk, studying a picture of Ray pinned to her wall. It's the same one Erik gave me months ago. Is it possible to look at a picture of somebody, over and over, and learn to love them?

When Alisha flitted into the room earlier to present me with a shiny new phone, she hinted that she blames Ray for the accident. He was driving. She also hinted that despite these feelings, she won't stop me from seeing him. It means she asks the occasional awkward question: How is he? Has he recovered from the accident? She knows he had a couple of fractures. Are we going out? Why don't I invite Sonya and Jaya over? She's trying not to push me, but she's anxious. She wants to see more of the daughter she knew, to reinforce her belief that she's still here.

She will be thrilled when I tell her I'm going somewhere with Ray on Saturday. I stare hard at the photograph, as if it can give me answers. Can I love him?

Love isn't so simple. It's not a word I can throw around.

I think of Sean. I miss him so much it's an ache, a longing

that starts in my belly and chews its way up into my throat. He's my best friend, my only real friend. But was it ever anything more than that? There were so many half moments, so many almosts. And he made it clear that he was not going to break the laws for it.

I can't keep doing this. I have to stop shrinking back. I have to stop clinging to the world by the lakes, the guardians and Mina Ma and Sean. I'm here now. I am somebody else now. I've got to be better.

There's a sound above me. I glance up. This is an old colonial house, and you can hear every creak and scrape. This sounded like it came from the attic. I haven't been up there yet.

I leave the room and head for the steps. The stairs don't creak beneath my feet. I have always been unusually light footed. I hover outside the attic door. It's slightly ajar. I can hear movement: the rustle of jeans, the sound of feet against the floorboards. I peep through the gap.

I see beautiful things. Paintings of mermaids, of rich colors, oils, sunsets and dark pirate ships on bleak seas. A woman standing on a cliff, watching an empty horizon, waiting. A sense of adventure stirs in my chest. I imagine sailing into open seas, seizing my fate in both hands. I imagine swashbuckling battles, swords and cutlasses and battle scars. I imagine desire, the raw passion of falling into bed after a long reckless day and kissing somebody. I think of lips touching the bent crook of my elbow, and I wonder where that memory is from.

I focus on the woman and the bleak gray horizon. I feel a pang as though I'm that woman and it's *my* skirt and *my* hair blowing in the wind. Then I blink and make myself step back from it, out of it, and I realize the woman looks uncannily like Alisha. Standing there, watching the emptiness. Waiting for something to come. Me? She wanted Amarra to come back so badly.

There are sculptures, too. A Greek goddess holding grapes. A pair of lovers who are neither mortal nor immortal but somehow both, fused together, crowns of leaves and twigs in their hair. The sculptures are clay, marble, and paper. No candle wax, but that was always *my* silly quirk. Paper birds, looming and enormous. I wonder if they will carry me on their backs, and if we can possibly soar out into the farthest reaches of the sky, until we've been swallowed up by the stars. Or will I need my own wings?

In the middle of these stories and this beauty is Alisha, and she's like a work of art herself. She moves around an enormous sketch on an easel. There's a look of such fierce concentration on her face that she's lovelier than usual.

I want to stand in the doorway for days, feasting on the beauty and absorbing every last bit of it. One look hasn't been enough, but I don't want her to see me here.

On my way back to my room, I stop in a pool of light spilling out of Neil's study. He's at his desk, examining papers with his glasses pushed up his nose. I think of all the times Amarra wrote about sitting with her father. *"We studied the fall of Rome today. I polished a really old knife in the study. Dad told me all about the Crusades."* She loved it, every minute of it.

I wonder if I ought to go in. Would it comfort Neil to have an echo of his daughter help him? As though he senses my gaze, Neil glances up. He seems surprised.

"Come in," he says in a friendly way.

I nod, going into the room. He gestures to the chair near his, on an adjacent edge of the desk, and shows me the papers.

"It's not very exciting, I'm afraid. They're copies of letters." He waves a magnifying glass at me. "It's slow work because my eyes just can't concentrate on text this small for long."

"I could read them out to you if you like," I offer.

He considers me for a minute. "I think we both know that wouldn't interest you for long."

"No," I try, "really, I—"

"I was her father," he says, gently interrupting me. "Believe me, I'd know her if I saw her."

I try to say something, but no words come out.

"Your gestures and mannerisms are different," he says, "and you have a different vocabulary. You do a good impersonation of her smile, but it doesn't look quite right. Your voice is the same voice, but it *sounds* different if you listen hard enough. I have no imagination," he adds ruefully. "When my sisters and I were young, they loved magicians, but I always saw through the tricks. Amarra was like that, too. She had a clear-eyed way of looking at the world. She saw through the smoke and mirrors so many of us construct."

"What about Nikhil?" I ask.

Neil smiles faintly. "Too smart for his own good, quite frankly. He sees clearer than any of us. But he's also a dreamer like his mother. He sees, but feels more."

I can't help noticing his repeated comparisons. Amarra was *like* him. Nik is a dreamer *like* his mother. He probably doesn't mean to, but he's underlining the similarities between them. Highlighting the crisscrossing lines that link their characteristics, personalities, mannerisms. Showing me *they're* the family and I am not part of it.

"I'm doing my best," I say.

"I have no doubt that's true," he says, quite kindly. "I don't mean to criticize you. But I'm too practical *not* to look and listen. I could have convinced myself I saw her. I could have tried. But that's not who I am."

I feel defeated, hurt at being so summarily dismissed. I can't help respecting him at the same time. He's not trying to be hurtful, he just loved his daughter.

"Give me a chance," I say, trying not to sound fierce. Keeping my voice quiet, level, like hers. "You might be surprised."

"Okay," he says.

As I turn to go, he adds something unexpected.

"Do you have a name?"

"That's not giving me a chance. . . ." I falter.

A sad smile elongates his features. "Until I see differently, don't I owe us both the courtesy of calling you by your own name?"

I suppose that's true.

"Eva," I tell him.

He nods. "You are important," he says. "Even if I can't quite believe my daughter survived, like my wife does, you've still given us reason to hope for something *more*. For life beyond death. It's why we wanted you in the first place. For that hope. And the absence of loss."

I look closely at him for a moment. For a man who claims to believe his daughter's dead, he's certainly not letting her go. She's still here, in everything he does.

When I return to Amarra's room, I stare down at the snake on my wrist. I want to tear it out of my skin, strip away the tattoo and everything else that Amarra did and made me do too. I look into the mirror and wonder if I am looking at her. What is this power the dead have over the ones they leave behind? It's strange and beautiful and frightening, this deathless love that human beings continue to feel for the ones they've lost.

"Where are you?" I ask her. "You haven't really gone, have you? I had this idea that I might be free if you were dead. But I'm not free; you've managed to trap me anyway. I've got to live your life and be you better than you ever were. Are you laughing? You've done it; you've died but you've stayed. You *must* be laughing. . . ."

• • •

160

Jaya's back in the school the next day. I have no choice but to sit next to her on the bus. "Hey, you," she says, holding out her arms to hug me. A lump lodges in my throat. She's so happy to see me, so sincerely and openly concerned. It's devastating.

"Hey," I say. I almost add "Are you better now?" but realize who I'm supposed to be in time. I say instead, "Feeling okay? Or were you trying to skip out on your test yesterday?"

She laughs. "Oh, please, that's a Sonya kind of thing to do. Yeah, I'm fine now, what about you?"

"I . . ." I find myself telling her the truth. ". . . feel a little shaky."

She nods. "Of course you do! It was such a horrible thing to happen. It's going to be a while before you're back to normal."

She's so understanding, so quick to excuse my behavior, it makes me feel guiltier. If she only knew.

Later in the day, at lunch, someone pulls out the chair next to Jaya and sits down across from me. I look up, and my heart jerks in shock: Ray.

Oh, God. How am I supposed to face all three of them at the same time without slipping up?

"Hi," he says, smiling at each of us, his eyes lingering on me. I look away. His hopeful, careful expression is too much for me. I can't forget how happy he looked when I agreed to go out with him over the weekend. Or how he asked me if I really *was* Amarra.

Why would he ask such a question? Why would he

imagine I might be anything else?

"Um," says Sonya, looking so astonished and irritated it's rather funny. "What the friggin' hell are you doing?"

"Eating lunch with you," he says. "Are you eating your tomato? May I?" He picks it out of her sandwich before she can say a word. Her face turns a worrying shade of purple, and I bite back a smile. It's quite obvious Ray is deliberately annoying her to amuse himself.

"Why would you want to eat here?" she demands. "I thought you didn't like me!"

"I don't," he says, "but I can put up with you for half an hour."

"Unsurprisingly, I still don't like *you*, either."

Ray ignores her and tweaks Jaya's nose. "Hey, Jay-Jay. Skipped a test yesterday, did we?"

She rolls her eyes and giggles in spite of herself. "Go away, Ray," she says, though her voice is friendly.

"Yeah, please," says Sonya.

"Why don't we ask Amarra what she thinks?"

"We already know what she thinks," says Sonya irritably. "Amarra never minds who sits with us, so don't think you're special just because you're her boyfriend. We need our girl time, you know."

"Hang out in the bathroom, then," says Ray. "I won't bother you there, I swear. I'm too manly to risk it."

"I doubt that."

"Want me to prove it?"

Jaya and I laugh. I can't help it. Even with my nerves strung so tight, I have to laugh at Sonya squawking and covering her eyes while Ray pretends to reach for his fly. He abandons the subject and goes back to his lunch, winking at me. I try to stop staring. I must have more of Amarra's hormones than I thought.

As the lunch bell rings, I wonder if I made a mistake, agreeing to see Ray on Saturday. Maybe if I'd backed away, said my head was a mess and I needed time, I would be safer. I'd be less likely to expose myself. He *asked* me if I was really her. I wish I knew what he meant by that. But it's too late to back out now.

I'm keenly aware of how dangerous this is. This illusion is fragile as the most finely blown glass, and at any moment it could shatter and cut us all.

When I get home that evening, all I want to do is go to bed, but I have to keep Amarra's face on for a while longer. Then I retreat to her room for a few precious hours on my own. When I sleep it's a deep, dreamless sleep. Peaceful.

And in the morning, it starts again.

I get through the rest of the week as best I can. I eat lunch with Amarra's friends, sometimes with her boyfriend. I sit in her classes and enjoy some of them. I laugh and play with her sister. I feel guilty every minute, but lucky too, because this is my life now and it's not really as bad as I'd worried it would be. The days congeal together, setting a pattern for the next few weeks, maybe months, and each day I learn a bit more about these people, this world, and the girl whose many roles I'm supposed to play. Sean, the theater boy, would say that rehearsals make you better at your part, and I guess he would be right to say so. Each day, I learn my lines a little better.

Each day, I lie better.

6

SPIDER

I stay in the car for a moment longer than I should, watching him through the open window. He's sitting on the steps of the patio area around Garuda Mall, and he hasn't yet spotted me. I can't see his eyes behind his sunglasses, but his head is pointed the other way. He looks like a model from an aftershave ad. No, he looks rawer than that. More interesting.

Alisha pushes her sunglasses up onto her head and squints past me at Ray. "What's wrong?" she asks. "Nervous?"

I nod. "It feels like it's all starting again." I can imagine how Amarra used to feel when they first went out, how nervous, how her heart stopped every time he looked at her, how she felt like she was constantly on her toes. It's a little like how I feel now. And it's how I felt last year, with Sean.

"The pieces will fall into place," Alisha assures me. "These things take time." She brushes hair out of my eyes. "You don't have to get out and see him today. You can call him, tell him something came up."

It's so tempting. He'd be disappointed, but at least I wouldn't have to keep lying. I feel like I'm caught in a web.

Each time I lie, I spin the web tighter around myself, until some days it's hard to breathe.

But I won't run away. I'll get out and I'll walk up to him. I just need to muster the courage to do it.

I will have to cling to my excuse: the supposed gaps in my memory, my uncertainty after the accident. There's no other way to be with him. No one ever trained me to be a girlfriend, a lover, a *love*—there hadn't been enough time, after discovering Ray existed, to start lessons and better equip me for it.

"No, it's okay," I say, "I'll get out now."

Ray suggested meeting here. Apparently it was one of their favorite places. They liked the air-conditioning inside, going up and down the escalators, eating at the food court, watching a movie, getting ice cream on their way out, just wandering.

"Have fun," says Alisha. "I'm going to drop some things off for next week's exhibition at the gallery, but I shouldn't be long. I'll call you on my way home. If you're ready to go back too, I'll come and get you."

"Okay. Thanks."

She drives off, almost hitting a car parked nearby on her way. As soon as I'm out of the air-conditioning, the heat hits me and sweat prickles on the back of my neck. I wish I could have put my hair up into a knot or ponytail, but I don't want to draw anyone's attention to the shiny white bandage I've taped over my Mark. Especially not Ray's. It's bad enough having to do it during PE.

I walk toward Ray, twisting my hands. He stands when he sees me, but he doesn't come any closer, just waits for me. His face lights up.

"What?" I ask, when I'm right in front of him and he's still staring silently at me. "Have I got something on my face?"

"No," he says sheepishly. "Sorry. I just always forget how beautiful you are."

My face burns hot.

"A blush!" he teases. "Hey! Point for me." I give him a bewildered look, and he explains, "Oh, maybe you don't remember that. You always gave yourself a point when you made me blush. We both did, but you had way more points."

It would be lame if I were to pretend I remembered this. Instead I smile and say, "Maybe we could start counting points from zero again?"

He strokes his thumb down my cheek, a quick touch before pulling his hand away so as not to alarm me.

"Sorry."

"If you're apologizing about the accident again, I'm not listening," I say, maybe a tad more firmly than Amarra would have. "I'm okay."

"You look okay," he says, and there's something in his voice that makes me tense. "Jesus, it's amazing, actually. I *saw* you, lying there in all the broken glass. I even tried to crawl to you, but I must have blacked out in seconds. There was so much blood. It drove me crazy when I woke up, not being allowed to see you until you came back to school. Not even being able to *talk* to you. I was so scared something was seriously wrong." He stops abruptly, as though aware of how much pain there suddenly is in his voice, in his eyes. He smiles to lighten his expression. "I expected you to have cuts, bruises, scars all over. But you don't seem to have a scratch on you."

My heart thumps very fast, and I have to swallow once or twice to moisten my dry throat. "I have scratches," I say, forcing myself to meet his eyes, trying to lift that glimmer of suspicion out of them. "But most of them aren't places you can see."

His face softens. That confusion isn't completely gone, but I think he believes me. "I know." He gestures at the sliding doors. "Let's go inside, I'm about to fry out here."

The air-conditioning is a blessing. The heat on my skin cools and I feel less sweaty, less edgy. I feel in control of myself again. I watch a last bead of sweat trickle down Ray's forehead, by his dark, dark eyes. I can't help looking at him; my eyes keep pulling that way. I don't know if it's the residue of Amarra's feelings or if it's the constant refrain in my head, reminding me that I am supposed to love him.

"Love him, then," a painfully familiar voice says in my ear. "Go on."

I jerk my head around. Sean always sounds so real.

"Amarra?"

I swallow back the silly, sudden tears in my throat.

"Nothing, sorry," I say. "I just thought I saw someone I knew."

Ray frowns down at me, concerned. "You okay?"

"Yes. Really."

This is ridiculous. I *can't* keep doing this. I can't look at Ray and wish he was Sean. I can't keep thinking about Sean. They belong to two different worlds; they shouldn't collide. I am Amarra. I must *be* Amarra. I have to stop thinking about Sean and everything else that belonged to that other life.

As if he could hear my thoughts, Ray reaches out and carefully takes my hand, linking his long fingers loosely with mine. The touch startles me.

"That okay?"

I nod and keep my fingers entwined with his.

He grins slightly. "I'd kiss you, but I might shock the old ladies." Irritatingly, I blush again. He quickly adds, "I mean, I wouldn't just pounce and kiss you. I know you're still shaky."

"I haven't forgotten you completely, you know," I feel compelled to say. "It's just a few pieces that are missing, that's all."

"Really?" There's something challenging in the way he says this, something almost desperate in the way he searches my eyes again. My heart sinks. He's looking for her and he's not sure if he sees her.

"Yes," I say, making myself squeeze his hand, though my voice chokes on the lie. "I know I'm different, but it's only for now. It won't last forever."

"I'm sorry," he says, "I didn't mean to make you feel bad. It's just that you seem different. It makes me think about what you told me—"

He stops.

"What I told you?" I prompt, alarmed.

"Never mind," he says, "it's not important. Do you want to go up to the food court? Or we can leave, go get dosas at Airlines if you want."

"Erm . . ." My eyes travel upward, past an escalator to the floor above us, where I can see the shiny, gleaming sign of a Crossword. I've obviously never been to one before, but I read about them in Amarra's pages enough times to know instinctively that Crossword means *books*.

Ray follows my gaze and starts to laugh. I notice his body relax slightly, as though I've done something to reassure him.

"We can go in there," he says, tugging my hand. "I know it's your temple."

I hop eagerly onto the escalator. Amarra loved stroking the spines of books, like I do. She loved reading, loved the smell of paper. She made a face at her father's Kindle because she didn't think an ebook was the same. She called it cheating and made him laugh. I feel an unexpected pang in my chest. Sorrow. Loss. For *her*. In spite of everything.

It occurs to me then, for the first time, that I have always been one of two. A copy. A mirage. I had her, even when I hated her.

Now I'm alone. Singular.

Something about the bookshop sets me at ease. It makes me feel more like myself and more like Amarra simultaneously. Consequently, Ray relaxes too, and for an hour we have *fun*. He affectionately rolls his eyes at my enthusiasm, and I barely notice that he's still holding my hand as I race around the store like a chicken without a head. Ray offers to buy me a book, but I decline. I sniff the spines, which makes him laugh so hard he chokes.

It sets me giggling too, and quite abruptly I flash back unexpectedly to another memory, of a zoo, and pulling on a boy's hand, and popcorn, and the smell of elephants under a bright blue sky.

I blink, trying to shake off the memory. I banish the flash of green eyes.

Ray is watching me and I catch that flicker of suspicion again. It keeps coming and going and probably won't entirely go away until I am flawless, constant.

"What do you think about?" he asks. "When you go away like that?"

"Nothing," I say too sharply.

His eyes narrow. I wonder if Amarra ever used that tone of voice in her life.

"I just—" I falter in a panic, trying to recover, fix the mistake. "I just remember things. They come back to me, stuff I didn't even know I had forgotten."

He doesn't say anything for a minute. He watches me carefully. There's nothing more I can say without sounding like I'm desperately scrambling for excuses. I think of Neil, his description of the ways I am different from Amarra, and I feel a paranoid surge of fear.

Finally Ray says, "Stuff about me?"

"Sometimes," I lie, the taste sour on my tongue.

He hesitates a moment. Then he kisses my forehead and I almost faint with relief. "Well, if it makes you feel any better," he teases, "I only think about you *sometimes* too."

"Liar."

"Yeah." He sighs. "I am."

I find a new book to fawn over, my hands still trembling slightly. Ray shakes his head but grins. He has no problem with reading a book, but it's obviously not the first thing he'd think of doing on a cold rainy afternoon. Still, he makes every effort to share my enthusiasm, and if he's bored, he hides it well. It makes me feel guiltier to see how much he loves her. It also makes me feel a stab of envy.

He will be so angry and hurt if he ever discovers my deception. He'll be in so much pain if he realizes she's gone.

He'll never forgive me. And for some reason, that bothers me.

Alisha rings me a little while later, to let me know she's leaving the gallery and can come get me if I want her to. I glance at Ray, who shrugs as though to say "it's up to you." Amarra would want to stay out with him. But the risk is too high. The more time I spend with him, the more likely I am to take a wrong step. So I give him an apologetic smile and ask Alisha to pick me up on her way past. Ray looks disappointed, but he accepts the excuse that my mother wants me home and resting as much as possible.

It's raining when I get in the car, and halfway to the house there's a patch of bad traffic, so we stay in almost the same spot for half an hour. Alisha puts some music on. Gipsy Kings. It's not enough to drown out the honking of impatient cars and trucks. There is no such thing as a quiet, orderly traffic queue in India. I roll the window down to get some fresh air, but all I can smell is dust and gasoline, so I put it back up. In the end I fall asleep.

The weeks following my Saturday with Ray have a certain rhythm. An exhausting rhythm. I've always had to work hard at learning Amarra, but there used to be breaks, respites, time to sit still and be myself with my guardians. I've never worked as hard at anything as I am forced to do now.

I exchange polite conversation with Neil and painstakingly pretend for Alisha. I watch telly—no, *TV*—with Nikhil and Sasha. They treat me like me when their parents aren't in the room, and it's nice. Soothing. I go to school and learn. I see Ray outside of school. I try spending more time with him, which is more enjoyable than I had expected, but it only leads to the inevitable slips. In response I can only pull away, and it heightens his suspicions. Whichever way I turn, I cannot convince Ray, not entirely.

When I can't avoid them any longer, I go out into

town with Sonya and Jaya, to Coffee Day, to a movie, to Brigade Road, where we sit on the steps of the Barista and eat flavored corn on the cob. I get through these hours by staying absolutely alert, my memory like a book I've propped open so that I can find answers the moment I need them. I muddle some things up, usually things Amarra never told me about, like the fact that Sonya once had a gloomy-rocker boyfriend they nicknamed Kurt Cobain. I make mistakes, but they believe me when I say my head's still not quite better.

I have one close shave before PE that December. It's a chilly winter and everyone is gearing up for the Christmas holiday. In the girls' bathroom, the talk is all about going to Goa and the beaches, who's going to which New Year's Eve party, who's decorating a tree, who's got to spend their holiday with millions of annoying aunties and cousins in Delhi.

While I change, I put my hair up into a ponytail. I've had to do it since my first PE class, but it never gets any easier. Keenly aware of the accident, Amarra's friends and classmates have restrained themselves from asking about the white gauze and surgical tape on the back of my neck. I knew their restraint wouldn't last. After all, it's now been more than three months since I arrived.

"So," says Sonya, choosing today, the *last* PE session of the calendar year, to confront me. "It's time you told me what the hell that bandage is doing on the back of your neck!"

"Sonya—"

"I'm only asking her, Jaya. I'm just worried there's something wrong that you haven't told us about." She stops in the middle of the bathroom in her bra and shorts, halfway changed. "It's not an open *wound*, is it? Shouldn't that have healed by now? It's been months!"

I tense. "It's an ugly scar. I don't like people seeing it."

"Since when do you care about having a scar?" Sonya demands. "You've never been vain in your life!"

"Sonya, leave it alone," Jaya says. "It's Amarra's scar, not yours."

"But—"

"I've never had a scar like this one," I reply.

She snorts. "It can't be worse than the scars on your stomach."

I stare at her in horror. Oh. God. I had completely forgotten about the stupid scars from the time Amarra was bitten by a dog, scars I never had. I've been changing in front of them for weeks now and it's obvious that no one has noticed their absence on my belly. Yet.

"Come on," says Sonya. "Show me? I won't make fun, I promise. It's not like having a scar is the worst thing in the world. You could have been *dead*."

I press my hand to the gauze, afraid she'll try to pull it off. "No," I say, too firmly. It's not like Amarra at all. Amarra would have sighed and given in to avoid a silly scene. But here I am, standing my ground in a fierce and entirely un-Amarra-like way.

"But—"

"Oh, for heaven's sake!" cries a high, clear voice from less than ten feet away. "Not *another* spider!"

Sonya shrieks and skitters six feet in the opposite direction. I look around. I don't see the spider; it's not anywhere near me. I search for the source of the cry and find Lekha, the girl who called Sam tactless on that first day. She's sitting on the edge of a sink and doesn't look very alarmed at all. In fact, she's clearly fighting the urge to laugh at the ridiculous spectacle Sonya and the other girls are making of themselves.

As the panic dies down, I can't help glancing over at her, my brow knit in confusion. Lekha and I say hello when we see each other, and more often than not we're the only two who raise our hands in English Lit. She seems nice. Funny. She says strange things, mixes her words up all the time. She and Amarra had known one another since they were little but didn't often see much of each other outside school, so I've never stopped to think about her.

But she has my attention now. There is no spider in the bathroom, I am quite certain of that.

"Don't be paranoid," I mutter to myself. If Amarra's best friends haven't noticed that I'm not her, why should a classmate who barely spends time with her?

I escape that PE class without discovery, but the Christmas break isn't much of a break for me. I still see a great deal of Amarra's friends, still see Ray. He seems more cautious, and it leaves me helpless because there's nothing I can do to be *more* convincing.

Over time, the strain begins to show. I never feel fully rested. The faint shadows beneath my eyes become purple bruises.

At night, I lie awake and think about danger. A man leaning against a lamppost with an old map. The zoo. The feel of Matthew's hand closed over on my wrist. Running off a train to Sean. Adrian Borden's golden eyes. When I finally fall asleep, I dream of strange things. Clock towers and Weavers and hunters prowling the dark. A sad-eyed woman, asking me what my heart wants. I dream of ghosts with Amarra's face, and green nurseries, and canals, and cities full of cemeteries and yellow fog.

But the most unsettling dreams are the ones of hourglasses and spiders crawling up the glass. I'm always trapped in the glass and fine white sand begins to fill it up. And I know that I'm going to be smothered if I can't break out of the hourglass in time.

7

MONSTER

For someone so tiny, Sasha's yawns are enormous. I can practically see her dinner. I stand at the top of the stairs while she and Nikhil watch telly below, and marvel at her.

"Shouldn't *you* be in bed, miss?" I ask with false severity.

Sasha giggles. "It's a Power Rangers thingy—"

"Marathon," says Nikhil.

"Marathon," she repeats. "Mummy and Dad said I could stay up and watch it."

I smile. Her parents spoil her rotten.

"Do you wanna watch with us?" Sasha asks, her eyes huge with excitement. "It's really good!"

Nik gives me a look that says otherwise, but he's also smiling. In the months I've been here, I haven't pushed him to like me. I haven't pressed him with attention or excessive kindness to try and win him over: it was always clear that he's too smart to be taken in by things like that. Instead, I have had the luxury of being myself. I've taken pains not to act like Amarra when I'm alone with him and Sasha. It was the right thing to do. He has slowly warmed to me. One time, during a late-night movie, he even fell asleep on my shoulder. It surprised me, both that he did it and that a slow warmth filled my chest when he did.

I curl up on the sofa next to Sasha and quickly grasp the general plot of the show: teenagers turned secret heroes make a habit of saving the world from ugly evil types.

"Dad told me and Sash that your name's Eva," Nikhil says. "I don't think he likes it when we call you Amarra."

I turn to look at him, my attention diverted. "It's true," I say cautiously. "I named myself after an elephant."

They love that so much, they make me tell the story.

"He said not to tell Mummy," Sasha says shyly when I'm finished, "but we can call you it when she's not here, can't we?"

"Yes," I tell her, "I'd like that very much."

"Nik says Amarra's not coming back," she says. "Is that true?"

"Yes," I say. "I'm sorry."

She considers this for a few minutes. Then she nods and becomes deeply absorbed in the show again. I stroke her hair.

I glance at Nik. He looks a little sad, but he smiles. "It's a good idea," he says, "you naming yourself. I've been thinking about telling my echo about it. He might like a name of his own."

"You have an echo?"

"Yeah," he says, like this should be obvious, which I suppose it should have been. Why ask for an echo for one child and not the others? "So does Sash. Didn't Amarra ever tell you?"

"No, she never mentioned it." I frown. "How did your parents afford it? One of my guardians once said it costs a *lot* to have an echo made."

"The Weavers made you and our echoes for free," says Nikhil, to my surprise. "Dad told me. He said they pick and choose how much they want to charge someone. There's no one else out there making echoes, obviously, so they can pretty much ask for as little or as much as they like."

I remember Matthew and the odd way he and Alisha behaved with each other. "I suppose the Weavers liked your parents."

"Yeah. Weird."

"Is it hard?" I ask Nikhil softly. "Having an echo?"

"Not for me. Kind of like having a pen pal. My echo is really nice. I don't know about Sasha's, obviously. I've never spoken to her."

"You *talk* with your echo? You *like* him?"

Nik nods.

I gaze at him, mystified. "But your sister *hated* me."

"I'm not my sister," says Nikhil, "and my echo's not you."

"But he might replace you someday. Don't you hate that that might happen? That he might be here with your family?"

"No," says Nik, so calmly I am exasperated. "I worry about what might happen to the people who love me if I die before them. I *like* knowing I have someone who will try to stop them from feeling so sad if that happens."

I stare at him in astonishment. My heart twinges at hearing Nikhil, not even twelve years old, saying these words to me. He is so amazingly unselfish, his thoughts so clear and unconflicted. It puts me to shame.

"I don't think of you as Amarra, anyway," he goes on. "So it's not like you've come here and stolen us from her. I think of you as Eva. I don't see you as someone who's replaced her. I see you as someone different who just happens to be here. I'd think of you the same way if you were both here at the same time." He glances up at me. "And I like you. You try so hard to make us feel better."

I try to smile back at him. It's a moment I will remember later, and always. A turning point. Until now I've been trying to make them feel better for *me*. Because as long as Amarra's family likes me and trusts that I am like their daughter, they will keep me. But as I stare into Nikhil's eyes, I decide that maybe it's time to start trying for *them*, too. Because if I *do* make them feel better in some small way, him and Sasha and even Alisha, that means something. It means they need me. I've helped. I've done, if only partly, what I was woven for.

"I like you too," I tell Nik.

"And me!" cries Sasha.

"And you," I say, mussing up her hair. I exchange a grin with Nik. "I like you best of all, Sash."

"Goody," she says, content.

I sit out the episode before going upstairs. There are only so many wisecracking superheroes and ugly villains I can cope with.

The first thing I see when I go back to Amarra's room is the Lake District postcard lying on her desk. Though I knew I could be punished for it, I sent Sean a birthday card in early November. A couple of weeks later the blank postcard turned up. Like old times.

I go to bed, but when I shut my eyes I still see the postcard. The painting of the lakes and hills makes me think of home, and Sean, and Mina Ma, and it makes my chest hurt. I keep seeing them. A tourist on the street might be Erik, a man in a bookshop could be Jonathan, a flash of blond hair and I imagine it's Ophelia. The smell of Mina Ma's hand cream, a popular brand in Bangalore, follows me around like a pup. Once I had to switch off an episode of the BBC production of *Robin Hood* because the actor playing Robin had hair just like Sean's. Every time I'm with Ray, I feel guilty, like I have broken a pact in some way, like I'm betraying them both. My past is haunting me and, like Amarra, it won't go away.

I can't sleep. I can't stop thinking about him. Frustrated, I turn the light back on and search for something to read. I've read every book on Amarra's shelf at some point in our lives, so I hunt for the book Sean gave me, *British Romanticism*.

It looks boring. I search for the blurb, but the back cover is blank. Touching the wrinkled spine, I notice for the first time that the cover is loose, made of old paper. I peel it away, revealing an old and tattered book beneath. The real cover has been blacked out with a thick felt tip. Bewildered, I flip through the first few pages.

I stop, frozen, on the inner page where the title of the book is usually repeated. I have to look twice to make sure I'm not imagining what I see.

Mary Shelley
FRANKENSTEIN;
or,
The Modern Prometheus.

"He didn't," I say out loud, in disbelief. My pulse races. Excitement and shock creep into my blood like a fever. "He *didn't.*"

Sean broke the rule nobody ever broke in our cottage. My pleading and coaxing had no effect on any of them. *Frankenstein*, and everything based on it, was forbidden. Sean never bent, in spite of all those times I asked, *begged*. Then, when he knew I would be leaving England, he did.

I stare down at the book, at the faded pages, the loose binding. I hesitate, frightened of it, of the secrets and story that I might uncover, things the Weavers never wanted me to know.

Very gingerly, I pick the book up again, flip the page, and start to read.

I read well into the night, tucked beneath a soft shawl,

eyes wide and worried as the terrible, terrible story unfolds. Bits and pieces stand out, voices from the book leap off the page and whisper in my ear. The voice of a man who made a person from scratch and paid a terrible price for rejecting him. Violence, darkness, tragedy. But something else, too. Strength. The creature, this monster, he wins. He beats the man who made him. More than that: he *destroys* him.

I read until I've finished and the clock tells me it's far later than I've been awake in weeks. When it's over, I put the book down and curl up into the smallest ball I can make.

"Sean, I think I've understood," I say very softly.

He doesn't reply. I can't conjure him up. Instead I think of the strangest thing: a girl from long ago, faceless and little more than a myth to me. An echo who once defied the Weavers.

And her lips move. She's telling me to defy them too. Because like Frankenstein's monster, I could win.

I've almost forgotten how hot it was when I first arrived. The nights are cold now. This is the only time of year here that the air is sharp and smells of stars instead of dust and spices.

No one at the house makes a fuss for Christmas, but I see Alisha cast worried looks at Neil over dinner, which makes me suspect that she wanted to but he asked her not to. He probably can't bear to celebrate Amarra's favorite holidays. Nikhil confesses to me later that the family normally decorates a ragged old Christmas tree, they have fun, the kids get presents. They skipped over Diwali this year, too: most Novembers, they went out into the street with lamps and soft Indian sweets and fireworks, spending hours out there with the rockets and sparklers and lights. The conversation takes me back to Mina Ma and the lakes, and our silly Christmases, and the one year Erik surprised her by bringing over little lamps and a box of noisy firecrackers around Diwali time. Our neighbors hated us that year.

As we ease back into school in January, I explore the city on my own. Bangalore unsettles me, with its bustle and sounds. I'm fascinated by the spices and scents and such peculiarities as spotting men hunkered around a tombstone in a cemetery, drinking tea out of steel cups. If I could have chosen to come here, on holiday maybe, I would have loved this place and everything around it: the hills, the forests, the temples and statues. I would have wanted to go see an elephant in the wild or try and spot a tiger or panther in the forest. Jaya's done these things; Lekha's done these things; they tell me about it and it sounds incredible.

But the city is the place that shelters Amarra's ghost. And yet being out alone is one of the few places I can let the mask slip away, and instead of walking *in* her shoes, it's like we're two girls, ghost and echo, walking side by side. No one looks twice at me. A couple of times I run into an old auntie or uncle of Amarra's, someone who pinches my cheeks and asks about school and the family, but these occasions are rare.

So I go out when I can. I try food off the streets. I buy

books at a little shop on Church Street. I drift through the malls looking for people I never find. I make a wish at a temple one silver morning. I wish to go home again.

Sometimes I have nightmares about the accident that killed Amarra. Awake, I try not to think about the bright lights flashing by and the motorcycle's tires screeching and the shattered glass as we—she—flew out of the car. Amarra's ghost hovers very close to me on those days. I wonder what she would have thought if she could see me, if she would have hated me even more, if, wherever she is now, she is willing me to fail.

If she does will that, she gets her wish. I make one mistake too many. It's careless and I have no excuse for it. My attention slips, only for a moment, but a moment is all it needed.

During lunch on a Friday, Sonya rummages about in my bag, emerging with a packet of Ruffles crisps.

"American Cream and Onion?" she says, wrinkling her nose. "What happened to the usual Classic Salted?"

I am bent over my desk, desperately trying to finish some geography homework I was too tired to work on the night before, and I am barely listening to her.

"I don't like the Classic Salted crisps," I say distractedly. "They don't taste of anything."

"What's a crisp?"

I look up at her, my mind still full of uninteresting details relating to rock formations and soil density. "What?"

"A crisp," she repeats. "That's what you called the chips just now."

She doesn't wait for a reply, simply opens the bag of crisps/chips and helps herself. I stare at her, my heart plummeting. Did she have to pick up on it? Did she have to question it? Worse, did I have to say it on a day when Ray is eating lunch with us?

I make myself look up at him, praying that maybe, just maybe, he didn't hear. But he did. Oh, he did.

The look on his face is worse than I could have imagined. He's stunned, like someone has hit him in the face with a sandbag. As he stares at me, his mouth moves wordlessly.

Such a small, insignificant mistake. And yet, to Ray, who knew every last nuance of Amarra's speech, it's the most significant thing in the world.

I watch his eyes dart this way and that, his mind fitting the pieces together, adding up all my mistakes, all those suspicious moments. I watch him relive every minute or day I have spent with him since I arrived. I watch the thing I dreaded most: the look of horror grow on his face as he realizes he touched me, laughed with me, held my hand, kissed my cheek and my forehead. And the whole time, it *wasn't her.*

"Amarra . . ." he croaks.

But he's not asking. He's not saying my name. He's calling for her, knowing she's not here. My bones rattle, icy cold.

Ray blinks at me, once, twice, rapidly. Then he gets up

and leaves the room, abandoning us without a word.

"What's with him?" Sonya demands.

I don't answer her. I spend the rest of the day feeling dizzy with fear.

In my distraction, I forget to take home a book I can't do my math homework without. I leave Sonya and Jaya at the buses and hurry back to the empty classroom. I find the book, turn around, and Ray is standing in the doorway. He must have followed me back to catch me on my own.

I take a step away, like an animal preparing its defenses. His eyes are dreadful and dark with hatred.

"I know what you are," he says harshly.

"I—"

"I've been an idiot," he says. "I should have seen it at the start. Jesus, I've spent whole days with you! I *touched* you." He covers his face. "I knew something was wrong. I knew you were different, but I *hoped*—shit, I've been so stupid! I believed you when you talked about how you hurt your head, how you had problems with your memory. What a joke. I *wanted* to believe you. I didn't want to *think* that she might be gone, because it means I killed her; it means she'll never come *back*—"

I retreat instinctively, as though the sound of his voice is a rush of air that has pushed me backward. He sounds like his pain and fury have been bottled up too long.

"Ray—"

"*Don't* say my name! Don't ever say it! I don't know how

you can stand to be what you are. Doesn't it make you sick, stepping in and stealing her life? Or do you not feel things like that because you're not actually a person?"

I take a deep, shuddering breath, trying to hide my hurt and my anger. I open my mouth to deny it, to tell him he's got it wrong, to convince him the way I ought to. But I can't speak. I can't do it. I can't look at him, not the way he is now, wracked with grief and fury, and tell him he's wrong. He'd be more likely to hit me than believe me. Rightly, too.

"Just go away," he snarls. "Why did they send you here? You're not even supposed to exist anymore!"

I stare at him. "What's that supposed to mean?"

"I thought—" He stops, almost visibly bites his tongue. His fists clench and unclench by his sides. "Why did you come?"

"I had to."

"Well, we don't want you here!" he almost shouts. "Stop pretending to be someone you're not; stop trying to be *her*. You're not! You're *nothing*, you're not even *human*." His voice drops, becomes low and deadly and pained. "You've been lying to everyone. But it stops now. I'll make them see how you've tricked us. They'll all see you for what you are."

"If you'd listen to me—"

"Why?" he demands. "What do I owe *you*? All you've done is lie to me. You let me believe you were her. Didn't you think we deserved to know she's gone?"

I try to say something, but nothing comes out; my lips

move soundlessly. Ray strides past the door. He turns back once to say one last thing.

"You're nothing but a cold, lying monster, *echo*."

The classroom door slams shut after him. I flinch and swipe angrily at my eyes, making sure no tears have slipped out onto my cheeks.

So that's it, then. I stare dully at the windows, the afternoon light, the sky. It's finished.

8

STOLEN

My force of will has never been tested so severely. As I get off the bus, it's all I can do to keep chatting to Nikhil and Sasha without breaking off, or crying, or frightening them. I do my best to seem normal. But only one thought runs through my mind as I look into their faces: their parents might go to prison because I made a stupid mistake. The ground beneath my feet feels shaky; it's not solid enough to hold me up anymore.

Erik *warned* me. He told me what exposure would cost us. I tried. I pulled it off for months. But I slipped in the end. I grew up refusing to be Amarra, and now I'm paying for that.

At the house, I settle Sasha in front of the telly and wait until Nikhil heads out to play cricket with some of the neighborhood kids. The moment he's gone, I race up the stairs. I can hear Alisha in her attic studio, clattering away, working feverishly on something new.

"Ray knows," I burst out before she can speak. "He knows about me. What I am."

Alisha's eyes widen. "You're not a what," she says. "You're

a *who*." She rubs her forehead, leaving behind a patch of paint. "So he knows about the new body?"

"Yes."

"But doesn't he know it's you?" she demands.

"He doesn't believe it is," I falter. "Like—like Dad." The word is alien to me. "He said he'd tell everyone in class, make sure they knew the truth. He could go to the police. Anyone else could. I just—I wanted to warn you. You could take Nik and Sasha and go away somewhere so the police don't find you. Leave the country—"

I sound hysterical, but I can't stop myself. I *can't* watch them go to prison. How can I let that happen to Nikhil and Sasha? Or to Alisha? After all this time living with them, I care. I even like Neil. He doesn't care much for me, but he's been kind to me regardless.

"Amarra," says Alisha, very calmly and firmly, "take deep breaths." She holds my face in her hands and looks me in the eye. "We're not going anywhere, not yet. If Ray won't listen to you, *I'll* talk to him. You know him. He always acts before thinking about it. But he's not cruel or cold. He'd never betray you."

"He doesn't think I'm that person," I miserably remind her. I think about that intense hate in his face. How the light died and he became someone else. I liked who he'd been: that he was nice and funny and moody. I liked it when he liked me. I never deserved it. I tricked him. I lied to him. Now he will always hate me.

"But you are that person," Alisha insists.

I nod. Even now, I have to pretend. I could tell her the truth, scream that they're right and I'm *not* Amarra. But I've seen the pain that truth has caused. I saw it in Ray's face only an hour ago. How can I tell her that her daughter's dead? If her own family won't take what little hope she has away from her, how can I?

"I'll talk to him," says Alisha. "If I can make him understand what his lack of belief will do to us, he may be willing to keep quiet." She straightens. Her eyes are anxious, but she smiles at me. "You stay here and watch Sasha, baby. I'll go see Ray."

"But—" I want to tell her it's futile, but she has to do this. She won't give up her life and her husband's life, her children's, if there's a chance she can make Ray understand how she feels.

So I step back. "I'm sorry," I whisper.

Her face softens. "Everyone makes mistakes," she says. "It's not a crime." For a moment, something flickers in her eyes, something that makes me wonder if she sees me and not Amarra. She blinks. "I'm the reason you're here. In a shitty situation. You can forget I said shit, by the way. Ray drove that car too fast, and he's also the reason you're here. We gave you a body and all these *rules*, shoved you into something strange and different." God, she could be talking to either of us. "When you've been put in such a small box, there are really only so many steps you can take before you hit something."

She kisses the top of my head, then walks past me down the stairs.

I sit on the steps and wrap my arms around my knees. I messed up, but maybe it would have happened anyway, sooner or later. Ray was never entirely sure of me. Amarra must have told him she had an echo. He always knew I existed. But if he tells the rest of the class, someone's bound to go to the police. I wish I knew how to protect us all. How to make sure Nikhil and Sasha don't lose something else.

Can they prove I am an echo? I don't know if the Mark can be removed with laser surgery, but it surely can't withstand a knife removing the skin? I almost laugh at how reckless and awful that idea is, but if I can replace the Mark with a wound—a scar from the accident splitting open, perhaps—if I can somehow replicate Amarra's old scars in time, maybe no one will be able to prove that I am not her. Or maybe they will. I don't know. I don't know how the Weavers and my familiars arranged this.

My panicked, rash thoughts tumble one after another as I sit there on the steps. It's only the thought of Sasha downstairs, knowing I should check on her, that makes me get up and go down again. I sit on the sofa with her and wait for Alisha to come back.

It's a couple of hours before she does. She goes to the kitchen to talk to Neil, and I run in after them. I don't know how Neil feels about me right now, but I have to know what happened.

"He was angry," says Alisha, "and in pain. He wouldn't believe me. He told me that you and I, Neil, we had no right to keep the truth to ourselves, that we aren't the only ones who loved her. And he wouldn't make any promises not to tell the rest of your classmates. He thinks they should know. But," she adds as both Neil and I stare at her in alarm, "he did say he wouldn't tell the police. He seems to understand that it's the kids I'm worried about."

She smiles. I can't help feeling relieved too. At least no matter what happens at school, Nikhil and Sasha won't suffer for this.

But Neil says, "Can we be sure someone else won't go to the police? If he tells her friends—"

"He seems to believe they'll keep their mouths shut," says Alisha, rather tiredly. "He says no one would show so little respect for Amarra's memory or so little care for two innocent children. I did try," she says to me. "I tried to tell him, but he refuses to believe you're you. I'm worried about how your friends will treat you if they won't believe it either."

"That's okay," I say, giving her the most reassuring smile I can muster. "Honestly, it's going to be fine. As long as no one tells the police, nothing else matters."

I catch Neil's eye, and there's a look on his face that tells me he knows I'm lying. If Ray tells everyone, he knows they will never forgive me either.

"You don't have to go back to school," he offers. It's kind of him. Kinder than I deserve right now.

I shake my head. Turning away from school will only reinforce his belief that I'm nothing like his daughter. It will only shake Alisha's belief. It won't make them any happier.

"They're my friends," I say, because that's my line and even Neil might believe it. "I can't *not* see them again. They're too important to me."

We look at one another in silence for a minute or two. Typically, it is Alisha who regains her composure first.

"It's time to eat," she says firmly. "Why don't we make Sasha happy and pick up some malai chicken from the club?"

I spend the night and the rest of the weekend fighting a constant urge to be sick, my nerves all knotted up into dread. Every time I think about school my stomach hurts, and I have to take Alisha's sleeping pills to get to sleep at all. I don't know who Ray might have talked to over the weekend. It wasn't Sonya or Jaya: both called me a couple of times and sounded normal. But Ray will have plenty of opportunities to talk to them and everybody else at school.

Neil offers to call school on Monday morning and tell them I'm not feeling well, but I say I will go. Alisha seems pleased. She's the kind of person who thinks hiding is the wrong way to deal with a problem.

I scramble to get ready, looking for a set of my uniform that's not in the wash, finally finding a spare skirt and shirt in the closet. I grab one of Amarra's favorite necklaces, for no reason other than I feel like I have to try doubly hard to look like her today, and I curse myself the whole way through. I so, so badly don't want to go to school today. Or ever again, really, but I have to. If I don't, the illusion breaks and I transform into an echo my familiars don't need to keep.

On the way to the bus stop, I have to be sick by the side of the road, a gesture that excites no little attention and thoroughly alarms Sasha and Nikhil. Nik suggests I go home, and he even offers to walk me back most of the way.

"It's okay," I insist. "I'm better now."

Hardly.

I straighten up, rub my eyes, drink some water, and get on the bus. As we rumble away, I fend off Jaya's concern, my tongue growing thicker and heavier with each mile that takes us closer.

When we arrive at the high school courtyard, I spot Ray immediately. He's on his own, at the far end, half concealed behind a wall sheltering the watercooler. He has his back to me. I take a quick look around the courtyard to see if anybody's looking at me funny. They don't seem to be, everyone's busy with the usual Monday morning chatter, and I turn my attention back to Ray.

I am so intent on him I walk straight into Lekha.

"Sorry."

"That's okay, I'm too sturdy to knock over!"

I'm about to walk away when I realize she's staring at Ray too, her eyes beady and alert, her head tilted to one side like a bird.

"Amarra?" she says before I can turn away. "I know you

feel like you're all on your own and there's nobody to rely on, but that isn't true. It will be okay, you know. No one's ever alone."

"I don't know what you mean," I say, stopping her midstep. "Why would I feel like that?"

Lekha raises her eyebrows, surprised. "We both know you're not the Amarra who was in the accident. Now it looks like Ray knows too." She tilts her head again, ignoring my shocked expression. "If I were you, I think I'd be feeling lonely. And scared. And I'd wear that necklace more often, it's very pretty, but that's beside the point." A smile brightens her eyes.

I open my mouth to offer a panicked denial, but she gets there first.

"Try lavender," she recommends. "Or sage! Don't you love the word *sage*? Such a nice *round* word. Math exams give me panic attacks. Sage helps. Or maybe I mean rosemary. I can never tell them apart."

She beams at me and wanders off to see a couple of her friends. I watch her go and I realize that, for the first time in two days, I could actually laugh.

Ray doesn't speak to me all day. But as far as I can tell, he doesn't speak to anyone else about me either. Once I catch Sam, the boy who first spoke to me on my first day at school, shooting me a strange look, but he looks away so fast I don't know if I imagined it. The waiting is agony.

He doesn't make me wait long. Just until PE, two days later.

I get changed as usual. I put my hair up, making sure the gauze is firmly taped over my Mark, and Sonya tries to get a look at it, also as usual. I swat her hand away and she laughs as we all traipse outside onto the fields to wait for the PE teachers.

We're about halfway across the field when I feel a pair of hands on my shoulders. I know the feel of those hands. He must have touched my shoulders any number of times on those days we used to spend together. But never like this.

Startled, I jerk forward, but it's too late to pull away. Ray's fingers bite painfully into my skin.

I stop, go still. A dull, resigned kind of relief sweeps over me. It's done, and I don't have to feel guilty about tricking these people any longer.

"What the *hell* are you doing?" Sonya demands angrily, and her voice is so loud that the rest of the class turns our way.

Ray ignores her. He's speaking to me, his voice harsh. "No one believes me," he says, with a short, humorless laugh. "I tried telling them, but they won't believe me. *They* think I've lost my mind. You know, maybe I have. Maybe that's what happens when someone you love dies."

"Ray," Jaya pleads. "Ray, stop—"

"Ray, this is crazy—"

"I'm not crazy," he tells them, and his voice is so sad. "I wish I was. I wish it wasn't true, I want it so badly to be her."

The field has gone very quiet. Ray grips my shoulders to

keep me from moving. He doesn't have to. I couldn't move even if I wanted to right now. My knees feel like jelly. I might be sick again.

"You've been on and on about some shit for two days, and I'm sick of it," snaps Sonya. "Why are you trying to convince us that Amarra's not Amarra?"

"It's not," he says. "It's an echo."

Sonya utters a sharp, incredulous laugh. "You're completely bonkers. Amarra doesn't have an *echo*. Ew."

Ew.

"She did," Ray snaps back at her. "She told me she did!"

There's a split second of shocked silence, and then Sonya's face turns purple. "She told *you* she had an echo?" she shouts. For a brief moment, she is outraged, jealous. A thousand times angrier with Ray than with me.

"Ray, you're hurting her," Jaya says very softly. "Can't you let go?"

"You don't believe me?" Ray challenges them. "I have proof this time, I can show you. Want to see that *scar* she's been hiding?"

In one sharp, savage move, he rips the gauze off my neck. He turns me around so my back is to the rest of the class. His face is satisfied, furious. Sad.

We both hear the gasps. Ray has been touched by a magic wand, transformed. He's not crazy, he's been wronged.

"There," he says bitterly. "Now you know what she is."

"But—" Sonya falters, her voice cracking in dismay. "But

that means . . . that means Amarra is . . . she's—"

Ray releases me abruptly. "Yeah," he says, and there's so much pain in his voice, "I know."

"No!" Sonya cries. "No, she's not! She's not!"

"Ask her," says Ray. "Ask her who she is. Who *it* is."

"I'm not an *it*," I say, stung by the injustice of this.

"So he was telling the truth?" someone asks in a hushed whisper.

I force myself to square my shoulders and be truthful. "Yes," I say, my heart pounding in my ears, "he was."

"I don't believe this," Sonya says. The girl who looked at me with such affection is gone. This girl detests the very sight of me. "You lied to us for months! You stole her life, you pretended—"

Angry murmurs build among the watching faces, like wasps in a small, confined space, and I force myself not to back away.

"I had to."

Even to my own ears, it doesn't sound like much of a reason. When you balance duty and law against death and grief, the duty seems worthless.

No one speaks for one shocked, shivering moment.

"I'm sorry," I say. "I never wanted to trick anybody."

"You're sorry?" Sonya repeats. "You're *sorry*? Do you even know what being sorry means? Do you even understand the difference between right and wrong? If I were you, I'd be crawling away in shame. But I guess *things* like you don't have feelings like that?"

I hear a hollow laugh. It's mine. I want to be patient, to turn away with dignity, but the jibe about my not even being human tips my temper over.

"I didn't ask for this," I say angrily. "I *never* asked for this. I've never had a chance to choose what I'm supposed to be and what I'm supposed to do. Never! I didn't come here because I wanted to; I didn't pretend to be Amarra because I enjoyed it. I *had* to be here; I had to do this. I have *never* been able to choose!"

Before anyone can reply, a figure flies across the field toward us. It's Lekha. I realize she's been missing all this time.

"The teachers are coming," she says in her high, clear voice, "and they're going to skewer us through the brain if we haven't started warming up by the time they get here."

"We're in the middle of something," Sonya snaps at her.

"Eff off," says Lekha agreeably. "That's short for *effervescence*, you know, which means 'do go and jump in a well.'"

A tiny, impossible smile tickles the corner of my mouth.

Everybody just stands around in a kind of angry, trembling shock. Ray makes a noise deep in his throat, like a hurt animal, and stalks off the field. Jaya starts to cry. I want to comfort her, but what use am I when all she wants is her best friend back? It's tempting, oh, so tempting to leave the field and leave school altogether. But I don't. There are any number of names they're going to call me and names they've called me already, but I'm not going to let them add coward to the list, too.

Somehow, impossibly, I make it through the day. And the next. And the one after. Things only get worse as the week winds down. The hostile remarks evolve slowly from "liar" and "thief" to insults aimed specifically at the monstrosity that I am. All my classmates have ever been taught about me was gleaned from rumors and overexaggerated news stories. I grow steadily more torn between guilt and fury. I know they have a right to be angry. I know they are suffering the aftershocks of learning Amarra's gone, but how long am I to be punished for?

On the other hand, the police never come. Whatever they think of me, no one has gone to the police. Not yet.

I have a feeling some of them want to, like Sam and Sonya. But if Ray told them what it would cost Amarra's family, it's worked. They've chosen not to tell. They've understood that it's not just me they would be punishing. And that, at least, is a very good thing.

Having exiled myself to my room over the weekend, I concentrate on homework. I read three tedious chapters for geography and make notes on a Second World War diary extract for history. I rework the tale of the mongoose and the snake for creative writing. I finish two pages of calculus for math. I reread a few chapters of *Wuthering Heights* and the last act of *Macbeth* for literature.

On Monday, I go back to school, same as always. I try not to notice the scowling, the hostility, the humiliating comments about my Mark, my stolen face.

I get to the high school but don't make it to the classroom.

On my way to get some water, the bell rings, and everyone scrambles to their classes. I don't realize there are people behind me until it's too late. I'm toppled, pushed, flung hard against the watercooler. It's tall, and made of steel and plastic, and it bloody hurts.

One glance at the faces around me is enough to tell me they're all young but unfamiliar. They must not go to school here. Beyond them, I see four of my classmates, Sam among them.

"You're joking, right?" I snap.

"It's only what you deserve," says a voice I don't know. Then my head is knocked back and hits the cooler again. Everything is a blur now and I scramble onto my knees. As one of them grabs me, I elbow her. She doubles over. There's another who catches me on the cheekbone. I make a spitting sound and throw myself at him. He cries out in pain and pulls away.

I wonder if that means I won.

As quickly as it happened, it's over. There's light again, the shadows have moved, and the bell has stopped ringing.

I can see shapes by the wall. My classmates. The strangers have disappeared. There's a girl who looks sick; so does one of the boys. Sam can't seem to look at me. I'm reeling in pain, in fury that I could have let this happen. I should have reacted faster, kicked harder. I want to shout at Sean. He told me echoes could be angels among mortals, but I can't imagine I look like much of an angel now.

Then I hear a new voice. I hear a trace of French and I tense.

"What the hell just happened?" Ray demands.

Someone mutters a reply.

"Weren't they expelled last year?" asks Ray. His voice is scathing. "I remember them. Really charming. Stayed friends with them, did you, Sam?"

"I play tennis with them," Sam says in a low voice.

"And they agreed to come and do you a little favor? That's sweet. If you were so pissed off you wanted to hit her, couldn't you have done it yourself? To do it like this—"

"Why didn't *you* hit her?" Sam asks. "Make her face look less like your girlfriend's? You hit *me* during football last year."

"You were cheating. That's like *asking* to be punched. And I don't hit girls."

"She's not really a girl."

"I don't care. What if they'd gone and killed her by accident?"

"It's not murder if it's one of those things," Sam mumbles, but he sounds uncertain.

Ray sighs. "Grow a brain, Sam. It can still get us all expelled. And those people who made her, the Weavers, they could get you for damages. You idiot. What d'you think she's going to do now, smile sweetly and forgive you?"

"Why isn't she getting up?" says one of the other boys.

"Shit, did they kill her?"

I see someone kneel down beside me. I jerk away.

"They didn't kill her," says Ray. He sounds angry. Because I'm alive? No, I don't think so. He's angry they did this. He hates me, but he knows what's right and what isn't. I feel a great pain deep in my chest. For a moment I hate him, too. I never wanted to care what he thought of me.

If you pretend you love a boy, maybe after a while you start to care. If you spend months with the traces of someone else's love and memories inside you, maybe those traces become a part of you. Or perhaps Amarra has nothing to do with this. Perhaps I care because I'm jealous of what she had. That kind of love. That kind of freedom *to* love.

I don't know anymore. I don't know what's real and what isn't.

"Ugh," I hear a girl saying, "don't let them ever come back on campus, Sam. There's a reason they were kicked out."

They disperse until there's only one shadow left. I turn my head away. I try to get up, but my legs feel weak and my head is spinning. There's something warm and wet in my mouth. It tastes rusty; it has a smell like roses gone bad.

A pair of arms hoists me to my feet.

"Get off me," I snarl. If I were a wolf, I could have bitten his hand off. Pity.

Ray releases me without comment, his face tense, his eyes darker than those of the boy who sat in the sun and smiled at the girl he loved. That photograph feels like a dream now.

"Why don't you leave?" he asks me. "Sam only did this because he's angry. He wanted to tell the police about you, but I made him swear he wouldn't. Nobody wants you here. How can you be sure someone else won't try to hurt you?"

"Is that a threat?"

"Of course not," he says irritably. "I just want you to go. It hurts like hell to look at you and see her face."

I straighten up. "This is my face."

"Just leave. Go, pack, do whatever. Haven't you realized you'll be better off that way?"

That puzzles me. "Why do you care whether or not I'm better off?"

Ray gives me a look that feels like burning. "Wish I knew," he says under his breath. "Good-bye, then. Have a nice life."

He stalks away. My body aches. What now? Ring Neil and tell him I'll be quitting school, thank you very much?

No. Of course not. I am not about to run *or* do the sensible thing. I will win this one.

I glance across the courtyard, at the classroom with the puke-colored door. My heart is still hammering. I'm so tired. I go to the bathroom to wash off the blood. It's not as bad as I thought. Only a bit of swelling and bruising.

I go back to class. Mrs. Singh will have just started Monday's double English Lit and *Wuthering Heights*. Her dry inquiry about my ability to read the time has no effect on me. I take my seat, enjoying the flabbergasted expressions on people's faces. Most of them, like Lekha, are simply shocked by the state of my face, their eyes huge. Nobody expected me to come back. I'm glad I did.

Mrs. Singh launches into a lecture about Heathcliff's apparently indisputable status as "a being of ultimate evil" in the novel.

I speak before she can ignore my raised hand.

"I don't think he's evil," I say. "I think he was sad and angry and he did some horrible things because of it, but he wasn't evil."

"I didn't ask you, Amarra—"

"I think," I continue, determined to be intrusive, "he's like Victor's Creature in *Frankenstein*."

"You mean the Monster," Mrs. Singh corrects irritably.

"No, I mean the Creature."

"Frankenstein himself referred to him as a monster."

"That was probably why Frankenstein lost everything. If he'd given the Creature a chance, taught him and raised him instead of rejecting him, well, things would have turned out differently, wouldn't they? If he had loved the Creature, they might both have had a much happier ending."

"*Loved* the Creature?" Mrs. Singh's glasses almost topple off her nose. "Gothic novels are not Hollywood extravaganzas! Why would anyone love what was made so unnaturally?"

Somebody laughs. Mrs. Singh appears to realize what she has said, and she flushes scarlet. My face grows hot under the pain.

Then an arm shoots into the air.

"I agree with Amarra," says a high, clear voice, without waiting for Mrs. Singh to call on her. "There was some good in the Creature. He even loved Victor. Same with Heathcliff. Doing a bad thing doesn't necessarily make someone evil. If you expect the worst, you're only denying someone a chance to be better. That's pretty much what Amarra said, and I agree. I," Lekha reiterates, lest anybody have failed to grasp her meaning, "*agree*."

Nobody knows what to say. I realize something that at once jolts and amazes me. By making my point far more eloquently than I did, Lekha has done something nobody expected. She has chosen a side.

Mine.

Mrs. Singh also seems to see that, somewhere along the way, battle lines were drawn. Her lips purse as though she has an especially sour lemon in her mouth. She sniffs and immediately sends me to the nurse to get my face looked at. But it's too late to quell the whispers or put out the fires. I go off to the nurse, smiling for the first time in days. Someone has chosen my side, and that is more than I ever expected.

9

SCULPTURE

It's weeks before I think of Lekha as anything but Amarra's classmate. But one afternoon after school, when I find myself sitting with her in Coffee Day, at the very table where Amarra sometimes sat with Sonya and Jaya, it dawns on me she's not just a girl in my class. She's a friend.

She makes me laugh, often *at* her, but she doesn't mind. She also tends not to listen to me. No matter how many times I tell her that "Palestines" are not what she thinks they are, she insists I must be wrong and that "Philistine" is in fact a country in the Middle East. I don't give up. She has no talent for metaphor, either, but insists on using it.

I realize she's also incredibly perceptive when she admits one day that she knew almost from the start that I wasn't Amarra.

"It's the way you move," she says. "You're too light on your feet. Like you're ready to run. Or you're about to growl and defend yourself. Like a hurt wolf cub. Lost but wolfy, you know?"

She shows me places in town I haven't yet visited.

Restaurants, rooftop cafés, cute little shops, and enormous stores. We go see movies at the multiplexes, buy peanuts off street vendors, visit shiny bars and hope no one questions our age as we order drinks with long, exotic-sounding names. We can never manage more than one or two because they're so expensive and we're poor teenagers. We sit under the hot sun and design costumes for famous literary characters: Lekha comes up with them and I draw them for her. We splash through puddles as we desperately try to hail rickshaws in the rain. I learn very quickly that the price a rickshaw driver will charge is directly proportional to the amount of rain rocketing down on the city at the time.

"Times like this," I tell her one hot April evening, during the last week of school before the summer, "you remind me of one of my guardians." She's pirouetting on the step in front of me, striking a ridiculous pose as I try to sketch her. "She's as dopey as you."

"A new word! Dopey. I like it. Like the dwarf. Does it mean charming and beautiful?"

"If you know the dwarf, you'll know it doesn't."

"Did you not think Dopey was adorable? Shame on you." She stops pirouetting, moving on to a contorted imitation of a plié. "Well? What does it mean?"

"In Ophelia's case," I say, smiling, "it means she has her heart in the right place, but her head is definitely full of dust and feathers and has a few necessary ingredients missing."

"Her name is Ophelia? Good grief. Has she done anything to ward off the evil eye?"

"Her father is a Weaver. I don't think she *can* ward off the evil eye."

"Creepy?"

"No," I say, "but I saw him on telly once and there was something cold about him, like he wouldn't let anything stop him from getting what he wanted."

Lekha abandons her posing. She sits down next to me. "Eva," she says, having by now coaxed my real name out of me, "I overheard someone in class talking the other day. About the Weavers. And hunters. You. All kinds of stuff. And normally I don't listen to a word anyone says about you but they did say *one* half-sensible thing. Ray used that Mark thingy-wingy"—she points to my neck—"to give you away."

I make a face. "We're supposed to hide them. Ray proved that doesn't always work, though. I think the Weavers decided it was worth the risk of exposing us." I give her a tiny smile. "See, this way we never forget who we belong to."

"Then . . ." Lekha hesitates. "Then you *do* belong to them? Completely?" I nod. "And they could destroy you if you didn't *be* Amarra properly?"

I nod again.

"Does that mean you're stuck here forever? But Amarra would have gone off to university. She was thinking of applying to places in the US and the UK and Australia. She used to talk about searching online for the best archaeology courses."

"It means I've pretty much got to go to university and study archaeology," I tell her. "Echoes are generally expected to do what their other would have done. I *could* study art instead. Or not go to university at all. But if I did that, Neil or Alisha could report me to the Weavers. They'd show them how different my choices are from what Amarra's would have been." I shrug. "Or maybe no one would say anything, maybe they'd just let it go."

"But that's unlikely. They'll want you to be like her."

"Exactly," I say. "So there's wiggle room, but they made me for a reason, Lekha. I have to stick by that."

"What about Ray?"

"What about him?"

"If he decides after all that Amarra *is* in you somewhere and he gives you a chance—would you have to be with him? Romantically?"

I nod. I think about Ray, winking at me that first lunch at school. The way he smiled, the way he looked at me. He was gorgeous. Temperamental, moody. He told me I was beautiful. He thought *she* was. He was rash and hot tempered and he was hers. He loved her. For a little while, he thought he loved me. And I pretended to love him.

Lekha stares at me. "Would you really be able to forget the guardian you told me all about? Sean?"

Would I?

Would I have loved Ray, really, truly, if I had just forgotten Sean? The sunlight dances off the pavement, making the air shimmer. I try to put Sean in this setting, imagining him with sweat in his hair and the sun in his eyes. His crooked smile broke my heart every time. He had the most amazing green eyes. He was irritatingly practical, grounded, clever. He broke the small rules for me but never the big one. He was there when I needed him and he was there when I didn't. I'd have loved him if he'd let me. But I will never know if he could have loved me. If he did.

I never forgot Sean. He was always there, a breath away, every moment I spent with Ray. He never left me alone. And I'm not sure he ever will.

"I don't know," I tell Lekha truthfully.

She shakes her head. "I think I'd have a coroner if I were you," she says. "I have a *very* low tolerance for turmoil."

"Coronary."

"No, sweetie pie," she says tenderly, "that's someone who works in a morgue."

I sigh.

"What are you doing out here with me, anyway?" I ask her. "Didn't you tell me last week that it's your mother's birthday today?"

"It is," she says, "but she's out of town, so I am as free as a daisy." This is a familiar refrain. Her mother is often traveling. "I always stay with my father when she's away. I like him. He never gives me veggies with my dinner."

I laugh. I stretch out in the sun, yawning on the steps. "I know we have exams starting in the next few weeks," I say, "but I'm *so* happy this is the last official week of school. I'm sick of being there every single day."

"You mean you're sick of everyone acting like you personally shot their dog," says Lekha.

I snort out a startled laugh. "That *is* rather how is it, isn't it?"

When it starts to get dark, we share a rickshaw back to our houses. I go in without any sense of homecoming. It will never be home to me, though it has become reassuringly familiar. The atmosphere never changes. It's peaceful, filled with the hum of conversation or Alisha clattering in her attic or Neil shuffling through papers in his study. But the peace is a tenuous thing, hovering on the surface, and if you shift too suddenly you could pop it like a balloon. And underneath is fear, and pain, and grief.

I stop long enough to thoroughly muss Sasha's hair before going up to Amarra's room. My last Lit essay of the school year is due on Friday, and I want to finish it tonight.

I'm halfway through when Alisha knocks on the door. "Busy?" she asks, surveying my neat handwriting and diligent attempt at homework with an amused look. It took me years to copy Amarra's handwriting.

"A bit," I admit. "I'm just stuck."

"Need some help?"

"It's this poem." I show it to her. "The question talks about truth and lies and how everything in the city is a mask, but all I seem to notice about the poem is how sad it is."

Alisha smiles faintly. "I know this one. It *is* sad."

"All I can see when I read it is that there's this man and he lost his world and now he wants to go back to the place he once belonged to. And it's sad because he *can't* go back; that world's not there anymore."

"Then say so," says Alisha. "Write that." But there's an odd note in her voice, and I look up at her. Her mouth trembles. What have I said? She tries to smile. "It's nothing. What you said just made me think . . . of something . . ."

I wait. She glances down at me before explaining.

"This city used to be a different world. When Neil and I were younger, we could get in the car and go driving late into the night, stop at an ice-cream shop or at the Imperial for biryani. This one time . . ." She laughs. "Your aunt Hema and I decided to be silly. I was eighteen. She blazed into my room late at night and said, 'Come on, Al, let's paint the town red.' So we got some red paint out of the shed, drove all over town, and painted random walls bright red."

I laugh. She smiles, too. "Do you remember when you were about four and we took you to the disco? We danced. You held my leg because you were dizzy and then you giggled and looked up at me and said, 'Mummy, the song's called "Dizzy," too,' and we found that so funny." She hums the song quietly. "It was a whole world," she says, "and it faded away."

There are tears creeping down her face, leaving glistening trails like the wet left behind by a snail. My throat is tight, and it occurs to me that she's crying because she can. Because she was once young and happy and silly and never knew anything about laws, or loss, or risks and sacrifices and desperate pretenses. Her whole, unfractured world is gone. And it's clear how fragile her belief in me is, how little of Amarra she must actually see when she looks at me.

I want to make her feel better, but I don't know how Amarra would have done it. I give her an awkward hug. She sniffles out an embarrassed laugh and looks around for a tissue, trying to compose herself. At the dresser, she finds the box of makeup Ophelia gave me when I left home. She brightens.

"Ooh, where did this come from?"

I tense, forming my reply carefully. "Someone gave it to me."

We spend the next half hour being silly with the makeup. Sasha joins in and demands we paint patterns on her face with lipstick. For the moment, at least, the pretense remains intact.

I'm in a good mood on Friday. I've been waiting for the end of the school year for weeks. I'm going to have to spend most of the holiday studying, until our exams are over, but I don't have to be back in school except on exam days. Not until July, anyway. Sean always started school in September and finished in June, but here we run from July to April; it won't be long before we're back for the new school year.

The last class of the day is English Literature. Mrs. Singh divides the class into pairs and asks each pair to talk for five minutes about a writer we've studied this year. I wait, fully expecting to be paired with Sam, which would be a very Mrs. Singh-like thing to do.

I've underestimated her. She pairs me with Ray.

I stay very still, arms folded on the table. In front of us, Ray's profile is dark, brooding, and Hamlet-esque in expression. I can almost picture him tearing his hair out.

Sam, who is supposed to be working with Lekha, comes to sit by her. He edges away from me, apparently convinced I'll choose this moment to wreak vengeance for my black eye and bruised face. I ignore him, watching Ray instead.

"And what do the two of you think you're doing?" Mrs. Singh demands, glaring at Ray and me. "Did I or did I not tell you to work together? Amarra, come forward."

"I'd rather stay here, Mrs. Singh," I say politely.

"Ray, move back, then."

"I'm staying here," he says through gritted teeth.

Mrs. Singh sends us both out of the classroom and slams the door after us.

"That was childish," snaps Ray.

"Ever heard of a pot and kettle?" I snap back, irritated.

I'm still aggravated hours later. He has a remarkable knack for getting under my skin. I scowl out the window on the bus, stomp loudly into the house, and bang mugs together as I make myself a drink. Trust him to ruin my good spirits.

Nobody else is home. Lekha is at the dentist's. There's no one to distract me.

Then I think of the attic. If Alisha's studio can't make me feel better right now, nothing else will. I go upstairs.

It's as beautiful as I remember. I've been here plenty of times since my first visit, but it never gets any less awe-inspiring. I stand in the middle of the attic and turn, absorbing each piece of this world as slowly as I can, savoring it hungrily, joyfully.

There are boxes in a corner of the attic. One is marked JUNK, so I look through it and find scraps of paper, wires, brushes, feathers. I pick out some tough wire and long black feathers.

Hot summer air flutters through the windows. I smell salt and earth and baked concrete, and it makes me want to be outside, high up in the air.

I twist the wire into a shape. At first I start to make a bird, a seagull or a crane, like the wax birds I used to give Sean. But I keep seeing something else in my mind. I stop to imagine the sculpture I want to create.

Wings, I think. Not a whole bird. Just the wings. I put my hands back to the wire and get to work. My supple fingers thrive beneath the coil as I pick apart separate pieces, heft them, twist them, shape them into the frame I need for the wings. I lose track of time, lose awareness of the real world beyond these walls. After I've made the frames, I retrieve a tube of superglue from a shelf. It's crude, but I'm not working to make something perfect. Slowly and meticulously, I stick feather after feather to the wire, blending, layering, the dark wings in my mind becoming clearer as they become real. It's fitting that the feathers are so ragged, unformed. Fitting for an angel the gods want to tear from the sky, who must ride on a bird until her broken wings heal.

Abruptly, I become aware of a sharp intake of breath. My concentration cracks. I look up at Alisha. She's frozen in the doorway behind me, her face so pale I'm afraid she's going to faint. My skin heats up and I stand.

"I'm sorry," I say hastily. "I know I shouldn't have. I should've asked, but I came up here and I saw all that stuff you were going to throw away. . . ."

I trail off, because it seems inadequate, and I don't think she's listening.

"Did *you* do this?" she whispers.

She moves closer, like a ghost, her eyes fixed intently, enormously, on my unfinished wings. I nod uncertainly.

She's quiet for a long time. She looks like she has stepped into a familiar world, but one that has lost all meaning.

When she finally turns to face me, there's a look on her face that makes me think this is the first time she is truly, properly, looking at *me*.

"It's sad," she says.

"I know." I trace a feather on the wings with my finger. "But they're supposed to mean things will be happy, in the end."

She nods.

"So what did you think?" she asks tentatively.

"About your work?"

She nods again. She's asked me what I think before, but always casually, with no expectation. This time it's different. This time she needs my answer.

I tell her the truth. "These things make me feel like I'm not in my body any longer. Like I don't have a body or a past anymore, but I'm still *more* myself than I've ever been."

Her eyes are shining with tears. "Yes," she says very softly, "that's what I wanted people to feel."

I wait, sensing she has more to say.

"She wasn't interested in any of this," she tells me. "You'd know that as well as anybody. She would never have made this."

She gazes at my wings, haunted. Her eyes brim and the tears spill down her face. Her voice breaks as she asks the question.

"She's not here anymore, is she?"

I shake my head. Then Alisha begins to weep, and I know that, for her, the pretending is over.

10

GHOST

The city is always quieter on Sundays. And Sasha is always at her most restless on Sundays. A couple of weeks into our holiday, she begs to be taken into town for the day.

The house isn't much fun for her. We do our best, Nikhil and I, but even we can't keep Sasha from noticing that her mother is in desperate pain and her father has finally given in to his own grief. They act normally when we're all together. They don't treat me any differently; they tease Nikhil about being an old soul; they laugh and smile and play with Sasha the way they always did. But she's not blind. She can see beyond it.

I take her out that Sunday, holding her firmly by the hand as we walk up our street. At the corner, I flag down a rickshaw. Sasha chatters excitedly.

"Where to, Sash?" I ask her.

She turns her face up to me doubtfully. "Anywhere?"

"Anywhere." I wince. If she suggests Mysore Zoo, I'm in a stew. Mysore is three hours away.

"Lunch?"

"That's all? Lunch?"

She nods eagerly. I can't help smiling. She could have had anything, and she picked lunch. Not long ago, an ordinary day out was such a treat for me, too. I hear a ghost of a laugh, a boy telling me I don't have to be ashamed, a flicker of green eyes. *Sean.* I swallow and push the memory away.

I consider the places I know and settle on a Chinese restaurant on Church Street. Sasha loves Chinese food.

I've been waiting for a blow. When Alisha realized Amarra was gone, I thought she'd be angry with me. But she's only grieving. I waited for her or Neil to decide they don't want to keep me, but it's been more than two weeks and they haven't said a word about a Sleep Order. Maybe they don't want to get rid of me after having gotten to know me all these months.

Either way, it has made being at the house quite stressful, and I am as eager as Sasha to get out for the day.

After lunch, Sasha and I go for a walk, past shops and vendors, ending up at Garuda Mall. It reminds me of my first day with Ray, but I don't protest when Sasha asks to go in. She loves riding the escalators up and down. I buy her a lollipop, and in exchange she solemnly agrees to go with me to the bookshop and *not* protest that she's bored. I lose myself in the aisles and the smell of paper. I am so immersed I don't realize my small charge has disappeared until I turn around to look for her.

Confronted with empty space, my stomach drops. I look

frantically around. There is no sign of her.

"Sasha!" I shout. "Sasha, where are you?"

When I find her at last, standing near the best-seller shelf, I almost collapse with relief. Then I realize that she has company. There's a dark-eyed boy with her. His T-shirt has French words over his breast pocket. My body tenses.

"Eva, look who I found," says Sasha happily, clinging to his hand.

I force a smile. "Oh, golly, what a treat," I say, hoping he can hear the venom in my voice.

Judging by his response, I think he did. "Better be more careful," says Ray. "You don't want to go back to the house and explain they've lost another child, do you?"

"That's a horrible thing to say, even for you," I snap. "Come on, Sash, we're going."

"She doesn't want to leave," says Ray angrily, holding up their entwined hands as if to prove this.

"Don't test me, Ray."

"Or you'll what?" His glower softens slightly. "I'm sorry I said that about losing her. It wasn't fair. But you could at least try to be friendly, for her."

"Of course," I reply bitterly, "*I'm* the unfriendly one."

I glare at him, but I also turn pink because he's right. It's not fair to frighten Sasha. I suppose it's a point in his favor that she's happy to see him. But he's not the smiling boy from the photograph. This boy is hard and heartbroken and bitter.

Sasha turns an anxious face up to me. She reaches out

with her free hand to hold one of mine, as if to show that she's not choosing Ray over me. Ashamed and touched by her gesture, I smile at her.

"Why don't you ask Ray if he wants to come with us?" I ask, hating each word. I don't want to spend time with him. I don't want to feel his bitterness, his grief, his hate.

Sasha's face lights up. "Will you, Ray?" she asks. "We're going to have coffee and ice cream, will you come?"

There's no way he can say no now. It's almost satisfying to see it's something he wants even less than I do. It also stings.

"Yeah, Sash," he says at last, "'course I'll come with you."

With Sasha happily chattering on, we go up to the food court. I find a table and avoid looking at Ray. He offers to buy the ice cream. I thank him as gracefully as I can.

"How's your holiday been so far?" he asks, politely enough.

"Fine, thank you. How's yours?"

"Fine too."

"Good."

I wince. I would rather have a black eye than make such inane conversation.

"What are you doing here anyway?"

"In the mall?"

"Yes."

"Wandering," he says.

But what I really hear is *remembering*.

"This place reminds me of you," I say, hoping to startle

him. It works. "Last time I was here, it was with you."

"When you were lying to me," he says, keeping his tone flat so as not to alarm Sasha.

"Yes, then," I say calmly.

Ray gestures at Sasha. "She called you Eva."

"Yes," I say, "that's my name." I cock my head. "That seems to surprise you. Did you think I *like* being a—what was it you called me? A cold, lying monster?"

He winces. "I'm not proud of that. It just came out. I'm angry because you lied. Because of *who* you are, not what you are. That's kind of irrelevant to me. I hope you know that."

"Thank you," I say. "I appreciate that."

He narrows his eyes. "Have you always been this, you know, confrontational?"

"Yes, I have a temper," I say wearily. "Why don't you join the line of people who have been bewailing it all my life?"

He considers me. "I get angry too."

"No! Really?"

"So you noticed?" he says, almost smiling.

"Do I have eyes?"

"She didn't lose her temper. She did get angry, but it was a calm kind of pissed off. She'd just tell you straight out, quite coolly, that you were being an idiot or that she was annoyed. But it took a lot to get her there. She was like those cows you see in the middle of the road. They seem so patient, they don't get worked up even with a gazillion cars honking at them."

I can't help smiling at the comparison. "I'm sure she enjoyed being called a cow."

A grin flickers over his face. "Yeah, I got a whack on the head for that once."

As the smile fades away, I can't help noticing how tired his eyes are, and I feel a quick rush of sympathy.

"I'm sorry."

"For what?" he demands, shifting back to anger in a flash. "Because she died or because you stole her life?"

Clearly he is not about to forgive me for that. Sasha looks up at the sharp tone of his voice. I tug lightly on a lock of her hair to distract her. She smiles anxiously.

"Because she died," I answer Ray, in a cheerful trill designed solely to reassure Sasha.

He doesn't reply.

"I'm not as wicked as you think I am."

"Yeah, I get that you were doing what you had to and all that. But I still think we deserved to know the truth. She *died*." He flinches in pain. "We had a right to know who we were loving."

I flush. "Yes, you did," I admit. "I didn't like lying to you. But it happened. So why are you still here? You could have had your ice cream, made Sasha happy, and left ages ago."

"Because I need to look at you." The intensity of his eyes is painful. "You look just like her. It's all I have."

"The last time we spoke, you said it hurt like hell to

look at me," I say. "Can't you make up your mind?"

"No," he says, "I can't. Because it does hurt like hell and sometimes I can't stand it. At school I had to avoid being in the same room as you. But these last couple weeks, not seeing you at all, were almost as bad." He stares bitterly into his melted ice cream. "I can't stop hating myself. I can't stop missing her. I'd do anything to get her back if it was possible. And sometimes when I *am* happy, it's because I see you and you're laughing. It's like seeing a ghost. For just one second, you're her and I forget she's gone."

I open my mouth to speak, but nothing comes out. I feel a throb in my chest, humming against my ribs. I search for something easy to say, something light to take that look off his face.

"It seems to me," I say rather severely, "that you could give Heathcliff a run for his money. Quite a moody git, aren't you?"

He grins, almost as if it was drawn out of him against his will. The smile shocks me, flashing phantomlike to the old photograph and the boy who knew how to be happy, who hadn't yet dissolved in rage and grief. It drags me through a tiny portal in my own mind, to the Eva who first looked at that photograph and wondered if she could love him.

"We've got to go," I say. "Thank you for the ice cream."

I'm on my feet before he can say or do anything. As we leave, I feel his eyes on me the whole way.

I pack Sasha off to her room when we get home. She has

a weekend's worth of journal pages to write for her echo. I run past her room and up the stairs, hoping for some time on my own.

But I only have a few minutes before there's a knock on the door. "Come in," I call out, half buried under the bed as I search for a pair of shoes I haven't worn in weeks.

Nikhil comes in and, to my surprise, shuts the door behind him. "Eva, can—can we talk for a sec? Please?"

He sounds so uncharacteristically hesitant, I crawl out from under the bed at once.

"Nik, don't be so bloody silly," I say briskly. "You can talk to me whenever you want to, you don't have to *ask*."

My manner cheers him slightly. He has an envelope in his hands that he keeps twisting, this way and that, round and round. It's a nervous tic I have never seen on him before.

"What is it?" I ask in a softer tone.

"It was, like, six months or something before Amarra . . . before the accident," he says, wincing slightly. "She asked me to keep a secret for her. I was the only one she trusted to help her. She—she gave me this." He taps the envelope in his hands. "She asked me to always keep it with me. I guess I . . . she—she must have thought she'd live a lot longer than—than she did."

"She couldn't have known," I tell him. "No one could have." I make him sit. I frown. "Do you want to go on?"

He nods miserably. "I have to. You have to know." He stares at me. "Amarra said . . . she told me that if anything happened to her, if she d-died before Mum and Dad did, that I should open this and read it. She asked me not to before then. She asked me to give the stuff inside to Mum and Dad."

"And you read it?" I say. I still don't see where this is going. "After the accident?"

"Yeah."

He doesn't say anything more. He opens the envelope and holds out its contents. A letter and a single sheet of paper.

"Here," he says.

"I don't think this was meant for me—"

"You need to."

So I unfold the single sheet of paper first and read it. It's typed all the way through, except for a dotted line at the bottom, where I see Amarra's signature carefully etched. I keep staring at the signature because it's the only thing on the paper that makes sense. The rest is a mass of words that blur and bend at angles.

There's a buzzing in my ears, I'm surrounded by angry wasps. Slowly, very slowly, words on the page come into focus.

Words like *Request for Removal*. And *effective immediately*.

"This is a Sleep Order!" I burst out in horror. "Amarra signed it? But this—this is *impossible*! She couldn't have done this, only familiars and Weavers can . . ."

I stop, the words trailing off like the last pitiful notes from a broken musical toy. Because it isn't true. It's *not* just familiars or Weavers who can pass the Sleep Order; I just thought so because I had never heard about it happening otherwise. But there must be some way it's possible. Mina Ma told me so, long ago, when she brought me scones to cheer me up about the tattoo. *Matthew* told me so. He said I was lucky Amarra had died before figuring out a way to destroy me.

Only she didn't. She worked it out.

I whip the Sleep Order out of the way and scramble through Amarra's letter to her parents, no longer hesitant. I have to know.

Dear Mom and Dad,

I'm sorry. I shouldn't have done this behind your back. I should have told you. I'm sorry about that.

I hate sharing everything with a stranger. She takes everything. She gets my stories and my memories and my photographs. You would want her to love you like I do, but she wouldn't. She could hurt you. She puts you in danger just by existing. I've been so scared thinking one day Nik and Sash and I will wake up and the police will be there taking you away. I can't do this anymore.

Now that I'm gone she'll be coming to live with you, and I don't want her to. She's not me. I don't want whatever second chance you think she could give me. I don't believe these second chances are possible. She's not me.

I found this blog online, where people like me were talking. "Others." Someone said they had found a way to get rid of their echo. I didn't know people like me could do it. I thought only you could. But it's true. I can do it. But only as long as you let me.

Please don't let her come. I've signed the Request for Removal. All you have to do is add your signatures to the bottom, under the bit where it says you're allowing me to do this, and then send it to the Weavers. They'll get rid of her.

Please.

I love you. So much.
Amarra

My mouth is dry. She didn't just hate me. She was *afraid* of me. She was afraid that I wouldn't just steal everything from her—I'd destroy it, too. I was the monster that haunted her nightmares.

And so she decided to destroy me first. In a funny, distant way, I actually admire that. It's the kind of thing *I* would do to protect what's mine, to protect everything I love.

I thought she was cool-headed, that she always gave in gracefully even when she didn't like something. Maybe that was true. But I was wrong to think there was no spirit in her or that she wasn't capable of doing everything in her power when pushed. She's proven twice now that she was capable of standing up and fighting back if she had to. She refused to tell me anything about Ray. And now she's killed me.

"Eva?"

That's Nikhil's voice. I should speak to him. I try to open

my mouth, but my throat is so dry I can't make any sound come out. The wasps are louder now. They're buzzing furiously.

I could laugh. I've spent all this time, all these months, trying to make my familiars happy. Trying to keep my promise to Mina Ma. Be good. Be happy. Keep the Weavers and my familiars happy. Make them want to keep me.

But in the end, it wasn't Neil or Alisha or the Weavers I should have been keeping my eye on. No, it was the one threat I thought had gone, the one I thought couldn't touch me again.

Yet her ghost has reached out and done it.

"Eva?" Nik says my name again. Louder. He looks so anxious, so unlike his normal self, it's heartbreaking.

"I'm okay," I lie, trying to moisten my dry mouth. "Nik, why do you still have this? Why didn't you give it to your parents after the accident?"

"Because," he says helplessly, "because when I read it I—I couldn't do it. I knew you'd die. And I didn't know you at all then, you hadn't yet come, but I knew you had feelings. That you might be a nice person. Amarra never knew those things, but I did, because I talk to *my* echo. If Amarra had known what I did, she wouldn't have wanted to hurt you either. So I—I hid it. I thought I could hide it forever and no one would have to know. And then you came and I *liked* you and I felt bad about not keeping my promise to Amarra, but I knew I couldn't—"

I put my arm around his shoulders and hug him. "You

did a very kind thing," I say softly, my voice shaking slightly. "But why give this to me now?"

He glances at the ceiling and I realize he's looking toward Alisha. He's been waiting for the ax to fall, too.

"After Mom realized—" He falters, and shrugs. "I don't think they'd ever just send you away to be hurt or anything, they're not like that. But I was scared someone would find the letter, I mean, if Mom doesn't think you could be Amarra, then she might not—"

I nod. "She might not feel like there was a good reason to keep me anymore."

"Yeah."

I look down at the letter, and at the Sleep Order, my fingers numb and my heart cold. "And now what?" I ask, half to myself, half to him.

"I want you to have it now." His voice is calm again, but underneath I hear a small, miserable note.

I look sharply at him. "Nik, you can't expect me to be objective about this—"

"I know that," he says. "But it's *your* life. You should get to decide."

I stare at him and wonder if I could have done the same thing in his place. If I'd made such a promise to someone I loved, would I be able to turn my back on it and do the right thing? Probably not. I'm not quite so selfless. But Nikhil is doing what he believes is fair. He's handing me my life back.

"Then I'm going to destroy this," I say quietly. My

stomach twists guiltily. It's definitely not the right thing to do, to keep Amarra's last letter from her parents.

But right now I'm safe. As long as Neil and Alisha don't see this, as long as they don't sign the papers and officially allow Amarra to pass the Sleep Order, I'm safe. I can't show this to them. My life is at stake. And I made promises, too.

I search Amarra's desk for the box of matches she used to light scented candles. I strike one, hoping to burn the letter and the Sleep Order together and toss the ashes in the bin.

Exactly at that moment, there is a knock on the door. Alisha comes in. "Eva," she says in the kind of voice that suggests she isn't used to using my real name, "have you seen Nik, he's not in his—oh, here you are! I was—"

She stares in confusion at the lit match, then at our guilty faces, and finally her eyes narrow in on the paper. We see the suspicion wiped clean off her face. We watch her go pale.

"Is that—is that Amarra's handwriting?"

"It's old stuff." Nikhil tries valiantly. "Eva's clearing the desk out—"

But Alisha's eyes are on my face and I can't meet them. I'm never this shifty.

"Can I see that, please?" she asks. Her hand trembles.

I blow out the match and give her the papers.

"Thank you," she says, in a funny voice. Almost like she understands what handing the letter over is about to cost me.

I close my eyes. Nikhil squeezes my hand, and in the dark behind my eyelids I listen to the wasps.

11

BOUND

I am an incorrigible eavesdropper. I always have been. I hover by the door of Neil's study, to listen in on his conversation with Alisha inside. I don't even feel guilty about it.

"But you've heard her," I hear Alisha protest. "You've *looked* at her. She's been here, what, eight months now? Don't you sometimes look at her and think she's just like us?"

"She isn't like us. She's been taught to look and act exactly like us, but she isn't."

Alisha's breath hisses through her teeth. "Sometimes I wonder if she's more human than you are."

I utter a silent gasp. There's silence.

"God, I'm sorry," she says. "I didn't mean that."

"Al, do you think I want to hurt her?" he demands. "Do you think I'm enjoying this?" His voice is raw, as though he has been weeping. "But this is the last thing our daughter wanted. The *last* thing. How can we even consider denying her?"

"I know that. Don't you think I know that? I feel like I'm spitting on her ashes by thinking this, but I'm thinking about what's *right*, and to have her destroyed—"

"It won't hurt," says Neil. "You know Adrian told us it's just like going to sleep—"

"You believed him, did you?"

"This . . ." His voice cracks. "This is the last thing she will ever ask us for."

"I know."

There's a pause, a tense silence full of anger and pain and love, and then Neil says, "Is this about the wings?"

I stiffen.

"What?"

"I saw the wings in your studio. Did Eva make them?"

"Yes, but that has nothing—"

"I think it has a lot to do with this," he says. "You always wanted a child who loved art like you did. Who had a talent for it like you."

Alisha's voice is cold as ice. "Are you suggesting I love my children less because they happen to be uninterested in art?"

"Of course not," he says wearily. "God knows you'd love them if they morphed into cannibals overnight. But you *did* hope, didn't you? You always hoped one of them would be passionate about it. Now there's a girl in this house and in many ways she is exactly the kind of child you wanted."

"You can't be serious!"

There's a fraught pause. Then Neil says, "Al, did you

ask Matthew to make her that way? To put that passion and talent into her?"

Alisha gasps. "No," she says icily, "I didn't."

"Do you think he might have done it to please you?"

"Matthew has no interest in making me happy any longer, Neil!" she snaps. "And considering neither of us has the faintest idea how they make an echo, I think this conversation is ridiculous and insulting. I would never try to *choose* what my children grow up to be."

"You know I didn't mean it that way," he says. "I just saw the wings and I thought—"

"I'm surprised you saw the wings and didn't see the obvious," says Alisha, rather miserably. "She made them, Neil. She made them because she's sad. They're wings. Wings make you fly. That's all she wants. To live. And fly. How can you argue that that isn't human?"

"I don't know," says Neil. "But I do know that if I have to choose between my daughter and her echo, and that's what you're asking me to do, I choose Amarra. I loved her the moment she opened her eyes. I didn't stop loving her when she closed them."

Alisha sounds tired, unsure. She's wavering. "I never realized how unhappy this made her. She was always so good about it. She so rarely complained about anything."

"But she *hated* it, Al. We made her write in that journal every week. We made copies of her photographs, asked her to tell us what we needed to know. She never believed this was her second chance. She never had arrogant hopes of living after death. She wanted the life she already had, and we made her share it with a stranger." I hear the snap of paper. "She was *afraid* for us. That we'd go to jail and she'd lose us! We were blind not to see it. And now she's *gone*. Doing this one thing she asks us to, it won't make up for that, but it's the only thing we can do for her. I *can't* not give her the only thing she wanted."

A sob breaks into Alisha's voice. "I just want her back."

"So do I," he says. "I want it more than anything."

There's a tremor in his voice. I think he's crying too. I don't want to listen anymore. I turn on my heel and almost bump into Nik. My heart sinks.

"Yeah," he says before I can ask. "I heard." He looks puzzled and lost, like a small child. "I thought they'd keep you."

"I don't think they can, Nik," I tell him gently, trying not to let my own hurt show. "Amarra's still so *real* to them. They don't believe she's in me, but they still feel her. They can't bring her back. They couldn't save her. All they can do for her now is carry out her last wish."

My hands are shaking. If I am honest with myself, I have to admit that I'm angry and scared and hurt, but I also can't imagine it could have gone any other way. I can't imagine *I* would have done any differently in their shoes.

I check that Sasha is occupied with her toys. Then I take Nikhil downstairs and make him some hot chocolate to calm him. He drinks it and stares quietly at the table. I wash up his cup, the spoon, and tidy the kitchen. I feel like someone has sliced me open.

When there's nothing left to do, I go back to Amarra's room, locking the door behind me. So that's it, then. I fling the cushions across the room, as hard as I can, over and over until my arms ache and the seams split. I sit down on the bed and try not to cry. Then I spring up again, furious. I can't just give up. I can't let them take me like a meek little lamb.

With a frenzied surge of energy, I start packing my things, only to unpack them again and put everything back in its place.

As terrifying as the open, unknown world is, my instinct is to run. To break free and cut loose and flee as fast and as far as I can go before they can find me and catch me and take me to the Loom. It's the only thing I can think of. It's my only chance.

But I can't run. Not because Mina Ma once said to me, desperately, "Don't run." But because I'm bound to the Loom by my own umbilical cord.

A tracker.

If I leave, if I do *anything* I shouldn't, they'll know. They'll find me. I have no way of removing the tracker. I don't know where it is.

I have no way out.

I'm sitting by the window more than an hour later, when someone knocks on the door. I unlock it and let Neil and Alisha in. Though red-eyed still, they seem composed. Calm.

Alisha's face is guilty. "Eva—" She falters and can't seem to go on. She covers her mouth, but to her credit, she doesn't look away.

"We signed the papers," says Neil. He doesn't sound like it gave him much pleasure to do so. "And we've sent them to London. By courier. They should be there in a couple of days. But I haven't called ahead to warn them that they're coming. They won't know about the Request for Removal until they get the papers." I don't say anything because I'm not sure what he's getting at. "If you were to— If you felt like you couldn't stay here any longer— We'd like you to know that we, ah, we wouldn't feel it necessary to stop you."

I blink at them. Once, twice. Then the penny drops.

"You're telling me to run away," I say. "That isn't possible. Didn't anyone tell you? There's a tracker somewhere in my body. They'd find me wherever I went."

"But . . ." Alisha begins, dismayed. "But then . . ."

They stare at each other. Then at me. It makes me feel slightly better, knowing that they *did* want to help me. That they don't want me to be hurt. So I smile faintly and say, "It's okay. I'll be fine." I've become a very good liar.

It's obvious they don't want to leave it at that, but I don't want to prolong this conversation, so I say, "Could I be alone now, please?" and they leave the room, reluctantly, and I let the smile slip off my face.

I don't sleep at all that night. I sit on the bed and make paper cranes out of a spare notebook. I read somewhere that if you make a thousand paper cranes, you get to make a wish. I work feverishly, relentlessly, through the night. My mind wanders. I think of crazy, outrageous, elaborate schemes and then laugh at myself for being fanciful. I am caught in a net. Every way I turn, I am brought up short.

And then, in the early hours, when my energy has burned out and despair sinks deep into my belly, I think about my guardians and how anguished they will feel when they find out. Will I see them one last time before the Weavers unstitch me? Do I even want to? I see a flash of Sean's green eyes behind my eyelids and I flinch. Do I really want their last memory of me to be right before I die? It will break Mina Ma's heart. I've failed her. I've failed them all.

I wait until eight o'clock the following evening, when I know Alisha will be in the attic. When she's upset, she spends more time making things.

I slip upstairs to the bedroom she shares with Neil and go straight to the table by her side of the bed. Her phone is there. She never takes it up to the attic with her.

It takes me less than a minute to find the number I'm looking for. I press the green button to dial.

One ring. My heart begins to race. Two rings. Three.

"Truly, I am astounded," a familiar voice answers, the drawl faintly punctuated with genuine surprise. "Two phone calls in as many days? You *must* be—"

"It's not Alisha," I cut in. "It's me."

There's a pause.

Under any other circumstances I would have laughed. Matthew Mercer is speechless.

"What do you want?" he asks wearily.

"You said two phone calls in as many days," I say. "Did Alisha ring you yesterday? Did she tell you about the—"

"The Sleep Order, yes, she did," drawls Matthew. "For a woman who has allowed this to happen in the first place, she seems peculiarly concerned about your safety. She rather thought I might be able to, ah, how did she put it? *Help you.*"

From the scornful way he says it, I can already see this is doomed to failure, but I have to try.

"I was sort of hoping you might help me, too," I say quietly.

"And why on earth would I do that?"

"Because you made me," I remind him. "You said it yourself. I'm your creation and you don't like destroying your creations."

"And you're enjoying this, are you?" Matthew sounds amused. I could strangle him.

"No," I say flatly, "I'm not. I hate asking you for help. But I'll regret it later if I refuse to try every possible thing I can think of. Amarra's papers will be there by tomorrow. You could revoke the Sleep Order. You could save me. I know you can. You can do whatever you want with us."

"True."

I wait. He doesn't say anything else. Despair and help-lessness claw at my throat.

"You *made* me. You'd be wasting that if you destroyed me."

"Again, true." I hear a yawn. "Are you going to keep telling me things I already know? If so, I'll have you know I have the attention span of a two-year-old and simply won't listen—"

"Please."

I hear a delighted chuckle. "Say that again. Do."

"No," I snap. "Will you help me?"

"I rather think not," says Matthew. I stare at the window. I was clutching at straws, and now the last straw is vanishing like smoke. "That said, you are aware that a Sleep Order cannot be enforced until an echo reaches the age of eighteen, are you not?"

I blink. "What?"

Matthew snorts. "Ignorant. All of you. It's preposterous, really. Doesn't anyone learn anything these days? Elsa insisted on it," he says, with a deep and heartfelt sigh. "She refuses to kill what she calls 'children.' Unless an echo has broken a law and is brought to us for trial, they cannot be removed until they are eighteen. And seeing as you've been a good little girl—well, hardly, but we'll disregard that for the moment—you are not *on* trial. So it will not be enforced until your eighteenth birthday."

"But I'll be seventeen in less than a week! That means I have a *year* left!"

I almost see Matthew rolling his eyes. "And in what way is that not a vast improvement on having a *day* left?"

He makes a good point. Hope prickles tentatively in my chest, like a seed looking for sunlight. A year gives me time to work something out.

"So that's all?" I ask Matthew. "You won't revoke the Sleep Order? You'll leave me with one last year?"

"Well, yes. Nicely put. Very succinct."

"Thanks," I say bitterly.

"Eva."

His tone keeps me from hanging up. I wait.

"As you have pointed out already, I made you, so you are not mindless or helpless. It would be insulting, quite frankly. So do not, I implore you, bore me by asking me for my help. Find your own way out of the noose."

There's a click as the line goes dead.

I should be angry with him, but instead I'm furious with myself. Why had I hoped he would help me? Because of the stupid, silly dreams of the pale green nursery and Matthew singing lullabies to my infant self? They're *dreams*. They were never real. Matthew won't help me. Neil and Alisha have condemned me and can't help me escape it. My guardians are far away, and if I were to try and speak to them, and the Weavers found out, I'd be breaking the law. That would mean going to trial, and trials trump Sleep Orders. After the things I have heard, I have no illusions that the Weavers would vote to save me at trial. That would mean losing the little time I have left.

Panic makes me feel dizzy. I have no more ideas. But I do have time. I force myself to breathe. One way or another, I must find a way out.

I stumble back to Amarra's room, weak-kneed and cold. I sit down on her bed, my bed, and wait for my seventeenth birthday, for the clock to begin ticking the last twelve months of my life away.

12

MINES

I leave the house on my birthday. Hanging around will only remind Amarra's family of the day their daughter and sister won't have. Instead Lekha takes me to lunch at a place called Koshy's, a Bangalore landmark. The food's amazing and we have fun, but she has to leave straight after and meet her father. "He's going to pick me up at the corner there," she says as we stand outside. "Sigh. I can't wait to be old enough for a real license."

"Ray drives," I say. "So does Sonya. They're not eighteen, are they?"

Lekha rolls her eyes. "I might be the only one who cares about having a real license before getting on the road. Ray and Sonya know *how* to drive. *I* know *how* to drive. But we're too young to do it legally."

"And Ray didn't get in trouble for that after the accident?"

"His lack of a license didn't cause the accident," Lekha points out. "So it wasn't hard to pay a police officer to ignore that teensy-weensy circumstance."

I will never understand how this city works.

"Are you okay?"

The question makes my face feel hot. I put on my best poker face. "Well, it would be nice if someone dropped a bucket of cold water on my head. How can it be this *hot*? I'm wilting."

"Oh, no," says Lekha. "Don't even try that innocent, ooh-I'm-a-delicate-flower thing with me. You've been quiet all day." She points a finger at me. "I thought I gave you specific instructions *not* to think about that Sleep Order boondocks today."

"I'm not sure *boondocks* is—"

"Eva!"

"I can't help it," I say quietly. "It's like my brain is counting down."

Lekha's face softens. She's been remarkably tough since she found out, apart from bursting into tears when I first told her. "You have a year," she says, regaining her brisk, no-nonsense manner almost at once. "You're going to find a way to stop this. *We'll* find a way. Now I admit I know next to nothing about the Loom and these wretched laws you're always going on about, but I am a troubadour and I *will* help however I can."

I bite back a laugh. "You meant trouper, didn't you?"

"Trouper, troubadour, quite frankly it's all the same to me. Should someone who has the Grim Reaper waving his sickle-scythe thing at her really be so concerned about words?"

"Fine," I say, defeated and smiling in spite of myself. "You're a regular troubadour."

She smiles and gives me a hug. "I won't let them kill you," she says. "I'll smuggle you away and stick you on my mother's coffee plantation if I have to."

"Thank you," I say, hugging her tight and feeling a bit more hopeful. "I may hold you to that."

After Lekha heads off to the corner, I walk the other way to the main network of streets, MG Road and Brigade Road and Church Street. I trace the roads, beating an invisible path into concrete so hot the air is rising off it, glittering like diamonds. In a couple of weeks, the first showers and storms will cool the country down.

Amarra's phone rings. I squint at the screen. The number's blocked, but there are only a few people it could be.

"Hello?"

"Happy birthday," says a voice I know well—oh, *so* well.

I stop, electrified, cemented to the concrete. The sounds of laughter and traffic and horns blur into stillness.

Sean.

"S-Sean?" I whisper in disbelief.

"I know it's been a while," he says lightly, "but have you really forgotten the sound of my voice?"

"Hardly. I never forget things."

He laughs. It sears through me. After all this time, all these months, it's like the earth has just exploded in fire and smoke.

"You're not supposed to call" is all I can say. "If they—"

"I thought you might like to hear a voice from another time and world. Even if it was just for a minute or two."

My body thrums with aliveness. It is agony, but I can't remember ever being so happy. I try to swallow a lump in my throat, but it won't go.

"Sean—" My voice cracks.

There's a pause, which lengthens. Then Sean says, "How are you?"

His voice is strange, as though someone has spread it like cheese over bread, spread it too thin. My heart pounds. Too fast. It makes me giddy.

"I'm all right," I say.

"That's a lie."

"So you've heard."

"Yeah," he says woodenly. "I've heard. We've all heard."

"Is Mina Ma . . . is she—"

"She's angry," says Sean. "She's swearing to cut off Matthew's unmentionable parts if he so much as hurts one hair on your head. Which means she's not yet sad. Look, we don't have to talk about this."

"I want to come home," I say very quietly.

"It would be nice, wouldn't it?" His voice is so expressive for a minute that I can see him. His jeans are creased, his shirt rolled back to the elbows and rumpled. He looks tired. He hasn't shaved in a couple days, his jaw's rough, his hair is messy. He looks . . . sad.

I want to see him so badly I could break something.

We're quiet again. It's not that I have nothing to say to Sean. There's just so *much* to say and I don't know where to begin. There's something fierce and silent blazing across the line.

"I'd better go," says Sean at last. "It's morning here. I've been in London, visiting this theater, and I only just got home. I need some sleep."

I know this is the last time he'll call me. This might be the last time we ever speak. I want to say something that tells him how I feel, but I don't know how.

"Eva," he says, and my eyes tear, "do you still dream of cities?"

"Yes," I say.

I hear the sound of him swallowing. "Do you dream of me?"

"Yes."

"I thought things might have changed."

"I haven't changed."

"No," he says. "I haven't either." He hangs up.

I put my phone back in my pocket but keep gazing ahead at the hot shimmering concrete. If I blink or move, the concrete will change, time will fracture, and I'll lose this, this moment with the sound of Sean's voice and the feel of him close to me. If I concentrate on the concrete hard enough, on that exact spot, I can feel his breath on my hair, his fingers on my skin. I can feel myself running off that train and into his arms.

But my eyes grow raw and blink against my will. I draw myself reluctantly back to the city, to the real world. I fiddle with the bracelet of shells that he gave me.

I keep walking. There's nothing else to do.

As I turn the corner, I realize my assessment of the Indian climate was off by a few days. It's beginning to rain. Within seconds it has turned into a torrential shower.

Around me, people are shrieking as they run for cover. The rain is warm. Before I can find a rickshaw, a car pulls to a stop beside me. A Scorpio, dark and faded and severely battered in places.

The passenger door opens. Ray and I stare at each other for a minute. He nods at the rain. "Do you need a ride back to the house?"

I hesitate, then climb in. "Thank you."

"No problem," he says. His jaw seems to be under severe strain.

"Are you following me?"

"Obviously," he says. "Didn't you see me outside your window last night with the night-vision goggles?" I laugh. He doesn't smile back, but his face twitches like he almost wanted to. "I was on my way home and saw you."

"Thanks for stopping. I'm impressed." I add mildly, "You still drive."

Ray's hands jerk on the wheel.

I could kick myself. "I didn't mean it like that," I say. "I was only surprised. If I'd been in your place, I probably wouldn't want to drive ever again." Ray glances at me. I look back earnestly. "It was an awful thing to say, but I really didn't mean it that way."

"Don't worry, I'm not going to cry myself to sleep," he says. He hesitates. "Not that it wasn't true. I did kill her."

"It was an accident," I remind him. "The guy on the motorcycle was going too fast, you didn't have time to do anything. Besides, she should have put her seatbelt on."

"It wasn't her fault," he snaps.

"I didn't say it was," I snap back. "I'm only saying you could blame anyone if you wanted to. The motorcycle driver, you, Amarra. I think losing someone is bad enough without blaming yourself for it, too."

He's quiet for a minute or two. Then: "How do you know all that? About the bike coming? That she wasn't wearing her seatbelt? Did someone tell you?"

"No." I hesitate before telling him the truth. "I saw it happen. I kind of dreamed it while it was happening."

Ray's face is a mixture of disbelief and fascination. His hands grip the wheel very tightly. "I didn't know that was possible. How does that work?"

"Well, you know how Alisha told you that echoes are imperfect? The Weavers are trying to fix that. One day, if they figure it out, we'll be spare bodies. And if our others die while they're still young, they'll wake up in the new body."

He nods. "That's why she thought Amarra was still here?"

"Yeah. And she was right in a way. I don't think she's

253

here the way Alisha believed she was," I add quickly, "but when they made me, they had to put some of her cells, some of her consciousness, into me. To make me grow the same as her. A small part of her was always part of me. It meant that sometimes, usually when I was asleep and my mind got quiet, I would dream bits of her life."

"Jesus," he says, "didn't that feel weird? Like you were spying?"

"There was nothing I could do about it."

"Did you ever—" He stops.

I get it. He wants to know if I saw them. *Together.* "No. I saw *you* once. Just your face. And I saw the accident. That's all."

We sit in uneasy silence for a few minutes. The rain has soaked me, and without the sunlight, it's cold. I huddle up. Ray flips a switch near the wheel. The air-conditioning turns warm. He doesn't say anything, but a little color creeps back into his face. His hands don't loosen on the wheel. His eyes are far away, following Amarra through the mist she vanished into. His anger and his grief fill the car like cigar smoke. I have no idea how to pick my way through it. I can only step cautiously, one step at a time.

I study his profile for a minute. A long minute. And I realize something.

"It was you," I say.

"What?"

"You're the reason she decided to get rid of me."

The lack of surprise on his face confirms what I'd guessed. He's known all along. "I thought you didn't know," he says.

"I didn't until about a week ago. But *you* did. You said something to me, months ago. You said I shouldn't even exist anymore. You thought I'd be long gone; you didn't think I would turn up."

"You weren't supposed to," he says, but not unkindly. "She said she'd done this thing where they'd get rid of you so that you wouldn't replace her if anything happened to her."

"She did it because of you. She wouldn't share you. I wondered. She put up with me all her life, but one day it was too much? I couldn't figure out what tipped her over. It should have been obvious. It was you."

Ray doesn't say anything for a moment. Then, carefully, he asks, "So does that mean you're going to . . . you know . . . that they'll—"

"Yes," I say, my voice flat as paper, "when I turn eighteen."

He glances at me. He doesn't say anything, but the expression on his face is almost one of regret.

Another difficult, awkward silence fills the space between us.

"We haven't gotten off MG Road yet," I say, looking out through the rain. "Is the traffic going to be this bad the whole way back?"

He nods. "It'll be jammed long before we get to Amarra's house. Could be over an hour before you get there. Do you want to stop somewhere and change clothes?"

"Where?"

"My house is about five minutes away. You're a bit shorter than my mother, but her clothes should fit you."

"Won't your mother mind?"

"Nah. She's in Paris with my grandparents this week."

"Have you been there?"

"Where, Paris?"

I nod.

"We used to go every summer," he says, "until a couple of years ago. I loved it. But with A-levels and everything, I have a much shorter summer break, so I don't get to go as often."

My phone buzzes and my heart leaps, but it's only a text from Lekha. I squirm guiltily. It was silly to hope it would be Sean again. I shouldn't be thinking about him at all, but I can't help myself. I can't stop picturing him living a normal life. Does he think of me much? Does he tell himself I'm the wrong person to be thinking about?

Ray pulls in through a pair of open gates and stops his car in front of a tall white house. It seems quiet, except for a dog barking.

"There's no one home," he says, "unless you count Sir Jacques."

"Sir Jacques?"

"My mother named him. He has some stray dog and some husky in him, so hell if I know what she was thinking. If you've ever seen a dog that looks *less* like a Sir Jacques . . ."

I follow Ray to the front door. He unlocks the house and leads me in. He glances at me, at the wet clothes, and then looks quickly away again. They've stuck to every line and crease of my body. I'm suddenly self-conscious.

A dog bounds into the room, padding toward us. He's a powerful animal, shaggy like a wolf, his teeth bared in a grin as he gambols around Ray. He's dark gray with white patches on his belly. The sound of his barking makes me want to step away, but I stay where I am.

After nuzzling Ray and sniffing me suspiciously, Sir Jacques licks my hand and wags his tail. I scratch behind his ears.

"Weird," says Ray. "He doesn't like strangers."

"Animals like me better than people do," I say truthfully. "They don't look at me and sense something's wrong."

Ray mutters something in French, too low for me to hear, and marches away. "I'll get you some clothes."

He returns in a couple of minutes with a silk shirt and tight blue jeans. "I don't think she's worn these in years, but they'll fit."

I thank him.

"I won't look," says Ray. He begins to turn away but jerks to a stop. I stop as well, my wet T-shirt halfway up my torso. I lower it back down. His expression has changed. "You don't have her scars from the dog bite," he says.

"Scars were one of the few things I didn't have to copy."

"But you have her tattoo?"

I move my watch a bit up my wrist to show him. The little snake gazes up at us. Ray shakes his head. "It's so strange how *like* her you are. You could *be* her."

"That was the point," I say.

He doesn't move, but I see his hands tighten into fists, his expression clear as the brightest of days. In many ways, Ray and I are alike. We can't usually hide what we're feeling. We have impulsive faces, voices that express everything.

I can see everything on Ray's face now, the agony, the thoughts rushing through his head. I see him marvel at how like Amarra I look. I see him remember that he's kissed my cheek and held my hand and touched my skin and it felt so like she did. I see him realize that, if he wanted me and I wanted him, I wouldn't feel any different from her. His expression flickers, tempted, angry, and rigid. I swallow.

"You're not her," he says. "You're only an echo of her."

"Only an echo," I agree, "and you're a minefield. I have to step around you so carefully so you don't blow me up."

He comes closer and reaches out to me. I wait, watching him, not breathing. After an eternity, his hand falls to his side again.

"You're not her," he says again.

"Turn around," I tell him softly. "I need to change out of these clothes."

13

PERFECT

Ray offers me coffee. He takes me to the kitchen, with Sir Jacques padding after us. "Why are you giving me coffee when you could just ask me to leave?" I ask him. "Is today one of the days when you need to see me? Or one of the days it hurts like hell?"

"You're surprised," he observes. How astute of him. "Because I haven't always been nice to you?"

"Yes, that would be why."

"I have manners."

"Oh?" I ask politely. "Have these manners been in Disney World the last eight months, then?"

"Funny," he says, then adds, "I told you no one wanted you here, and that was a nasty thing to say. But I've been angry. I say some not-nice things when I'm angry. Does that mean I can't be a nice person?"

"Depends. *Are* you a nice person?"

He flashes me a suspicious look. "Do you always ask this many questions?"

"Yes. Should I have mentioned that earlier?"

There's a pause in which he stirs his coffee, somewhat violently. Sir Jacques growls low in his throat, a contented sound.

"Sugar?" says Sir Jacques's master.

"Yes, please. Four teaspoons."

His expression is slightly stunned as he counts the teaspoons into a cup. I notice he only has one teaspoon of sugar in his coffee. One more than Sean, who likes black coffee, one less than Mina Ma, who likes hers a little sweet, and certainly far more than Erik, who could run out of all the types of tea in the world and *still* wouldn't drink coffee. I listen to the clinking of the teaspoon against the sides of the cups. It's such a familiar sound that I'm transported, to a place that smells faintly of hand cream, and the hills rising in the distance through French windows. I am spooning sugar into cups of tea and coffee for my guardians.

The clinking of the spoons has stopped. I focus on Ray's pale face and grief-stricken eyes and pull back to reality. I wonder if I'll ever stop half living by the lake, wanting it.

"What does your heart want?" It's the question the woman with sad eyes asks me in dreams. I wonder if she knows the answer. There's such sorrow in her voice, as if she knows what I want and knows already that those things are stars in the sky, entirely out of reach, no matter how high on my toes I stand and stretch for them.

But stars sometimes fall.

"So," I say to Ray, pushing my fragile hopes into a corner,

"you're not as angry with me as you used to be?"

"I don't know what I am," he says, clunking coffee cups down in front of me. "It's so strange to see you and hear you and you're so much like *her*. It's painful, but also *nice*." He watches me, on my knees with his dog that doesn't like strangers. "You and me, we're not as different as I thought. As people." He clears his throat. "I didn't expect to like you. I blamed you for stealing her life. I can't just forget about that, but I can't be angry all the time either. It's bad enough missing her every single day without being angry, too. I don't even know if I like *you* or if I'm confused because I want *her* back so badly."

I listen to the extremes of his voice. His feelings are so exposed. He has a wild, reckless way of making choices and gestures, but he also has an earnestness I like.

"So maybe we could be friends?" I say softly, treading cautiously among the mines. "You get to see her face whenever you want, and I get to hang out with you."

"Why would you want to hang out with me?"

I wonder why myself. Spending time with him confuses me, makes me wonder who I am. Who I am supposed to be. But there are parts of it that are nice, too.

"You seem okay," I say, "and spending time with you is what Amarra would have done. You know I'm not her and I don't particularly like being her, but there are rules I have to live by."

"I figured the rules wouldn't matter. If you only have a

year, why bother? I mean," he adds hastily, "I don't really know . . . I didn't mean you have nothing left. . . ." Sheepish guilt crosses his face. "I should shut up now."

I shake my head. "It's fine. It's not like I forget about it if no one mentions it. You're right, it doesn't seem like there's much point. But a year's something."

He holds his cup between his hands and gazes at it intently. "I don't know if we'd ever really be friends," he says at last. "Too weird."

"Doesn't matter," I say. "At least we're not still at each other's throats." I lift the edge of the drapes and look out the window. "It's stopped raining. I'd better go. I'll return the clothes at the exam next Thursday."

Ray and Sir Jacques follow me to the door. I briefly glimpse the conflicted, wounded look in Ray's eyes. How much must he have loved her, I think sadly.

"I miss her, too," I say at the door. It's a tiny truth I hadn't acknowledged even to myself. "All my life she's been there. I've listened to her voice. I've watched her on film. I've read her words in those pages. Sometimes I can't believe none of that will ever happen again. Sometimes I wonder who I am without her. She's always been there. It's rather lonely now."

"Yeah, it is. Happy birthday," says Ray.

I walk as far as I can go before the humidity and the noise become too much. Then I flag down a rickshaw. The traffic is still quite bad, and the city rattles slowly past the open sides of the rickshaw. I answer the driver's friendly questions in

Kannada. I know it better than I do Hindi; I can barely speak a word of that. Mina Ma was disdainful of Hindi. "North Indian languages," she'd say scornfully. "No need for *them*."

Alisha is on the sofa when I get home, her legs tucked against her chest. She turns toward me when I come in, and then away again, as if the sight of me is much too painful. I see her eyes are red. Her brow is furrowed.

"I made you a cake," she says.

I stop. "You didn't have to do that," I say.

"It wasn't any trouble. Sasha insisted."

"Thank you."

"Eva?" she says before I can turn away. Her voice bursts out of her like she tried to stop it but failed. "I'm . . . *sorry*."

I nod but don't reply. There's nothing I can say. It's been tense at the house since we found out about the Sleep Order. It's like someone reached in and turned the place inside out and nothing fits quite right. Nikhil won't speak to his parents. Neil and Alisha seem strained when they speak to each other. The warmth and tenuous trust that gradually set in over the months since I arrived is shaky now, the equilibrium shattered. Everyone puts on a good face for Sasha, but no one wants to tell her that one day I'll be leaving and won't come back.

Sometimes I almost wish that Nikhil had handed over the letter right after the accident. At least it would have spared them this. They'd never have met me. They'd never have felt guilty. They'd still be mere photographs and stories in my head; none of us would have ever truly started to care. I would still be in England, spending my last months with Mina Ma and Erik and Ophelia and Sean.

I go upstairs. "For someone who died," I mutter at an imaginary Amarra, "you've done a very good job of hanging around."

But maybe that's what the dead do. They stay. They linger. Benign and sweet and painful. They don't need us. They echo all by themselves.

That night, as I lie in bed, my thoughts start to look like a ballroom. It's painted the color of burnished silver, the color of a Bangalore sky after the rains. In this ballroom there are angels and monsters, and Seans, and Rays, and echoes and others and guardians and Weavers and hunters, and families distorted in broken mirrors, and they are waltzing, to and fro, with one another. I fall asleep very quickly that night, too exhausted by the mess in my mind to think any longer.

Over the next few weeks, I find myself bumping into Ray more often than I can pass off as coincidence. I see him at exams, but I also see him at the places I usually go. I wonder if he comes out hoping to see me. See *her*.

"He loved her, but he wanted her, too," Lekha says one time, hushed, as though discussing the greatest scandal of the nineteenth century. "You look like her. It must be hard for him, wanting you."

"I don't think he does."

"I'm not interested in what you think," she replies. "I'm much more interested in my eyesight and intelligence, both of which"—she blinks to adjust one of her contact lenses —"are above par. Now the next time I'm with you when you *run into* him, I'll investixplore the situation. Then I'll be able to tell you what's what, all right?"

After the promised encounter, Lekha says, "It's *very* complicated."

"How ever did you work that out?" I say bitterly.

Ray and I spend a long time together when we meet on these occasions. He gets angry less. We often snap at each other, but it's without malice, and we talk, usually about Amarra.

"Did you like her?"

He waits curiously for a response. We're walking to the school gates after an exam. Ray has offered me a ride back to the house.

"No," I say truthfully. "I didn't like her much. She always seemed to be doing things to make me miserable, like swimming in the winter and getting a tattoo. At least that's how I saw it. I brought out the worst in her."

"Yeah, I think you did," he says. "She was amazing. She made me feel better just by smiling. You made her feel insecure, unsafe." He smiles wistfully. "It's weird, but the thing I think about most is how she used to wash her apples before eating them. I know you're supposed to, but she was the only person I knew who actually did every time. I laughed at her and she said that even if *I* was dumb enough to eat a worm or traces of dog poo, it didn't mean *she* was." He kicks at a stone on the ground. "I always wash my stupid apples now."

Other times, he asks me about my childhood, my time with my guardians. Like Lekha, Ray's terribly curious about what it was like, growing up an echo, and I don't mind talking about it. It's nice to wander back, to feel the cold and the water of the lake on my fingers and breathe in Mina Ma's tea on a chilly afternoon. I tell Ray about Sean: about how Ray and Sonya and Sam thought I should have been ashamed of what I am, but Sean showed me I didn't have to be. How Sean took me to the zoo and I found a baby elephant called Eva.

Ray frowns, his expression, for once, unreadable. "Did you two—"

"No," I cut him off. "That's against the laws."

"Can't imagine that stopping you," says Ray, quite accurately. "It wouldn't have stopped *me*, and I get the feeling we have that in common."

"It could have killed me," I reply. "So it stopped him."

"But you wanted to—"

"We're not talking about this," I say hotly. "What do you care anyway?"

He glares at me. "I don't."

A few days after that, at Coffee Day, I ask him something I've wondered about for so long.

"Why did she get her tattoo?"

"Doesn't seem like she was the tattoo type, does it? She wasn't. Sonya couldn't believe it was real. Amarra's mother almost had a heart attack when she saw it."

"So why'd she get it? Why the snake?"

From the way he hesitates, it's clear Amarra's tattoo had more to do with me than I realized. "She wanted something beautiful," he says, "but also something she couldn't trust. She said you were like the vases glassblowers make. Fragile and pure and lovely, but a sharp piece can cut you in two. So she chose the snake. It's all nice to look at, but it's a *snake*. She didn't want to forget that the shiniest, prettiest things can be the most dangerous."

"If she hated me so much, why did she do everything she was supposed to? She kept her Lists, wrote her pages for me, told me stuff she probably didn't want to."

"She loved her mum and dad," says Ray. "It was important to them. So she did it. That's the kind of person she was."

I gaze out the window at a pair of crows pecking at a discarded box of KFC wings. "But then there came a point when she couldn't do it anymore," I say. "*You* came along. And she asked to have me removed."

"She didn't know what you were like," says Ray defensively. "She expected you to be a robot or something, steel under the flesh. For all we knew, you could have been in a pod or a freezer until it was time to replace her! She hated you, but she would never have tried to destroy you if she knew that you were, you know, like *this*. With feelings and thoughts. She was better than that."

"All right," I say, rubbing my wrist, where my tattoo stings.

"Are they real?"

I blink at him. "Are what real?"

"Your thoughts and feelings? Or do you just react to things the way you've been told or taught to?"

"Of course they're real," I say indignantly. The cheek of him. "Are *your* feelings real?"

He reaches across the table toward me. His fingers very gently brush against my throat, a light, tracing touch, like butterflies' wings against my skin. I jerk back, and all over my body my skin prickles with goose bumps. I think quite suddenly of a zoo, a house, a light thumb on the soft skin of my wrist. Of a dream, when somebody's lips bent to my elbow.

"You felt that," says Ray. "You felt it like she did, like normal people do. Last year, when we used to go out on weekends, I sometimes touched you and you reacted like she did."

"Don't do that again," I say.

There's wild hope in Ray's eyes. It's like a fever. "I talked to someone a couple days ago," he says. "She said Amarra might not be gone."

"What?"

"She might still be alive. In you. The way it's supposed to be. Don't you think it would explain why her mother was so sure she saw her when she looked at you? And maybe the only thing stopping her from *waking up*, or however else you want to describe it, is you. Because you have your own mind and your own personality, so you're kind of stamping her out."

I stare at him in disbelief. "You can't be serious," I say. "Was this person a Weaver?"

"No, but—"

"Then she doesn't have any idea what she's talking about," I snap. "*No one* knows what we're capable of except the Weavers. No one understands us except them."

"She seemed to know what she was talking about," says Ray, gritting his teeth. "Why won't you even consider it?"

"Because it's outrageous. Amarra's dead, Ray. You can't *wake her up*. I know you want her back, but I'm *me*."

I stand, ready to leave, my fingernails digging into my palms. Ray follows me out onto the street. His face is pleading, desperate.

"If there was a chance—"

"All right, let's pretend," I repeat angrily. "Let's pretend there's a chance. So what happens now? You know me. You know I think and I feel like you do. Will you ask me to disappear, *die*, so that she can wake up?"

"It wouldn't be like that," he says. "You have to know I don't want to hurt you. You don't have much time, anyway—"

I could slap him. "Charming. Throw that in my face."

He flushes. "That just slipped out."

"But it doesn't make this any better. Do you really think becoming Amarra is a way for me to escape being killed?"

"Isn't it, though? The woman I talked to, she said you

wouldn't die or anything, you'd just be different. She said that if it worked, Amarra would wake up and you'd have done what they made you for. You'd be perfect."

"Well, it seems to me that she's off her head," I snap. "I think I'd know if there was someone else sharing space in my body."

"Why would you? You told me you've always had her there, a part of her anyway, so maybe it wouldn't feel any different—"

"Stop! This isn't possible. And even if it was, it doesn't sound like *perfect* to me. It sounds like I'd be escaping the Loom, but I'd be dying anyway. I wouldn't just step aside and sacrifice myself so Amarra can have another life. There are people I would give everything for, but she isn't one of them."

"You were made so she could have that second chance!"

"She didn't want it!" I shout back. People on the street are beginning to stare, but I don't care. "She didn't want me, remember? I don't owe her a bloody thing. She wanted her one life and she had it. You love her, you want her back, and I understand that, but all this"—I raise my hands, show them to him—"all of me? This is *mine*. You don't get to think about taking it away."

I turn on my heel and run away. This time, he doesn't stop me. I leave him shocked and dark-eyed on the pavement, in the blazing sun.

14

JUDAS

The fight on the pavement effectively ends our "accidental" encounters. Ray and I don't have another exam together until the beginning of June. English Lit. It's the last exam for most of us. It's also the first time I see him again.

Whenever I think of what he said, I taste anger and hurt. I also feel guilty for my outburst. It was unfair not to listen, not to stay calm and explain things better.

And who am I to judge Ray for putting his hope in outrageous ideas when *I* spend every day thinking of insane and impossible ways to elude the Sleep Order?

He doesn't look happy when I spot him outside the exam room. But he's not angry, either. I'm used to his temper, but today his shoulders are hunched and his head hangs low, as though there's a cold wind on this summer's day. I try shrugging it off as we file into the exam room.

The exam goes better than I'd expected. It's even relaxing, to forget about the real world and concentrate on Lady Macbeth and Heathcliff and Cathy and Keats instead.

After the exam, Lekha skips in circles around me as we

leave, singing under her breath about holidays and freedom and death to all exams.

"Hey," says Ray, coming up behind Lekha. "Sonya's decided to have an end-of-exam party at her parents' farm tonight. Everyone's invited. Do you two want to go?"

"I don't think she'll want me there," I point out.

He shakes his head. "She said you could come if you wanted. Asked me to tell you."

Lekha raises her eyebrows. "And why is she being so magnanimous?"

"Dunno," he says. "So. Going?"

"I can't," says Lekha, disappointed. "I'm going away with my mother for the weekend. I told you so last week," she adds, as though Ray is personally responsible.

"Yeah, but even if I'd told *her* so, it wouldn't have changed her plans. You do know we're not exactly best friends, right? She won't do anything to oblige me."

Lekha sighs. "Alas. Take notes. I want to hear all about it later. Conceal *no* gossip from me, unless it involves Sam, in which case I just don't care. Are you going to go, Eva?"

"I don't think so. Isn't her farm halfway out of the city?"

"I can give you a ride," Ray offers.

I frown at him. "Why?"

"I guess it's my way of apologizing for the other day," he says. He glances at Lekha, who rolls her eyes and takes six pointed steps away. I stifle a smile. Ray gives me a miserable look. "I shouldn't have said those things."

"It's okay. I didn't mean to get so angry."

"You could let me make it up to you. I figure that if we went to the party, everyone else will see us there. If they see *us* being friendly, they might decide they have no excuse not to act the same way."

He has a point. And it's a sweet thing to offer to do.

I nod cautiously. "Okay."

He gives me a rather twisted smile in response. He doesn't seem over the moon that I agreed, but I let it go. Lekha, who has obviously been listening in, skips back to us. "Can we get out of here?" She shepherds us in the direction of the gates. "I could fry an egg on my head right now, it's so effing hot. And I need to get home and pack for this weekend in the wild."

"You do know that saying *effing* makes you sound like a dimwit, right?" says Ray, sounding almost normal.

She beams back at him. "And *you* know that saying *dimwit* makes you sound like a dimwit, right?"

We separate at the gates. Ray goes off to his car, after asking me if picking me up at eight o'clock tonight will be okay, and Lekha and I go to find her mother's car and driver. We're about halfway back to Amarra's house when Lekha sits bolt upright.

"Do you think Ray means tonight to be a sort of date?"

"No," I say. "He's just trying to be nice."

"And he likes being around you," she says shrewdly. "I can tell."

"I'm not so sure *like* is the right word for it. He sees *me* and he's talking to *me*, but he sees *her*, too. He has to. We look the same."

"Heavens, I don't know how you cope," says Lekha. "It boggles my brain."

I eat dinner early that evening because of the party. I help Neil cook, and while we're eating, I tell them I'm going out. I don't know if I'm supposed to ask permission. But of all people, *Nik* is the one who asks me when I intend to be back, which makes the others laugh.

"I'm probably not going to want to stay out late," I say. "I should be back by ten-ish. I'll call if I'm going to be any later."

I don't particularly want to be there well into the wee hours. My classmates don't like me, no matter what Ray hopes to achieve, and if they keep feeling that way, it's going to be an uncomfortable evening.

It takes me twenty minutes to decide what to wear. I'm tempted to wear the black dress Mina Ma gave me, but it's too nice for a spontaneous end-of-exam party. I don't want to look overdressed. Amarra's style was casual and classy and it's a style I like, but it leaves me very little room to go out tonight looking like *me* and not like she would have done.

In the end, I choose a pair of black leggings and a silvery tunic and I find a pair of black heels in the closet. I feel almost silly, spending this much time thinking about something I will only wear for a few hours, but I really want to look like me.

I don't bother with makeup, apart from black eye pencil. I clip my hair up into a loose knot. There. I smile. *Now* I look like me. We aren't going out in public, just to Sonya's house, where everyone already knows what I am. And if they're going to treat me like an echo anyway, why hide?

I'm ready in time and waiting outside when Ray drives up.

"I thought I'd have to wait," he says when I jump in. "Amarra took half a year to get ready if we went out anywhere."

"Was it worth it?"

"Every time," he says, his eyes sad.

We make polite, strained conversation the whole way to Sonya's farm. For once, Ray is more tense and uneasy than I am. His grip on the wheel is so tight I can see the veins pop in the backs of his hands. I wonder if he regrets asking me to go with him.

"Why are you so jumpy?" I ask.

"Why do you always ask so many questions?"

"Why are you answering my question with another question?"

He makes a half-irritated sound. "This could go on awhile."

"I can ask questions till I'm blue in the face," I assure him. "So I wouldn't try to compete. And you still haven't answered me."

"I still don't want to," he replies.

I stare out the window, watching the flickering tubes of the streetlights flash by. They look like falling stars when Ray drives fast enough. The pattern is hypnotic. And eerily like the lights racing by on the night Amarra laughed in his car, flew through the shattered glass, and died.

I wonder if she felt any different that night. If she knew somehow, instinctively, that she was in danger. Does anyone know?

I shudder with cold, wondering why I thought of that.

"Why didn't she have her seatbelt on?"

"A lot of people don't bother wearing them here. Road laws are often held in contempt."

"But *she* must have been the seatbelt type. She washed her apples, for heaven's sake. Why didn't she have her seatbelt on that night?"

"She was small," he mutters under his breath. "As you probably know. If she had her seatbelt on, she couldn't reach far enough to kiss me." He touches his neck. "So she took it off."

I wish I hadn't asked.

Sonya's farm is tucked away off the street, up a winding dirt road sheltered by trees and half-broken fences. There are ten or twelve cars parked in the large yard in front of the house when we get there, and I can hear the low throb of music. I feel a nervous twinge in my stomach. Out of the corner of my eye, I see Ray checking his watch, looking strained and rather white. What on *earth* is he so edgy about?

Maybe he's worried about what his friends and classmates will think of him, hanging out with his dead girlfriend's copy. It could go over very badly.

I reach for his hand and give it a tentative squeeze before letting it go. "Ray? Thank you for trying to change their minds about me."

For some reason, this only seems to make him look slightly sick. "Come on," he says.

It's not as bad as his anxiety made me fear it would be. Sonya must have told people that I would be coming, and that Ray would be bringing me, because no one looks particularly surprised. People greet Ray and only a few seem a touch frostier than usual, their eyes *judging*, questioning. Sam avoids me, but others say hello, though they don't say my name. They probably don't know what to call me. "Amarra" is a bit of a faux pas now.

No one stares. They have their own lives. They go back to whatever they were doing before we came in: chatting or finding a drink or attempting silly dances on Sonya's makeshift dance floor.

Ray and I find a table littered with bottles and cans by the kitchen doorway. As Ray pours a Coke into a glass, I spot Sonya in the kitchen. She's alone and on the phone, with more drinks on the counter behind her. She waves her hand desperately at Ray.

"I think Sonya wants to talk to you," I say. "Maybe she doesn't like your shirt?"

Ray smiles almost unwillingly. "It's definitely going to be abuse of some kind," he says. "I'll be back in a sec."

He crosses into the kitchen to see what Sonya wants. I put my bag down on the table and stay where I am, drinking my Coke as fast as possible to look like I'm doing something. A girl called Tara, the older sister of someone in the class, strikes up a conversation. I only last ten minutes with her before the combination of Coke and nervousness makes me need the bathroom. I ask Tara if she knows where it is, and she points helpfully up the stairs. I thank her and follow her directions. I knock on the bathroom door first to make sure there's nobody in there already, before going in and turning the lock. The music becomes a dull throb through the door. There's a window open in the corner and the fresh air is lovely.

On my way down, I almost collide with Ray on the stairs. He looks like he's downed three or four shots of vodka since I last saw him.

"Ray, are you—"

He puts a finger to my lips, stopping me. He isn't moving like he's been drinking. His hand is mostly steady.

"You're beautiful," he says. "She was. Is. Was. You are too. You both are." He leans close and I am too startled to step back. "I called you a monster once. But you're not. *I* am."

His head draws in and he kisses me. So light, like the swipe of a fingertip against my lips. My heart jolts in shock. I respond instinctively without any thought or will of my own. I can't breathe. I can taste the vodka on him. He tastes bitter.

Ray pulls back and rubs his eyes like he can't understand how he ended up here. He leans his head against the wall. "You have to get out, Eva."

"Wh-what?"

"You need to go," he says. And I realize that behind the slightly drunken desire, the pain, the memories of someone else and of me, there's something else. Guilt.

Fear.

"What are you talking about?" I ask more sharply. My heart's still pounding. My mouth is dry and raw and soft. I bite my lip, trying to bite away the lingering traces of the kiss.

"Come with me." He takes me by the elbow and pulls me back up the stairs. To the first door on the right. Behind us, someone hoots, someone else makes a lewd comment, and I turn red. But Ray ignores them and pulls me into the room and slams the door shut behind us.

He takes me to the window and draws the curtain back. "There," he says urgently.

"You're going to have to explain—"

"Just look," he interrupts me.

I look. I have no idea what to look for, so at first I see nothing. Just the cars already parked outside, including Ray's. The trees. The dirt road. And far beyond, twinkling between trees and fences, the faint lights of the main road about half a mile away.

Then I see someone moving. There's a car parked behind Ray's that wasn't there before. It pulled in after us. There's a woman standing by the passenger door, rummaging around inside. She's in her twenties, in tight jeans, a leather jacket. I don't recognize her. I watch as she pulls something out of the car, and then my eyes travel down to an odd bump at the bottom of one leg. Like she has some padding around her ankle.

My knees wobble. Suddenly I am somewhere else, staring at a man with an outdated map, and Sean's voice is in my ear. His hand has clamped down on my elbow. He's afraid.

The woman reaches into her car to pull something else out. She moves quickly, but not quickly enough. She hikes up one leg of her jeans and shoves two shiny things into a sheath strapped around her calf. They both flash in the lights from the house, flashing silver.

Knives.

In an instant I understand, though I can't quite believe it. I turn to look at Ray, disbelieving, incredulous. This can't be happening.

"Is she a hunter?" I ask very quietly.

He nods, jaw working like he can't bring himself to speak.

"And"—something inside me splinters in two—"you brought me here so that she could find me?"

He nods.

15

SILVER

I had laughed about the hunters. They were blind tigers. I used to tease Mina Ma about them; I'd threaten to run amok and end up in their clutches. And I never quite believed the man Sean and I saw *was* a hunter. They were always a lesser threat. They should never have found me.

"Congratulations," I hear myself say. "You beat Amarra and the Weavers to it. You've killed me."

He shakes his head. "She hasn't seen you yet. She doesn't even know what you look like! You can leave before she finds you—"

"It's too late for this," I say, dashing tears off my face. "Do you think *warning* me changes the fact that you brought me here in the first place?"

"You have to understand," he whispers, "I only wanted her back."

I stare at him. The pieces click together.

"That hunter," I say, pointing at the window in shock, "is *she* the woman who told you all that stuff about how Amarra might still be here? How I'm stamping her out?"

The look on his face makes the answer obvious. "Sonya found them," he says. "At first she was angry and wanted to punish you for lying to us. I guess she blamed you for being there when Amarra wasn't. She found a website, told them she knew an echo. She wanted them to take you away, but she didn't want you *dead*. They told her they wouldn't kill you." His words come out in a rush, tumbling out; he's pleading with me to understand. "They said that if Amarra's soul was still alive, they could bring her back. They told her she needed to get you somewhere quiet, not public, so they could examine you. They didn't want a scene. She thought about using the party and—"

"And then she told you about it," I say, "and you talked to the hunter and she was sweet and told you exactly what you wanted to hear."

Ray stares bleakly at me. "I didn't agree to this as easily as you think," he says. "I wanted to think of another way. I want her back so badly, but I wasn't happy about this. You and I, we spent all that time together. I know you. I *care*. I never wanted to hurt you."

A ragged sob creeps up my throat. "I don't care what you wanted!"

"She was just so sure. The hunter, I mean. She was so sure we could get Amarra back."

"If you weren't blind with your obsession and your grief, you wouldn't have believed a word she said! Hunters want to destroy us. Not our souls, which they don't even believe we have. Not our minds. All of us. She wasn't going to try and bring Amarra back. She's a *hunter*, for god's sake. What did you think they did to us? *Cuddle* us?"

"Why do you think I'm here?" he says desperately. "That's what Sonya wanted to talk to me about. She said she was on the phone with the hunter and things didn't sound right." He grips me by the shoulders. "You *have* to get out of here. It's not too late, you can—"

I jerk away. "Don't touch me."

"Eva, please. Let me help you get out."

"I don't want your help," I say. Hot, salty tears burn their way down my face. I wipe them away. "I don't care what you thought you were doing. I don't care how many lies you believed. I don't care how much you loved Amarra or how much pain you're in because you lost her. You brought me here to die."

I turn away from him and stare out the window. My blood feels frozen with fear. The hunter is still outside, scanning the farmyard, the trees, taking stock of the area. It's started to rain. I shiver, thinking of the knives strapped to her calf. I have only a few minutes before she comes looking for me.

I can't believe this is happening.

I thought a year would never be enough time. But it seems such a luxury compared to a few minutes.

My hurt freezes into stone. Maybe I haven't yet thought of a way to protect myself from the Sleep Order. But here?

Here things are different. I will escape. I will not allow myself to be killed by a hunter.

"She doesn't know what I look like?" I ask Ray flatly.

He shakes his head. "I was supposed to point you out."

"Then I'll walk right past her."

I pull the clip out of my hair, letting it fall and hide my Mark again. Without so much as a last look at Ray, I leave the room and start for the stairs, knitting my hands tightly together to keep them from shaking.

"Hell, he's quick," a boy on the landing remarks, grinning, taking in my tousled hair.

I ignore him and stalk past.

I am almost at the door when I see Sonya open it. The hunter's on the other side. I stop in my tracks. Someone's left a cigarette on a table, unlit, and I snatch it and continue toward the door. Sonya looks stressed and frightened. My hands are shaking and it's all I can do not to look up at the hunter. I force myself to ignore her and look at Sonya instead. I smile.

"I'm going to have a cigarette outside," I say, waving it at her. I slip carefully past the hunter. "Jaya shouted at me for blowing smoke in her face."

I wait for Sonya to expose me, but she only presses her lips together. She turns back to the hunter. "Um, I think she's upstairs with Ray."

Good girl, I think savagely.

The door closes behind them, leaving me out in the

chilly night. I don't have much time. The rain has slowed to a fine silver drizzle. I drop the cigarette to the ground and scan the dark dirt road. What am I supposed to do? Walk to the main street? Try and catch a rickshaw this late? I feel for Amarra's phone in my pocket, then realize my leggings don't have pockets. My stomach clenches. The phone is in my bag inside the house. *Idiot.*

Unless—

I study the wooded area by the dirt road, trees and broken fences stretching out across the farm all the way down to the street. It might be my only chance. If I've vanished, the hunter will have to give up and leave, find other quarry somewhere else. She'll search the house, but she can't search Sonya's entire farm in the dark.

If I can conceal myself among the trees and wait her out, I can call a taxi once she's gone. I'm not going back with Ray, that's unthinkable.

Heart pounding, I hobble past the parked cars. These shoes hurt. But I press on, slipping into the dark of the wet earth and heavy trees beyond. A squirrel brushes against my leg, making me gasp in shock.

I hide behind a damp tree trunk and lean my head and trembling hands on the wood. My heart is hammering so loud I can't hear much else.

Too soon, the house door slams open. I stiffen in terror, pressing closer to the tree.

"How can she be gone?" I hear an unfamiliar female

voice demand. "What the hell does that mean?"

"She's not in the house. We looked."

They draw closer to the hunter's car. And to me.

"Why would she leave? Did someone warn her?"

"I wasn't with her," Sonya replies. "I was watching out for you. I don't know when she went." She can't quite hide her relief, however, which makes the hunter's face darken.

"And you?" she demands of Ray.

He plays the angry, defensive role very well. "No one told me I had to watch her every single minute," he snaps, but he's kicking at the ground, a sure sign that he's nervous. "Sonya asked me to keep her busy, so I took her upstairs and tried to talk to her. Distract her, you know. Maybe she looked out the window, saw something that scared her."

"I wasn't standing here polishing an *ax*," the hunter says coldly.

"She's paranoid. I guess the Weavers taught her to see everything as a threat. She said she needed the bathroom. I couldn't follow her *there*, could I? But she was gone awhile, and when I went to check, it was empty."

The hunter paces back and forth. "Stupid kids," she says in frustration, loud enough for all of us to hear.

My forehead is covered in icy sweat and rain. I lean my head on the tree again, swallowing. Ray and Sonya don't speak. Sonya, loud, bold Sonya, looks small and scared. Ray has his hands in his pockets and keeps kicking at the ground. I see him glance at the trees, wondering where I might have gone. The hunter paces, coming alarmingly close.

"We have to find her," she growls at last. "I'm not leaving without having a look around."

"You're going to search all this?" Sonya gestures at the wide expanse of farm and trees. "It'll take you all night!"

The hunter swears violently, but her shoulders sag in defeat. I am about to let my breath out, let the relief surge through me like pure oxygen, when I see her slam to a halt. She's paced back in my direction and she stops, staring at the ground. She tenses like a fox.

"These weren't here when I arrived," she says excitedly.

"What wasn't?"

"Tracks," she says. "Footprints. The ground's wet from the rain. Don't these look like a girl's high heels to you?"

Ice fills my lungs. My shoes. I didn't think about my shoes. Out in the yard, Ray is horror-struck.

"I'm sure it's not—" he starts.

"I'm sure it *is*," says the hunter, hiking up her jeans. A flash of silver, and there's a knife in her hands. "She went this way. She couldn't have gotten far. Not in those heels."

"Why do you have a knife?" Ray asks angrily, though he knows the answer. "You said you'd just examine her—"

"Of course," says the hunter sweetly, her eyes fixed on the trees. I'm too afraid to move. She will see me. "But I need to keep her from running away, don't I? Echoes are dangerous. I know, believe me. I watched my husband's echo destroy everything we loved. I know what they're capable of." She smiles back at Ray. "It's just a silly little knife. Won't do anyone any harm."

Sonya shudders. "This was a mistake," she says miserably, futilely. "We don't want—"

"Too late," says the hunter.

I don't think about it. Adrenaline flashes hot through my body and I move. I rip the high heels off my feet and start running. It gives my location away, but I can outrun her. Tigers are fast, but deer run faster.

My bare feet recoil at the rough earth, the sharp twigs, and the puddles, but this is no time to be fussy. I race through the trees, aiming for the main road. I push violently through the undergrowth, scrambling over broken bits of fences. I run so fast my lungs burn and my legs ache, my blood roars in my ears.

I can't stop. I hear her running behind me, not far away, all teeth and tongue and hunger. I have the strangest thought: *I want Matthew.* Matthew with his lazy drawl and his casual mockery and his utter lack of care. With his songs in my dreams.

I am his creation. He values that. He might be willing to destroy me. But he will also make sure no one else does.

Especially not a hunter.

The thought of his scorn makes me plow on, through the pain, the burning in my lungs. I am a creature, a girl, life stitched from nothing. I am eerie and frightful. And I'm stronger than all of them. I can't allow any hunter, or

Weaver, or betrayal, to defeat me. Believing that is all I have. It's all that might save me.

So I run, outrunning her until I can't run any longer and, inevitably, I falter. There's a cramp in my side. Not far from the main road, from the lights and the smell of gasoline and concrete, I slow down.

She pounces.

We tumble to the earth, slipping over a fallen log, crashing onto wet leaves. I see a blur in the dark, a sharp silver streak, and I twist out of her reach. The knife catches my leg instead and I howl in pain. Fire spreads through my skin. Blood mixes with the rain.

I fend her off, twisting her knife hand away from me, but she's stronger. Bigger. Trained for this. I try to wriggle away. She digs her knee into my slashed leg. I gasp through my teeth.

"It doesn't have to hurt," she hisses, "if you stay still. If you go quietly."

I utter a pained, broken laugh. She should have asked Ray and Sonya about me before trying to kill me. They might have told her I don't go quietly.

Something digs into my back. I reach for it, hoping for a stone, but my fingers close around my hair clip. I must have held on to it after unpinning my hair. It cracked under my weight. I can feel the pieces.

My finger slips over a tooth of the clip. It's sharp. *Sharp.*

I seize the broken teeth and strike at the hunter's face.

My knuckles catch her lip; the teeth catch her in the eye. She drops the knife with a squeal and clamps her hand over her eye. I flex my good leg to kick her off me. Blood drips off my bare foot into the ground. I can barely feel it, it's only a shadow lost in the agony of my leg.

My leg buckles as I try to stand, but I force myself up. The hunter reaches for my foot, hoping to unbalance me. I whip it out of reach and run.

I leave her behind in the leaves and the dirt and race for the street. I stumble past a blind beggar, past a tea shop, race down the street with people staring, looking for the nearest rickshaw. It isn't the safest way to travel this late, but that seems laughable now, after surviving a knife-wielding hunter.

Three rickshaw drivers refuse to take me anywhere. The fourth grunts and nods when I name the general area of town I want to get to. He demands double the meter fare. Resigned, I agree.

My head drops against the side of the rickshaw as we rattle down the road. I hurt all over. I wonder dimly if the hunter will come after me. She'll have to get to her car if she wants to, and by then I'll be long gone.

When we're a street or two away from the house, I tense. The driver pulls up to traffic lights.

"Where do you want to go, madam?" he asks curtly in Hindi. I just about understand it. "Left or right? You know the road name?"

I don't answer. I take a bracing breath and dart out of the rickshaw, dodging through waiting cars as the lights glow red. I hear the driver swearing, shouting after me, but I don't falter. I have no money to pay him with. And his charging a hurt, bleeding girl double the usual fare makes me feel an awful lot less guilty about running away.

I race through a side street and cross onto Amarra's. My knife-cut leg crumples under me. I keep going, dragging it along. The house is only a hundred yards away now.

I sway on my bare, bleeding feet. It feels like my chest is on fire. I make myself take a step forward. Then another.

Faster. I can get there. I break into a run.

Just when I think I might have survived this after all, I stumble. I trip over broken pavement and fall. It is cold and hard and I can't get up.

I stare at the sky, which swims above me like dark water. I try to roll over onto my knees and push myself up, but the movement sends a sharp pain through my side. I'm too tired to do this. My eyelids flutter shut. I let the liquid world fade away.

16

WAKE

I am home again. I can see everything, as though I am on a cliff top, about to jump. The Lake District has the bloom of spring. Sunlight glimmers through the clouds and dapples the forest floor. My eyes follow the English oaks, the pines, the old trees, past the rocks and the stones, the damp, dewy paths, and go to the very top of the hill, where I can see the gleaming lake and the hills that scallop the silver sky.

The image flickers. Broken.

Flash, a shard of light, a ripple through the dark, like a bad picture on the telly or a flash of lightning in the shape of the bolt in my Mark. *Flash*.

Sean. His eyes. Green. Gold flecks of light shimmer across them. They look like being alive under a hot red sky. I silently swear that I will trade everything, every breath and every last particle of my soul, just to get to keep him.

"Look at me," he says. His voice is so fierce, so raw, I *must* be dreaming. Sean's voice is never like that.

Pain clouds my vision and I blink slowly. Dark, light,

dark, light. There's a shadow in the light. Angular, green-eyed, devastating. Dark hair. Short, straight. Like sparrow feathers. I reach for one of the feathers. It's too far away.

The shadow leans down and kisses my hair.

"Wake up," he pleads.

Flash.

There. My back garden. I know it so well. There's a little girl playing on a swing, a guardian pushing her, up, down, up, down. I recognize them. Little Eva, a younger Jonathan. I kneel on the damp grass. "Where have you gone?" I want to ask him. I look to the house and see familiar shapes against the light: Erik by the doors, guarding, always guarding. Ophelia is some way behind him, staring at something far away. I glance around to see Mina Ma right behind me, watching for the dark, wicked things that might come when I'm not looking.

I look back at the swing and the guardian. The swing is empty, but Jonathan keeps pushing it. "Where have you gone?" I ask him again. "Where have I gone?"

"I'm tired," I tell Mina Ma. "I came a long way to come back home."

The empty swing sways and the lake laps the shore. She wipes my tears away with a brisk hand. She smells of love and salt and butter.

Flash.

• • •

293

"Oh, good. Shining the light at her eyes must have helped. She's waking."

I open my eyes. Unhappily. I wanted to be home. Not here. I am in a bed in a clean room that smells of bleach. A hospital room. There's an empty chair by the window. Tubes in my arm. A monitor nearby, beeping in time to the beat in my chest. A flimsy green gown on my body. A man in a white coat is touching my wrist, shining a flashlight into my eyes. I squeeze my eyes shut until he stops. He says something, but it sounds muffled by pillows. Being awake is painful.

He says something and leaves the room. I want to close my eyes now that he's left, but there is somebody else beside me. I turn my head very carefully.

There's a bandage wrapped around my leg. A cast on my left hand. Bruises down my body. My head is throbbing.

But I made a deal with whoever was listening. Every breath, every part of my soul. Just to be with him again. And here is what I traded for.

"Eva," says Sean, and his voice is hoarse, raw, but it's not a dream.

PART THREE

1

PEACE

"You came," I say.

Sean's expression is drier than desert sand. "I did," he says, "and your surprise is somewhat insulting. Did you really think I wouldn't? That Erik might say, 'By the way, Sean, Eva nearly died,' and I'd say, 'Oh, all right then,' and go on with my life?"

"You're still sarcastic," I say happily, though my voice sounds like it has been run over by a tractor. "You haven't changed much. You look older."

He smiles in spite of himself. "I am older. You sent me a birthday card."

"I remember."

I drink some water. Someone must have given me painkillers, because nothing hurts quite as much as it should. I can't stop looking at Sean. I've longed to see him for months, and here he is. Tears slide down my face and he brushes them away. I want to touch him, but it hurts to move. I smile up at him. I must look awful. God. I must *smell*.

Sean's eyes are red and tired. I watch them while he

absently strokes the back of my unhurt hand with his thumb.

"Have you been crying?" I ask him.

"No," he says, rubbing his eyes self-consciously, "I just haven't had much sleep the last few days."

"You're lying."

"The hell I am," he says, and changes the subject. "You've been in and out of consciousness for a couple days now. I've tried to be here the whole time. I guess your head was pretty banged up. I haven't been your only visitor, though. Your familiars have been here. A girl called Lekha was here a couple of hours ago. Nikhil's barely been pried from your side. He found you, you know."

The hard, cold road swims back into memory. "How?"

"He saw you fall," he explains. "He says you told him you'd be back by ten and you're never late. So when it got to eleven and you weren't answering your phone, he went out to the gate to wait for you and make sure you came back. And he saw you."

I sniff, wiping my nose. "He likes me," I say.

Sean goes to the window to refill my glass. When he returns, he says, "Do you want to tell me what happened to you? We still don't know how you ended up there. Amarra's boyfriend, Ray, he rang the night you got hurt. Your familiars say you went to a party with him"—his tone becomes carefully neutral here—"but you were alone when you came back."

"I was," I say. "But I did go to the party with Ray."

His expression is very blank. "I see."

"We've spent time together. It's messy. He can't forget her and he can't stop seeing her when he looks at me. And I can't forget that I'm not her. I can't forget *you*." The mask on his face slips. "But there were times when he was Ray and I was Eva and we both knew it. I cared what he thought of me. I don't know. I only know something went badly wrong and here I am."

"Wait." Sean's face darkens. "You mean *he* put you here?"

I shake my head. "Not like that. He thought he could get Amarra back."

I'm telling this in the wrong order. My head doesn't feel right. Fuzzy. Like my body's juddering too fast and my head can't keep up.

"The doctor said you'd probably be in shock," he says quietly. "Look, just rest, tell me about it later."

I take a deep, shaky breath. "No. Now. But you're going to say 'I told you so.'"

"I wouldn't—"

"Well, you should. Because you *did* tell me so and I didn't listen. See, it was a hunter."

And then I tell him. From the start. My voice falters and I muddle things at first, but as I keep speaking and remembering, the musty fog in my memory clears up. I tell Sean everything, stumbling over the kiss, hesitating at each turn to try and read his eyes. He doesn't say anything. He just listens, his jaw tightening, until I have finished.

"Jesus Christ," he says.

I shake my head. "I used to *laugh* at the thought of being picked off by a hunter, remember? I thought there was no chance they'd ever find me."

"Well, let's face it, the odds were slim they'd have found you if it hadn't been for those two," says Sean in a flinty voice.

"They didn't do it to hurt me," I say, trying not to think about Ray kissing me and telling me to get out. "I think they just want Amarra back."

Sean makes a noise in the back of his throat that doesn't sound very forgiving. In spite of what I've said, I have to admit I don't feel very forgiving either.

"Do you think the hunter will tell the police about me?"

"I doubt it," says Sean, "Hunters act on their own. That's why they exist, they've never trusted the law to get rid of you."

I let out my breath in relief.

"You drive me bloody mad, Eva," he adds, "and I'm convinced you're a lunatic, but you're the only person I know who could have gotten out of that."

I smile lopsidedly. "Thanks." My mouth feels sticky. "Can we talk about something else? I may be sick if I keep thinking about this."

"Are you hungry? Do you want me to go get you something?"

"No!" I cry. Sean goes very still. I let my breath out in a rush as the panic subsides, and I look sheepishly up at him.

"Sorry. I didn't mean to burst out like that. I just—I just don't want you to go. I'm still afraid I've been imagining you all this time."

"Silly," he says affectionately.

I wrap my hand around his index finger. "It's good to see you, Sean."

"It's good to see you, too."

He draws the chair up to the bedside and sits down, legs sprawled in front of him. "See? Not going anywhere," he says.

"How are they? The others?"

"They're all right," says Sean. "Ophelia now lives in London so she can be closer to her father. Mina Ma's retired from the Loom, but she hasn't left the cottage. Erik's helping the Weavers revise some laws about how echoes are raised. None of them wanted to take charge of another echo. They miss you." He stares down at the sheets. "We were told not to get involved when we heard about this. As far as we're concerned, your chapter's closed."

"What'll they do if they find out you came?" I ask worriedly.

He shrugs. "I wanted to come after I heard about the Sleep Order, but Erik reminded me that it would only have gotten us both in trouble. But I couldn't stop myself after this."

"I thought you cared about following the Weavers' laws."

"I decided to break this one."

"How un-Sean-like of you."

"Tell me about it," he says, smiling. "But I can always count on you to make me feel like the cautious one again."

I lift my tube-wrapped hand and tuck it in his. "Stay?"

"Until you're better," he promises.

I never want to get better.

The next time I see Nikhil, I give him a big hug. "Thank you," I whisper in his ear. Not just for spotting me when I fell. For being out there in the first place, worried because I was late. When I draw back, he's smiling, that sweet smile I've come to know so well.

"Eva, are you okay?" Sasha demands, climbing onto the bed and sending an instant bolt of pain through my chest. Sean pulls her off before she can sit on my broken wrist.

"Yes," I gasp through the pain, "I'm fine!"

I leave the hospital at the end of the week but am prescribed bed rest while my ribs and leg recover. My broken wrist takes longer to heal and aches almost constantly. The first time I look in a mirror, I'm shocked to see two small red scars on my face, one down my left temple, the other an inch below my right eye. They upset me at first, but Lekha tactfully points out that this is a small price to pay for survival.

Neil and Alisha insist that Sean stay with us while he's in the city. They like him. He's easy to talk to. Uncomplicated. There are no ghosts or shadows or pretenses where he's concerned. He's also polite and helpful, which makes him a lovely guest. He is given Sasha's room, and she moves in with me for the time being. I daresay they all realized that if Sean hadn't stayed close, I might have thrown a fit worthy of cracking Mount Olympus in two. As the days slip by, I dread the moment he will leave again.

"What are you going to do?" I ask him one afternoon. I'm hobbling on my leg as he steadies me. I try to keep my balance, regain the strength in my muscles. "When you go? You've finished school now, haven't you?"

He nods. "I think I'm going to spend the summer in London. I've been going back and forth a lot this past year, theater stuff mostly. I might just take my things down and camp out there for a few months. I still have Loom work to do, but I'm thinking of quitting in September when I start university. Erik reckons they'll let me go without a fuss. I've already signed the confidentiality forms."

"Meaning you're not allowed to talk about the Loom to anyone who isn't involved with it?"

Sean nods, steadying me with one hand. "Not one word. The Weavers keep their secrets. And they run the Loom with an iron fist. They've been getting careless lately, though. Erik told me so. He said Adrian messed up while making two echoes this past year and he doesn't even care."

"Life and death's not big enough for him anymore," I say drily. "What else could he possibly be obsessed with?"

"Living forever? Isn't everyone obsessed with that?"

"But not you."

"What good's forever when everyone else is gone?"

"Hmpf," I say, annoyed. "Don't you have an *ounce* of romance and adventure in your soul?"

"No, not really. Should I?"

I tug my hand away from his in a show of pique and try walking on my own. My leg buckles and he grabs hold of me, catches me, before I fall.

"This is the moment when you scoop me into your arms and proclaim your desire to make me your own," I say.

Sean laughs and helps me hobble back to the bed. "Scooping you up isn't going to fix your leg," he says. "Do you want to try again?"

I nod. But even as I try to balance again, I'm conscious of a terrible, certain fear. That when Sean leaves, so will the peace. And the joy. For the first time the house is quiet and restful, and Amarra's ghost is silent, and I can keep my thoughts away from hunters and Weavers and Sleep Orders and the relentless clock ticking down my time.

But I keep quiet about it. I don't tell him how badly I want him to stay. Or how badly I want to go with him. To see him again, only to lose him once more, will be agony.

No, I don't tell him. How can I? Echo. Guardian. Echo. Guardian. We were never meant to stay together. Never meant to *be* at all. They never say what happens to the guardians who break the laws. Am I supposed to risk Sean's life?

Sean helps me balance upright. "Matthew brought you

here, didn't he?" he says. "What did you think of him?"

"I don't know," I say. "I don't trust him. I don't like him. But he's Erik's friend. He can't be all bad. And—" I hesitate. "It's silly, but he *made* me. That matters. I feel like it ought to matter to him, too."

"It's not silly," says Sean. "There's more of him in you than there is anybody else. More than Amarra, or Neil, or Alisha."

I don't answer.

"They're not kind people, he and Adrian," he says. "Brilliant minds, but they're not kind. Two of the most dangerous men in England. They don't seem to have any pity or mercy left. Erik told me that, too. He said they weren't always like this. They've changed. Matthew, especially. Erik's afraid the Loom's gone wrong."

"Was it ever *not* wrong?" I ask.

He can't answer that. How can we know? We weren't around two hundred years ago when the Loom first stitched a life.

In the wake of being attacked, of almost dying, I can't shake a painful awareness of time. Each night I lie awake, cold. I can't sleep. It's been weeks since my seventeenth birthday, and I can't stop thinking of how little time ten months really is. And how I am not saving myself by staying here.

But how *not* to stay here? If I left, my god, that would probably kill me anyway.

"What's the matter?" Sean asks me early one morning, after Sasha has gone to school. We're alone in Amarra's room. Grayish sunlight spills onto the bed. I catch a glimpse of myself reflected in a window. I look ill.

I stare away from him, clutching the sheets tightly in my fists. "I'm okay," I say. He knows what the Sleep Order means. He doesn't need me to remind him that I am not going to survive here much longer.

2

MISTAKES

I have two visitors while I'm recovering. The first is Lekha, who comes by on most days. She often brings a movie with her, something she's bought off the man on Commercial Street who sells DVDs cheap. Neil has moved an old television and DVD player to my room for the time being. We rarely watch the movies, though: Lekha talks her way through them. Nikhil and I are used to her, so we only laugh, but Sean is constantly perplexed by her sketchy vocabulary.

The other visitor, who comes only once, is Ray.

I wake one evening to find him standing by the door. I scramble upright, pulling the covers to my throat. He looks guilty. He looks like he's tearing himself to pieces with it.

"I have five minutes," he says. "Nikhil wasn't happy, but Amarra's mother said I could come in. She's waiting at the bottom of the stairs to get rid of me when my time's up."

I stare at him in silence. He doesn't seem to know what to say.

"I don't look like her anymore," I say at last, gesturing to the scars on my face. "Happy?"

"I'm sorry," he says. "I'm so sorry."

I stare back at him. "Is that it?" I ask. "Because you can leave now, if that's all. I'd like to sleep."

"Can I just say something?"

"I'd rather you didn't," I say. I sit up, both of my arms aching as they push me upright. "You warned me and I appreciate that. But I almost died—"

"I didn't take you there so you'd die!" says Ray. "We were friends. I wasn't *pretending* I liked hanging out with you all that time. You know how it was. I saw her, but I also saw *you*. I like you. I—I never wanted to throw all that away."

"But you did. You say you didn't want to kill me, but if things had worked out like you hoped, I wouldn't be here anymore. You'd have given away my life to get her back. That means I never want to see you again. Please leave."

Ray swallows. "But—"

"No," I say, and to my horror my eyes fill with tears. "I don't want to listen anymore."

He stands very still, very quietly.

I wait.

"I'll be around," he says at last, "if you change your mind."

I don't reply.

He turns abruptly. I wonder if Alisha's about to come in to tell him his time's up. But it's Sean, and his eyes are dark and the look on his face makes me shiver.

"Get out," he says very quietly.

Ray bristles. "Who're you?"

"The only one of us who *didn't* take Eva off to die," says Sean. "What more do you need to know?"

Ray's face darkens. "I was only talking to her—"

"Leave," says Sean, "or I swear I *will* kill you."

I watch Ray's hands fist by his sides. Sean's eyes narrow. I almost fall over trying to get out of bed.

"Are you joking?" I demand, knowing fully well how ironic these words sound coming out of my mouth, "A brawl? Really?"

"Eva—"

"I want you to leave, Ray." I cut him off. I'm so tired.

Although it's obvious he doesn't want to, Ray backs down. The anger blows out of his face and he nods. He stops at the door to look back once. "I mean it, you know. You'll never know how sorry I am."

When he's gone, I sit down on the floor and swallow back a sob. Sean sits down next to me. I lean my head on his knee and breathe in and out. I'm tired of being afraid. I'm tired of being hurt. I'm tired of having no control over my life. This has to change.

I go back to sleep a little later, but it's fitful and broken. I wake with a start, shivering, and I look around for Sean. He's still there, sitting in the chair by the window. There's a tray of sandwiches and cold lime juice next to him.

"Your leg seems better," he says. "You practically sprang out of bed back there."

"It feels better today."

Sean hands me a sandwich. "Eat."

I eat.

"I'd take you back with me if I could," he says, quite out of the blue, and my heart stutters with longing. "I'll probably drive myself crazy worrying about you when I leave. Would you come with me? If you could?"

"You know I would."

He sighs. "I'm sick to death of worrying. I've spent months doing it. About whether you were safe, if you were happy. I even worried about whether or not you were with *him*. How childish is that?"

"Does that mean you were jealous?" I ask, smiling.

"Finish your sandwich" is all I get by way of reply.

So I do.

By mid-June, I am able to walk properly again. My wrist is still in a cast, still broken, but I feel more like myself. A small part of me wants to play up the pain when I feel it, to keep Sean here longer. But it isn't fair to him. He has a life to live and it's not here.

And my life? I have a life to fight for. Frankenstein's Creature did unspeakably awful things, but he *beat* his uncaring creator.

I must too.

"I wish we could run away together," I tell Sean dreamily. "I wish we could go away, you and me, and disappear. I think we could do it if we were together. I'd get in less trouble if I were with you. You'd laugh more if you were with me. We'd be like Cathy and Heathcliff. Harry and Hermione. Liam and Noel."

"I didn't know you liked Oasis."

"*You* do, though, don't you? You brought that CD to the cottage and you used to play it when it got late. You'd fall asleep on the sofa. And I'd come turn it off."

"Well, I'm not sure they're the best example anyway," Sean points out, handing me a coffee. "Nor are the others. None of them exactly ended up together."

"*That* doesn't matter. What matters is what they did together, what they could achieve side by side. We'd be unstoppable if we were together."

"I suppose," says Sean. "You and I could burn the whole world down."

I gaze at him for a long time, until his brow creases and his eyes grow wider. I watch my own disbelief mirrored on his face. I am thinking of that unthinkable alternative.

"You know it's not possible," he says.

I nod. "But if it was," I say, "I'd go. I swear. I would go and never look back."

There is such freedom in the words. For just one minute, I am flying, high into the sky, among the stars and the shining planets.

"I'd disappear. One night, before the dawn, *poof.* Like magic."

Sean smiles faintly. "Where would you go?"

"Anywhere. I have that deposit box Erik and the others set up for me. Maybe there's money in it. They said it would help me have a life."

"And how would you survive? You've never been out there in the world. Who would help you? Anyone who did would be punished. But that's nothing compared to what the Weavers would do to *you* when they found you and they *would* find you—"

"I wouldn't expect your help. I wouldn't ask you or Mina Ma or the others to risk so much for me. They did it enough while I was growing up." I swallow. "I think I could make it. If I was clever and fast enough. If I only had the chance."

"But you don't," Sean says very quietly.

"No," I say, the lump in my throat hardening, "I don't. I never will have that chance."

It would have been a risk, throwing my life on the line to escape the Sleep Order. It might have been a fatal mistake. If I had found a way to get rid of the tracker, and run, and the seekers had found me, I'd have gone to trial and lost the rest of my time. But at least I'd have lost it by choice. Because I chose to take my chances with the unknown. It would have been on my terms. Not Amarra's.

"I'm sorry," says Sean.

I turn my face away to hide my despair and pain from him. We're silent for so long I wonder if we've forgotten how to speak.

I swallow and clear my throat. I force a smile. "Do you want to play chess? It's been a long time since we've played."

"Longer still," he teases, "since you've beaten me."

So we play. I win the first game. But there's not much satisfaction to be had in the victory, not when I know that *I'm* the king, white or black, and I have been thoroughly checkmated.

Until an unexpected move knocks every piece off the board altogether.

"All right," says Sean. "If you're willing to take your chances with a life of being on the run, I won't stop you."

"It doesn't matter. They'd find me before I left the city. Matthew knows too much. And there's the tracker—"

"The tracker's the only thing that stopped you these last weeks," he interrupts, "but you could get around it if somebody told you where it was. If they took it out for you."

"Well, yes, but who would do that?"

"Your guardians could," he says, "and one of them would."

And just like that, *checkmate* becomes only *check*, and I see a single shining, gleaming way out.

3

FLIGHT

My coffee rattles in my hands. I have to put it down. I stare at Sean in disbelief, shaking my head. "You'd do that? You'd take my tracker out?"

"Yeah."

"But they'll know it was you. They'll find out you were here and know you did it, you'll get in such trouble—"

"Not if they can't find me," he says.

"Excuse me?"

"Not if I run too," he says.

"What?"

"You said it, Eva. You said we could do it together."

"But you have a life—"

"Yeah," he says. "But I'd rather have one with you."

I stand up. Pain shoots through my muscles and I ignore it, glaring at him. "You must think I'm terribly selfish or terribly stupid," I say. "I won't let you do it. You mean too much to me. I forbid it—"

"You can't *forbid* me," he says, smiling ruefully. "I'll follow you if I have to."

I rock slightly on the balls of my feet. I'm standing on a floor that is tilting beneath me. Like a bird with a cage door thrown wide open, I hover, dazzled by the open skies but frightened.

"The thing is," says Sean, his eyes very green and sad, "there's nothing I wouldn't do for you."

I feel a sharp, stuttering jolt in my heart. I blink, once, twice. How do you protest something like that?

"I wish you wouldn't do *this*."

"And I wish *you* wouldn't cut and run," says Sean. "They've never forgiven a single echo who has dared to run. But staying here isn't going to save you."

I claw desperately for any alternative. "I can live with getting myself in trouble if I fail. But you? You can't ask me to do that."

Sean raises his eyebrows. "I'm not asking."

I twist my hands together and make shapes with my fingers. I could argue until I'm blue in the face, but he's not going to change his mind. And maybe it's not fair of me to try and make him. Wouldn't *I* follow him if our roles were reversed? Wouldn't I want him to let me?

"Thank you," I say brokenly, digging my fingernails into my palms. "I know this isn't easy for you."

He gives me a slightly suspicious look. "That's it? You're done arguing?"

I nod.

We stare at each other for a long time. I feel like we can

hang on to this moment if we don't speak. We can tread the line between being safe and taking this risk, and the moment someone says a word, this becomes real.

"We'll need money," says Sean at last, and it crashes down on me, that we're really going. My knees wobble.

I nod. "I need to look in that deposit box, see what they put there. And then—"

I break off. It's easy to imagine running. Frightening, exhilarating, but nevertheless easy for me to picture in my head. The reality, on the other hand, seems somehow colder. If we run, we'll have to run all our lives. If we make it, if we elude the seekers, we could be running for *years*. Long enough to get jobs, grow up, maybe even grow *old*. We'd have to survive out there indefinitely. Sean might be able to turn around and return to his old life if he chose to, but *I* can't. If I run, I can never stop.

"Yeah," says Sean, almost as if I said all those things out loud. "So are you sure this is what you want?"

I swallow. "Yes."

He considers me a moment and then nods. "Well, I have some money too. I have most of the money the Loom paid me over the years and the money Dad left me when he died. But we'll have to use cash as much as possible." He rubs his forehead, a worried gesture. "And there's—"

Someone knocks on the door. Sean goes quiet at once. We both look up guiltily as Neil pokes his head in.

"We thought we'd order pizza for dinner," he says.

"Pepperoni okay with both of you?"

I find that my brain can't quite understand the word *pizza*. It's too normal, too mundane, to fit into my tumbled feelings. Neil looks between us, slightly puzzled.

Sean recovers first. "That sounds good to me, thanks," he says, and he sounds so perfectly at ease I can only marvel at it. "Can I help set the table or anything?"

"Don't worry about it, we'll just eat out of the boxes." Neil gives me another odd look before leaving.

When we're alone again, I make a sheepish face. Sean shakes his head. "You need a better poker face."

"I know." *Pizza* is still bouncing around my head, still making no sense whatsoever, merely an unwelcome interruption. It makes me remember there's a household, a world, beyond this room. There are people who expect things of me. Am I really thinking of leaving Nik and Sasha? I gnaw my bottom lip, then push these doubts away. "What were you about to say when Neil knocked?"

"I was going to ask about passports," he says. "Do you still have the false one Matthew used to bring you here?"

I check Amarra's desk. "It's here."

"You'll have to use that one if we want to leave this country. And I'll have to use mine. But the Weavers will be able to track them. We'll have to stop using them as soon as we can."

"We could stay here," I say. "Not use passports at all."

"You're illegal here," Sean reminds me. I almost want

to hit him. There's something diabolical about the way he thinks of everything. "Do you really want to worry about the police finding out what you are, on top of everything? And anyway, if you want to get a look in that deposit box—"

"We'll have to go back to England," I finish, chilled to the bone.

"Yeah."

"*England*, Sean."

"I know, Eva." Sean doesn't look happy. "It's a little too close for comfort, but it might be our only choice right now."

I can't help thinking that, as unnerving as such proximity to the Loom is, it also means we're closer to Mina Ma, and Erik and Ophelia and Sean's mother.

Typically, Sean guesses where my thoughts have gone. "We can't see them," he says quietly. "You know that. The moment they find out we've run, they'll be watching everyone they think we'd go to."

"I know!" I say testily, biting back my disappointment. "It was just nice to imagine."

I study my hands, the lines in my palm. Everything has its consequences. You can't win a war without losing something. The price of survival could well be never seeing Mina Ma or my guardians or Nik or Sasha or Lekha ever again.

"What about after we've emptied the deposit box?" I say. "Can we get our hands on passports that the Weavers won't know about?"

"Sure," says Sean, "I'll just email my connections in the

criminal underworld, shall I?"

I glare at him. "Sometimes you really need a smack."

He gives me a lopsided smile.

"Well," I say, abandoning the false-passports idea, "it sounds like thinking ahead isn't going to help us now." Sean actually looks pained. I resist the urge to rub it in. "Sean, as much as you feel like it'll kill you not to have every stupid detail worked out, we can't know what to expect. We need to work out what to do *now*. And then figure out the rest when we need to."

"Fine. Then we need to get a flight out of here. We'd better avoid the London airports and fly into Manchester instead."

While Sean gets on Amarra's computer to look up flight schedules, I try to think of how we're going to get to the airport. I reach for Amarra's phone and dial Lekha's number.

"Okay," she whispers, by way of greeting, "are you in trouble again?"

"I—"

"No, don't answer that! They might realize you're tipping me off. We need a code word! Oooh, I have it! If the hunters have you, say *shoelaces*. And if it's Ray, say—"

"Aside from how ridiculous that is in itself," I say, choking on a giggle, "why on earth are *you* whispering?"

She laughs. "I have no idea. It seemed appropriate. So you're *not* in trouble?"

"Not as such."

"I need to teach you how to reassure people, because that was a shoddy attempt at it."

I smile. "Do you remember telling me your mother taught you to drive?"

"Not in the slightest," she says cheerfully, "but you always remember things, so I daresay I did. She taught me when I was a wee tot."

"Please tell me you've practiced since."

"A few times."

"How many is a few?"

"Once."

I sigh. "And you definitely don't have a license?"

"No," says Lekha, before adding with a snort, "not that *that* matters in this city, but I *do* like to obey the law—"

"Think you could break it this one time?"

There's a pause. Lekha sounds resigned. "Good god, they *have* got you, haven't they? Are you in a pool of your own blood again? Do you need me to pick you up?"

"No," I say. "*Really.* I'm at the house. But I'm leaving. At the end of the week. And I could use your help."

"I didn't know you drove, Lekha," says Neil, peering past her at the faded Zen parked by the front gate.

She beams at him. "I do now."

"Legally?" he asks doubtfully.

"Well—"

"Never mind," he says, "the less I know, the less I worry."

I wave hello to Lekha from the top of the stairs. My stomach is in knots. She looks cheerful as ever, but I'm quite sure she's putting it on. She didn't hesitate for an instant when I asked for help, but she seems to share Sean's view that running away is more likely to get me killed than save my life.

Neil shuts the front door behind her. "I hope you're staying for lunch. We've made too much."

"Oooh, can I? Something smells amazing!" Lekha turns to me and says, innocently, "What do you think about going out *after* we've eaten instead?"

Neil looks at me in surprise. "You're going out?"

I haven't gone anywhere since the hospital, and though I worried my sudden decision to do so might rouse Neil or Alisha's suspicions, Sean and I couldn't think of any other way to leave the house quietly. This way, we might even be out of the country before someone realizes we've left for good.

"They won't stop me," I told him. "They even suggested I disappear. Sort of. They won't stop us if they catch us slipping out."

"They might not," Sean admitted, "but if we flaunt it in their faces, they might feel like they have to lie to the Weavers later. It could get them in trouble."

Now, I force myself to meet Neil's eyes and babble, "Sean wants a souvenir to take back to his mother."

"Sounds fun," says Neil. "Fresh air will do you good."

He hesitates over his next words. "But do be careful, Eva."

"We will," Lekha assures him.

I smile weakly. Lekha takes me by the elbow and steers me upstairs, her bright eyes growing wide in panic as soon as we're out of earshot. Her fingers tighten.

"Are you really going to do this?"

I nod.

"Eva—"

"You can find me," I promise her, though I know the risks would be enormous and it's likely neither of us will be able to find the other again. "When you've finished school and you're out in world, come find me. I'll tell you where I am. Don't even *try* saying good-bye, because it's not."

"I hope not," she says softly.

We walk into Amarra's bedroom and stop short, because Nikhil is standing there, staring at the two bags on the floor.

"I told him they're both mine," says Sean quietly. He's by the window, elbows on his knees. "But he doesn't believe me."

"That's *yours*," says Nik to me, pointing at the dark green duffel bag, the zippers locked together. "You brought it with you when you came."

"Nik—"

"Are you leaving?"

It's just a question. Not a demand for the truth. I can't bear to look in his eyes, but I do. "Yes," I tell him, "I am. I have to."

"Is this because of the hunter?"

"Kind of. But it's more than that. I don't think I'll survive if I stay here. The Weavers will come for me."

Nikhil shifts his weight from foot to foot, considering. Then he nods, a slight jerky bob of his jaw.

"But maybe . . . like in a few years . . . when we're older . . . maybe Sasha and I could see you? We could find you—"

"I'd like that," I say softly, "very much."

I kiss him on the forehead. Nikhil is nearly my height. He will grow up to be such a wonderful boy. My heart squeezes tight. I've known them all their lives, he and Sasha. I watched them take their first steps on film. I heard them laugh. I pretended to love them for so long, and somewhere along the way, it stopped being pretend. I didn't expect a small part of me to *want* to stay. I didn't expect to miss them already.

After Nik leaves the room, I let out a heavy breath. "I don't know how I'm going to make it through lunch."

"*You* don't know?" Lekha demands. "What about me? *I'm* the messenger. And you know what happens to the messenger!"

"Speaking of," I say. "Here." I hand her a piece of folded paper. "You can read that if you like, it's a note for them. Can you give it to them after you've dropped us off?"

Lekha puts the note in her bag. It took me a long time to write it. I didn't really know what to say. In the end, I was honest.

I'm sorry to leave without saying good-bye. Thank you for giving me somewhere to stay and looking after me these last ten months, especially when I was hurt. You've been very kind and I hope you will all be happy.

P.S. Sean says thank you for letting him stay and that he's sorry he had to leave like this. He thinks it's rude, but we couldn't think of any other way.

Neil calls up that lunch is ready. Sean and Lekha go downstairs, and I go up to the attic to tell Alisha we're eating. When I step into her studio, I notice a difference immediately. On the wall straight ahead of me, hanging from a hook, is a pair of wings covered in black feathers. My wings. For the echo who was going to live forever.

"They're not finished," I say, embarrassed.

Alisha shakes her head. "Things don't have to be finished to be beautiful. But if you ever want to come in and finish it, you're welcome to."

I swallow. "Alisha, I . . ."

Her wide eyes focus on me. Eyes just like mine. I almost said good-bye. I almost hugged her. She stares at me. It's like she sees right through me. "Is something wrong, Eva?"

"N-no," I say. "I just—I just came up to tell you lunch is ready."

This is harder than I'd expected.

I eat slowly at lunch, partly out of anxiety, partly to make this final meal with them last a bit longer. When we're finished, I go back to Amarra's room to make sure I've packed everything I might need. I check my bag. False passport. Photographs. The bracelet Sean gave me. Indian money. A few British coins. *Frankenstein*. Erik's envelope and key. I double-check everything and have just finished when Sean comes back upstairs. Lekha trails behind him rather reluctantly.

"Do you *have* to do this?" she asks. "Here?"

"We have to leave the tracker here," says Sean, "so that anyone checking up on her will think Eva is still in this house."

"So they won't know it's out immediately?"

"Not until it loses power. It's like a battery being charged. When it's out, it will start to wind down, and it should set an alarm off at the Loom when it dies. But her body's been charging this tracker for almost a year now. It could be days before it loses power. Or hours."

Lekha shudders. "Well, do *not* ask me to help, because removing things from people's bodies is just not a talent of mine. *I'll* be shutting my eyes."

But she opens one eye and watches with a kind of disgusted fascination anyway.

I feel slightly squeamish myself. I pull the chair over to the window so that Sean gets the best light. I look up at him for a moment. He's soaked in sunlight. "From what I remember, the tracker is in your back," he says. "Erik told me. It's about an inch to the right of your spine, three inches above your tailbone, and about a third of a centimeter beneath the surface of your skin."

"How are you going to get it out?"

He reaches into his pocket and pulls out a Swiss knife. He opens out the blade and says, "How do you think?"

"Great," says Lekha, "absolutely spectacular. I should not have eaten lunch."

I feel the blood drain out of my face. I'm not afraid of a single *cut* after the blows I've taken already. But there's something awful about knowing it's coming.

Sean reaches for Amarra's box of matches. He sets one alight and holds the blade of the knife over the flame for a minute or two. I swallow back a sour taste in my mouth.

"Turn around," he says gently.

I hike my T-shirt and kneel in the chair, screwing my face and forehead up in anticipation of pain. I wait, and there it is, a flash like fire. I gasp.

"Sorry." He cuts into my skin. I imagine the knife sliding in as easily as if I'm butter, but this can't be what really happens. It's a sharp, raw pain, as though it's taken a lot of his will and nerve to actually break the surface of the skin. Skin is tougher than I had imagined.

"Is it out?"

"It is now." He shows me. It's tiny, little more than a black dot, a miniature capsule covered in blood. I take it from him and lean my head against the back of the chair, tired, aching. He touches my shoulder. His thumb brushes against the bare skin below my ear. My skin prickles pleasantly.

Sean cleans the cut and puts a bandage over it. He throws blood-soaked cotton balls into a tiny plastic bag. My back continues to throb, but it's bearable. I leave the blood on the tracker and wrap it in an antibacterial wipe, leaving the wipe under Amarra's bed so no one notices it for a few days. Sean and I wash our hands in the bathroom.

"It's done," I say, a little breathlessly.

"The tracker's gone now."

"Thank you."

"You're welcome," says Sean.

Lekha shakes her head at me. "I spent seventeen years without any unnecessary turmoil," she says happily, "seventeen years! Then *you* turned up and here I am, aiding a fugitive, watching a minor surgical procedure take place in a bedroom, witnessing firsthand the agony and the despair of star-crossed lovers . . ."

"We're not star—"

"Don't bother," I tell Sean. "It's not worth arguing with her."

He lets it go. "I think Neil and Alisha were still at the table when we left, finishing their wine. I'll go talk to them. It should keep them from coming out and seeing you take the bags to the car."

I toss Sean's things to Lekha and collect my stuff. Sean leaves the room, and we soon hear his voice in the dining room. We wait a couple of minutes before going down too.

We make it out to the car without running into anyone. Lekha sags against the front door in relief and says she'll wait outside while I get Sean. I go back indoors. The slit in my back is throbbing, and I'm quite sure I will be sick any minute now.

I go upstairs to find Sasha, busy writing her journal pages for her echo. "Hi, Sash," I say. "I'm going out with Lekha and Sean, so I won't be here for a while, okay?"

"Can I come?" she asks eagerly.

"Not this time. You have to finish your pages, don't you? Come here," I say, heart snapping in two. "Give me a hug before I go."

I scoop her up and she puts her face in my neck, nuzzling like a cat. I laugh and squeeze her tight. I hold on too long and she wriggles, looking at me worriedly. I let her go. She drops back onto her bed. I smile to wipe away her concern.

"You be a good girl."

"I'm always a good girl!" she says indignantly.

I blow her a kiss and force myself to leave her. I find Sean in the dining room and tell him Lekha's waiting for us.

"Have fun," says Alisha. "See if you can find a jade elephant at one of the shops. They make lovely souvenirs."

"Bye," I say. Sean, master of the carefully blank face, says a light good-bye and grips me by the hand. He pulls me out of the house before my expression gives us away.

I don't look back. I can't. The sky and road are singing to me and I have to run. I have to fly. Or stay and wither, die by a Weaver's needles and loom.

Sean gets in the back of Lekha's car. I get in the passenger seat. We don't leave at once. We sit there silently, absorbing the fact that once we start moving, there will be no going back. Then Lekha blows out a huge exaggerated breath, turns the key in the ignition, and jolts forward before stalling. I laugh in spite of myself. She addresses the car with a number of rude words. She starts again and we glide down the street. We've left. We're gone.

We've each chosen. All of us. To take control or to stand back. To stop a friend from risking her life or to help her do it. To follow or not to follow. We will have to live with our choices, whatever the outcome.

"Isn't anyone going to talk?" Lekha demands, after exactly three minutes of silence.

"Radio?"

She huffs and turns it on. The song playing is "Stop Crying Your Heart Out." By Oasis. It seems like a sign. It makes me feel more hopeful.

"Why is the traffic so bad?" Lekha wails at intervals. "It's driving me bananas!"

"I can drive if you like," I offer. I've been watching her do it. I've watched Ray. I think I can figure it out.

Sean makes a noise in his throat. "As bloody if."

"You drive then. You're the only one of us with an actual driver's license."

"No one's touching my mother's car," says Lekha. "I can

live with the traffic. I have bathed an elephant in a river. I can handle *traffic*."

In spite of a few starts and stops and a great deal of unladylike swearing from Lekha when a motorcycle zooms by and nearly takes her mirror with it, we sail out of the traffic in good time. From there it's one long straight road, and Lekha cheers up no end.

At the airport, she can only park by the departure doors for a few minutes before security will come shoo her away. We hop out of the car and collect our things.

"Be careful," says Lekha. "And call me. Whenever. So I know you're still alive."

"I will. Will you get back okay?"

She nods tearfully.

Then she wraps her arms around me and hugs me tightly. I hug her back, even harder if that's possible, and whisper, "Thank you for this. Thank you so much."

"Good luck," she whispers back. "Never eat sushi at an airport."

Then she kisses Sean on the cheek and jumps back in the car. We watch her drive off. I sniffle. I think I might miss her the most.

"Come on," I say, "let's go be star-crossed lovers and court disaster."

Sean laughs. I realize how much I've missed hearing the sound of it. I've always been able to make him laugh.

We pass through the airport scans and checks without

incident, but I can't relax, I am as tightly wound as wire around a spool. But when we're finally on the plane and we haven't caught a whiff of the police or a Weaver, I realize that we've done it. We've gotten away.

By the time we take off, I am fast asleep.

4

RISKY

Sean puts a coin in the pay phone and dials a number. We don't dare use our phones. For all we know, my tracker has died and the seekers have been after us for hours. I stand rigidly a few feet from him, arms crossed tightly over my chest, and watch the crowds. Manchester Airport is busy and chaotic and I don't like it. A seeker could be anywhere. I am terrified I wouldn't spot one in these crowds until it was too late.

I open my mouth to tell Sean to hurry, but he glares me into silence. I turn back to the crowds. I've been gripping my shoulder bag so hard my fingers are numb and the strap is slick with sweat. I feel sticky and edgy and bone tired. We've been traveling for the better part of a day, with only a few broken hours' sleep on the flight. But I will have to get used to feeling this way. I ran away. I can't now expect my life to be restful.

"Done," says Sean, coming up behind me. "Let's get to the train station."

I feel smug for a moment. "Not leaving me behind, then?"

We argued about this through most of the flight. My key unlocks a safe-deposit box in London. Sean wanted to take the key and go fetch its contents himself, leaving me in Manchester and far away from the Loom, but I refused to be left behind.

"Compromise," says Sean. "We both go to London, but I go alone to empty the box."

I consider this. "Okay. That's fair."

He looks relieved. I'm an exhausting person to argue with.

"Who did you call?"

"A friend in London. I was trying to find a safe place we could stay while we're there. Just for a night or two. It'd be dangerous to linger in London much longer than that."

"Hotel?"

Sean shakes his head. We start walking through the milling crowds in the direction of a sign for the train station. "We'd be better off saving our money while we can. I thought we could hide out at a theater. There are rehearsals going on, but the place will be deserted at night, and we'll just do our best not to be seen during the day."

This sounds very risky, but I have no better ideas. I rub my arms to fend off the cold and look back over my shoulder. I keep expecting to be pounced on at any moment.

The sun is dazzlingly sharp outside. At the train station Sean goes to buy tickets while I stop at a shop to find us some lunch. It's hard letting him out of my sight. We're more vulnerable on our own. There's always a blind spot. Somewhere we won't see them coming from. I choose the first sandwiches I see and throw in some chocolate bars and bottled drinks. My hands aren't steady. I have to fumble in my bag for money.

I spot Sean making his way toward me. I stare at him for a moment or two. It's funny, feeling so pleased and yet so frightened at the same time. It's been months since I have felt like my fate is firmly in my hands and not vanishing out of reach like a floating lantern. I am in danger out here, but I am alive, and if I can keep outrunning them I will *stay* alive. Having to look over my shoulder, being constantly afraid, it's not perfect. But it's worth it. It has given me my life back.

And it has taken Sean's old life away. Suddenly my throat feels scratchy. I swallow. One day I will make him go back. I have to.

"Stop looking at me like that," he says.

I rearrange my face. "When's our train?"

"In about ten minutes."

I hand him a sandwich and we eat as we walk, taking a flight of stairs down to our platform to wait. My bags and shoulders feel heavier with each passing minute. Sean looks as tired as I feel.

By the time the train pulls in and we find our seats, I feel half in a trance and no less edgy. It's getting harder to stay awake. I sit next to the window and rub my eyes and look out at people passing by.

That's when I see him. His blue eyes are like knives.

At first it's only a dream. Not quite real. The fear is a cold trickle sliding slowly, lazily, up my spine. Then it freezes into panic and my eyes snap wide open.

The train begins to move, but my gaze is glued to the platform. Where is he? He was there a moment ago!

I leap up and climb over Sean into the aisle.

"Eva, what—?"

I ignore him and race down the aisle as the train moves away, pressing myself to the windows to try and spot him again. A hand closes over my elbow and I jump and turn, ready to fight him off, but it's only Sean and he looks worried.

"What the hell is going on?"

"I saw—I thought—I thought I saw—"

He steers me back to our seats. People glance our way, but I don't care. I sit down, certain I am about to be captured. Or that I am going mad. Imagining things that aren't there.

"Saw what?"

I lick my dry lips and look at Sean. "Matthew."

"Where?" He sounds calm but he looks around, eyes wary, alert, searching for any threat. "On the platform? Watching us?"

"It was only for a second. I saw him." Doubt punches a hole in my voice. "At least I could have sworn I did. But then I looked again and I couldn't spot him. Maybe—maybe I imagined it."

"You haven't slept much. And you're scared. It's probably

normal to start seeing bad things all over the place. If it *was* him, we'd be in the seekers' hands by now."

That should make me feel better, but I can't help thinking of Matthew, who likes to play games, and the way he looked at me as he watched me run off my *last* train to see Sean, and how it would be so like him to turn up and vanish again, leaving me behind to question what I did or didn't see.

"Try to sleep," says Sean.

But I don't. He doesn't either. The Loom feels an awful lot closer.

5

SAFE

It's late when we arrive in London. The sun is long gone and false yellow light spills out into the roads. We get immediately into a taxi. Sean gives the driver the name of a street. I dig my nails into my palms to get rid of some of my tension and only half listen as the driver makes Sean aware of his views on the traffic, the government, and the weather. It's not a long drive, and soon we're getting out again and paying and thanking the driver and then he's gone in a puff of fumes.

"It's this way," says Sean. "I didn't want to tell him exactly where we were going, so we have to walk a bit."

I'm exhausted, but I haven't forgotten that Matthew *could* have been in Manchester watching us, and I say, "Take us the wrong way first and cut back after a while. Just to make sure no one follows us there."

Sean seems impressed that such caution occurred to me. I give him a dirty look and follow him down the street. I don't really think we're being watched right now. There is no one in sight, and even the seekers would leave *some* trace of their presence. Still. I want to step carefully. Especially in the Weavers' city.

Eventually we make our way to a large cobbled square that looks like it would be busy during the day. There's a fountain in the middle, an ornate thing where people drop pennies and make a wish. My footsteps have slowed to a trudge and I can barely move anymore. Sean isn't much better.

"In here." He tugs my arm, leading me down a narrow, dark alley. It seems like the ideal place for someone to be mugged.

Halfway down the alley, Sean stops and wiggles the doorknob of a door on his left. It turns. He glances around to make sure there is nobody in sight and pushes open the door. He steps aside to let me in first, then follows me in and shuts the door behind us. I hear the sound of a lock turning. I can only assume Sean's phone call involved him asking someone to leave the side door unlocked for us. I don't like that someone else knows where Sean is tonight, but I let it go.

Sean takes me through the dark theater without difficulty. He's obviously been here plenty of times. I concentrate on picking out the smells of paint and new carpet and try not to think about things in Sean's life I know nothing about, like theaters and friends, and how he will soon have to leave those things behind.

He stops at the rear of the theater, behind the stage, and reaches for a poker propped against a nearby radiator. He raises the poker above his head and hooks it onto something in the ceiling. It's a door to the loft. He drops the door and lowers a ladder. We climb up and pull the door shut behind us. The loft is clean and quite full and smells like freshly laundered clothes. It must be where they store costumes and equipment.

Sean flicks a switch, and bright gold light spills out of a single bulb hanging from the low roof. It fills the loft with color. Blinded, I blink at him.

"We should black that out," I say when I can see again. I point to the single window at the far end of the loft. "Someone might see the light and wonder who's up here this late."

"Good idea." Sean drops his bag next to mine. "Look in these trunks. There might be cloth you can use. I'll go check the props for mattresses and sheets and lug them over here."

I open the nearest trunk, releasing a fresh wave of that clean-clothes smell. I sift through the costumes and material carefully. I move on to the next trunk. In the third, I find rolls of black velvet. I unroll the material, find some pins, and steal a piece of black cardboard from the props section.

I cover up the window and clamber across the loft to help Sean. We drag two mattresses into the space we have appropriated for ourselves, and Sean goes to fetch pillows. I check the trunks again and find clean sheets and quilts.

Immediately I want to drop down onto my mattress and go straight to sleep. I resist the urge and smile up at Sean.

"We're lucky."

"Nah," says Sean, grinning back. "There are bedroom scenes in this play. I knew they'd have bedding. I'd better write a note and pin it to one of the trunks," he adds, and pulls a face. "'Dear Mrs. Brown. Sorry if we left a mess behind. We probably had to leave in a hurry. We're on the run, see. Bit of an emergency. Yours penitently, S. J. Franklyn.' Yeah, she'll love that."

Laughing for what feels like the first time in days, I pull my nightshirt out of my bag. "I could burn these clothes, I've been in them so long," I say.

"There are showers right below us. Attached to the dressing rooms. Tempted?"

"You've just made my day."

"Come on, I'll show you where they are."

I add a towel, hairbrush, shampoo, soap, and clean underwear to a pile with my nightshirt, and follow him down the ladder again.

When I'm finished, I climb back up. Sean must have finished showering already, because his hair is wet and there's still water drying on his forehead. He's sprawled on his mattress like he tried to wait for me but couldn't stay awake. I throw his quilt over him and curl up on my own makeshift bed. I am asleep in seconds, and for once I don't dream of anything at all.

"Eva, wake up." Sean is speaking above me. Beyond him I can hear birds and distant voices. The cobbled square out

340

front? The theater below us? Probably both. "Eva, come on, wake up. We have a problem."

Even that can't jolt me awake. My muscles feel sore and warm and sleepy. I squeeze my eyes open. I look at my watch. It's almost noon. I could probably sleep some more, but Sean is now crouched next to me and his eyes are very green and very impatient.

His words finally get through to me. I sit bolt upright, my heart sinking all the way to my toes. "What do you mean? What problem? Have they found us?"

"No, nothing like that," he says, handing me a hot chicken wrap in blue paper. "Eat that. I've been up about an hour. I slipped out and got us some breakfast. I also went online at a shop. I didn't want to turn my phone on, but I wanted to look up your deposit box, find the address on a map, the nearest tube station, that kind of thing."

"And?" I feel calmer now that I know we're safe. I bite into my wrap. It's delicious.

"It's gone. The place where they stored your stuff, I mean. They went bankrupt and closed last year."

I stop eating. "All that stuff is lost?" I ask in dismay.

"It shouldn't be," says Sean. "They'd have called everyone who stored stuff with them before they closed. Erik would have emptied the box and moved the contents somewhere else. But there's no way to know where—"

"—without asking him," I finish. I bite my lip. "And the Weavers will be expecting us to try reaching him or Mina Ma."

"Hence the problem."

I eat my wrap slowly. Sean paces the loft and I frown, trying to think, but my brain still feels half asleep.

"What about Ophelia? She might know where Erik moved the deposit box. If she's been living in London this past year, he probably had to ask her to move it for him."

Sean glances at me. "They're going to be keeping an eye on her, too."

"True. Except she's Adrian's *daughter*. He trusts her. You know what Ophelia's like. She used to get so upset when Mina Ma said harsh things about the Loom. She believes in Adrian. Loves him. He must know that." I rub sleep out of my eyes. "But he doesn't know that, in spite of everything, Ophelia never told tales about me. She always stuck by me."

"True."

"And if the Loom's not tracking her, they won't know if we call."

"I don't know," says Sean, considering. "I still don't think they'd ignore her altogether." His brow knots unhappily. He can't think of an alternative. "Fine. She may be our best bet. We'll make the call from a pay phone a safe distance away, just in case."

"You'd better do the talking." I am quite sure I'll burst into tears the moment I hear Ophelia's voice. I want to talk to her so badly. To all of them.

Sean stops pacing and nods. He has a look on his face that tells me he's made up his mind. "I think that would be better anyway. It means you can stay here."

"But—"

"It's safer, Eva." I can't argue with that. "We agreed I'd go empty the deposit box on my own anyway. I'll call her, find out where it is, and go deal with that. When I'm back we can figure out what to do next."

I don't like it, but I have to acknowledge it makes far more sense than my going with him. I'm the one who broke free; I'm the one they want to find most. I can't go running around London without care. Until we're well away from this city, I have to lie low.

I get up and wrap my arms around myself. I don't think it's cold in here, but I shiver. "Sean, be careful."

He opens the trapdoor and pauses by the ladder. He smiles. "I'm not you," he points out. "Of course I'll be careful."

After he leaves, I get dressed. I make my way cautiously out of the loft to use the bathroom and wash up. I can hear voices, sounds echoing through the theater, but the dressing rooms seem quite deserted. I hurry, glancing edgily behind me every couple of seconds to make sure no one is coming, jumping at every sound. I fill our empty drink bottles with water and steal a few biscuits from a tray in the dressing room for good measure. No sense leaving the loft more than absolutely necessary.

I take my towel, toothbrush, and the bottles back up and close the trapdoor. Sean can't have been gone more than half an hour. I occupy myself by tidying up the loft, nibbling biscuits and flicking through one of the books I'd packed. When I find I can't concentrate, I try instead to think of where we could go next.

I check my watch compulsively, but the passage of each moment is agonizingly slow. Sitting here and waiting is unbearable.

Restless, I turn off the light and carefully pull aside a section of the covering on the window. I look into the street and the square far below. It's busy, as I'd guessed, bustling with stalls and people. Farther away, I can see bits of a gleaming river between the rooftops and church spires across the city. I open the window a crack and breathe in the open air. It smells warm and summery, like wet grass and onions and barbecues, but it doesn't warm me up. My hands are ice cold.

He's been gone almost two hours. I abandon the window, covering it back up, and flip the light on once more. Desperate for something to do, I press my ear to the trapdoor and make sure all seems quiet below. Then I sneak down again to refill the bottles.

Only this time the dressing room isn't empty. There is a man standing by the wall, studying a poster, almost like he was waiting for me.

He turns around. I catch a glimpse of silvery chain mail before terror obliterates everything but the gleam in his eyes.

"Matthew," I croak.

"I prefer *Sir* Matthew," says the Weaver, with a smile like a hungry tiger.

6

PUPPETS

I want to run away, but some force holds me fast. I reach for
something, anything, to steady me, and my hand closes over
the door frame. My fingers bite down so hard my knuckles
turn white.

"So what now, Matthew?" I ask, biting back a whine of
panic. "You ask me to come quietly and I say you can go to
hell?"

He rolls his eyes. "Of course you refuse to be reasonable.
Have you never considered giving in gracefully?"

"I'll give in gracefully when the time's right. But until
then, I'm not going gently into any good night, thank you
very much."

"You needn't take that tone with me," says Matthew,
smothering a yawn. "Effusive thanks will do nicely."

"What for?"

"I don't know if you have bothered to look around,
dearest Eva," he drawls. "If you had, you'd have noticed that
I am alone. If I *had* intended to take you to the Loom, I
would have brought Theseus or Lennox. Seekers. Powerless

I am not, but I have no desire to wrinkle this new shirt in a brawl with you. It therefore stands to reason that I am *not* here to capture you."

This makes very little sense to me. I swallow, trying to moisten my dry mouth. "How did you find me?"

"I," says Matthew, "know everything. Have we not discussed that at length?"

"Were you in Manchester yesterday?"

He smiles but ignores the question. "I rather think it would be prudent to move this little chat somewhere more, ah, *discreet*."

I don't like admitting it, but he has a point. I show him the way up to the loft, stamping down on my terror, trying to think. A few minutes ago I wanted nothing more than for Sean to be back. Now I hope he stays out awhile longer. I can't let Matthew get hold of him too.

Once we're upstairs, I keep my eyes fixed on Matthew, the way you might watch a snake for sudden movements.

"Why?" I ask. "Why *didn't* you bring a seeker?"

"They're busy," says Matthew blithely, "and I rather thought everything would turn *so* tedious and predictable if I did. If you return to the Loom now, you will go to trial and tragically perish. And *I* will have no new material for my definitive encyclopedia on echo behavior. You asked me for help once," he adds. "And I told you to find your own way out. Which you have done. More or less. I have to admit, I wasn't sure you would have the nerve to run. I'm impressed.

It's been so entertaining that I am most intrigued to see what you do next."

I stare at him in disbelief. Hope blossoms in my toes and begins to creep upward. I try to read his expression, but it's impossible.

"How would the other Weavers feel about you not taking me back?"

"I daresay they wouldn't be surprised," muses Matthew. "They've long since given up trying to predict my actions or understand my motivations."

I don't take my eyes off him. He found me and he's letting me go. I can't quite accept it. This is a Weaver. *Matthew.* It can't be this easy.

"I don't trust you," I say. "You're not doing this to be kind."

"I have never had a reputation for kindness," Sir Matthew reflects, "and I am only heroic if it suits me."

I ignore that. "What do you want from me? Do you want me to be grateful? Thank you on my knees? You're only doing this so you can entertain yourself watching me squirm. I'm a puppet and you want to pull the strings. I'm only safe from you as long as you find this amusing. The moment you get bored, you'll send seekers after me." I shake my head. "Soon I'll be far away. I don't care if you come after me or not. I ran away to survive. To win my life back. Not to let you mess about with it. I won't be played with. And I'm not going to thank you."

Matthew gives me a long, hard look. I see amusement, but something else, too, something I can't put my finger on.

"You *should* thank me, you impossible little brat," he says at last, pointing a finger to the tip of my nose. "If I don't play my games, how long do you imagine you can outlast the seekers on your own?"

"I'm not on my own—"

I stop, biting my tongue in chagrin. But Matthew doesn't look like this is news to him. "And by that I suppose you mean Jonathan's son?" He shrugs dismissively. "He hardly counts anymore. I don't expect you will ever see him again."

My blood freezes. My voice is hardly more than a whisper. "What does that mean?"

"A little birdie's been chattering," says Matthew, examining his fingernails. "A *girl* birdie. I did mention the seekers were busy, didn't I? The little birdie told Adrian that you would be going to a bank in the city to empty a certain deposit box. This was, oh, an hour ago. Naturally the seekers made haste to get there and wait for you."

I'm going to be sick. "Ophelia? She *told* Adrian?" A bitter taste fills my mouth. I've loved her most of my life. I always knew, we all knew, that she was loyal to the Loom. But she kept my secrets from them despite that. I didn't think that would change. I *trusted* her.

"Of course she told him."

"Sean." I choke on his name. *I* told him to call her. This

is my fault. "God. They'll find Sean. But—but it's *me* they want. They—they will leave him alone, won't they? They won't hurt him or take him away?"

"What a sweet, innocent thought." Matthew casts his eyes skyward. "And totally incorrect. He broke our laws too. If I were you, I'd write him off and get the devil out of here. Flee with your life like you so grandly wanted."

"I can't do that."

"Going to go after him, are you? You don't even know where he is."

"I can call Erik and ask him about the bank. Thanks to Ophelia, I don't have to be careful about contacting him anymore. It's too late for that now."

"You are being absurd."

I scramble for my shoes. "I have to find Sean before your seekers do. I might be in time. Get out of the way!"

"No." Matthew puts his foot down on my boots. I try to pull them out from under him, but he is immovable. I straighten up, ready to hit him, and he gives me a cold, dry look. "You will not be in time. I have no doubt they've found him already. If you go out there, you will also be captured, and as I have already told you, *that* does not suit me one bit. Do be sensible for a change. *His* capture does not mean death. *Yours* will. Tedious. Predictable. Remember?"

"Move!"

"And this is what he would want, is it?" he drawls, refusing to budge. "He'd *like* it if you went out and threw yourself into the jaws of the waiting beast? He'd be happy, would he?"

It's the last thing Sean would want. He will never forgive me if I am captured because of this. But he's out there and if there's still a *chance* I can help him—

"I can go barefoot, you know," I hiss through my teeth.

I see him move, but I am standing too close to him. I can't get out of the way in time. His hand closes over my throat.

I gasp. Oxygen vanishes from my lungs. My hands claw frantically at his, but everything goes dim and dark at the edges. Then it's all gone.

7

ECHOES

I groan against the floorboards. I must have bumped my head because it hurts. I open heavy eyes and blink at the empty loft.

My confusion lasts only a second before it is wiped out by fury. I crawl to my knees. Matthew's gone. My watch tells me I've been out cold for twenty minutes. My boots are on my feet. He must have put them on. His idea of a joke. I could strangle him.

What did he think this would achieve? That if he delayed me I would change my mind? I'm not an idiot. I *know* the odds are slim. I know how unlikely it is that I will get to Sean in time. The seekers probably already have him, and if they are still waiting, hoping to draw me out, I won't stand a chance at getting away. But I can't turn tail and run and abandon him.

I get to my feet. My mouth tastes like dust and fear and rage. I hesitate, staring at my boots. They feel heavy. Weighing me down.

Matthew was right about that much. The sensible thing

to do would be to run. Sean would want me to. He wouldn't want me to waste our efforts, everything he's given up for me, by going back for him. And Erik will step in; he will try to persuade the Weavers not to send Sean to prison. They may let him go. I make a bitter sound in my throat. It's not likely to happen that way. But the voice of reason in my head, the one that sounds an awful lot like Amarra, tells me how much smarter it would be to run.

Only I *can't*. The Eva from before, who lived by the lake and knew so little of loss and loyalty and blinding terror, she wouldn't have even recognized the sensible thing. She'd have been on her way to find Sean by now. But me? I recognize sensible and not sensible. I am still here looking at my boots. But I am also still going to go.

I find some aspirin in Sean's bag and take two for my throbbing head. Then I search for cash, not knowing how much I will need to get to the bank, and stuff whatever I can find into my jeans. I have just closed my fist over a last five-pound note when I hear it.

The ladder.

A creak. Someone is on the ladder.

I whirl, almost tripping over my mattress. If it's someone from the theater, I'm stuck. What am I supposed to do, fight them and run? But the trapdoor flips open and it's not a stranger, it's the top of Sean's head.

I sway unsteadily on my feet. I think I might faint. I drop the five-pound note. I'm going to kill him.

"What the *hell* happened to you?"

He looks slightly alarmed. "Er, I went to get your stuff. Did I imagine the conversation we had before I left?"

I almost bite him. I am dangerously close to tears. "But— but the seekers! I thought I'd never see you again. . . . I thought you were in trouble—"

"I got away."

He sounds calm. Too calm. There are scratches on his arms. A bruise under his right eye. *I got away.* That's all he says?

"I hate you!" I sob. "Go away! I don't care what happened to you! I wish they'd caught you!" I throw myself down on the floor and cross my arms so tightly they feel numb.

Sean walks carefully toward me, but the tiny glimmer of amusement in his eyes only annoys me more.

"Go away!" I say again, sniffling. "Or *I* will. I can't bear it! I can't make it through a lifetime of *you* going missing every five minutes!"

"Okay."

I scramble to my feet. "No, I didn't mean it! Don't go away!"

"I wasn't going to," he says, the corner of his mouth twitching like he can't help himself. "But if it's all right with you, I'm going to kiss you now."

And before I can say or do anything, he does.

I stop trying to talk. His fingers tangle in my hair. He puts a hand against the wall behind me, trapping me in place.

My heart beats very fast and a fierce, shocking *wanting* spreads through my skin, to my fingers and toes and belly. His other hand bites into my back, pulling me closer. I lick his tongue. He groans softly and pulls back, just a little.

His eyes stare dizzily down into mine. His breathing is uneven. It feels like stars are bursting into flame across my soul and I am sinking deeper and deeper into a hot, spinning sky. I run my fingers over his lips.

"I can't live with losing you," I whisper, "and for a while there, I thought I had."

He reaches for my fingers, tangles his hand with mine. "That's how I feel every single day," he says brokenly. "*Every* day, Eva. Your life is dangling by a thread. And I'm scrabbling to hold on, but it keeps slipping through my fingers. I'm here because I can't stand not to be. It's not some big noble sacrifice. I *want* to be here. I don't like the world without you. I need you to be alive."

I wipe the back of my hand across my nose and blink away tears. "And I need you to be, so don't ever scare me like that again," I say, pushing at his chest.

He steps back. "Wait just one minute. How did you know about the seekers?"

"Matthew told me."

"Matthew!"

"He was here." I tell him what happened, almost word for word. His eyes narrow, rather dangerously, when I get to the part about my wanting to go after him, but he lets it go for the moment. My lips twist with dark humor as I finish: "And then he knocked me out."

Sean is incredulous. "What is he up to? All this, it's really just because you impressed him by running away? Because you *amuse* him?"

"I don't know. I don't understand him. He says no one bothers trying to anymore, and I can see why."

"I can't believe he knocked you out!"

"I can," I say darkly, "but never mind that. Ophelia told Adrian I'd be at the bank." The sharp, cold sting of betrayal hasn't gone away. "Did the seekers find you?"

He nods. "I talked to Ophelia, she told me where to go, I got there, talked to the manager and gave him the key. He brought me the box, I emptied it, zipped everything up in my jacket pocket, didn't have any problems. Then I walked out of the bank and saw them. One of them was missing an ear, and the other had scars across his face. But the eerie thing about them is how quiet they are. They know exactly how to go unnoticed if they want to. And they *watch*. Their eyes are so steady. I knew who they were as soon as I saw them. I legged it."

"But that bruise . . . those scratches—"

"They caught up to me in an alley," says Sean. "I think they'd been right behind me the whole time I was running, but they were just waiting for me to end up somewhere quiet. I got lucky. A car backfired in the road and startled one of them enough that he let go of me. I fought the other one and ran. Got in the first taxi I found, got out at the next traffic light, and went halfway across the city to sit in a Starbucks until I was sure they hadn't followed me. We can't hang around," he adds. "The sooner we're out of London, the better."

I feel shaky imagining how close he came to being captured. I swallow. "We have no reason to stay here now that you've got the stuff. We could get on a plane. Or a train. Anything."

"We're going to have to think this one through," he says, taking his jacket off. "Now that they know we're in London, they'll be watching the stations and airports to catch us on our way out."

I open my mouth to offer ideas, to say something sensible, but all I hear is:

"You kissed me."

I grimace. It's like the words were sitting on the tip of my tongue all this time, waiting for an opportunity to burst out.

Sean almost blushes. "What, d'you want me to apologize for not being gentlemanly?"

I half laugh, half choke. "It was a surprise, that's all."

He looks down at me and his expression shifts. He looks sad, like he's watching a wave come toward us and he has no way of stopping it from crashing.

"I shouldn't have done it."

"We've broken every other law. What's one more?"

He shakes his head. "It's different now. It was always wrong for us to feel like this, we knew that. But when they were just feelings we kicked under the carpet, we were safer. They couldn't punish us for something we hadn't done. Do you remember that night, ages ago, in your room? Don't you think I wanted to kiss you then? But I didn't. And now I have. Now we *have* broken that law."

There's a truth in his words I can't deny.

"If we're caught," he says, "this could mean the difference between forgiving and condemning you. They don't need another excuse to destroy you."

"Do you *want* to kiss me?"

He nods. I lean over and kiss him. I've been longing to since we stopped.

"Don't," he says, pulling me closer. "We *can't*. This is the last"—he kisses my neck—"last time."

When he eventually pushes me away, it's a positively indecent amount of time later. Heat has crept up my neck and all the way to the roots of my hair.

It hurts somewhere deep in my body, deeper than a lung or a stomach or a heart. The world I knew has folded in on itself. I kissed him. He kissed me. In the last couple days, I have broken every law I've ever lived by. I feel like singing. I also feel guilty. Ray flickers in a corner of my thoughts. I was supposed to love *him*. Sometimes, when he looked past Amarra and saw me, sometimes, then, I even thought I *could* love him one day. I was never supposed to betray everything the Weavers wove me to be. I was never supposed to love anyone else.

"Did you eat anything at Starbucks?" I ask, and somehow, miraculously, I don't sound like I'm stunned or breathless. I sound blessedly normal.

He shakes his head. He looks slightly shaken.

I hand him a chocolate bar. He gestures wordlessly to his jacket. I follow his lead and ignore what's just happened. As badly I want to, I know we can't sit here kissing and pretending everything is shiny and okay.

I unzip the inner pocket of his jacket and remove the contents.

A debit card with bank details. I have no idea how much money is in the account, but anything will help. I feel a surge of love, of incredible gratitude for my guardians.

A shiny disk with no label. It looks old.

And a wax bird.

I stare down at the bird and something swells in my chest. I run my fingers over the ridges in the wings. This is one of mine. I don't think I have a distinctive style or anything, but I recognize what I once made. It was one of my early birds, made clumsily and happily in a corner of my bedroom while Mina Ma slept, a dark, delicious secret to be kept from everyone, even from Sean, who I hadn't yet met at the time. I put the bird under my bed, and soon after it wasn't there anymore and I forgot about it.

"You were the only one who ever knew I made these,"

I say softly, stroking the wings. "How did it get here?"

Sean runs a fingertip down the bird's beak. He smiles faintly. "I think it's their way of telling you they always knew," he says, "and they never tried to stop you. They never told the Weavers about it. I reckon it's their way of reminding you how much they love you."

My throat closes up. I want suddenly to be little again. I want to follow Mina Ma around the supermarket, listening to her complain bitterly about "having to stick to a ridiculous list *peppered* with things you can't get your hands on in this wretched country." I want to hold Erik's hand and run down the lakeshore, pulling him with me. I want Jonathan to push me in the swing they made for me for my seventh birthday.

And Ophelia—

I can't. I can't even think of her.

"What do you think is on this disk?" I ask Sean, forcing myself to focus on the here and now. I hold the disk up to the light, watching it shine.

He crumples up the chocolate bar wrapper. "This place is full of sound equipment," he says. "There's got to be some kind of portable CD player somewhere." He checks his watch. "It's still early. They won't have finished rehearsals yet, but we can't wait forever."

"I think there was an old radio thing in the dressing room below us. It might work."

"I'll go have a look."

He isn't gone long. He returns with the radio a moment

later. "Dressing room wasn't empty," he says ruefully, "but I don't think they paid much attention to me. They're used to seeing me around."

We need to leave. Quickly. Sean plugs the radio into a socket in the wall. It doubles up as a CD player, with a little slot to pop the disk into. Sean presses play.

The sound is scratchy, from the age of the player or the recording or both, but we can still hear everything. At first we hear only a few muffled sounds, footsteps and creaking and the sound of a door opening and closing. Then a voice:

"Erik! To what do I owe this unexpected visit?" Matthew's voice. It's a little different. Younger. But unmistakable all the same.

And Erik's reply. "I came to give you my answer. I can't do it."

"Why not?"

"You know why not. I've seen what happens to them when they break your damned laws. I'd be mad to become responsible for one of them." There's a pause and a gurgle in the background, and I realize there's someone else in the room with them. A child? A baby? "I couldn't possibly teach her and raise her without coming to care for her. And then if she were destroyed, I couldn't bear it. No. I have no intention of leaving the Loom altogether. But I can't be one of *those* guardians. I can't take charge of this little thing."

"I can't ask anybody else!" Matthew snaps. "There *is* no one else!"

"You have plenty of guardians willing to—"

"None I'd trust with *her*. You've been here as long as I have. I need you to be part of her life. *Look* at her, Erik! Look . . . when I pick her up, she *smiles* at me!"

"How dare she," says Erik drily.

Matthew snorts, sounding remarkably like the Matthew I've met. "I only mean it's obvious the child can't tell a good thing from a bad one. No one in their right mind smiles so unreservedly at me. She will be trouble. I can tell already. Soon she will have to leave me—leave the Loom and go north. She *needs* to be guarded. You're the only guardian we deign to listen to. You're the only one who can keep her safe."

I don't think I've ever heard Matthew's voice sound sincere. I don't think I've ever heard him *ask* for anything. It's a shock.

I look at Sean, and it's obvious he's thinking the same thing: Erik was having this conversation on purpose. He must have hidden a recorder in his pocket. But why?

"I'm assuming this *is* the echo of Neil and Alisha's first child?" Erik asks. "Amarra? That's her name?"

I tense, listening so hard my ears twitch.

"You know it is."

"Matthew." Erik's voice is very careful. "I understand why this one is different. I understand that this isn't easy for you. But you have whims. You change your mind in the blink of an eye. You wish for her to be guarded today, but as

361

soon as she bores you, you won't care what happens to her."

"That is an outrageous slur on my character—"

"Shut up for a minute. You've changed. And I'm not entirely sure I can trust you. What good is *my* keeping her safe if she isn't safe from you? If she is in trouble, how much do you truly think *I* could do to save her? Only a Weaver can save her."

Matthew lets out an exasperated breath. "What do you want? My word that if she is ever in trouble, I will do my utmost to save her?"

"It might make me change my mind."

A long, tense pause.

"What exactly are you trying to do, Erik?"

"If you want me to move north for this child, risk my heart, I want a promise in return. You will protect her if she needs you."

Another pause. I realize I'm holding my breath. My ears are ringing. None of this makes any sense to me. It seems like a dream, intangible voices and echoes from long ago that are no longer real or solid or true.

"I have one condition."

Erik sighs. "Here we go."

"I will do what I can for her. *If* she proves herself worthy of it."

"For heaven's sake, Matthew—"

"That's my condition, Erik. I know what I'm asking of you, and so I will give you my word. But I'm not about to risk life and limb for some mewling shrimp of a thing who won't even *try* to save her own skin."

"You *care* for that mewling shrimp of a thing—"

"Only because she's a living, breathing piece of a lost dream." There's scorn in his words, like he's mocking himself. "It's sentimental rubbish and I daresay I'll get over it. The other, the real baby, that girl belongs to Neil and Alisha. But *she* belongs to me. I lost Alisha, but this—"

Silence. All we can hear is the scratching of the recording and the muffled sounds of the baby in the background.

"All right," says Erik, after an eternity. "Keep your condition. But making me a promise isn't enough. You've made declarations before, and you have a rather unscrupulous tendency to weasel your way out of them. This time I want you to give *her* your word."

Matthew's tone changes. He's addressing someone else. "I promise."

His only reply is a delighted baby laugh.

"Thank you," says Erik.

A creak, footsteps, the sound of the door opening again. And then Matthew's voice: "You were always going to change your mind. No matter what I promised."

"I suppose we will never know, will we?"

"*I* know," says Matthew. "Haven't I ever told you? I know everything."

The door closes and the recording goes quiet.

8

DROWNING

Sean presses stop and takes the disk out. He wipes fingerprint smudges off the shiny surface but doesn't speak. He seems as at a loss as I am.

"Why didn't Erik just tell me about this?" I eventually say. "If he made this recording all those years ago because he thought I might need it, why didn't he *tell* me?"

Sean shakes his head. "Matthew was his friend. Still *is* his friend. He wouldn't have wanted to tell you something that would betray Matthew's confidence. So he put it on a disk and put the disk in a safe-deposit box. He knew you'd never touch the box unless you really needed it."

I stare silently at the disk and rub my arms to keep warm. I don't know how to feel about what we've just heard. I can't help thinking about a pale green nursery and a laughing Matthew. I bite my lip angrily. They were just *dreams*, and the recording might make them feel more concrete, but it would be silly to fall into the trap of expecting anything from Matthew now.

"Did you know?" Sean asks. "That Matthew may have once loved Alisha?"

I shrug. "They acted weird around each other. And I overheard Neil and Alisha once. They said things that made me wonder if there used to be something between her and Matthew. Not that it matters," I add. "Whatever it was is long over now. Erik only wanted to help me. But if Matthew ever did care about Alisha or me, and I don't believe he did, he doesn't any longer."

"He's different now," says Sean. "Bitter. Maybe he can't love anyone anymore. Maybe he and Adrian are no longer loyal to anything but each other, who knows? I just can't help wondering why he bothered to find you here, only to let you go. Are you really so sure it wasn't because he *wants* to keep you safe?"

"Yes!" I say, and to my horror, my eyes fill with tears. I blink them sharply away and hold on to the anger instead. "I *am* sure. I don't even believe he was telling the truth in that recording! I think he wanted something from Erik so he said exactly what Erik needed to hear. Everything Matthew does is tricks and games and lies."

Sean stares at me, and there's a mixture of doubt and pity in his face. "That doesn't mean we ought to just forget about it."

"I wasn't planning to. Maybe that disk *can* help us. I don't know." I stand up. "We'll have time later on to think about the disk and find a way to use it. When we're safe, settled somewhere, we can work it out. But right now we need to leave."

"Yeah, we do. And soon."

"Any ideas?"

We both think about it. I latch on to the problem gratefully, glad to push the disk into a boxed-up corner of my mind, and eventually Sean perks up.

"Cromer. It's not a long-term solution, but it should do us fine for the next few days until we're sure where we want to go next. It's on the coast. We can get there on the train and then a bus, I think, but we can look that up. I have a great-aunt who lives there. She likes me. Hates my mother. Hated my father. She's never visited our house, and my dad would never have mentioned her, so the Weavers will have no reason to know she exists. They might get to her eventually, but we should still be safe there for a little while."

"I don't like that you always have good ideas," I say, my annoyance halfhearted at best.

He smiles. "If it's any consolation, I don't know how to avoid getting caught on our way out of London. Even if I had my car, it wouldn't be very smart to use it, and the seekers will be keeping an eye on public transport."

I consider that. It's all too easy to come up with elaborate, outlandish possibilities, but when I was little, Erik taught me that the simplest solutions are usually the best. An image of Ophelia swims to the front of my thoughts. What could be simpler than repeating a mistake that has already gotten us in trouble?

I brighten. "I think I may have a way."

We pack up and make sure to leave the loft exactly as we found it yesterday. As I stuff a few empty wrappers into my bag, I dislodge a photograph. It's one I took only a couple of months ago: Nik and Lekha and Sasha. Nik is standing by the window and Lekha is crouched on the floor next to Sasha, helping her with some wooden blocks. I made them look up and smile when I took the photograph. I'm going to find a way to call them soon. Find out how they are. Let them know we're safe.

A hollow ache swamps my chest. I have only been gone a couple of days, and yet it feels like I left them behind years ago. Them and Mina Ma and Erik and Ray and everything. All of it far behind me and I am drowning in my future and only Amarra still has hold of me.

I put away the photograph and pull out a pack of cards instead. Sean and I play until we sense the theater has gone quiet. Then we pack the cards, take our things, and leave.

We slip out into the square, past the wishing fountain, and onto the street. Sean is clearly on edge and I can't relax either. We both look back, this way, that way, making sure nobody is likely to surprise us. But somehow we manage to talk, too. Almost like a normal boy and girl walking down the street. We talk about music and books and funny things we remember from our lives before I went to Bangalore and where we'd most like to live while we're running.

A long walk later, we stop at a red telephone box and dial a number. My heart quickens, but I take a deep breath.

"Hello?"

The sound of her voice tears holes in my carefully rehearsed speech. I want to scream and cry and wrap my soul around her voice and hug it tightly. My hands curl into fists.

"I want to know why."

Ophelia gasps. "Eva?"

"Don't bother tracing this, I'm not going to stay on the line long." I don't even have to pretend to sound upset or angry. My voice splinters. "I thought—I thought you *loved* us."

"I do!" Her voice is so clear, so sincere, it almost does me in. "I told him *because* I do! I never wanted to hurt you, but you're not safe there, Eva, don't you see that? A hunter almost killed you and if they find you again—"

"And you thought I was better off with Adrian?" I wipe my eyes. "You thought the Loom was a safer place for me?"

"But they won't—"

"No! That's not good enough. I'm going to go now. Tell him what you want. We're flying out of the city tonight. And I will never call you again."

I hang up. My hands are shaking. Sean pulls me closer and I bury my face in his shoulder. He tightens his arm around me.

"Think it'll work?" I say thickly.

His heart beats under my ear. I listen to the rhythm, feeling the slow rise and fall of his chest. He shrugs. "The phone call was reckless and emotional. It'll fit what they know of you. If we're lucky, they'll believe every word you said and they'll concentrate all their attention on the airports." I step back and look up and he smiles crookedly. "It was a neat trick, Eva."

"Only if it works."

We take a taxi to Victoria Coach Station. I study the bus schedule while Sean keeps watch. We figure out a complicated route, taking a series of buses across East Anglia until we eventually end up in Cromer, and get in the queue to buy tickets. It's not yet quite dark outside, but the colors have gone dimmer, the sunlight glowing orangey-gold across the street.

We're third in the queue when a small child in front of us says, in a loud stage whisper, "Mum, look at that man! He doesn't have an ear!"

I stiffen.

"Hush, Terry, don't be rude! And you mustn't point—"

I'm not listening anymore. My heart is pounding too loudly. Next to me Sean is so still he could be made of stone. Then he turns his head and looks over the top of mine.

"Is it them?" I whisper.

He nods. His face is dark and set. "The same two."

I risk a peek and spot them. There are two young men standing patiently by the exit. There is nothing terrible or sinister about them, nothing except the quiet, watchful manner they possess, just like Sean described. One is blue-eyed with short reddish hair and scars across the left half of his face. The other is blond with sweet eyes and a missing ear. They are unmistakably echoes from the Loom's Guard. And they've seen us.

Sean's hand tightens on mine. "Run."

He didn't have to tell me. I am already running, pulling him with me. We run in the opposite direction of the exit, past little old ladies and happy families, down a flight of stairs and out into the underground bus depot. I hear footsteps behind us. Close behind us. I think of the rifles and dogs I saw at Dubai airport during our layover before our flight to Manchester. I remember how the hounds would growl and snap if you got too close. The seekers are the hounds. Persistent and strong and sure. If we don't outrun them, they will chase us down and drag us under, to the dark of the Loom.

They're on the stairs. I look around in panic and dart sideways into the small space between two parked buses.

"Here, quick!"

Sean follows. We kneel on the ground, trying to keep out of sight, our breath coming in short, sharp bursts. It's a hot summer day and the depot feels like an oven. I could be sick from the smells of sweat and grease.

"They found us too fast!" I whisper. "How could they have known we were here? They should have been watching the airports!"

A pained look flickers across Sean's face. "They must have known we were at the theater." He closes his eyes. "They must have followed me back earlier. All that taxi hopping and hanging around Starbucks didn't shake them off as well as I'd hoped."

I squeeze his hand tightly. "It's not your fault. You couldn't have known. We came all the way *here* without having the faintest idea they were watching us. They're very good. This is what they do. It's *not* your fault—"

He clamps a hand over my mouth. "Shh," he says in my ear. In spite of the heat, I feel my body turn cold and prickly. "They're behind the next bus."

I peer around him, looking under the bus, and catch sight of two pairs of legs about thirty feet away. Sean releases me and straightens cautiously. He looks the other way, his brow creased and his eyes searching the depot.

"We're going to have to run before they find us." He points to the yawning entrance at the front of the depot where the buses drive in and out. Beyond it I can see glimmers of dusky sunlight. "It looks like that's our only way out. Are you ready?"

"Now?"

"Now."

We burst out from between the buses and run for the opening. It's so far away. I run faster, as fast as I can. The sunlight grows brighter. I can only just hear the seekers behind us. I don't dare stop to look. They're so precise. They don't call after us or make threats. They simply follow us. Sean's hand feels like the only solid thing in the world.

We're going too fast, and out in the street we stumble into traffic. Sean rips his hand away, his momentum taking him forward, and I fall back. Tires squeal. I run around the car and find Sean on the ground.

"Sean!"

I rush to him, but he's already on his feet. The driver of the car swears at us, but nobody stops to listen. Sean grabs my wrist and we run ahead again, but the seekers have now closed most of the distance between us. There's a cramp in my side, and I feel like I'm being torn in two.

We reach the opening of a tube station. I start down the stairs, but a little boy gets in my way. I stumble to avoid running right into him, and I fall past him down the stairs. The world spins upside down. I crash to the bottom. My head hits the railing.

Pain. Black spots dance in front of my eyes.

A young man takes my hand to help me up. I stare past the dancing spots and see that he has blue eyes. There's no malice there, no spite. He just looks tired.

"This won't hurt," he says.

But it does. In my hand. Only a little bit, like the prick of a safety pin. He puts a needle back in his pocket. I blink at him. And then I can't blink properly. My hand goes numb, and then my arm, and it spreads all the way into the rest of me. The pain in my skull vanishes. I try to speak, but I can't feel my way around my own mouth. My knees give way and the blue-eyed man catches me as I drop.

My eyes are open, but I can't struggle. He carries me away. I can't stop him. I can't feel a thing.

9

LOOM

I see only what is straight ahead of me. A blue-eyed stranger's shoulder. The back of a seat in a car. A tall, ornate gate. Hallways. A flight of stairs up a tower. A tiny window. Then Sean. His face is over mine. He is speaking, but his words don't make much sense. He touches me, but I don't feel it. I try to tell him I'm still here, but I can't. Not yet.

When the feeling finally starts to come back, so does the pain. My head is on fire. It's not the sharp, quick flash of having someone cut into your back. This is a slow burn, a candle held to a single focused point inside my skull, burning hotter and hotter. I hear a low, pained moan and realize it's me. At least I can make sounds again. I thought they'd turned me to stone.

"Eva." Sean sounds almost sharp with relief. "Can you sit up?"

It takes me another minute, but I show him I can.

"I think I'm okay." I test my voice. Flex my fingers. Both shaky but working. "Though my head hurts like you wouldn't believe."

"Theseus told me it was temporary, but I wasn't sure I believed him." I look at him, confused, and he explains. "He's the seeker with the scars. The blue-eyed one. The other one is called Lennox." He makes a sound in his throat. "They were almost nice. Introduced themselves and everything. They even took me back to get our bags. The staff at Victoria wasn't happy about the way we dropped them and ran. I found them still trying to decide whether or not to call a bomb squad."

I feel a sharp surge of dismay. "I didn't see you in the car. I couldn't, my head was turned the wrong way. I hoped you'd gotten away."

"I stopped struggling the moment Theseus stuck the needle in your arm," says Sean. "Wasn't going to let them take you away alone."

"You should've kept running."

He rolls his eyes. "You're an idiot if you thought I would."

He looks as bad as I feel. Blood has congealed on a gash halfway down his arm; there are cuts and scrapes all over his exposed skin. I put a tentative hand to my head and feel my hair matted with dried blood. I wait for panic, for terror, but I only feel exhausted. We've lost.

I think we're on a bed of some kind. The room has stone walls and a window. It's also curved like a slice of a tower. It's not a cell, but it has that sort of feel, with its narrow bed and narrow window and heavy wooden door. My boots are on the floor.

"What was it?" I ask, carefully readjusting my body so that I can lean against the wall behind the bed. "What did he stick me with?"

"Apparently it's some kind of serum Adrian developed. It causes temporary paralysis."

I shudder. "It was horrible. Like you're screaming and struggling in a cage but no one can hear you." I lick my dry lips. "We're still together."

He almost smiles. "I yelled the place down when they tried separating us, so they put us both in here."

"You look awful."

"So do you. Positively ghastly, really."

We laugh, the slightly hysterical laugh of the soon to be destroyed.

"Honestly?" I say. "You look kind of sexy."

"So the bloody, battled look gets you going? And here *I* thought my intellect and wit would be enough."

I smile up at him. "I thought you looked sexy before you were bloody and battled."

A faint flush creeps up his neck, but he grins lopsidedly. "Wish I could say the same for you, but you definitely look sexier with your head half bashed in."

His worried eyes undercut the desperate humor, and soon neither of us is smiling. Cold slips under my skin.

"Are we at the Loom?"

He nods.

I saw photographs of the Loom once. Not of a room

like this, but of outside, the way it looks from the street, beyond the grounds. It is sprawling and austere, with spires and chimneys and a tower at the western corner. It looks like it was once a cathedral and once an opera house and at some point a home to a gentleman who kept his mad wife shut away in the tower.

Bile rises in my throat. I force myself to my feet. My head feels so heavy. I stumble across to the window and breathe in the clean air. When I feel a little better, I look out at the skyline of London. From here, with so many of the new, shinier landmarks out of sight, the city looks hundreds of years old. I have stepped into time and wandered backward to a place where waifs threw themselves in the gleaming river, and chimney sweeps scurried through the dirt, and Weavers and hunters first began their war over life and death.

I am about to turn back to Sean when something catches my eye: letters have been scratched into the windowsill. I try to make them out and realize it's a sentence repeated several times. I AM HENRY WILLOW. I AM HENRY WILLOW. I AM HENRY WILLOW. Who was he? I conjure up memories of long-ago lessons with Erik. I know the first Weaver at the Loom was a Henry *Borden*; I know he made the first echoes here and the Loom has passed down through his family since. But who was Henry Willow? I trace my fingers over the letters. I feel like I understand him. Whoever he was, he was also a prisoner like us. How long would they have to keep me here, in this cold, lost room, before I too tried to scratch my name to remember who I was?

Shivering, I stumble back to the bed and curl up next to Sean again, burrowing close to him for warmth. He puts his uninjured arm around me.

"I think we're in trouble," he says, quite matter-of-factly.

I don't reply. I don't know how we can both escape. All I know is it's *me* they want to destroy. I've got to get him out one way or another.

A new noise makes my stomach clench. We both go quiet and listen. It's the sound of voices outside the heavy door.

I shrink closer to Sean, all my muscles tensing for attack. The door creaks open. Ophelia steps in, fluttering cautiously by the opening.

"Why haven't they seen a doctor yet?" she asks someone out of my line of vision. She sounds worried. "Look at them!"

She steps into the room but doesn't come any closer. Whatever she sees in our faces, it makes her stop.

"Don't look at me like that," she says softly. "I didn't *mean* for them to hurt you. They didn't mean to either, but they have rules. They had to stop you. Oh, Eva. I didn't want to turn you in, but you *are* safer this way. Why can't you see that?"

"Because I was safer out there," I say angrily, "away from the Weavers. Why can't *you* see that?"

"You understand, don't you, Sean? This was the only way I could protect her!"

"*Protect* her?" Sean demands. "What about protecting her from *them*, Ophelia?"

She shakes her head frantically. "But it's not like that at all! The Weavers will vote to save her when she goes to trial. You'll see."

"They've never voted to save anyone—"

"I asked," she says. "I asked my father. Eva, he knows how important you are to me. He said he'd make sure you were spared as long as you were reasonable. And you *will* be reasonable, won't you?"

"Ophelia," says Sean, "your father is *not* going to save her!"

"He wouldn't lie to me!"

"I thought *you* wouldn't turn me in," I say quietly. "People can be wrong."

Ophelia's eyes fill with tears and, impossibly, I feel guilty for upsetting her. "I thought it was the only way to keep you safe," she says. "I'm sorry I hurt you. I'm sorry you hate me right now but I—I did what I thought was b-best! I didn't lie to you. I *did* want to help you. I love you too much to do otherwise. And anyway," she adds, taking a deep breath, "you'll see for yourself in a minute. He wants to talk to you. He's on his way up to the tower."

My heart misses a painful beat. Why would Adrian Borden want to talk to me?

Ophelia glances out into the hallway. "He's here."

A shadow appears in the doorway.

It's a man. About Matthew and Erik's age, late fifties. He is standing absolutely still, but it's the contained stillness of a jungle beast. His shirt is creased; he is wearing socks but no shoes, and there is a feverish cast to his skin that makes me think of Victor Frankenstein, working all hours, day and night, to achieve the impossible. Words pop in my head like corn. *Grave-robbing. Rumors. Obsessions.* I make them go away and I look up into the golden eyes of Adrian Borden.

His voice is quiet, but it reminds me of thunder. Thunder tightly boxed. It makes me afraid of what will happen if the box is broken.

"Take the boy to the next room," he says. "I want to speak to her alone."

Sean and I don't budge.

Adrian makes an impatient sound. "Now."

One of the Guard walks into the room. It's the blue-eyed seeker with the scars. Theseus. I try not to hate him. This is the only life he's known.

"Please come with me," he says very politely.

"Sean, please," Ophelia begs, "for Eva's sake. They're just *talking.*"

Sean's eyes take in everything without expression. Then he stands up and follows the Guard out of the room.

"Don't worry," Adrian tells me, "I will have him brought back after we've talked. Ophelia," he adds, with a shade of something like warmth in his dark, indifferent voice, "I'd like you to leave, too."

Ophelia leaves the room and shuts the door quietly.

"May I?" Adrian gestures to the chair by the battered old desk.

"It's your Loom."

He smiles. It's not a nice smile. "Yes, it is, isn't it? I thought you may have forgotten that."

I don't answer. My heart pounds.

"Do I frighten you?"

I shake my head defiantly.

"I think I do," he says, amused. "But you put on a bold face. I like that." He moves the chair to the edge of the bed and sits down. He rests his elbows on his knees and looks at me for a moment or two.

I force myself to look back.

His eyes sharpen to gold points, splintering me. I swallow.

"I expect you understand that when an echo runs away, breaks from their purpose as you've done, they forfeit the life we've given them." Adrian straightens the rumpled edge of the bedsheet. "It's been thirty-four years since I inherited the Loom. In that time, three echoes have tried to run. All three were subsequently destroyed. Do you see where this is going?"

"Did you come here to tell me what I already know?"

He raises his eyebrows. "Matthew told me you weren't the meek sort," he says. "I usually put everything he says down to exaggeration, but with you I see he was spot-on. It's obvious you're one of his, you know. Uninterested in rules. Reckless. Temperamental. My echoes tend to be more calculating and more restrained. Elsa's are gentler."

I don't know what to say to that, so I stay quiet.

"I assume Ophelia told you she has asked me to spare your life at your trial?"

I nod carefully.

"Echoes are rare beings," says Adrian. "We gave you life. You were nothing before us. Bones and dust. I think it's a terrible waste when your lives are destroyed because you've been so careless with them. For that reason I'm willing to indulge my daughter. I will spare you."

Hearing it from him, in a voice that leaves me in no doubt that he means every word, it makes me take a sharp breath. Everything I have ever heard about Adrian, everything in his voice now, tells me that he does not play games like Matthew does. He's ruthless. He will do what it takes to get what he wants. He won't dance around it because it amuses him.

And remembering this makes my hope gutter and die again.

I will spare you.

"And what would you want in exchange?"

"Your help."

"*My* help?"

"We made you," says Adrian, his eyes like two bright sparks, "but there's still so much about you we don't fully understand. So much potential that could be harnessed. I have created life, but that isn't enough. What if I could find a way to prolong it? What if we *perfected* you? I could transform the world. Defeat death. If I could prolong my own life, I could work for another hundred years, another thousand, if it came to that. It's unthinkable to me to die before I achieve everything I intend to. We have broken one of the greatest barriers set on humankind. I've stitched life from dust and bones. I will break the others."

I open my mouth, but nothing comes out.

"Unfortunately . . ." He sighs. "I can't experiment with these ideas without studying echoes. You tread the line between life and death. You could be very useful to me. You're young. Healthy. Whole. If you gave me two years of your life, even less perhaps, I could study you."

I stare at him in horror. "Why can't you create an echo just to study him or her?" But even as I say it, I realize what a terrible thing that would be. To create someone to be nothing but a guinea pig, a tool to be played with.

"I have," says Adrian, without pity. "I once created two copies of an other, instead of one, and kept the second. Naturally, the familiars weren't aware of this. But creating an echo isn't as simple as snapping my fingers. It is a difficult and time-consuming thing, and I have to save my time for copies like you." He shrugs. "Others have been persuaded to help me in the past. But I'm not quite *there* yet. You would live here and be completely cared for. Any pain that resulted from the experiments wouldn't last long. When I've learned all that I can from you, you would be free to leave."

"Don't you have to ask the other Weavers before you

give me a choice like this? What if Elsa or Matthew thinks I should be destroyed?"

"I doubt they will feel strongly enough to disagree with me," says Adrian, unperturbed.

Then he must believe Elsa will simply be happy to spare somebody's life—but what about Matthew? Is he so sure of their friendship that he knows Matthew won't care enough to object to this experiment?

"This is your only way out," Adrian adds, in a harder, colder voice, "the only way to survive now."

"You said you'd spare me. From trial. But what about the Sleep Order? I ran away to escape it. If I help you, will you revoke that, too?"

"Like I said, you would be free to leave. Bear in mind your familiars signed the order. It was their choice to make. I can't force them to take you back. If, when the time comes, they refuse to take you, we will have to find an alternative life for you. But I will revoke the Sleep Order. You will live."

"And what if I'd rather die?" I ask him.

"You *will* die," he assures me. "The way things stand, you won't last long at trial." His gold eyes are pitiless. "I'm offering you a chance. Take it."

I swallow hard. I know exactly what I want to tell him. I don't even have to think about it. The thought of being treated like a toy for months, of putting my fate in Adrian's hands because he wants to do the impossible, is appalling. It saves me from trial. It saves me from the Sleep Order. But at such a heavy price.

And then, before I can offer an impulsive, passionate reply, a little voice in my head reminds me to stop and *think*. It sounds like sense. It sounds like Amarra.

And it tells me to ask him one more question.

"What about Sean?"

"The boy?"

"Yes. If I agree to this, what happens to him?"

Adrian cocks his head and considers me. His gaze is shrewd. "What would you like to happen to him?"

"I forced him to help me," I say, weighing each word carefully, "so it doesn't seem fair that he should be punished. If I agree to stay, I want him to be allowed to leave. Now. I know you can't let him be a guardian anymore, but I want that to be his only punishment. You can't hand him over to the police or lock him up or whatever it is you do to guardians who break your laws."

"Very well," says Adrian, and from the tone of his voice I know he doesn't believe a word of my lie. "He can leave. Right away, if you like." He is dismissive. "I don't care about the boy. He doesn't interest me."

I take a deep breath and let it out again in a rush of relief. I swallow back the sour taste on my tongue.

"Then I'll stay. I'll help you."

"Very good." Adrian stands. "I told Ophelia you'd make the sensible choice. We'll begin work tomorrow."

Tomorrow. I shiver. That leaves me very little time.

Adrian opens the door. Ophelia and the blue-eyed Guard are on the other side. Ophelia looks so anxious it's almost difficult to stay angry with her.

"Bring the boy back," says Adrian, sounding satisfied. The Guard nods and steps out of sight. Adrian smiles at Ophelia. She looks relieved. It's a slightly nicer smile than any he gave me. "We've worked something out."

I don't think she knows what he offered me. He glances at me. Waiting. My tongue sticks to the roof of my mouth. I could tell Ophelia everything. Tell her that her father set a price on my life. Tell her what the price is. It looks like he's been a good father to her, and I get that she only turned me in because she believed I'd be safe with him. I'm sure there is something good there that she sees and loves. But I could tell her the truth and take it away. I could destroy her love for him. Destroy her.

And he knows I won't.

"I'm so glad," Ophelia says, smiling at me. "I told you it would be all right, Eva. This has all worked out for the best."

"It has." Adrian sounds pleased. Now that he has what he wants, he can afford to be generous. "Give her a moment alone to say good-bye to the boy."

"You mean he's—you're letting him go?"

The Guard returns with Sean. Adrian glances at me. "Five minutes," he says, and turns back to the Guard. "Theseus, send someone to fetch the boy's things."

Then he strides away and they shut the door again.

"What was that?" Sean demands. "Why are they giving me back my stuff?"

I gulp. I didn't expect the words to claw their way so painfully through my throat. "I— They've let you go," I say. "You're leaving."

"What are you talking about?"

I tell him. My tongue feels thick and heavy and the look on his face makes it a thousand times worse, but I tell him everything.

He stares at me, deathly white. "You can't do this. You can't make me leave."

"You can't *want* to stay here!"

"Not *here*, Eva. With *you*."

"You have a life," I say as the first tears slip down my face. "And if I'd said no, you would've lost everything. I don't know where they'd have sent you. This way neither of us needs to run. Neither of us will be in any danger. This is the *only* way I know to save you. Sean—" My voice cracks. "*Please*. Let me do it."

He dashes at his eyes. "You're asking me to leave you here, to become nothing more than a neat little puzzle for him to use and break, one of his experiments—"

"Yes."

"Eva—"

"Please."

Sean gazes at me for a long moment, his dark green eyes burning straight into mine. I want to look away but I can't.

"All right," he says. I flinch at how polite his tone is. It's worse than outright anger. "If this is what you want, God forbid I stop you."

He crosses the room to the door and knocks so that they'll let him out. At the last minute he turns back and kisses me fiercely and I taste blood and tears and something else, something so Sean-like I want to grab hold of his shirt and never let go. When he pulls away, I catch a look in his eyes that tells me he will never forgive me.

Then, just like that, he's gone.

Sunlight turns dust motes in the room to gold. I watch them swirl in the air. I feel a thousand times worse than I did half an hour ago. I feel raw and bruised and the red-hot pain in my head hasn't gone away.

I don't have much time. Tomorrow Adrian means to start studying me. Today is nearly over. If I want to escape the Loom, escape a choice between certain death and Adrian, I have to find a way out soon. I close my eyes. If nothing else, at least I got Sean out. If I can't do the same for myself, at least I know he won't suffer the consequences of my choices.

Amarra used to read books about battles. Great heroic battles. Swords and shields and knights and honor. Battles like that don't happen anymore, yet I feel like I am caught in one. Once I may have hoped to fight for my life with all those things: swords and shields and knights and honor. But I don't have a sword. My shield is broken. I don't know what is and isn't honorable anymore. And now I've sent my knight away.

10

COST

They give me water and a late dinner, but I eat very little. I search the tray for anything I can use as a weapon, but they've been careful; there are no forks, no knives, no sharp ends.

Ophelia comes to see me a few times. She stays long enough to tell me that Erik is on his way to London. I find that slightly cheering. I want desperately to see Erik again.

"Eva?" Ophelia pauses before leaving. It's a desperate attempt to reach me. "Please talk to me."

She sniffs and kisses the top of my head. I don't pull away from her, but I don't reply. I want to tell her I understand. I get it. But that it hurts anyway. I trusted her and she knew it and used it against me.

"I love you. Remember that."

After she leaves, I curl up on the bed with a lump in my throat, exhausted with pain and hurt and just plain tired after a very, very long few days.

I try to catch a few hours' sleep and regain some energy. But it's not very restful. I dream of a nursery and a clock, and

Matthew sings me songs about beautiful, eerie things. I wake up and don't feel much better.

It's bitterly lonely in this tiny room. The words scratched painstakingly into the window seem clearer every time I look at them. I imagine scratching I AM EVA under I AM HENRY WILLOW.

I look for a way out. I check the window, but it's much too small for even someone of my size to squeeze through. It's too high off the ground anyway, and there's no ledge or foothold nearby. I try everything. I scrape at the wall, but the walls are too thick and solid for me to scratch my way through. I search for holes or vents in the ground and find nothing. I test the door, but the wood is solid. Not that breaking it would help me: I'd only tumble out at the Guard's feet. Theseus is polite, but I haven't made the mistake of underestimating him. I have no doubt he will be quick to use his knife if I attack him first.

At least I got Sean out. It's the one good thing I keep repeating to myself, over and over, each time trying not to remember the look on his face or the way he kissed me before he left. He's safe. That's something. It might even be enough.

I hear a sound at the door and jerk upright.

The key in the lock. I wrap my arms around my knees and watch the door warily. Ophelia? I'm aware of a smidgeon of hope: Erik?

The door swings open. I see a plump, sturdy woman with a fierce face and hair like the round-topped ashoka trees.

All the breath is sucked straight out of my lungs.

Mina Ma clomps her way in and deliberately bangs the door shut behind her. She's all strength and fury. I throw myself into her arms and promptly burst into tears. She smells like butter.

"Hush, child, enough of this," she says briskly, but her words don't mean anything, not when she's clutching me as hard as I'm holding her and she sounds like she's trying not to cry herself. "We have better things to do with our time."

"W-what are you d-doing here?" I blubber, trying and failing to get a grip on myself. I never dreamed I'd see her again. I never thought they'd allow it.

"Why do you imagine I'm here?" she demands. "What a goose. I came as soon as I heard they had caught you."

"And they let you see me?"

Mina Ma gives me a brief, smug look. "I chose to ask the right Weaver. I have been talking to Elsa." Her face darkens. "She has been telling me some strange things. About you and Adrian Borden."

Heat creeps up my neck and it's all I can do to meet her eye. I wipe the last of my tears away. "So he's already told her what he offered me?"

"Yes. Also that you *agreed*."

I bite my lip. I don't know what to say.

"She also mentioned that part of the offer involved letting Sean go." Mina Ma's eyes narrow on my face. "Interesting, eh? You wouldn't have agreed to this monstrosity just to make sure Sean was safe, would you?"

"I—" I try to look her in the eye. "You know about the Sleep Order. I had to do whatever I could to survive."

"And you will stay here? *Help* him?"

There's something about Mina Ma's tone that makes my lies wither. "No," I say, letting out a heavy breath. "I had no intention of staying if I could help it. I meant to find a way out. But there's no way out of this room. I have no ideas left."

A grave look crosses her face. She watches me for a long time. Then she reaches into the folds of her sari and carefully withdraws a steak knife. My mouth falls open.

"I don't like it," she says. "Knives, they're not nice. But this is not a nice situation either."

"Didn't they search you before they let you see me?"

Mina Ma almost snorts. "After the way I stood there abusing them? I assure you, they wanted to get it over with as quickly as possible. At any rate, I don't think they understand saris, poor things. They didn't even think to look in the pleats."

I choke on my own laughter. It dies almost immediately. It was too strange a sound in this desolate room.

Mina Ma sighs. "My advice," she says reluctantly, "is to use that on Ophelia. No," she adds, when I recoil, "I don't mean it that way. I mean you should threaten her with it. Make the Guard think you will cause her harm if he doesn't let you go. We can only hope she will be sensible and realize you don't *actually* intend to hurt her. We don't want to scare her. Not," she says darkly, "that she doesn't deserve it. But I suppose she thought she was doing what was best. She always tries so hard to please everybody."

I stare at the knife, wondering if I can really threaten someone with it, someone I love. Mina Ma tips my chin up.

"Be brave," she says, "and everything will be all right. I will go get Ophelia. I will tell her you want to talk to her."

"Wait. You knew I would want to get out? You knew I never intended to stay here with the Weavers?"

"You may have been gone for the better part of a year," says Mina Ma tartly, "but you're still the girl I raised. It wasn't *Erik* who taught you to be sneaky, I promise you."

I put my arms around her and hug her tightly. I don't think I've ever been so scared or unsure in my life, but I'm going to get out. One way or another I will get past the Guard and find my way out of the Loom.

"Thank you," I whisper.

"No," says Mina Ma, "thank *you*. Thank you for being mad enough to run. I could not have borne it if you had stayed and allowed the Sleep Order to destroy you."

She wipes her eyes and marches to the door. She bangs on it.

"Oy!"

I hide a grin as Theseus unlocks and opens the door. He looks terrified of her. I actually feel sorry for him.

When I am alone again I pick up the knife. It feels cold

and alien in my hand. What if I make a mistake and the knife slips? What if I hurt her? My stomach roils and I squash the feeling. I have to do whatever it takes, or there's no point trying to escape.

It can't be more than twenty minutes before I hear the key in the lock again. It feels like an eternity. Each minute I wait drains a little bit more of my nerve.

As the door opens my heart begins to race. Too fast. Too loudly.

"I'll wait for you on the tower stairs," says Mina Ma. It sounds like she's talking to Ophelia. I know she's talking to me.

"Eva?" Ophelia looks tentative. Hopeful.

I almost give up. The *look* on her face. To threaten her now seems like such a dirty trick. Then I remember that I wouldn't be here if it wasn't for her, and the pounding of my heart becomes a roar that drowns everything out. Mina Ma walks away and vanishes down the stairs. I take a step forward and press my shaking hand and the flat of the knife to Ophelia's ribs.

"Sorry," I whisper. I hope she believes me. I hope she understands why I'm doing this. I hope I don't make a mistake.

The Guard recoils. His blue eyes widen. "Where did you get that knife?"

"You didn't search me properly when you caught me. That was a mistake." My voice sounds amazingly calm.

I hold on to that sound, I cling to the calm. "Could you please step away from the stairs and let me pass by? I won't let Ophelia go until I've gotten to the bottom of this tower. But I'm not going to hurt her unless you do something stupid."

"Eva, please—"

"Don't." I cut Ophelia off, and there's a tremor in my voice for the first time. "Don't make this any harder."

I cautiously walk toward the stairs. I have one hand clamped around Ophelia's arm to make sure she doesn't try breaking free of me. The other keeps the flat of the knife against her ribs. Tiny drops of sweat trickle down my back.

Theseus backs up but refuses to get out of the way. He's blocking my only way out. He has drawn his knife and holds it with the point down. Unthreatening.

"I can't let you leave the tower," he says quietly.

"I have a *knife* in my hand!" I snap. "Do you really think I won't use it? Do you think Adrian will be happy you obeyed orders and allowed his daughter to be hurt?"

"I do what I'm told."

"And I'm telling you—"

"I do what the Weavers tell me to."

Ophelia makes a piteous sound. She looks so hurt and bewildered, I would have relented if my life weren't at stake. Even so, guilt burns holes through my skin.

"Do what she says, Theseus," she pleads.

"I can't," he replies. His voice has an odd sticking sound, as though he isn't used to speaking unless it's necessary.

"Forgive me. But I can't let her leave."

A low thrumming fills my ears. Panic. Butterfly wings against my brain. Nobody moves. I flick frightened eyes between Theseus and Ophelia, between the knife in my hand and the one in his. He doesn't waver. And I realize that this isn't a time to be standing still and trying to think. I have to act. I have to do *something*.

I throw the knife at the Guard. I don't aim for him. I don't want to hit him. I just throw it in his direction. I pray that no matter how devoted to the Weavers he is, he is still human enough to react.

He does. His eyes widen and he ducks out of the way. He slams back against the wall behind him as the knife clatters past him down the stairs.

I let Ophelia go and run. I have just reached the stairs when Theseus, on his feet again, springs forward. The knife flashes. I skid to a halt and skitter backward. The stairs are blocked again, the knife missing me by inches.

And maybe it would have been okay if it had ended there. He'd have put me back in my room. Nothing would have changed.

Only Ophelia sees the knife flash and cries out, "No! No, don't hurt her!"

I see her run at his arm, try to stop him.

"Don't—" I scream.

The Guard jerks back. I try to imagine what he must have seen. A woman rushing at him. The stairs right behind him.

If she pushed him, ran into him, she would have sent them both tumbling down the stairs. They could have broken their necks. He swings his arm around to stop her, but this makes the knife swing around too. It takes a split second, but even then I know, I can see, that he doesn't mean to *use* the knife. It simply gets in the way.

There's a horrible squelching sound. And a ragged gasp.

I cover my mouth to stop a second scream.

Theseus drops the knife in horror. The blade looks almost black in the lamplight.

"I—I didn't mean . . . I didn't—"

I rush to Ophelia's side. At the same time Mina Ma comes running up the stairs. She wouldn't have been far. She must have heard my scream.

She gasps. "Ay Shiva, what have you done, you silly boy?" She kneels on the floor and gently lifts Ophelia's head onto her lap. "You!" she barks at Theseus. "Give me your shirt! We have to try and stop this bleeding."

Theseus obeys. Mina Ma balls the shirt up and presses it to the wound spreading a dark stain over Ophelia's dress. She looks so small, her blond hair spilling across my hand. Her eyes stare at me for a few minutes, shocked, pained. Then she smiles.

Then her eyes close.

"No!" I shout. "No! Ophelia!" A sob bursts through my chest. "No!"

Someone kneels beside me, reaching for her pulse, at her

throat, at her wrist. I realize it's the Guard.

"Get off!" I push him away, sobbing. "She's hurt and you did it!"

But that isn't entirely true. I held a knife to her and put her in that position. *We* did this. Both of us.

"It was an accident," the Guard says hoarsely. His blue eyes are wide. "I . . . I didn't want to do any harm to anyone."

I don't argue. How can I? He is the enemy. He does whatever the Weavers ask of him. He may have killed echoes, maybe ordinary people too. But in spite of all that, I know he didn't mean to use the knife on her.

Mina Ma's voice is unsteady, but she makes herself sound calm. Quiet. "Enough," she says. "Stay calm. You must go get some help."

He hesitates. Glances at me. "But the girl—"

"Do you think I can't control an echo I raised from babyhood?" Mina Ma demands. "Idiot! Go! Quickly!"

Theseus goes. I barely hear him running. He has a swift, sure way of moving. His feet make so little sound. Like mine.

A weary misery floods me. I don't know what to do. Ophelia is bleeding, and it's my fault this happened. Everything I care about, everything I love, is slipping away.

"Eva."

Mina Ma's voice is firm. Deliberate.

"It's time for you to go."

"What?" I stare at her in dismay. "But—but Ophelia . . . I can't leave her—"

"I will look after her. That Guard will bring help and she will heal. You must get out while you can. You will never have a chance like this again. Eva!" She reaches over Ophelia to shake me. "You *must*. For my sake. If you don't, you will be condemned to die. Or at the very least, you will be forced to honor the agreement you made with Adrian."

I choke on the words. "And Ophelia—"

"The wound is not as bad as it looks," says Mina Ma steadily. She looks me in the eye. "She *will* heal. She will be fine. You must go *now*."

I stroke Ophelia's cheek. My thumb leaves a bloody stain. She wanted me to forgive her, but I didn't. She betrayed me and I almost destroyed her. I fought to save Sean. I fought to survive. And I've done it, I've found a way out of the Loom, but at what cost? There's always a price. I stare down at her face and all I can think of is five little ducks, five little ducks, of the ducks going over the hill and far away and of fewer and fewer coming back, each one vanishing. . . .

I gaze back into Mina Ma's eyes. Ophelia will be okay. She will get better. Mina Ma wouldn't lie to me.

"Go!" she snaps.

I swallow a sob and run.

11

GREEN

I must be less than a dozen steps away from the bottom of the tower when I hear footsteps running close by. I duck into the nearest alcove, behind an old suit of armor, my heart racing. I can't get the thought of Ophelia and that dark stain on her dress out of my head. My skin is soaked in cold sweat.

Theseus and a woman in a white coat hurry past the alcove, up the stairs. I must have heard the doctor's footsteps. Theseus is too quiet. They don't see me.

I wait until the footsteps have faded away before continuing down the stairs. I slow at the bottom. Warily. I look around, checking the hallways. There is no one in sight. I don't know my way around the Loom. I don't know how to get out. I can't use the doors. They will be guarded. Right now all I can hope for is to find an empty room on the ground floor and get out through a window.

Without being seen.

In a minute Theseus will reach the top of the tower and will see that I've escaped Mina Ma. I have to be quick. They will start looking for me.

I run down the hallway and turn the corner, choosing my path blindly, letting my feet choose the way for me. They don't falter. They keep running. Like they know where they're going. The pillars and stone of the Loom tower above me, and a host of gargoyles leer down from the walls. I try doors as I run farther away from the tower. Most of the doors are locked, and the windows in the hallways are sealed with double-glazed glass.

There's an archway ahead. I pass through it and the decor changes subtly, becoming woodier and paneled, slightly warmer than the stone. I reach for a doorknob but stop when I hear a sound. My heart jolts. *Listen.*

Someone pacing. Voices behind the door. I strain my ears, but the words are muffled. Is that . . . Matthew?

I don't wait to hear any more. I race down the corridor until I reach a door that opens when I turn the knob. I almost weep in relief.

I rush in and close the door quietly behind me. There's no lock. It doesn't matter. It will have to do.

Each breath feels like a needle is being pierced through my ribs. I lean back against the door to catch my breath. I sound like an old man with a rattling in his chest. I take a moment to breathe in and out. Slower and slower until the needles are gone.

Something flutters against my cheek. I almost let out a cry, then realize it's only a dirty gray cobweb that must have shaken loose from the door when I opened and closed it.

The room is full of cobwebs. It looks like no one has come in here in years. Not even to clean the place. I stare at the dark shadows of furniture and cobwebs dangling like nooses from the ceiling.

As my eyes adjust to the dark in the room, I see the outline of a window across the room. It's large and deep and covered with blinds, but I can see moonlight behind them. That's my way out. I pick my way carefully across the room but stumble into something. I stifle a yelp and grab hold of it to keep it from falling over. Someone might hear the crash. It moves in my hand. Like it's rocking.

A crib. Or a rocking stand with something on it. I feel for it. A basket?

For a baby?

I stumble over to the wall and feel for a light switch. Eventually I find one and press down. A lamp flickers to life in the ceiling. It lights everything up: the cobwebs, the rocking basket, the clock, the thick layer of dust, the sad look of neglect. And it lights up the walls. The wallpaper is green. A pale green, faded with time.

This is a nursery. *My* nursery.

My head swims dizzily, and I have to hold on to the wall for support. For a moment the dust and the cobwebs are gone and the room is bright with sunlight and toys. I have yellow pajamas and the basket is being rocked. It was real. I lived here for a little while after I was made. Matthew rocked me and sang me songs about cities. Once, the bitter, drawling

402

Weaver *laughed*. Did he love me? Because he made me, made me for Alisha? I don't know. But I know he laughed. They weren't just dreams. They really happened.

And then I was taken away to be what an echo is supposed to be. And no one's come into this room since. Not after I left it behind.

"Oh my god," I stammer into the silence.

If the dreams were real, it means the recording was too. Everything on the disk Erik gave me really happened. And those things, they weren't just real: they were *true*.

Because if they weren't true, if Matthew made us a promise he never intended to keep, then this room would be long gone by now. It would have caused him no pain. He would have repapered it and thrown out the furniture and used it for some other purpose. And he would have forgotten. But it's still here, exactly the way I left it, and that means he hasn't forgotten. If the room still exists, so does a part of the Matthew who swore he would save me.

I reel from the shock. I am swallowed by my life, by seventeen years, and suddenly I can see everything, but it has been stripped bare and the only thing that shows up is the color green. Green wallpaper. A scarf on a lady at a shop. Mina Ma's sari. Finger paints. The grass beneath an elephant's stamping feet. A balloon. Sean's eyes. Green wallpaper. I began in green and may now end in green. I was given a life in a green room. And now I've come back, after all this time, and it's in a green room, once again, that

I must take back that life.

The clock chimes once. It's a broken and lost sound, like there's not much left in the clock. It makes me jump.

I dig my fingernails into my palms. My eyes drift to the window, but I turn away. My heart is a bird. Fluttering against my ribs, trying to break away, but I ignore it. I sit down in an old rocking chair, among the dust and the ruin, and I wait.

Five minutes. Ten. Fifteen. Then I hear footsteps in the corridor. More than one pair, and none of the Guard among them. The treads are too loud and too firm.

The door opens. Adrian stalks in first, Matthew a reluctant step behind him. He doesn't want to enter the room. But he does.

Adrian's eyes burn with the coldest hate I've ever seen. He opens his mouth to speak and then closes it again. For a brief moment he looks uncertain. They expected to burst in here and find me in a panic, trying to break out of the window. Or to find me already gone. But I'm here and I'm just sitting in this chair, watching them. It makes them wary.

Matthew narrows his eyes. Adrian glances at him and back at me and his voice is icy. "Would you care to explain what the devil she's doing, Matthew?"

"Meaning what?"

"Meaning . . ." Adrian takes a threatening step in my direction. I can almost see his fingers itch to close around my throat. "She was waiting for us. Why would she do that?"

Before anyone can say anything more, there's a clatter of footsteps down the hallway, and then a woman sweeps into the room. She's not alone; Erik and Mina Ma are with her. I feel a rush of warmth at seeing them. Erik's eyes widen and he makes a jerky move, as though to grab me and hug me and conceal me from Adrian, but he stops himself. Mina Ma seems furious. For a minute it looks like she is going to demand to know why I'm still here and expose the part she played in my escape.

"You're Elsa," I say to the other woman. "Elsa Connelly." Her hair is still golden and her face is calm and unlined, but there's a hint of steel in the line of her mouth. Her eyes reveal her to be older than she looks: they're sad and weary.

I've dreamed of her, too. She stood in my dreams with sad eyes and asked me what my heart desired.

"Yes," she replies, almost kindly, "and you are Eva. Is that correct?"

I nod.

"That is *not* her name," snaps Adrian. A chill skitters down my spine as his eyes burn gold into me. He didn't look at me with so much hate before. Now it couldn't be clearer that he wants few things more than to kill me and be done with it.

"Eva," says Erik, looking pained, "you understand that you will go to trial, don't you?"

I start to reply, but Adrian cuts in. "I think we can dispense with the formalities and get it done here. Now. We have an array of charges to choose from. Any one of them is enough to allow us to be rid of her." He gives a bitter laugh. "Taking her own name, running away, consorting with a guardian, causing the death of a guardian—"

"What?" I stand up and stare at him. "What are you talking about?"

Adrian takes a step closer. I brace myself, but he makes no move to touch me. "Are you telling me you've already forgotten about Ophelia? My daughter has been cold less than an hour and you've already forgotten what you did?"

"Cold?" I repeat stupidly. Horror grips me so tightly I can't breathe. "*Dead*, you mean? But she's not! She wasn't hurt that badly, she was okay—"

I catch Mina Ma's eye and the words die on my lips. She doesn't even look guilty. And I know from the look on her face that Ophelia *was* hurt that badly. She was never going to heal. A pain builds in the back of my throat, a silent scream itching to come out. She smiled at me and she closed her eyes and she never opened them again.

For half a second I am so angry with Mina Ma I am almost sure I will never forgive her. But it's gone as quickly as it comes, because I realize it's no different from what I did to Sean. She lied so that I would run. She lied to save me. How can I hate her for that?

"Adrian, that was a tragic accident," Elsa interjects. She looks terribly sorry for him, but she is firm. "Theseus told us what happened. This child is no more responsible for

Ophelia's choices than you are."

His expression doesn't change. He knows it would never have happened if I hadn't threatened her with that knife. That's all that matters to him.

My legs can hardly hold me. I felt so strong a minute ago, and now I want to crumple and fade away. I can't make Ophelia and death fit together. A fresh spasm of pain rocks me. Am I going to hurt everyone I love in this desperate bid to survive?

I could step back and let them have their trial and end everything. The fight has almost all gone out of me. Almost. And then I remember the way Sean kissed me as he left. How alive I felt. And I think of Sasha in her little pajamas with her too-big yawns. And I glance at Matthew, who has been silent so far, and there is a hard, mocking, *waiting* look on his face that makes me straighten my spine once again.

"You made a promise once."

My voice echoes into the dusty silence. Matthew's eyes flicker. Adrian looks at me in disbelief. And then his eyes turn, hard and accusing, to Erik.

"He didn't tell me anything." I speak carefully so that I need only tell as few lies as possible. I rub my eyes, rub away the tears. "He didn't say anything. I was there too. Remember?"

Adrian gives a sharp laugh. "This is outrageous. Matthew?"

"There is a teeny, tiny, *infinitesimal* possibility," says

Matthew, idly studying his fingernails, "that Eva may be correct."

A terrible silence. When Adrian speaks, his tone is dangerous. "And what, precisely, did this promise involve?"

"Matthew swore to save Eva if she was ever in danger from the Loom," says Erik.

Matthew clears his throat. "I seem to recall the promise was contingent on her proving herself worthy."

"I am worthy." I look him in the eye. "You want me to run? I've done that. Fight my way out? I've done that too. I'm here, aren't I? You told me to find a way out of the noose and I did. I ran away. I would still be running if you hadn't gotten lucky. Your seekers found us because they were *told* where to look." I can't make myself say Ophelia's name. It hurts too much. I point to the window. "It wouldn't have been hard to climb out of there and escape. You wouldn't have found me here if I hadn't chosen to wait. Amarra tried to take my life from me, and I cut out my tracker because I had no other choice. But now there's another way. I've done everything in my power to save myself. Now I need you to honor your promise."

My hands are shaking, but I knit them tightly together. In the silence all I can hear is the sound of my heart. It sounds so alive.

"You can't be considering this," says Adrian at last. His eyes are on Matthew. He sounds like winter. The icy winds that cut your skin like knives. "You can't sidestep a trial and a Sleep Order because of a promise you once made behind our backs."

"*You* would have done it," says Matthew. "*You* sidestepped everything only hours ago, when you made her your offer. That was somewhat behind our backs too."

Adrian's lips become a hard, flat line. "*My* offer would have kept her under our watch. It would have kept her under control, which is something you have all failed abysmally to do."

"That I can't deny," Matthew admits.

Adrian glances bitterly at him. "And I suppose you will insist on taking her side."

"Don't be absurd."

Adrian smiles faintly. Almost ruefully. "How did she cause so much trouble?"

"Good question." Matthew studies my face. "She looks so small, so fragile. How *did* you turn the Loom upside down, Eva?"

"I just wanted my life back," I answer.

"Oh?" Adrian's eyes glitter. "And so you fought for it. Whatever the cost. Matthew, would you truly ask me to let her go now? My daughter is dead."

"Do you imagine Eva will ever forget what winning her life back cost?" Erik demands. "Do you really not believe Ophelia's *life* is a steep enough price to pay? You weren't the only one who cared for your daughter. Eva did too."

"Funny," says Adrian, "she didn't act like it. Threatened

her with a steak knife, didn't she? Or was that supposed to be a loving gesture?"

"Adrian—"

"That's enough." Adrian's voice is quiet, but it echoes like thunder through the auditorium. It silences everybody. Only Matthew looks at ease. He even looks like he's conferring a great honor on Adrian by deigning to remain quiet. "We will put her on trial and she will be punished."

"You can't ignore everything Eva has said," Elsa cuts in. "You can't just pretend Matthew never swore he would—"

"And yet you can see I am ignoring it rather successfully, Elsa. People sometimes keep their promises," he acknowledges. "People like Erik, for example. For all your faults, Erik, you do have an irritatingly moral streak. But not Matthew. When has Matthew ever been honorable?"

"People always expect the worst of me." Matthew sounds mournful. "But I will grant I am not exactly trustworthy, and alas, I *have* proven duplicitous in the past, so there is an outside chance I may have deserved that."

Erik's jaw tightens. "What you swore that day, in this room, that was different."

"It makes no difference to me." Adrian puts a hand out and seizes me by the back of my neck. "There is nothing stopping me from destroying her now. This very moment." I try to wriggle free, but his fingers are steel biting into my skin. It feels like he could rip me apart with just that one hand. His eyes are not on me. They're on Matthew. Waiting.

"Well? Will you stop me?"

Matthew seems particularly interested in his fingernails today. "Go on, then."

"No!" Mina Ma shouts.

I struggle wildly, but the grip on my neck only tightens. Erik takes a step forward, and Matthew puts up a hand to stop him. Rage radiates off Mina Ma like ocean waves during a storm.

"He won't do it." Matthew smiles at Adrian. "You would no more stick a knife into me than I would into you."

Does that mean he still cares about me? Otherwise I have no idea how destroying me could correlate in any way to Adrian sticking a knife into Matthew. It seems to make sense to Adrian, because he lets me go. I look between him and Matthew, and for some reason I think of an elastic band tying them together: a band made up of friendship and loyalty and secrets and the dark obsessions of the Loom. When they make conflicting choices the band is stretched and pulled, but it is elastic, so it doesn't break. Instead, the two ends snap together again. And I understand that I'm a force pulling at one end and no matter how far I pull, the ends will always snap back together. No matter what Matthew chooses to do about his promise, he will always be on Adrian's side. There is not much left of the man who sang lullabies in a pale green nursery.

But there might be *just* enough.

"We *could* go to trial and satisfy your thirst for blood,

Adrian," says Matthew. "But it would be such a waste of time, and I am due to have tea with a *very* important person in the morning. Let the girl go. Revoke the Sleep Order. We can't have her running around, doing what she likes, so send her back to her familiars. I think you'll find they are willing to keep her." Suddenly he looks tired and bitter. "I'm done talking about this."

"I agree," says Elsa. There's a funny look in her eye, like she's watching the world she knows collapse and that pleases her. "If we *did* go to trial, Adrian, you would be outvoted."

I don't dare feel relieved. Not yet. Winning my life back, having it in my own two hands again, it doesn't seem real yet.

Adrian doesn't speak for a long time. His silence is far more chilling than any open rage. Then he smiles and I shiver. Beneath the smile is fury, and grief, and hate. He will never forget how Ophelia died. He will never forget that he wanted to punish me and I got away.

"I see I *am* outvoted," he says, "this time. Very well. You may leave." He goes to the door and stops beside it. "I have no doubt you will return. You don't seem to be very good at obeying my laws. I will be here when you come back. And somehow I don't think there will be many promises to rely on when you do."

No one says anything for a long, long time.

"Erik, could you be so kind as to put her on a flight back to Bangalore at the end of the week?" Matthew asks, breaking the spell. "And do keep an eye on her until then."

He glances at me and there is a brief, bitter, faraway look in his eyes. Then he turns around and walks away.

Adrian pauses before following. He shakes his head. "It need never have come to this. If you had done as you agreed to and stayed to help me with my work, none of this would have happened." *Ophelia.* Unspoken but there, hanging above us like an ax. She would still be alive if I had only made a different choice.

"I couldn't have stayed," I say. "I will never stop being sorry about Ophelia, but I couldn't have helped you. Not like that. I won't be your monster."

"You've always been our monster," says Adrian. "Don't ever forget that."

I watch him go. Elsa is the last to leave, and she sweeps away, with a cool, calm dignity I envy, after giving me a long and searching look. I don't know what she's looking for.

When they're gone, my knees give way. I sit down on the floor, on the ragged, dusty rug, and swallow a hard, dry lump in my throat. Mina Ma holds me tight and I feel her love and her relief, every bit as tangible as her arms.

"Thank you," I say. She hears me and so does Erik, but he doesn't turn around right away. He is staring at the open doorway.

Mina Ma frowns up at him. "Erik?"

"The Loom is coming undone at the edges," he says, turning back to us. "Adrian and Matthew have both shown that they will bend their laws for their own ends. Adrian can no longer see beyond his obsessions, and with Ophelia gone"—his voice cracks—"that will only grow worse. For so long it has been iron and steel, and now the edges are fraying and the Loom is beginning to unravel. If it is hit in the right place, it may even fall."

"Does that frighten you?" I ask him.

"I don't know. I know I was frightened for *you* until a moment ago." He crouches on the rug, looking me in the eye, and he gives me one of his faint twinkly-eyed smiles. "Don't look so sad. Most echoes only leave the Loom once. When they are first stitched. Few leave it twice. That is something. Today you won."

Everything has changed. *I* have changed. I have to keep changing. Growing up. Learning to be careful while the Loom watches me closer than ever, while Adrian waits for me to slip. But that, there, *that* hasn't changed. When I was little, the Weavers were the dark, frightening monsters under my bed. They still are. Watching. Waiting.

I won. And I have paid dearly for it. I have earned Adrian's hatred. We've unmasked the Loom for what it is: whims and obsessions and cruelty and all of it, unraveling. I sent Sean away and he will never forgive me for that. And then there is Ophelia. I will never be able to forget that. Things will not just magically go on the way they did before I began fighting for my life. Before Bangalore and before Amarra and the Sleep Order and before the Loom.

I wonder if the police will investigate Ophelia's death or if they will turn a blind eye, unwilling to come too close to the Loom and to the strange, eerie games it plays with life and death. I wonder if Adrian will let me go to her funeral. Not that that matters. To me, Ophelia can't be a body in a coffin in the earth. She's laughing and smoking cigarettes in the garden of a cottage by a lake, sniffling over birthday cakes and frantically searching a dictionary for the meaning of a big word. The cottage by the lake is now over the hill and far away, and Jonathan and Ophelia and the other little ducks are there, and if I dream hard enough maybe, like the song, I will go after them and find them and one day all the little ducks will come back.

12

LAST

My flight is in the morning. I watch the sun reflecting rainbow colors on the windowpane of our hotel room. I don't know what I will do when I go back to Bangalore. I will give Sasha a big cuddle and hug Nik and Lekha and wait to see what happens after that. Ray led the hunters straight to me, but we will be at school together and I can't avoid him forever. When I think about him, everything becomes murky and confused. Sooner or later we will have to talk to each other. I will have to confront the hard and complicated tangle of Amarra and him and me.

The truth is, there is only so much space given to a single life. And I think I will always have to fight Amarra for our shared space. She will always be the ghost in the mirror. I have defeated her, but I won't be rid of her. Tomorrow I will go back to that life we share. My guardians and I will separate for good. I haven't seen Sean since I made him leave me, and I don't even know if he's safe. Erik promised to find out, though we both know I will probably never see him again anyway.

I get up. Mina Ma has gone to one of the shops nearby to get us some dinner. I leave her a note, check that my hair is concealing my Mark, and go out.

It's funny walking down a street in London without looking over my shoulder. I take the tube to Oxford Street, where I still have about half an hour before the shops close. I buy presents for Lekha and the kids and an ice cream off the street because I've barely eaten all day. Later, when I get back on the tube, a dark-haired, green-eyed boy glances my way and smiles, and I have to look down at the floor because the longing in my chest is so intense it's unbearable.

"Go away," I silently tell the ghosts, swatting at them like flies. It doesn't bother them. They follow me anyway. Reflections in the dark glass of the tube. Fragments of memories whispered in my ear. *He* won't leave me alone.

I look at the dainty, delicate bracelet on my wrist. It's knotted with shells off the beach, rough and small and flawless. He gave it to me. I look at it as though looking long enough might conjure him out of memory and into reality. If I could ask for anything, anything at all, it would be to see him again one last time.

But I fought for my life and I won. Perhaps that means I can win anything. Perhaps I can find a way back someday. Back to him.

Instead of going straight to the hotel, I get off at Covent Garden. I glance around. I know I'm in the right part of the city, but I'm not sure which way to go.

"Excuse me?" I say to a girl passing by. "I'm looking for this place. . . ." I describe it for her, and she gives me directions.

I end up back in the cobbled square. Next to the fountain.

The theater looks different in the dusky daylight. It doesn't look like our sanctuary. I stand in the light and watch the color of the clear, cold water in the fountain change as the sun drops lower in the sky. The square around me is alive. The markets haven't yet closed down for the day, and butchers, fishmongers, and housewives walk past me. I stand there as the water changes from blue to pink to gold.

I look into the fountain and see the pennies. And I laugh to myself, but I take a penny out of my pocket anyway. I drop it into the fountain and watch it spin until it hits the bottom. I want a wish. I could wish for an awful lot of things, but I've only dropped the one penny, so I take a deep breath and make one wish.

I wish as hard as I can.

I look up, and there he is. Like magic. He has his hands in his pockets and his face is bruised. It still looks like a war zone. He stands at the other end of the fountain. Too far away. But he's alive and he's safe and I wished and now he's here.

He raises a hand. Like he's waving. Like a hello. Or a good-bye. I try to raise my own. I try to open my mouth and speak. But nothing works. I can only watch him. He looks like a mirage. But then a child bumps into him and he helps her up and that makes him so solid, so real.

The fountain is bright gold between us. His eyes are the green of marbles and lagoons and nurseries and lights in the sky in the north. If I go to him he will taste of kisses and battles, of knights and promises. I don't know how long we stand there. It could be minutes. Hours. Days. For the longest time we just stand there and look at each other across the water.

ACKNOWLEDGMENTS

Enormous thanks to my agent, Melissa Sarver. For believing in me, for fighting for this book, and for just generally being all-round fantastic; and thanks, too, to Holly Root, for pointing me to Melissa.

To my editor, Sara Sargent, for being so much fun to work with, for remembering every romantic moment, and for loving Matthew (almost) as much as I do; and to Alessandra Balzer, Donna Bray, and the rest of the team at Balzer + Bray, for taking a chance on Eva and her story.

To Sarah Hoy and Michelle Taormina, for designing an amazing cover; to Anastasios Veloudis, for the gorgeous artwork; to Rosanne Lauer and Brenna Franzitta, for catching every inconsistency and making sure my disastrous typos don't see the light of day; to Caroline Sun and Olivia deLeon, for getting the word out about *The Lost Girl*; and to marketing director Emilie Polster and her assistant, Stefanie

Hoffman, for turning my manuscript into a real, live *book*. I honestly can't thank you all enough.

To my parents, for being funny and clever and raising me in a house so full of books, it's astonishing it hasn't collapsed.

And finally, to Steve. For making me believe this book was worth it. For a real–life love story. For everything.